The Thankless Child

The Fourth in the Hippolyta Napier Series

by

Lexie Conyngham

ISBN: 978-1-910926-49-9

Cover illustration by Helen Braid
www.ellieillustrates.co.uk

DEDICATION

Thanks again to lovely beta readers Kath, Nanisa and Jill!

Dramatis Personae

Ballater Folks
Hippolyta Napier, domestically incompetent
Dr. Patrick Napier, her husband
Ishbel, Johanna, Wullie and Wullie's dog, the household staff
Mrs. Kynoch, proprietor of a school for young ladies
Mabelle Ash, Georgina Pullman and Grace Spencer, young ladies
Strachans and Strongs, local families

Those from round and about
Peter Middleton, farmer in Tarland, interested in young ladies
Johnnie Boy Jo, interested in rich wives
Dod Durris, sheriff's man, interests as yet unspecified

Visitors to the area
Lord Tresco, an injured peer
Mr. and Mrs. Dinmore, of Dinmore's Banking House
Mr. Ravenscroft, precisely related to Lord Tresco
Mr. Hendry, his sons and his daughter, formerly of Tobago
Adelina Price, a commercial artist

Lexie Conyngham

Chapter One

'What an amusing thing if he should marry one of us!'

A surge of giggling filled the air at the other end of the parlour, and Mrs. Kynoch rolled her eyes.

'Too many novels,' she murmured. 'More tea, Mrs. Napier?'

Hippolyta Napier grinned, and held out her cup and saucer. She hoped Mrs. Kynoch would offer her more of those delicious little biscuits, too: now that Mrs. Kynoch had come into money it was even more of a pleasure to visit her – though her company was, as always, the chief attraction. The hot tea was welcome, too: the hearth was empty of anything but a screen to block the draughts from the chimney, and though the day was almost sultry outside, here in the parlour, a long, broad room with low windows, it was cool if you sat too long. It did not seem to be bothering the gossiping girls.

'They do seem a little different from your old pupils, Mrs. Kynoch.'

Mrs. Kynoch sighed, though there was a glint of satisfaction in her eyes.

'I still find time to teach the more promising village girls,' she said, 'for the sake of my sanity. When I set this school up for the daughters of plantation owners, I had thought that, being far from the fashionable cities, I might receive sensible girls who wanted to learn useful skills for their future lives in a healthy environment. Alas, few of them have anything you might call sense. But the healthy environment is certainly a draw, after the West Indies: really, some of them are so weak when they arrive! But you know that.'

Hippolyta's husband was the local doctor. Patrick had

9

learned quite a bit about the after-effects of tropical diseases in the last few months, but fortunately none of the girls had brought anything contagious to the healthy spa town of Ballater, open to the fresh air and cooling waters of Deeside. She glanced over at the girls, the pupils, as they clustered together for their chatter. They sat so close that the flower petals of their broad summer skirts pressed together, their heads of carefully managed curls turning eagerly from side to side. They certainly seemed content in their new home. Only two sat a little to one side. One was a girl with a striking face, a longish, slightly flat nose, slow brown eyes and a high forehead, surrounded by swathes of honey-coloured hair. Her expression was sulky and bored, her gaze resentful as she watched the huddled gossips. The other – one could not escape the word 'attendant' – was much less attractive, small and mousy with an eager face and hair of no particular colour. Her curls, no doubt the result of much effort, were already sliding away into nothing, and her gown was much less fashionable than that of the first girl, who sat aloof in silk and lace. Hippolyta admired both the silk and the lace, but thought them a little too sophisticated for a schoolgirl.

'Is she new?' Hippolyta asked, keeping her voice low.

Mrs. Kynoch, who even with money to spend was never going to look fashionable, knew at once without looking round the object of Hippolyta's curiosity.

'She's been here about a week. Georgina Pullman is her name. She's one who would no doubt rather be in Edinburgh or London. We are a little slow for her here.'

'Hm, I should think so! You'd have to work hard to penetrate that boredom. It looks almost deliberate.' Hippolyta was distracted for a moment as the dog at her feet, a creature constructed from many sources, stirred and contemplated some kind of action. The golden cat who stooped to live with Mrs. Kynoch opened one eye and stretched an enormously long paw, and the dog froze, instantly subdued. Hippolyta scratched the cat's head, and was acknowledged. She hoped it would also tolerate the white kitten she had brought for the girls to play with: needless to say, the kitten was on the lap of one of the gossiping girls, and not anywhere near Miss Georgina Pullman, where claws might catch and tear something expensive. 'Who has attracted their eye now?' she asked. 'I cannot think of many local bachelors of a good age.'

Mrs. Kynoch shrugged.

'The season is a promising one, nevertheless – just look amongst the visitors to the town. There seem to be any number of handsome young men I'll need to watch around my girls! I hope I'm quick enough.'

'Some of the men are less than at their best, though, surely, if they are here to recuperate their strengths.' Ballater, a new village still, had been built to accommodate the visitors to the spa at Pannanich and all those who derived benefit from the clear Deeside air. But Mrs. Kynoch's lips twitched.

'Aye, maybe! But you know well how quickly some of them brighten up when they come here, and then the next thing you know they'll want some pretty feminine company! And then there are some who are just here to attend on an elderly or sick relative, and the time hangs even more heavily on their hands.'

'Oh, do you mean the Hendrys? I met them only yesterday at tea with their sister and the invalid father. They seem amiable enough – and I should not have called either of the young Mr. Hendrys particularly handsome,' she added.

'The elder, perhaps, in a sharp kind of a way,' said Mrs. Kynoch, though she acknowledged with a nod that this unsuitable discussion of the appearance of young men had a practical application here, 'but no, not the younger. But you know what young girls are like!'

It was not that long, Hippolyta reflected, since she had been a young girl herself, after all. She had only been married four years. She glanced again at the two groups of girls in the parlour. The teacups rattled as more giggling bubbled around them, and Miss Pullman's mouth grew even more disparaging. The girl beside her, whom Hippolyta recognised as a longer-standing pupil at Mrs. Kynoch's school, gave the other girls a wistful look but clearly valued her place by Miss Pullman's side more, torn though she was. Hippolyta thought she could almost hear her sigh. Mrs. Kynoch gave a slight nod towards Miss Pullman.

'Father is a very wealthy plantation owner, I gather: mother died when she was a baby. I should have expected him to send her to suitable relatives in some fashionable town, as I mentioned, to find an appropriate husband, but my minister friend in the West Indies wrote me to say – well, that there are no relatives, for one, and that the father was anxious that his daughter should be taken in hand, as she had developed some independence of thought that was unlikely to be appealing to a good husband. From which, having met the young lady, I gather that he did not mean an intellectual streak or unfeminine tendencies to intelligence,' Mrs. Kynoch met Hippolyta's eye significantly, as she had quite an unfeminine tendency to intelligence herself, 'but that he has allowed her to become spoiled, and I am to discipline it out of her. I, discipline that?' Her eyebrows rose sharply. 'He would have done well to send her ten years earlier. I fear she is long past discipline now.'

It was unlike Mrs. Kynoch to allow herself to despair, but Hippolyta could see her point. Miss Pullman did not look like the kind of person who would admit the idea that she was anything but perfect, but at the same time she clearly did not take such satisfaction in those around her. Mrs. Kynoch might find her current pupils more frivolous than her previous ones, but she had built up a pleasant little community in the first few months here in her new property. Hippolyta would not like to see it spoiled by a bad apple.

Dinnet House certainly deserved happy inhabitants: over the last few years it had seen unpleasantness enough. When Mrs. Kynoch, widow of a previous minister in the parish, had come into money unexpectedly from a cousin who had connexions with plantations in the West Indies, she had at first been inclined to refuse it. Then, to everyone's surprise, she had conceived an ambition to extend what had been a tiny school for local girls, teaching them to whatever standard they wished in whatever time they could afford, into a greater enterprise for those families desirous of sending their daughters back from the plantations to a homeland that was completely unfamiliar to the girls, but was healthier and provided some kind of education and introduction into a modest level of society. She had taken the empty Dinnet House for the purpose. Not all Scots settlers in the colonies were wealthy: many of these girls would be destined to set up little businesses as milliners or dressmakers, music teachers or even governesses, genteel enough but nothing startling in society, unless they by chance married well in Scotland. As Mrs. Kynoch had indicated, most of those who were recommended to her school had no greater aim than that, and she taught them needlework and writing and accounting accordingly. What Miss Pullman expected was less clear. Whether she would find it in Ballater was also moot.

Mrs. Kynoch now was stirring, setting her cup and saucer back on the tea table and pushing away her chair.

'It seems a shame to be sitting indoors on such a glorious day, and the heat of midday has diminished now. Shall we take a turn outside? The front lawn is pleasantly shady.'

'That would be delightful.' Hippolyta set aside her cup and saucer as Mrs. Kynoch rounded up the girls and their shawls and parasols. The cat regarded them indulgently but the dog, which belonged not to Hippolyta but to her serving boy, rose at once at the chance of a walk and hurried to the front door, where they all drew in helpings of the fine mild air. It really was very summery.

The lawn was shielded from the road beyond the walls by a narrow stand of trees, and bound on the other side by the short drive from the gate to the front door. Mrs. Kynoch had the wherewithal now to have it kept neat, and it was a popular promenading spot for the girls, particularly as it allowed them to keep an eye on any visitors approaching the house. The house itself, Hippolyta fancied, was beginning to lose the grim visage it had taken on over the last few years, though perhaps it was only the sunshine.

'This weather is so fine, Mrs. Kynoch: we ought to organise a picnic somewhere before it breaks,' said Hippolyta, enjoying the cool grass under her boots. She had been wearing summer petticoats for weeks, but the layers still inhibited any fresh air about her. The fashions of her childhood had been chilly in the winter, but the fashions these days were much more suited to colder weather, with tight waists and padded sleeves. She glanced down at the skirts of her best summer visiting gown, with its sprigs and ribbons of blue and yellow on white, and sighed. It looked much cooler than it really was.

Miss Pullman and her little friend were walking close by, and Mrs. Kynoch nodded to Hippolyta.

'Georgina? Mabelle? Come here, please. Georgina Pullman, and I'm not sure you know Mabelle Ash? Girls, this is Mrs. Napier, the doctor's wife.'

Mabelle, instantly forgettable, made her curtsey and smiled

pleasantly. Georgina looked as if she felt Mrs. Napier, a mere doctor's wife, should be introduced to her and not the other way around, but she lowered herself stiffly into some form of respect.

'I hope you are enjoying your stay in Ballater,' said Hippolyta, feeling very old.

'Oh, yes, Mrs. Napier!' said Mabelle. 'I feel ever so much better here – though I miss my mother terribly! But Mrs. Kynoch is very kind!'

'And you, Miss Pullman?' Hippolyta persisted.

'I daresay,' said Georgina. 'It seems a pleasant enough place to linger for a little.'

'How long do you intend to stay?' Hippolyta asked, surprised – and not at all disappointed.

'Oh, as to that – my father will no doubt send me on to friends in Edinburgh shortly,' said Georgina, already casting about for someone more interesting to talk to.

'Not until the season, surely,' said Hippolyta, unable to resist. Georgina glanced back sharply at her, not happy to have been caught out in ignorance of such a thing.

'Does Edinburgh have a season, too?' asked Mabelle, happy to learn. 'Surely there are not torrential rains or hurricanes! That is what we have at home.'

'Well, no, not exactly,' Hippolyta admitted, 'though sometimes it can feel like it. The social season, when the galleries have exhibitions and the theatre is open and there are dances at the Assembly Rooms and everyone is in town and inviting everyone else to dinners and suppers, that is in the winter. I mean,' she added, remembering that the West Indies was a strange place on the other side of the world, 'from about September to about April.'

'I shall be there, no doubt, this winter,' said Georgina, nodding.

'I hope you enjoy it,' said Hippolyta, a little ambiguously. Mrs. Kynoch trod gently on her foot.

'I don't suppose I shall be there,' said Mabelle, then brightened. 'But no doubt there is plenty of entertainment to be had in Ballater!'

'We shall make sure there is,' said Hippolyta, warming to her even if she had befriended the much more aloof Georgina. 'There will be dances and dinners here a-plenty. Some visitors even stay for the winter so the society is very pleasant and varied.'

'How lovely,' said Georgina absently, the lack of curiosity showing her intention to be far away by then. 'Oh, look: someone is coming to call.' She frowned, and Hippolyta, following where she was looking, felt sure she knew why.

Along the drive, at his usual solemn pace, came Mr. Durris. More than that it was difficult to say at first: he was well presented, neatly dressed if not at the peak of fashion. He was strongly built and not unattractive. Yet there was something about him that was – neither here nor there. For a girl interested in her rank in society, as Miss Pullman seemed to be, there was nothing here to tell her whether the acquaintance of this man was something to be pursued or shunned. Mr. Durris, sheriff's officer in these parts, was a difficult man to place. He was, however, a friend to both Mrs. Kynoch and Hippolyta, and they smiled a welcome before he was close enough to speak. The dog, too, rushed to greet him and had its ears ruffled for its trouble. Georgina, unsure of herself at last, pulled away to a little distance, just in case. Nevertheless she held herself in a pose Hippolyta was sure was designed to catch the attention of any suitable man: Georgina was ready for any eventuality.

'Mrs. Kynoch,' said Durris, bowing correctly. 'And Mrs. Napier: I am glad to catch you here too.'

'That sounds solemn, Mr. Durris! I hope it is not bad news.'

'I hope not, too, Mrs. Napier,' said Durris, without smiling. 'Are you taking a turn about the lawn? Perhaps I might walk with you.'

He does not wish to be overheard, thought Hippolyta, as Mrs. Kynoch agreed. Hippolyta caught Georgina watching curiously as the three of them set off again around the grass, keeping their distance from the groups of girls. Georgina nudged Mabelle and they followed, but not too closely. As far as Hippolyta had seen, Mr. Durris had not even noticed Georgina.

Mrs. Kynoch was enquiring after Mr. Durris' health – not, as convention would next dictate, after his family, for as far as they knew Durris had no family. He was not a man to talk much about himself, though, Hippolyta reflected: for all she knew he could be one of fourteen brothers and sisters, and have a house full of aging parents, a wife and a nest of children. She was not even entirely sure where he lived.

'News, all the same,' he was saying, and she paid attention. 'Johnnie Boy Jo is back in the parishes.'

'Oh, dear, is he?' Mrs. Kynoch's expression was more sorrowful than distressed, though there was an element of that, too.

'Who is Johnnie Boy Jo?' Hippolyta asked at once. Both turned to look at her.

'Goodness, has it been that long? I wonder where he's been?' asked Mrs. Kynoch, meeting Durris' eye.

'Up north, the story goes,' said Durris, but not as if he was very sure. 'So it must be, what, five years or so? If you have never heard of him, Mrs. Napier.'

'I certainly have not,' she said. 'Are you going to tell me?'

'Oh, of course, dear!' said Mrs. Kynoch. 'But goodness, to be away so long! Has he changed at all? Will we know him?'

'He has not changed a bit,' said Durris. 'He is the same as if he had walked away yesterday.'

'Who is he?' Hippolyta's patience, never great when her curiosity was aroused, was wearing very thin. 'Or what is he? He sounds like a racing dog!'

'Oh, he's a man, dear.' Mrs. Kynoch's eyes again met Durris'. His lips, uncharacteristically, twitched slightly.

'He's not the kind of man one would want about a school for young ladies,' he said, recovering. 'And you should watch yourself too, Mrs. Napier. No doubt he'll be excited to be back.'

'Poor soul,' said Mrs. Kynoch, nodding. 'He's not found his rich wife, then, yet?'

'No, nor like to.' This time Durris did allow himself the slightest smile.

'Johnnie Boy Jo is a poor simple man,' Mrs. Kynoch explained at last, 'who claims he is looking for a rich wife. His methods, I'm afraid, are a little unorthodox. He waits about in quiet parts of the town and around, and when a respectable woman passes he – well, he reveals himself.' She turned a little pink.

'Good gracious!' Hippolyta was overcome with an urge to giggle. She tried not to choke. 'And – and he's been away?'

'Yes, he disappeared – well, as we said, it must be five years ago or so. No one knew where he had gone.' She made a sorrowful shrug. 'I suppose we thought he might have died, sleeping out in ditches and so on as he does.'

'Does he have family about?'

'No one that will own him, anyway,' said Durris. 'He is not from Ballater – no one is quite sure where he calls home. The story goes that his mother kept him in the house for years, only let him out when she came with him to church or to market, but when she died he – he wandered freely.'

'Oh, he's harmless, poor soul,' said Mrs. Kynoch. 'It's just a little alarming, when one is on one's own and is confronted with – well, that. But he's never touched anyone. I suppose I did indeed think he was dead: I had not thought about him these past years. I wonder why he's come back?'

'I wonder why he went away? I always thought perhaps someone had threatened him, someone's husband, perhaps?' Durris' curiosity could be strong, too. Clearly Johnnie Boy Jo had not dropped so far out of his thoughts as he had from Mrs. Kynoch's.

'Oh, I had better find a way of warning the girls,' Mrs. Kynoch sighed. 'Though no doubt some of them will find the whole idea worryingly fascinating.' This time she met Hippolyta's eye. The giggling girls would giggle all the more at this news.

'Can't you stop him?' Hippolyta asked Durris.

'The parish constable will be keeping an eye on him,' said Durris. 'It's not really something for me to comment on.' Hippolyta made a face. The parish constable was not a figure who inspired respect or even confidence. Durris sighed, as if agreeing.

'Well, best we all keep in company, then, I suppose,' said Mrs. Kynoch. 'Mr. Durris, Mrs. Napier and I had just mentioned the idea of a picnic. If you were not too busy, would you be able to join us? Apart from the fact that we would all feel much safer, you are really part of the village here!'

'A picnic for the whole village?' Durris queried.

'Well, maybe not the whole village,' Hippolyta conceded. 'We've only just thought of it, but the weather is so lovely. The minister and his wife, the Strongs, the Strachans, you know – some of the visitors to the spa, perhaps. Those Hendrys, do you think, Mrs. Kynoch?'

'Perhaps – the boys and their sister, anyway. I don't know

if Mr. Hendry elder is fit to attend such a thing.'

'We can ask. And your girls, of course, Mrs. Kynoch.'

'Yes ... There's a pleasant young man by the name of Middleton who has formed a connexion with one of my girls while he's been here. He seems eminently respectable, and I should like to give them the chance to meet at a social occasion.'

'Of course – we shall have to work out how to manage food and tables and chairs and things. Where shall we go?'

'Oh, not too far!' cried Mrs. Kynoch. 'It takes so much more organisation!'

'I shall talk with Mrs. Strachan and the Strongs,' said Hippolyta, determined now to carry the project through. 'Mr. Durris, if we say next Saturday, would you be able to come?'

'Unless something happens to detain me, I should be delighted, Mrs. Napier.'

'And let us hope that Johnnie Boy Jo does not make an appearance,' said Mrs. Kynoch. 'If we are fortunate, his stay here will be fleeting!'

Durris nodded. A thought occurred to Hippolyta.

'What does Johnnie Boy Jo look like, then? I feel I should be warned!'

'Middle build, a face that's neither old nor young but a little of both, sandy fair hair,' said Durris at once.

'And usually a smile,' added Mrs. Kynoch.

'A smile?' Hippolyta queried.

'Oh, yes. He's a friendly sort,' said Mrs. Kynoch. 'He has no idea that he's doing anything wrong, however often he's told. There's really no harm in him.'

'Well, that at least is good to know,' said Hippolyta.

Chapter Two

Hippolyta Napier had another call to make when she had reluctantly left Mrs. Kynoch to the organisation of late afternoon lessons. Yesterday she had gone to tea at Mrs. Strachan's (and she must return there to consult Mrs. Strachan about the picnic, for Mrs. Strachan was a leading light of Ballater society and, even more importantly, her husband owned the excellent grocery warehouse in the town). While there, she had made the acquaintance of a summer visitor to the town, someone she was keen to meet again, and it was an appropriate time to pay her own call on the visitor.

Adelina Price, the visitor in question, had taken lodgings to the Tullich side of Ballater, a little outside the main habitation, and Hippolyta was glad she had waited until the day was a little cooler to pay her visit. The road, which led back to the main commutation road from the west to Aberdeen, was not shaded in the least, though it was flat and easy to walk. To Hippolyta's right, as she kept her eyes open for the cottage she sought, was first of all the fine inn that accommodated wealthier visitors to the area and met every coach and carriage that arrived. After that there was a clear view to the river, the rumbling, rambling Dee, beautiful when it rolled along peaceably in its own bed, but prone now and again, as Hippolyta well knew, to terrifying swells that surged over the shallow banks here, sweeping across the loop of land where Ballater lay, and leaving destruction in its spreading path. It had been a hot summer when it had last spectacularly burst out, and the heat now, though very welcome for crops and ripening fruit and old men with stiff wintery limbs, had a hint of threat to it that no long-term inhabitant of Ballater could completely ignore.

Nevertheless the view was extremely picturesque: the far bank of the river, by contrast, rose steep and wooded up to Pannanich where the springs that fed the spa brought forth their reddish, metallic waters, and where the original baths were. She could see the building pale through the dark trees, and the line of the road that followed the south side of the Dee back to Aberdeen.

Here on the north side the way was quiet until she reached a row of three or four cottages, facing the road and the river, busy enough with washing parched in the sun and children playing on the skirts of the highway. The house she sought, she was sure, was the farthest, so with a wave and a word to the children she walked on past. The end cottage was no worse than the others in terms of dilapidation or untidiness: these were estate cottages, and though the landlord was absent the factor saw to their upkeep with a fairly easy eye. Hippolyta was about to open the gate and walk to the front door when she noticed a rough wooden shelter raised to one side of the cottage, open on two sides to the air, and within it two figures, one of whom was the lady she sought. It took a moment, pausing at the gate, for her to realise what was happening. A man was arranged on a chair, rather an indoor sort of chair for such rough surroundings, holding a book in his hand and his chin awkwardly angled. Mrs. Price was standing some feet away, at an easel, sketching at something with quick movements – presumably a portrait of the man. Hippolyta cleared her throat.

'Hello!' she called, and the man jumped. Mrs. Price looked round, and smiled. 'Is it all right if I interrupt?'

'Mrs. Napier, isn't it? Of course – if you don't mind if I carry on working.'

'Not at all.' Hippolyta opened the gate, wide skirts brushing the low wall to either side, and ventured to the shelter. It offered a little tantalising shade. 'Good day to you, Mrs. Price.'

'Good day to you! This is Mr. Hendry – um, Mr. Lennox Hendry, isn't that right?'

The man, who looked as if he would have stood politely if he thought it was allowed, shook his head slightly.

'Mr. Richard Hendry, at your service, ma'am. Lennox is my older brother.'

'I beg your pardon,' said Mrs. Price, not particularly concerned. 'I have a commission for both brothers, which is most generous of their father, Mr. Hendry elder.'

'I think he thought we might as well do something useful with our time while we're here, instead of wandering the hills and dales in search of entertainment,' said Mr. Richard Hendry, out of the corner of his mouth.

'You may speak, Mr. Hendry: I'll tell you when I want you to keep your face still.'

'May I see? I understand completely if you say no,' said Hippolyta quickly. 'I paint landscapes, myself, and I don't always want someone commenting on them over my shoulder.'

'No indeed! But yes, make yourself free,' said Mrs. Price, generously. 'I am at the planning stage, as you see.'

Hippolyta realised at once that Mrs. Price was an accomplished artist. Even in the sketch she could recognise Richard Hendry's awkwardness, his amiability, and his puzzlement over what he was doing with a book in his hands. It promised well for an accurate final portrait, even though it might not be one his father would care to pay for.

'I like to start with the full picture,' said Mrs. Price, 'and then smooth things over as I go.' She met Hippolyta's eye and there was a spark of humour in her own. Hippolyta, nodding, realised that the final portrait probably would be what the father wanted. Mrs. Price was working off her accuracy in the sketch.

'Please, take a seat if you will. There is lemonade on the table – do you mind helping yourself?'

Hippolyta did so, gratefully.

'Mrs. Napier, did you say?' asked Richard Hendry. 'Are you by any chance related to the local physician?'

'Indeed – I'm his wife,' said Hippolyta at once. It still gave her a little thrill to admit it, and she hoped that would never go away.

'He's been attending my father. Seems a decent fellow.'

'I could not say otherwise!' said Hippolyta, laughing. 'I believe I heard that you were here from the West Indies?'

'Indeed, from Tobago,' said the man. 'Everyone is talking of the heat here at the moment, but this is a pleasant spring day for us, you know.'

'Goodness, I don't think I should be able to live in such a place!'

'It takes a certain fortitude,' he agreed, with a hint of self-approval. 'But I suppose one grows used to it. I was born there,' he added, his smile admitting that he had had an advantage. 'But my parents have certainly found it a struggle at times. My poor mother succumbed to yellow fever when we were children, and my father's health is not good.'

'I am sorry to hear it,' said Hippolyta.

'Face, Mr. Hendry,' said Mrs. Price sharply, and he froze into some semblance of the pose she must have dictated to him. Hippolyta watched them both as Mrs. Price busied herself on the canvas. The artist was somewhat older than Hippolyta - in her middle years, in fact, with a soft, wrinkled face as of one who spent time squinting at her subjects, perhaps often outdoors like this. Her eyes were quick, and her mouth determined. Her clothes had been fine once, but had been altered and adapted to conform to something like fashion, and the colours were faded in a way Hippolyta would have expected to find unattractive but which were actually rather pleasing: they were worn with taste and a degree of absent-minded style. Her boots were dusty, as though she had spent the morning walking, and her hands were black with charcoal dust, a state with which Hippolyta was all too familiar.

Richard Hendry was rather a contrast. Hippolyta reckoned he was younger than she was, perhaps around twenty, with dark hair and sallow skin befitting his time in the West Indies. His mouth seemed ready to smile but his nose was soft, his eyes lacked much in the way of intelligence and his chin was weak. Hippolyta grinned at herself. There, she thought, a man condemned in only a few words. No time wasted there!

'So you paint landscapes, do you, Mrs. Napier? I can't be doing with them, myself. All those leaves! Perhaps a desert, though … But people are my favourite. Do you paint commercially?'

'Oh! no, no I don't,' said Hippolyta, slightly shocked at the thought. 'But I do take it seriously.'

'Watercolours?'

'And oils.'

'Serious indeed. May I see them some time?'

'Of course. I was going to ask you to come to tea, if you're not too busy. I'd be delighted to show you a few then. I'm not very good at people, though: animals, sometimes, if they stay still long enough, but I can't seem to do skin very well.'

Mrs. Price snorted, but not disparagingly.

'Each to their own, Mrs. Napier. Animals, now: that can be challenging enough.'

'Cats, mostly,' Hippolyta admitted. There were so many cats in the house that one or two could usually be found stationary somewhere. The dog was obedient, but she would consider it a triumph if she managed to paint a hen – even the one that spent most of its day in Patrick's study. 'Would tomorrow suit you?'

'Certainly – where are you?'

'The white house opposite the church,' Hippolyta explained, 'but everyone knows where Dr. Napier lives. Oh, and be careful out on your own: there's an odd man about.'

'An odd man?' Richard Hendry queried, forgetting not to move. 'What kind of odd man?'

'Oh, just one who behaves peculiarly,' said Hippolyta, trying not to blush. If he had not been there, she might have been more explicit to Mrs. Price. 'Don't allow yourself to be caught!'

But she had a feeling, as she left them to their session, that it would take a good deal more than Johnnie Boy Jo to intimidate Mrs. Price.

'I'm no doin' that again!'

Hippolyta, expecting to be greeted with a polite good afternoon and a curtsey, was a little taken aback, but Johanna the new maid was in full flow as she answered the door.

'She's doin' it a purpose! Fit kind o' a wye is that to behave? Chappit tatties a' ower the floo-er!'

Wild strands of hair snaked from beneath Johanna's cap, as if joining in her remonstrations. Her bony fingers were fisted on her hips, demanding satisfaction.

'Johanna! Johanna, I've said before that if you expect me to understand you, you must speak more slowly and carefully.' Heavens, she would never have had the nerve to say such a thing to their incomprehensible old cook – gone but not forgotten - but this lassie was much younger and Hippolyta felt she had a little authority. 'What's happened?'

'That quine you tell me's your cook. Fit wye is she a cook?

She's drapped the pan again!'

The dog, nose in the air, understood faster than Hippolyta did, and darted off to the kitchen to help tidy up. When Hippolyta arrived, the dog already had its nose in the spilt mound of mashed potatoes, despite the cook's best efforts to push it off with her foot. She was almost in tears.

'Ishbel! What's the matter?'

'Och, Mrs. Napier, I'm that sorry! Ken I broke my wrist? And it just gave way and left me.'

'Oh, dear!' Ishbel's wrist had healed, but it was not strong. 'Johanna, you know Ishbel has trouble lifting heavy pots. Perhaps if you helped her she would be less likely to spill them?' Out of the corner of her eye she noted a pair of bare feet sticking out from under the kitchen table. She decided not to comment.

'Ah'm no here to lift tattie pots. That's a cook's job.'

'It's also the job of a maid of all work, which is what you are. Is that not the case? And you address me as ma'am, remember?'

'The minister says last Sabbath that it's no right for one man to own another, nor a woman neither. Did you no hear him?'

'I did not, Johanna – ma'am, remember? – you well know I was worshipping elsewhere. Nevertheless he was quite right. No one should own anyone else.'

'Then you canna make me cairt them waichty pots – *ma'am*. You dinna own me.'

'You're quite right,' said Hippolyta, wondering if everyone else's servants in Ballater were so troublesome. Beside her, Ishbel had pulled out a ragged handkerchief and was heartily blowing her nose, while the dog, undisturbed, ate the potatoes with enthusiasm. 'We don't own you. You are free to leave at any time,' she added, tempted for a moment to open the garden door and show her the route, 'but you did tell me you wanted to learn how to be in service and all the skills of a maid. If that's the case – if you want to go on to work in a grander household than this – then you must learn the skills and the manners required. But you are not owned by us, and helping the cook is part of your work, and carting weighty pots,' she translated carefully, hoping she had caught it correctly, 'is part of helping the cook, particularly when she is still recovering from her injury. Do you understand?'

Johanna sniffed, but it was nothing to do with tears. She stood there defiantly, staring past Hippolyta's shoulder.

'Johanna? Do you understand?'

'I suppose. *Ma'am.*'

'Very good,' said Hippolyta, though it really was not. 'Now, help Ishbel to clear up, out of human kindness if nothing else.'

'Oh!' said Johanna in surprise. 'Human kindness? Well, aye, I suppose.' And to Hippolyta's astonishment she hurried to fetch a cloth and a bucket, and set to with a will. Hippolyta tried very hard not to meet Ishbel's eye, but it was difficult.

'Will you have enough potatoes left for the dinner?' she asked.

'Aye, ma'am, those ones were for the morn's morn,' said Ishbel, somewhat obscurely, and curtseyed.

'Good, good,' said Hippolyta, and retreated to her own part of the house. The parlour was inhabited only by a few of the household's numerous white cats, and Hippolyta sank gratefully on to the sopha, her hands over her face. One day, she swore to herself, she would run an orderly house. But how?

The parlour door opened, and she jumped. But it was her husband Patrick, sandy-haired and handsome, and even more welcome than the cats.

'Trouble?' he asked, coming to sit beside her. His arm slipped around her waist straightaway, and she leaned into him.

'Oh, only Johanna. And Ishbel – should her wrist not be better by now? She can't manage weights very well.'

Patrick raised his eyebrows.

'It can happen,' he said. 'Strength sometimes comes back slowly, though she's young and active. I thought Johanna was supposed to help her?'

'Johanna lacks the natural deference necessary in a servant.' Hippolyta sat up and made her face solemn as Patrick's eyebrows stretched again. Hippolyta laughed. 'That's what Mrs. Strachan said. It's what made me take her on, really. I thought perhaps …'

'You could succeed where Mrs. Strachan had failed?'

'Well, no, obviously … but I thought that if I did succeed, by some chance …'

'You'd prove you had some hope of being a good housewife?' asked Patrick, teasing but gentle.

'Well – yes.'

'You're fine, my darling,' said Patrick, pulling her back towards him. 'Now that Mrs. Riach has gone the meals appear on the table at the right times, the laundry is done, and the place is clean enough for us and for visitors. What more do you want?'

'A little domestic harmony would be nice! Servants that get along together, and don't resent one another, and don't retire to their rooms with a brandy bottle – though to be fair that was only Mrs. Riach – and don't quarrel over their duties.'

'Wullie is peaceable enough, is he not?' Wullie was the owner of the dog, a kitchen boy who would have worked at the Napiers' house for nothing if it meant he could keep himself and his dog away from his big brother at home.

'Wullie still hides under the table when anyone starts arguing,' Hippolyta sighed. 'But he's always willing to help if people ask him nicely.'

'We may have to see Johanna on her way, then.'

'Oh, let's try for another week, shall we?' Hippolyta was not ready to admit defeat yet. 'And I'll tell her she's on trial. If I could be able to say that I had managed to keep her a month …'

'That would be longer than Mrs. Strachan?'

'Well, a month and a day, then. Like in a fairy tale.'

'That would be a year and a day, my dear.'

'Yes, but I'm not sure I'd last that long!'

They laughed, and sat back on the sopha comfortably. She loved the clean smell of him, knowing how rigorously he washed his hands between patients. Cats immediately sensed the availability of their laps, and appeared for attention.

'What have you been up to today, my dear?' Hippolyta asked.

'Oh, nearly all visitors, I believe,' he said. 'I could almost wish for a second physician in the town in the summers, now, we are so busy. Today I attended on a Mr. Hendry, who is here to recuperate some strength after years in Tobago. He owns substantial plantations – no doubt Mrs. Kynoch will want a few words with him.'

'Oh! I believe I met his son. One of his sons.'

'Indeed? He has a daughter, too, a pleasant enough girl. Where was the son? Attending on Mrs. Kynoch's school for young ladies seeking profitable marriages?'

'Now, that's not fair, and you know it!' Hippolyta waved a finger at Patrick, and the cats wiggled their ears in alarm. 'That was not Mrs. Kynoch's intention.'

'No, perhaps not, but it is clear that her present pupils have not, between them, the wit of her village girls.'

'Then she has all the more work to do, and should be supported appropriately! Some of the girls are hardly silly at all. And there's a new one, very striking to look at.'

'Silly or not?'

Hippolyta considered.

'Spoiled, apparently, but by her appearance not so much silly as sulky.'

'Then if she finds a husband around here I pray it is one of the visitors and not a local. When the visitors go and the winters are cold, we want no sulky neighbour to join our social circle.'

'Anyway, it was not there that I met Mr. Hendry – Mr. Richard Hendry. Do you remember I mentioned yesterday that there was a lady artist at Mrs. Strachan's tea? Well, I called on her – out by Tullich – and she was painting his portrait.'

'Was she any good?' Patrick regarded his wife thoughtfully.

'It was beginning well, but she was only at the sketching stage.'

'Have you invited her to call?'

'Yes, of course. I liked her.'

'And you can discuss painting with her.' He nodded to the parlour walls, where several of Hippolyta's landscapes were on display.

'I had hoped to, yes. Do you know, she asked if I were a commercial artist?'

Patrick was silent for a moment.

'Had you considered selling any of them?' he asked, without emphasis.

'Well, no, I had not.'

'Hm,' said Patrick. Hippolyta frowned, but he went on. 'Well, I shall be delighted to meet her, if I have the chance. I have another new patient, too – a peer, no less!'

'Really?' Hippolyta sat up, then hesitated. 'A peer without his own physician?'

'He's a young man: I think he has not considered such things yet. He had a fall from his horse and broke his leg, and did not let it mend properly – a lesson, perhaps, to Ishbel. He's an active man and did not want to rest, and now he has to, and on impulse, I believe, came here for the air. Henry Tresco, his name is: Lord Tresco.'

'Handsome?'

'I should say that the young ladies at Mrs. Kynoch's will be quite a-flutter if they chance to see him. And he's rich, I should say, and is as yet unmarried.'

'Oh, dear! I don't think any of the girls is likely to be considered suitable for a lord. There will be broken hearts! Is Lord Tresco well enough, do you think,' she carried on, a thought striking her, 'to attend a picnic?'

'If he can go in a carriage, yes, I should say so. He's growing bored already: he would make the effort, I believe. Why, where is this picnic?'

'In my imagination at present. But Mrs. Kynoch and I thought it perhaps a good idea, while the weather holds. She has a courting couple she wishes to observe, and it would be an opportunity for the visitors and the locals to do something together, don't you think?'

'It sound delightful, in this weather,' Patrick agreed. 'But where?'

'Perhaps to Loch Kinord? Do you think we could find enough carriages and horses to take everyone?'

'I think we might,' said Patrick comfortably. 'The Strachans' carriage is larger than they need, we can take three if all are slim, and several of the visitors have their own carriages here. Including Lord Tresco, if you are determined to invite him.'

'It is not every summer that we have handsome young peers visiting! Of course I want to invite him. And at least at Loch Kinord we should be out of the way of Johnnie Boy Jo.'

'Johnnie Boy Jo?' Patrick sat up, and the cat on his lap leapt away. 'I thought he was long gone.'

'He's back, apparently. Mr. Durris came to tell Mrs.

Kynoch.'

'Durris did? Then it's true.' Patrick appeared to consider. 'Then be very careful on your walks, my dear.'

'Mrs. Kynoch says he's harmless,' Hippolyta protested. She feared having her freedom curtailed.

'He may have been harmless before,' said Patrick, 'but I have known of men like this. They never grow better, and they usually grow worse.'

'Worse?' She shivered at the look on his face.

'Yes, my dear. Much, much more dangerous.'

Chapter Three

'So if Saturday would suit you and the girls,' Hippolyta said, 'then we shall complete the plans. Mr. Strachan is already ordering extra supplies of cold meats and pies, and the Misses Strong have threatened to make punch.'

'Lemonade would be more appropriate, surely? I should not like the girls to attend some drunken debacle,' said Mrs. Kynoch, 'but yes, Saturday would be perfect. I believe the weather will hold, from all everyone is saying. I'll tell the girls this evening at supper.'

'The house seems very quiet, Mrs. Kynoch,' said Hippolyta, turning slowly on her heels. 'What have you done with them all?' They were standing in the darkish hallway, which Mrs. Kynoch had had painted as bright a white as her paintmaker could manage to counteract the gloom. But the cold tiles and shiny wood still echoed emptily, and no number of floral displays, cheery as they might be, brought much delight to the place.

'Oh, the pupils are out in the walled garden. I thought it perhaps safer for their perambulations than the front lawn with – you know, after Mr. Durris' warning. And the weather continues so fine that they have their needlework out there now – and some visitors. Will you join us? I came in, in fact, to call for more tea.'

'That would be lovely, thank you, Mrs. Kynoch,' said Hippolyta, and followed her hostess through the house and into the gardens at the back. The bright sunlight made nonsense of the weight of Craigendarroch's rocky hill looming beyond the garden walls, turning it into a painted backdrop, green, grey and purple, of little consequence. In the foreground, though there was less in the way of open lawn for walking on, there were crisp paths amongst the beds, cheerful flowers bloomed and girls busied themselves picking raspberries and strawberries, filling little baskets with scarlet and crimson fruits in abundance. It had been a good year so far: if Mr. Strachan could stock up with sugar, they would have jams and jellies all winter – and if the girls, fingers and mouths bright with juice, could manage to leave any fruit in the baskets.

There was quite a little party around a table under a large parasol, the bright sun cutting shadows across faces and hands and bright summer dresses. Apart from the girls, Hippolyta noticed that there were two or three men to entertain them, and to one side, in the shade of a tree, Miss Pullman and her little friend Mabelle sat apart again. On this occasion, though, there was a reason. Miss Pullman was sitting for her portrait. Mabelle, it was clear from the angle, was naturally not to be portrayed.

Adelina Price had set herself up, businesslike again, with easel and canvas, and was working away with little regard to anything else going on around her. Hippolyta admired her focus, distracted by her even as Mrs. Kynoch brought Hippolyta into the circle under the parasol.

'You'll no doubt have met Peter Middleton, Mrs. Napier,' Mrs. Kynoch murmured, pointing out a young man Hippolyta believed came from Tarland direction but had been spending rather a good deal of time in Ballater recently. He was the one she thought Mrs. Kynoch had been referring to the other day, when she mentioned wanting to encourage a courtship amongst her girls, but there did not seem to be one girl in the group to whom he was paying particular attention, instead watching Adelina Price work a few yards away. His brown eyes were soft and dog-like, his lips pursed in contemplation. Hippolyta suppressed a smile. She would not have thought that Adelina Price, shabby and middle-aged as she was, would have bred such interest, except perhaps in a fellow artist. Was Peter Middleton a painter? She had had the vague idea that he was a prosperous farmer.

She pulled herself back to what Mrs. Kynoch was saying, particularly as it referred to the young man next to her, who was pushing himself to his feet with the aid of a silver-mounted stick.

'Lord Tresco,' said Mrs. Kynoch. Hippolyta curtseyed.

'Mrs. Napier,' said the young man, and even his voice fitted with the swept-back yellow hair, the fine brows, the authoritative nose. Hippolyta was slightly surprised there was a girl in the place who was not in a swoon. 'How do you do? I gather it is to your husband I am indebted for his treatment?'

'He is the town's physician, yes,' she found herself saying, and hoped her smile did not look as silly as it felt. When Patrick had said the man was handsome, he had not exaggerated. 'And I am sure he would insist you sit down, regardless of good manners!'

Lord Tresco bowed.

'Thank you, that is most thoughtful. Dr. Napier is insistent that I rest, which, I must confess, goes against my natural inclinations.'

'It is never easy for active people,' she agreed, and sat to make it less awkward for him to resume his seat. He eased himself down with care, and favoured her with a rather lovely but entirely proper smile.

Mrs. Kynoch cleared her throat.

'And our other guest, Mr. Lennox Hendry.'

Hippolyta dragged her attention away from Lord Tresco.

'Mrs. Napier. Charmed,' said Lennox Hendry, bowing almost into Lord Tresco's face. 'Your husband's attending to our old pa, I believe.' If there was the least disparaging glance down at Lord Tresco, and comparisons drawn, Lord Tresco remained politely oblivious. Hippolyta, angling her bonnet away from both of them, sought for a change of subject. It presented itself quite readily.

'I believe you are to sit for your portrait with Mrs. Price, Mr. Hendry?'

Hendry, whose upper lip seemed designed for the purpose, sniggered.

'Oh, yes! Village life, eh? Everyone knows everyone else's business. Yes, Pa wants a record of each of us, he says, and she seems skilled enough. My brother was sketched day before yesterday, and she tells me it's half finished already. Makes me wonder if Pa's being had: there can't be much to it if it only takes a couple of days.'

'She certainly works quickly,' said Hippolyta, not quite sure how to defend Mrs. Price against that, when she had not herself seen a completed portrait yet.

'And now she's working on that creature there.' Lennox

Hendry nodded towards Georgina Pullman, a curious expression on his rather sour face.

'Perhaps the commissions came at around the same time – or she has seized an opportunity, when the light is good.'

'Pretty girl, int she? And well set up. If she does it well and flags it around the place, there'll be others queuing up to be painted,' said Lennox cynically.

'She is indeed a very pretty girl,' Hippolyta remarked, interested to see the effect on Lennox and on Lord Tresco. But it was Peter Middleton, forgotten behind her, who leapt to agree.

'Isn't she? A real beauty!'

There was a clatter of china through his wistful sigh, and they all turned back to the table. One of the girls had risen abruptly and was marching off towards the house, shoulders tight. Hippolyta could not see her face, but if the girl had been trying to hold in tears she would not have been surprised. She looked back quickly at Peter Middleton. His face had assumed a sheepish look, but he twisted again in his chair to continue his observation of Georgian Pullman and her portraitist. More of the former than of the latter, Hippolyta now realised.

'Excuse me,' she said suddenly, 'I must go and say good afternoon to Mrs. Price. Please do not think of standing, Lord Tresco.'

He nodded gratefully, but Lennox Hendry made a show of rising and assisting Hippolyta with her chair. Then, to her irritation, he followed her over to where Adelina Price was working.

'Good afternoon, Mrs. Napier,' called Georgina Pullman. It seemed that the girl was disposed to be friendly to Hippolyta as she saw her as the organiser of the forthcoming picnic. 'I trust all is going well with your plans for our excursion?'

'Quite well, thank you,' said Hippolyta, feeling a little like a housekeeper. 'I believe we will go on Saturday, if that suits you still.'

Miss Pullman considered a moment, then replied,

'Yes, that will be quite suitable, I believe,' much as if the whole outing depended on her attendance. 'You'll have mentioned it to Lord Tresco? Oh, and Mr. Lennox Hendry, of course,' she added, her tone changing from one name to the other in a way that was not subtle.

'I have not, as yet,' said Hippolyta, trying to keep her own tone mild. 'No doubt in due course – and Mr. Hendry,' she turned to Lennox who was smiling toothily beside her, a little too close, 'perhaps you would convey the invitation to Mr. Hendry and to Miss Hendry? I have not had the pleasure of meeting them yet, but I am sure all would be most welcome.'

'A picnic, is it?' said Mr. Hendry. 'That would be another way to stave off the boredom, I suppose. Where are you off to?'

'To Loch Kinord. If you came here direct from Aberdeen, you will have passed the road to it between here and Dinnet. It is but a few miles, not too much of an inconvenience if you have a carriage with you.'

'Oh, yes, Pa has a carriage, of course. I'll mention it to him. Is it a big party?'

'Fairly big,' said Hippolyta, hoping that might put him off. She was annoyed with Georgina Pullman for putting her in the position of having to invite Hendry, to whom she had not taken an instant liking. 'Around two dozen, if you all come too.'

'Daresay,' he said, grinning. 'And Miss Pullman, you are to attend?'

'If the day looks favourable,' she replied, offhandedly.

'Oh, of course, if the weather breaks all will be cancelled,' said Hippolyta, detesting both of them now. 'And you will be left to your own devices,' she could not help adding, hoping that the pair of them would go off somewhere and leave the rest of society alone. But the words, casually said, seemed to trip something in Miss Pullman's mind. She looked thoughtful. 'But those who know these things are quite convinced that the weather will hold well past the weekend.'

'We were told it would be cold and wet.' Hendry shivered.

'What, by the weekend?' Hippolyta was alarmed.

'No, generally. In Scotland,' he added. 'That's what they said before we left Tobago. Well, it's cold enough, but it's nothing like what I would call wet.'

'No ...' Hippolyta could talk about the weather like anyone else, but this seemed not to demand a response. Lennox Hendry appeared to take a grim satisfaction in not being drowned, but the mere thought took Hippolyta back to the Dee bursting its banks.

She shivered, but the other two paid her no heed. Georgina Pullman looked at Lennox Hendry as if he represented some particularly revolting memory, then glanced away. Mrs. Price sighed, and Georgina, recollecting that she was being sketched, overdramatically rearranged herself into her original pose.

'Will that do?' she demanded.

'Perfect, Miss Pullman,' said Adelina Price, with the precision of long practice with clients. On reflection, Hippolyta wondered that Georgina Pullman was paying to have her portrait painted: she seemed vain enough, but had her father given her that generous an allowance? Then it struck her that perhaps her father had requested that she sit: that might explain better Georgina's lack of patience with the artist. And it would make sense, even if she had only left the West Indies recently, for her to have a painting to show him that she was well, though perhaps a miniature would have been easier to send to him.

'Will Lord Tresco not be kind enough to come and talk to me while I'm stuck here?' Georgina asked, batting her lashes as if to flick away the shadows of leaves that touched her fair skin. 'He simply must come over here. I shall be so bored without his company, frozen in this miserable pose with no one around to talk to.'

Hendry's face seemed to stick at that, though he bowed and left. Hippolyta was surprised to see that he was, in fact, going to speak to Lord Tresco. She cleared her throat.

'I should imagine that Lord Tresco is trying to rest his leg, as his doctor ordered,' she suggested.

'You can't expect me to put up with Lennox Hendry,' said Georgina, as if it was an entirely reasonable sentiment. 'I have known him since he was in skirts. Well, his brother, anyway: Lennox is a little older.'

'You lived near them in Tobago?' Hippolyta asked in surprise.

'Not near them, as such. A neighbouring estate,' said Georgina, already distancing herself from the Hendrys. 'But Tobagan society is very limited, you know. One is constrained to associate with all conditions of people one would not necessarily entertain in, for example, Edinburgh. Or London, or Harrogate, or simply anywhere with an idea of fashion.'

'Or Ballater,' Hippolyta could not resist adding, just to see Georgina's reaction. It was very much as she had imagined it would be, though Georgina managed to restrain herself from expressing fully her thoughts on Ballater society. It was probably just as well.

'I imagine I shall not be in Ballater long enough to appreciate completely its range of delights,' Georgina said, her pretty teeth only very lightly clenched.

'Really? What a shame that is,' came a voice, and to her surprise Hippolyta found that Lord Tresco had chosen Georgina's charms over his doctor's instructions, and had managed to cross the grass to where Georgina was posing. Georgina blushed, and an expression of annoyance chased across her face to be followed by the sweetest smile Hippolyta had yet seen there.

'Lord Tresco! What a pleasure! Mabelle, let Lord Tresco sit down.'

Mabelle, forgotten in the conversation, leapt to her feet and shuffled her chair towards Lord Tresco, who shook his head at once.

'Not at all, Miss ... Miss Mabelle,' he said. 'I am quite content to stand and admire the view.'

'My husband will be most displeased with you if you do,' said Hippolyta firmly. 'Mabelle, let us find you another seat.' But already Peter Middleton, who had been watching, was bringing over another seat for Mabelle, his eyes only on Georgina for approval. Mabelle, however, fluttered around it and thanked him several times before offering the seat to Hippolyta. She declined it, and remained standing, as from her vantage point she was able to see what Mrs. Price was doing as well as hear what Georgina was saying. If she managed not to be annoyed by it, it was disturbingly entertaining. She could already imagine how she would describe the scene to the Misses Strong, two of the greatest gossips in the town. But Georgina was already speaking again to her receptive little court.

'Lord Tresco, there is to be a picnic – on Saturday, is that not what we arranged, Mrs. Napier? – I hope you will be able to come with us.'

'How very kind, Miss Pullman. I shall look forward to it – Mrs. Napier, I hope that you do not mind if I intrude? Perhaps this is just an excursion for the townsfolk.'

He had managed it nicely, she thought, without putting Georgina down for inviting someone to an event where she was not the hostess, and without assuming he could attend just because he was someone of importance.

'Not at all, Lord Tresco,' she said with a smile. 'The invitation is to be extended to several visitors, and you will be most welcome if you are able to come.'

'With Dr. Napier's permission, then!' He made her a little bow from his chair.

'What has Dr. Napier to do with it?' demanded Georgina. 'He is not issuing the invitations, I think.'

'No, but he is instructing me on how to ensure my silly leg makes a full recovery. I am therefore most keen to oblige him,' said Lord Tresco. Georgina cast a look at the leg in question, as though such a thing as an injured limb had no right to be part of someone on whom she had bestowed her favour, but again she just managed to say nothing. Perhaps she was learning, Hippolyta thought: after all, she was very young, and in the mixed society of Tobago perhaps she had had few good examples to show her how to behave. She wondered how much good effect Mrs. Kynoch might be able to have on her in the short time she planned to be in Ballater, but if anyone could set a good and worthy example, it would be Mrs. Kynoch.

Mrs. Price was slowing now in her sketching, filling in delicate details with her charcoal in a way that Hippolyta envied at once. Her fingers itched to copy the moves. Georgina's face was coming to life on the canvas, pretty and petulant, her hair and lace and gloves, fan and parasol all outlined in strokes of remarkable accuracy. The agate necklace at her throat, a touch of darkness in the light-and-shade composition, caught the eye. At last Mrs. Price stood back, arms folded – a habitual posture, Hippolyta judged, noting her worn elbows – and considered the sketch.

'Show me,' said Georgina at once.

'Not yet,' said Mrs. Price, just as imperious. 'This goes home with me and the paints are applied. You would not wish a display of something unprepared, would you? You would not appear in the street in your shift and petticoats?'

Mabelle's jaw dropped at such indelicacy, but Mrs. Price

was simply being forthright. Georgina Pullman considered.

'But *she* can see it. Mrs. Napier: she can see it.'

'Mrs. Napier,' said Adelina Price, in words that Hippolyta would repeat gloriously to herself in private moments for months, 'is a fellow artist, and I value her opinion. Well, Mrs. Napier?'

Glowing, Hippolyta considered, trying to find the right words.

'I think it will be an excellent likeness, Mrs. Price, and a delightful painting.'

'Thank you. Now,' she said, briskly covering the canvas and its frame with a cloth in such a way that the charcoal would not be rubbed, 'I shall attend you on Saturday with the completed painting. Mr. Hendry, I shall expect you tomorrow at noon for your sitting.'

'But the picnic is on Saturday,' Georgina objected.

'I hardly think the picnic party will leave at nine in the morning. I shall be here then. If you are not, or if you are abed, then I shall take the painting away again.'

My word, thought Hippolyta, I wish I had the nerve! Georgina's lips were set in a surly line and even Lord Tresco, with his excellent manners, was obviously fighting laughter, while Mabelle was stunned at this treatment of her friend. Through their silence Adelina Price folded her easel, tucked it and the canvas under her arm, and marched off, bonnetless as she had been as she sketched, and vanished into the house to take herself home. Hippolyta felt like applauding.

Mabelle and the gentlemen had stood hastily as she had left, but Georgina stayed in her chair, staring straight ahead as Adelina Price strode past her. Mabelle watched the artist go with a kind of regret in her eyes, and Hippolyta, seeing that she had missed being served tea, drew her over towards the tea table to find her a cup.

'She is rather an extraordinary woman, don't you think?' Hippolyta suggested, handing the full cup on its saucer to Mabelle. She took it clumsily, but caught it before it spilled.

'She frightens me!' Mabelle confided, once she had taken a substantial gulp. 'She's so sure of herself!'

'But talented, I think,' said Hippolyta, hoping that they were talking about Mrs. Price and not about Georgina Pullman.

'I'm sure the portrait will be excellent.'

'I hope so: Georgina will be so cross if it isn't perfect,' said Mabelle. 'Such a waste of time, she'll say.'

'And money, no doubt,' said Hippolyta a little rudely, her mind still on the matter of who was paying for this commission.

'No, no, not money,' said Mabelle at once. 'Georgina wasn't paying Mrs. Price. Mrs. Price asked if she could paint her, as a favour. Because she's so beautiful, you know.'

'Really?' Hippolyta was astonished. She had thought Adelina Price would be the kind of artist who chose the interesting and challenging over the beautiful. But then, in a way, Georgina was indeed challenging. If Mrs. Price did as she had said when Hippolyta had watched her painting Richard Hendry, and made a first, telling sketch then smoothed away the characteristics the sitter would not want to see, then removing Georgina's spoilt petulance to leave only the beauty that would please her to see would be an interesting task, no doubt. 'Well, of course, Miss Pullman is lovely,' she said quickly, in case Mabelle thought she had doubted that. 'Are you both looking forward to the picnic, then?'

'Oh, well, yes, I suppose so,' said Mabelle. 'It will be an adventure, no doubt. I suppose we aren't really going out into the wilds, are we? There will be plenty of men in the party to shoot any bears, or wolves, won't there?'

'There will be a few men,' said Hippolyta, 'but no guns, and no need to shoot bears or wolves. I don't believe the wildlife here is half as ferocious as the creatures where you come from, you know. We have snakes, sometimes, but they are only small and frightened, and it is rare to die from their poison. And the spiders and frogs are quite harmless.'

'Goodness! No bears at all? And what about the deer? With those extraordinary horns?'

'Antlers – well, yes, they look alarming. But actually they are very shy,' Hippolyta reassured her. 'They are most unlikely to invade a picnic, whether the men be armed or not.'

'And what about Johnnie Boy Jo?' She spoke the words as though she were invoking a hobgoblin. 'Would an armed man frighten him away?'

'I don't believe,' said Hippolyta firmly, 'that any of us has anything to fear from a creature like Johnnie Boy Jo.'

Chapter Four

Adelina Price had been to tea at the Napiers' house, had admired the cats and Hippolyta's landscapes, and had been all a good guest should be, even covering her shabby gown with a fine lace shawl in honour of the occasion. The Misses Strong, also invited, had found her fascinating, and were keen to have their likenesses taken by her. Now it was Hippolyta's turn to go again to the little cottage in Tullich for tea in Mrs. Price's parlour, though Mrs. Price had warned her against expecting anything out of the ordinary.

'And I shall be walking with you,' said Patrick at breakfast. 'Johnnie Boy Jo has been active again not far from there at Tomnakeist, so you're not going alone, I'm afraid.'

'It will be a pleasure to have your company,' said Hippolyta with a grin. 'No doubt it will make the walk seem all the shorter.'

'As to coming back ...' said Patrick, 'I'm not so sure. Perhaps I can find someone to visit in that direction.'

But this turned out to be unnecessary. Hippolyta had thought Mrs. Price might be reluctant to admit a male guest to tea, but that was not the case.

'The famous Dr. Napier! I hear of your expertise at every turn. I should be honoured to serve you tea in my humble accommodation!' The tone was sarcastic, but Adelina Price's face was friendly.

'I couldn't intrude,' said Patrick.

'Not at all. Please come in. If you have been protecting Mrs. Napier from the local troublemaker, then no doubt you intend to wait around to walk her home again, so you might as well make yourself comfortable and no doubt put up with a great deal of talk about paints and canvases, which I suspect you are well used to.'

'I have grown to tolerate it quite well, I think,' said Patrick solemnly.

'He simply goes and plays his pianoforte,' Hippolyta explained, 'which is of course so much easier to ignore.'

'An artistic household, then! But you don't draw, Dr. Napier?'

'I was constrained to draw at medical school,' said Patrick. 'Anyone who saw my efforts there is unlikely to ask me to portray anything again.'

Mrs. Price smiled.

'And Mrs. Napier, do you play?'

Hippolyta made a face.

'To about the same standard as Patrick's drawing. I am allowed, on occasion, to turn the pages.'

'Then you seem perfectly matched! Please, come in to my little parlour. The woman who accommodates me here is a fair cook, but there will be nothing fancy. Could you take a – what is it called? A buttery? You know I am from England and such things differ from county to county on these islands.'

'But a buttery, well made, is a delight,' said Patrick quickly. He nudged Hippolyta discreetly, but she had come across butteries before – just not usually at a lady's tea table.

'I think one could live on a single buttery for a day or so,' said Mrs. Price. She stepped to a door and, pushing it ajar, called something to someone beyond. 'Please be seated – Mrs. Napier, you are very welcome to wander and look at paintings, just as you allowed me in your parlour!'

Hippolyta was delighted: she had already begun to scan the paintings and sketches that hung on rough nails along the whitewashed walls. There were one or two landscapes, and she could see that Mrs. Price had not underestimated her own skills: there was something too lush and green, an unnatural glow, about the trees and plants she had tried to portray. It was strange, because her portraits, which made up the vast majority of the canvases, were so lifelike they seemed to stare out into the room, fellow guests at tea, ready to eat any number of butteries.

She certainly worked quickly, for one of the completed portraits was that of Georgina Pullman, luminous under her parasol, her pale summer gown catching flakes of sunlight amongst the shadows of the leaves. True to her word Adelina Price had painted out the petulance, the spoiled child in the young woman, softening the mouth and the eyes into charm and loveliness, the face that Hippolyta had glimpsed so briefly in the smile that had been bestowed on Lord Tresco.

'She's lovely,' Patrick remarked, watching from his chair. 'That's not one of Mrs. Kynoch's young ladies, is she?'

'Briefly, if you listen to her. Miss Georgina Pullman, eager for the lights and glitter of Edinburgh or London.'

'Yes: a rather exotic flower for Ballater, I'd have thought,' Patrick agreed.

'And rather less amiable than I have portrayed her,' said Mrs. Price drily. 'I should think Mrs. Kynoch would be glad to see her go.'

'Mrs. Kynoch,' said Hippolyta, 'has a very clear sense of duty towards her girls, for their moral education as well as their practical skills.'

'I'm sure she has: but I should think Miss Pullman would be more resistant than most.'

'She'll be delighted with this,' said Hippolyta, her eyes drawn again to the golden-green light Mrs. Price had captured, veiling the painting like a window. 'Oh, and you've finished that one, too! You really do work quickly!'

'Time is money, they say,' said Mrs. Price, with a twist of her mouth.

'I've seen him,' said Patrick. 'That's one of the Hendry household, is it not? The younger son?'

'Mr. Richard Hendry, yes,' said Mrs. Price. 'Not, perhaps, the more handsome of the two sons.'

'Perhaps not,' Hippolyta agreed, 'but he seemed the more pleasant of the two.' Again, as she had promised, Mr. Richard Hendry looked more intelligent, firmer of character, in the finished painting.

'There I could not disagree,' said Mrs. Price. 'His brother Lennox is still on the easel: I sketched him this morning.'

'May I see?'

Mrs. Price hesitated a moment before nodding.

'You know what to expect, Mrs. Napier.'

The easel was propped against the wall, a cloth over it held clear, as before, by a light wooden frame. Hippolyta lifted the cloth with care, and at once the sly, confident face of Lennox Hendry seemed to flicker into black and white life.

'Good gracious,' said Patrick after a pause. 'He could be in the room.'

Hippolyta flashed him a smile.

'Isn't it good?'

'Yet I have told Mrs. Napier I cannot paint landscapes – you see how vague the background is in any of these pictures! I envy her facility with foliage and pasture, the depth of distance. She should consider exhibiting in Edinburgh, Dr. Napier.'

'Really?' Patrick's face was half delight, half confusion. 'I know I enjoy them. Do you believe they would be appreciated more widely?'

'I certainly do,' said Mrs. Price, 'and I speak as one whose work has appeared in the Academy on more than one occasion. I do not care to boast about it – unless I wish to attract a particular type of customer,' she gave a little sardonic smile, 'but if it will assure you that I know of what I am speaking, then there you are.'

Hippolyta and Patrick exchanged glances. The possibility seemed very distant.

'Maybe one day,' she said, 'but I'm flattered that you think I should be of that standard!'

'Will you be painting on Saturday at the picnic?' Mrs. Price asked. 'Is the place picturesque?'

'Oh, very,' said Patrick. 'It is a most historical site: there was a castle on an island there, and it is believed there was an ancient monastery to the north – a stone with a cross carved on it was dug up ten years ago or so. Then there is the Burn o' Vat, a curious rock formation. There is plenty to see – and plenty to paint, I should think!'

'But I probably won't paint on Saturday,' Hippolyta added, feeling how pink her face still was. 'Not in front of everyone. I like to go and paint on my own, you see – which would be very awkward with portrait painting!'

'I think,' said Mrs. Price, 'that you and I are each well suited to our chosen subjects. Well, I had hesitated to accept the invitation for Saturday – there is plenty to be done here - but I look forward to visiting such an interesting place. Do you take a great interest in historical artefacts?' she asked Patrick, just as the tea arrived. Hippolyta returned to her seat: the butteries smelled hot and salty.

As Patrick talked eagerly about a possible Roman fort to the south of the loch, she turned back quickly to her perusal of the walls, her mind dancing. Her paintings on the walls of the Academy in Prince's Street? Where she herself had so often gone to see the latest masterpieces by Nasmyth or John Watson Gordon or David Wilkie? She chuckled silently at the very thought. What nonsense! And as for selling any of her paintings – would that be entirely respectable? Even assuming anyone would buy them, would society accept such a thing? What would her mother and sisters say?

Only half listening to Mrs. Price's conversation with Patrick, she let her eyes wander over the display of art on the walls. Face after face stared out at her, pale ovals against green or brown or blue or dark velvety red – the backgrounds were certainly not the portraits' strong point. Then something different sprang out at her: a painting where the background was a sandy yellow, and the subject's face was not pale at all. She glanced at Patrick and Adelina Price: they were absorbed in a discussion of mediaeval monasteries they had both visited. She slipped from her seat and crossed the parlour for a closer look.

She was not sure why she had not seen the portrait before, for it was set at eye level – always the best position in the Academy, she reminded herself – around two thirds of the way along the opposite wall, over an old kist that sat on the floor beneath it. She leaned over the kist to study the painting. It was a finished work, not one of the charcoal sketches, but it did not seem to be one waiting for collection by its sitter – for one thing, the man in the painting wore clothes which were not particularly fashionable: his breeches were narrow and his coat close-cut, but he stood with confidence, one hand, clutching gloves, on his hip, the brim of his hat in his other hand and his head tilted a little as if he wanted to ask the painter a question when she had finished. And the man's complexion … how had she caught that colour, the depth of that mahogany brown, the glint of light on his cheekbones and nose? It was remarkable. She stared at the painting so intently that she did not notice silence fall behind her.

'Ah, you have found Joshua!'

Mrs. Price's voice was light, but when Hippolyta turned to face her her expression was a perfect contrast.

'What a wonderful portrait!' said Hippolyta.

'It has a purpose, too,' said Mrs. Price. 'You will have read in the newspapers about the campaigns to abolish slavery. To abolish it in the colonies, I mean, and forthwith.'

'Well, yes,' said Hippolyta, glancing at Patrick. She had taken to reading his newspaper more carefully of late, feeling that she was growing uninformed. There was no slavery in this country, not since the famous case of Joseph Knight so long ago. A slave brought to British shores was a slave no more. But the same could not be said of the colonies, the plantations where Mrs. Kynoch's young ladies had grown up, where the Hendrys no doubt carried on their business in Tobago. The money Mrs. Kynoch had inherited which had helped her set up her school had come from sugar. It had meant some misgivings on Mrs. Kynoch's part, but they had been overcome through some machinations of Mrs. Kynoch's own.

Mrs. Price also looked at Patrick, considered for a moment, then went on.

'I do not know how you view the actions of women in the political sphere of life, Dr. Napier ...'

'Go on,' he said.

'But I am part of an association of women who are campaigning and petitioning to abolish all slavery forthwith. Some of us are artists. We paint particular paintings – such as that one – and sell them to those who support us and are happy to show it by displaying our art on their own walls. And the proceeds of these paintings go to our funds, of course. We have set up schools to educate the slaves when they are freed – and some masters even permit their slaves to be educated now, to increase their value. We are not proud: we will teach them all. I hope you are not shocked.'

Hippolyta looked to Patrick, sure that the question was directed more towards him.

'It is a worthy cause,' he said. 'And, if women are to be involved politics ... it seems to me both the right cause, and the right way to go about it.'

'Miss Strong, whom you met the other day,' said Hippolyta

with a grin, 'would like to make speeches in Parliament!'

'Ah,' said Mrs. Price, 'that seems a step too far for me! But women have immense influence, don't we? Even if it does not always seem so?'

'Do we?'

Mrs. Price smiled.

'Do you buy your sugar from Mr. Strachan's warehouse in the village?'

'Well, yes, of course.'

'And is that where most of the women in the parishes buy their sugar?'

'It is, I suppose: there are few other warehouses. Some might buy directly from grocers in Aberdeen.'

'So if the women in Ballater decided, together, not to buy sugar from Mr. Strachan's shop any more, it would materially damage his sugar sales?'

'It certainly would.'

'Where does his sugar come from?'

'I'm not sure ... but I think I see what you mean. If we all insisted that his sugar was from – somewhere where it was not produced by slaves, then ...'

'Then he would no doubt attempt, at least, to find such sugar to sell you.'

'Goodness, yes, I suppose he would!'

'But the painting,' said Patrick, who had also risen to look more closely at it, 'you have not sold it yet?'

'No, Dr. Napier, I have not. Nor is that one for sale. There are others aplenty if you care to purchase one, but that one I intend to keep.'

'Do you think you will buy one?' Hippolyta asked tentatively as they began their walk back from Tullich to Ballater.

'One of the slavery paintings? It depends how much they cost, I suppose, and whether the others are as good as that one. It is outstanding.'

'I know, isn't it?' She paused: it would be the perfect point to introduce a discussion on the possibilities of showing her own work, or even of selling some of it. But somehow her tongue stuck, and Patrick said nothing. Probably he would not approve. Would he? He indulged her in so much, she knew – and she was grateful to have such a husband – but then every now and then he remembered that he needed to be careful of his reputation, for people would not call in doctors whose wives were in the least bit wayward. If he said nothing, then it was most likely because he did not want to say no but knew he would have to. She bit her lip. 'Perhaps we could ask her. I didn't see any similar paintings there today.'

'Perhaps she didn't bring any with her to Ballater, for fear the place should be full of plantation owners. As indeed it seems to be at present.'

'Mrs. Kynoch's school girls. And the Hendrys, of course. I suppose all of them own slaves, or their fathers do. It – it makes one quite shivery to think of it,' she said. 'Some of the girls seem so nice and pleasant, and yet …'

'Yet when Mrs. Price talks of abolition forthwith, it does make me concerned,' said Patrick thoughtfully.

'But surely if it is to be done – and it cannot not be done – then it should be done as soon as possible! I know the plantation owners want compensation, but –'

'I'm thinking rather of the slaves,' said Patrick. 'Yes, to lose all one's labour in an instant would be detrimental to one's business, but think of the slaves. You are suddenly free, yes, but with what? With what food, or money, or belongings? With what means of earning any of them? It is possible, of course, that their erstwhile owners might employ them, but if your business depends on an unpaid workforce, then will you be able to afford to pay all of them? I should think most owners would only take back a few, the basic requirement to tend the plantations.'

'And would the slaves go? I mean, when they are not slaves any more? One reads of such ill treatment – would one go back, even paid, to a master who had treated you like that? Goodness,' she said, 'it is not as simple as I thought.'

'Nothing ever is,' Patrick sighed. The road was quiet, with hardly anyone about to disturb the hot dust on the road, and they shared what little shade Hippolyta's parasol could offer. He touched her hand as it rested on his other arm, absently tender. 'Mrs. Kynoch's girls have been brought up amongst slaves – brought up by slaves, indeed. Some of them, I suspect, had a slave as their mother. It is hard to condemn them for a choice they did not make.'

'But –' Hippolyta was about to go on when she was interrupted by a cry from somewhere up ahead. They stopped.

They had passed the few cottages that clustered around the ruined kirk and graveyard at Tullich. Ahead the road ran between fields, with only a small stand of trees on the left to break them, just where the road crossed a little burn. They could clearly see two figures by the trees, just at the edge of the road. One was a woman.

'I do believe that is Miss Pullman,' Hippolyta found herself whispering, though the couple were some distance away. 'I think I recognise her summer gown.'

'And the man?' Patrick was tense.

'I don't know. I can't see clearly with the shadows of the trees.'

They watched, not sure now what they had heard. Hippolyta was sure Mrs. Kynoch had no idea that one of her charges was out here on her own with a man: she would definitely not approve. Then the man clearly reached out for the girl, and they heard her scream.

Patrick was off in a second, bounding along the road, shouting as he went. Hippolyta, as best she could, flipped her parasol shut and ran after him.

'Leave her alone!' Patrick was shouting. 'Don't touch her!'

Johnnie Boy Jo, she almost gasped aloud. It must be Johnnie Boy Jo. What on earth was Georgina Pullman doing out here on her own when someone like Johnnie Boy Jo was about? Had she not been warned? She trotted after her husband, flourishing the closed parasol like a lance. Wasn't he supposed to be harmless? But then Patrick – Patrick had said – Patrick had clearly said that people like that only get worse. She was panting in the heat, her corsets gripping her ribs in a vice, and sweat pouring down under her shift, when she reached Patrick and the others, flinging herself into the pool of shade under the trees as if it were a cold bath.

'Mrs. Napier too! Good heavens,' said Georgina Pullman, a little too calmly for Hippolyta's liking. She turned to look at the man. It was not some strange wanderer at all. It was Peter

Middleton, erstwhile admirer of one of Mrs. Kynoch's longer-standing pupils. He too seemed more annoyed than anything.

'Was this man bothering you, Miss?'

'Miss Pullman. Georgina Pullman. And this is Peter Middleton from ... Tar something, isn't it, Mr. Middleton? My husband, Dr. Napier.'

'Miss Pullman,' said Patrick, focussed. 'Are you in need of assistance?'

'Against him? No, not at all!' Miss Pullman was dismissive. Peter Middleton flushed to the roots of his hair. 'Mr. Middleton was about to take his leave.'

'But Georgina!'

'Miss Pullman, I think you mean,' she snapped, and the anguish in his face was painful to see.

'Perhaps it would be best, just now, Mr. Middleton,' said Patrick, in the voice in which he suggested a particularly unpleasant form of treatment to his more stubborn patients.

'But may I not ...? May I not visit again?' asked Middleton, his eyes only on Georgina.

'As to whether you visit Dinnet House or not, that is quite immaterial to me,' she said, tossing her head in a way that made Hippolyta dearly desire to slap her. 'I shall not receive you.'

'Best to go, Mr. Middleton,' Hippolyta murmured to him. 'Things will seem much better tomorrow, no doubt, and there is nothing to be done now.'

Middleton's gaze fell to the ground, and he breathed deeply for a moment or two. Then he lifted his head, straightened his coat, and turned on his heel. He had walked only a few paces when he half-spun again.

'I shall be at the picnic tomorrow!' he said, defiantly.

'I shan't notice whether you are there or not!' returned Miss Pullman, and spinning on her heel she made for Ballater. Patrick and Hippolyta exchanged glances, and followed her. She walked fast.

'Miss Pullman, did he harm you in any way?' Patrick asked, catching her up first.

'Him? Harm me? I should think not. Offend me, yes, perhaps, but it was nothing that I am not used to. Men conceive of the most extraordinary ideas, do you not find, Mrs. Napier? Or perhaps,' she added, looking Hippolyta up and down briefly and taking in the sweaty breathlessness, 'perhaps you do not.'

'Then we shall escort you back to Dinnet House,' said Patrick grimly. 'You should be able to find a refuge from my hapless half of the species there, should you really wish it.'

Hippolyta, though, was quite sure she did not. Miss Pullman, in fact, was far too interested in men for her own good.

Chapter Five

It was clear before the shutters were even opened on Saturday morning that the weather had not broken. The sky was already deep blue and cloudless, and when Hippolyta splashed cold water over her face and arms from the jug on the washstand, it was not quite as cold as she would have liked it. The day was already warm.

'You're up early,' said Patrick, greeting her at the breakfast table with a kiss. 'I thought we were not to depart for another hour or so.'

'I know,' said Hippolyta, 'but I thought I would just pop up to Dinnet House first, and make sure that all the girls have a seat in some carriage or other.'

Patrick looked at her over the top of his book.

'I'm sure Mrs. Kynoch would send word if there was a problem,' he said. 'What's the real reason?'

Hippolyta sighed: he knew her far too well.

'Mrs. Price was to bring her portrait of Georgina to Dinnet House this morning at nine o'clock. I should like to see Georgina receive it. Surely she will be satisfied with it: Mrs. Price has done her beauty justice and eliminated all her surliness.'

'Well, I suppose I have known you take more risk than that in the cause of your unending curiosity,' he said, resigned. 'But I think you are perhaps over-optimistic. Miss Pullman will see it at most as an appropriate gesture of appreciation of her charms, not as anything out of the ordinary.'

'Well, then, she is more of an ungrateful fool than I had already thought her,' said Hippolyta, uncharitably.

'Just try not to intrude, my dear. It is a matter between artist and sitter, however much you might like one and dislike the other.'

55

Hippolyta, marching up to Dinnet House, told herself that she did not dislike Georgina. I simply find her difficult, she explained firmly, and a little ridiculous, and I must remember that we are all young once and she has years yet to improve. And I myself am far from perfect. So there.

She grinned at herself, and transformed it quickly into a greeting to some passing farmhand who tipped his cap in surprise. Wondering what on earth he thought of her, she turned in at the gateway of Dinnet House.

She knew as soon as she reached the front door that she was a little too late. Georgina's voice, which could be sweet if she tried, pierced the wood with the sharpest tones.

'I don't see how you could possibly think I should want such an ugly thing. When I am in Edinburgh I shall have Papa commission a portrait from a proper artist, you know. I have no need of that object.'

Hippolyta eased the door open a little, just in time to see Georgina flick her fingers dismissively at the lovely painting. It was propped on a chair. She backed away, but could not resist stopping to listen.

'Now, you have taken up enough of my time. I must complete my toilette for the picnic. You would be advised to do the same.'

'You are an ungrateful little savage! When I think –'

There was the sound of footsteps, and an unladylike grunt, smothered at once by an outraged gasp. Hippolyta knocked smartly on the door, and caught Mrs. Price, one hand out towards Georgina. Georgina's mouth was open in shock, but at the sight of Hippolyta she turned and stalked up the staircase without a backward glance. Hippolyta cleared her throat.

'Ah, Mrs. Price! I hoped to catch you here,' she said, as if nothing untoward had happened. 'Do you need transport to the picnic? We have a little trap, with just room for three, if you would like to join us.'

'Mrs. Napier! Ah – yes, that would be most welcome. Let me just …' She dropped the cloth with which the painting had been wrapped back over it again, and tucked the bundle under the stairs where it was least likely to be noticed.

'Is that Miss Pullman's portrait?' Hippolyta could not help asking.

'Yes: apparently it does not meet with her approval. Never mind,' she added, and Hippolyta was surprised to see a glint in her eye, 'I have other uses for it.'

'I'm sure it would sell well,' she remarked, but Mrs. Price looked surprised.

'I suppose it would,' she said. 'Now, do you want me to go back with you now, or shall I call later?'

'No, no: we should be ready to go imminently.'

It would have been pleasant if the pony pulling their trap had gone fast enough to cause a bit of a breeze, but the pony in question had firm ideas about the expectations it was prepared to meet, and having three passengers was not one of them. The other carriages and traps were no faster in the sunshine, and it was almost noon when they finally turned off the commutation road to climb the side road towards Tarland. Hippolyta slipped down from the trap and took the pony's head to encourage it: she was the only person the pony would not bite.

The road rose steeply enough through stark birch woods, the leafy white columns punctuated frequently with dead trees where the horseshoe fungus had sapped them of all their strength.

'Look, girls,' Mrs. Kynoch liked to turn every day into a school day, 'see how the cup of the fungus always faces upward – and when a tree falls, the cup slowly turns itself around so that it still faces upward.'

Some of the girls in her carriage craned to see. Georgina, though, hid her face, unexpectedly disturbed.

'The fungus moves on its own? That cannot be right!'

'Aye,' remarked Miss Strong from their trap, 'it's no so bad when it's a sunflower seeking the sun, eh?'

About a mile up the road there was space for drawing the vehicles off the road. Two men waited there for them. Hippolyta was pleased to see that one was the sheriff's man, Dod Durris, while the other was Peter Middleton, Georgina's rejected suitor from the previous day. That might be interesting, she thought, but Middleton went straightaway to the Strachans' large carriage and opened the door, assisting another of Mrs. Kynoch's pupils from it with every sign of affectionate attention. Hippolyta recognised her as the girl who had so precipitately left the tea table when he had admired Georgina. He must have decided to abandon Miss Pullman for his previous sweetheart – no doubt a sensible move, if the previous sweetheart could be placated.

Mr. Durris came to greet them as Hippolyta released the pony from its harness. Patrick, helping Mrs. Price from the trap, turned to greet him and introduce them. There was general bustle as the Strachans' servants, some of them sent in advance, came to take the horses to graze while the picnic guests sorted themselves out, opened their parasols, adjusted their gloves and hats, and surveyed the area. The last of the girls stepped from the Strachans' generous carriage, followed by a middle-aged couple Hippolyta had barely seen before – more visitors.

'Mrs. Napier!' Mrs. Strachan called. 'I don't believe you have met the Dinmores? Lord Tresco, have you met?'

Lord Tresco, fiddling with his stick, stumbled.

'Dinmore!' he said, in obvious surprise. 'I had no idea you were here!'

'Nor I you!' Mr. Dinmore was a contrast to Lord Tresco, though they greeted each other with evident friendliness. He was a short man, almost entirely bald, with a decisive face and clever eyes. The two men shook hands. 'We are near neighbours, Mrs. Strachan, in London: indeed, Lord Tresco has been kind enough to take me in on occasion!'

'That was only once, Dinmore, and you were more than welcome!'

The men laughed, then Mr. Dinmore turned to Hippolyta.

'I beg your pardon,' he said. Mrs. Strachan, waiting patiently, made the introductions, and Mr. Dinmore brought forward his wife to present her.

'Are you staying in the village, or up at Pannanich?' Hippolyta asked. Mrs. Dinmore was paying little attention to Hippolyta, but looking about her with interest.

'In the village, of course,' she replied shortly. Hippolyta decided she would not waste too much time on the woman just now, though she took in her expensive gown and elegantly arranged grey hair – appropriate for her age, but with more than a nod to current fashions.

'Well, I hope you are enjoying your stay. And I'm delighted you were able to come to our little picnic!'

'Do we eat straightaway?' demanded Lennox Hendry, dusting his sleeve and examining the results on one pale glove.

'Not here, surely, in the middle of the road.' Lord Tresco broke off from his chat with Mr. Dinmore, leaned on his stick and smiled. 'Is that the loch I see through the trees there? I assume that is where we are going.'

'Will you manage?' asked Georgina sweetly, nodding to his leg. 'I'm sure something could be contrived here for your convenience.'

And no doubt, thought Hippolyta, she could also contrive to stay here with him.

'I think I might be permitted a little exercise,' said Lord Tresco, with a laugh. 'Is that not so, Dr. Napier?'

'If you go gently, yes, my lord,' said Patrick patiently. 'And avoid rough ground if you can.'

'There, I have my instructions!' said Lord Tresco amiably. 'And I have every intention of obeying them, Dr. Napier. The path to the loch looks manageable.'

'But I had hoped first of all to take the girls to see Burn o' Vat,' said Mrs. Kynoch.

'Oh, yes!' said Hippolyta at once. 'It is most interesting!'

'What is it, then?' asked Lennox Hendry, as if he had resigned himself to any number of miseries today.

'A rock formation, carved by the flowing waters,' Patrick explained.

'And very picturesque,' Hippolyta added, nodding at Mrs. Price. The artist smiled.

'It sounds worth a walk,' Richard Hendry, glancing at his brother, seemed intent on being more accommodating. 'How far is it?'

'Oh, only along there.' Patrick waved. 'Not too far for anyone to walk.'

'Except Pa, of course,' said Richard Hendry at once. He peered back into the closed coach he had just left. 'Pa, you won't want to go, will you?'

An older man pushed his head out of the Hendry carriage window, reminding Hippolyta of an elderly hen considering the weather.

'Where is the meal to be?' he asked, his voice thin.

'Down there, isn't it?' Richard Hendry glanced about for confirmation as he pointed to the loch below.

'Then Rebecca and I will walk down there while you go. Rebecca,' he spoke back into the carriage, his words lost in the upholstery. Richard opened the door, and a girl who had to be his sister stepped out lightly then turned to help her father.

'What's the matter with him?' Hippolyta whispered to Patrick.

'Too long in an unhealthy climate,' said Patrick. 'Worn out by fevers and flux. There's hardly anything left of him.'

'Will he recover?'

'He has good days and bad days.'

Mr. Hendry's legs seemed too thin to support him as his feet fumbled for the narrow step of the carriage. Miss Hendry was slim and slight, but took his weight on her arm without apparent effort, pulling him free of the vehicle to stand, breathless, on the dust of the road. Two little figures scrambled out of the carriage behind him, busy with rugs and baskets designed less for a general picnic, Hippolyta thought, and more for the specific comfort of Mr. Hendry. She wondered that he had managed to come at all.

Mr. Strachan, who had probably seen Burn o' Vat more times than any of them, volunteered to escort Mr. Hendry and his daughter to the picnic site, and the Dinmores elected to join them – Mrs. Dinmore's hand was urgent on her husband's arm, drawing him away - while the others set off at an easy pace, forming and reforming little groups already, along the path to the rock formation.

It did not take many minutes to walk along the easy, winding path through the birch trees, though the heat of the day intensified as they went. A stream dogged the path, and the trees dripped with lichen, while a thick upholstery of moss softened the rocks. A rounded cliff face began to rise to their left, and the high ground on their right curled to meet it until the path came to a sharp corner at a tumble of stones, and carried on steeply up the hill to their right.

'We have a choice of ways here,' Mrs. Kynoch explained. 'If you wish, you can climb up there and look down on the Vat from above. Or, if you prefer, you can come this way.'

'What way?' demanded Georgina. 'There is no way in there.'

Mrs. Kynoch grinned, and the orange feather on her bonnet quivered.

'Follow me, if you please!'

She led the way to the rocks. They were wet, and looked as if they should be slippery, but in fact they had a grip almost as tight as pumice stone. The party followed as Mrs. Kynoch turned a corner between two tall rocks, and vanished. In a moment, they were all through the short tunnel, scrambling not to step in the stream, and found themselves gasping with delight.

The rocks had immediately opened up into a large, smooth hollow, a natural arch on each side allowing shelter from the bright sunlight that sliced across the cliff above. The floor of the hollow was thick grit flooded in places by the burn, which tumbled into the hollow in streamlets and waterfalls down a wall of stones at the far end. High above them tree branches webbed their view of blue sky, and roots dangled down the damp cliff face.

'Goodness,' said Mabelle, 'it is almost tropical!'

'I want to see what's up there,' Lennox Hendry announced, and began to scramble up beside the waterfalls.

'Oh, me too!' said his brother, following. Patrick turned to Hippolyta and took her hand, but the climb was easy enough and at the top they found themselves perches in grassy hollows amongst the boulders, able now to see further upstream. The little glen was lush and green, the stream contained to a deeper channel but still with little beaches of the pinkish grit where it skipped the corners around the rocks. The air was balmy, even the breeze failing to lift it. Down in the hollow Lord Tresco looked about him with pleasure, and raised his stick as if to assure Patrick he had no intention of attempting the climb. Patrick grinned back. One or two of the girls did risk it, but most, including Georgina and Mabelle, stayed below. Hippolyta smiled to herself. For young ladies brought up in such a dangerous place as she thought the West Indies, they were very careful of themselves – or perhaps they were expecting bears and wolves.

The picnic site, arranged with parasols and seats and

cushions and tables full of the best Strachan's grocery warehouse had to offer, was enticing after their efforts.

'Shall we eat now, while the food is still fresh?' asked Mrs. Strachan with a look at her husband.

'Oh, yes!' called Miss Strong, whose appetite was rarely known to fail.

'And before it grows really hot,' added Hippolyta, who was also more than ready for her meal.

No one objected, so they arranged themselves about on rugs and cushions, with the older and frailer members of the party on chairs by the table. Rebecca Hendry sat by her father, reaching for snippets of food for him as his fancy took him, and Hippolyta had a better chance than before to take a look at her. She quickly decided she had not been missing much: Rebecca Hendry was certainly attentive to her father but seemed neither resentful nor particularly doting. Perhaps they spent so much time together they had no conversation left, but certainly she said little, and her face lacked animation.

'Are you to paint Miss Hendry, too?' Hippolyta asked Adelina Price quietly.

'It has not been mentioned,' she replied, and looked across at the woman. 'I'm not sure I should be that eager to do it. She's … there's somehow not much there, is there?'

'That's what I thought,' said Hippolyta, pleased that Adelina agreed. 'I'm sorry, my dear,' she added to Patrick, who was listening, 'but it's true.'

'Now, that's interesting, though,' Mrs. Price went on, nodding. 'Look at the little girls.'

The girls, servants presumably, who had busied themselves with rugs and baskets in the carriage, were now seated almost under the table at Rebecca Hendry's feet. Two little white caps crowned their heads and they sat quietly in neat, plain dresses: Hippolyta was not clear about children's ages, but she thought they might be around six and eight. Two little shadows in the larger shadow of the table: both were dark-skinned.

'Now there's a thing,' said Mr. Durris, sitting a little straighter.

'What?' asked Hippolyta.

'I just wonder,' he said, 'if Mr. Hendry knows the law.'

'You mean you wonder if he thinks they are still slaves?' asked Patrick, frowning.

'Surely he must know,' said Hippolyta. 'They're probably just maidservants. They look a lot better than ours,' she added ruefully.

'I should like to paint them, all the same,' said Mrs. Price. 'Think how a painting of those two would touch the hearts of anyone supporting our cause. I wonder ...' She slipped away into her own thoughts. Durris and Patrick began to discuss the legacies of various tropical diseases as demonstrated by visitors to Ballater, and Hippolyta scanned the rest of the party, interested to see what Georgina was up to now.

Inevitably, she had secured a seat next to Lord Tresco, and was conversing with him with great assurance. She did look fine, in her summer gown with pale green ribbons, and the matching feathers in her bonnet. Perhaps she thought she was winning his favour, but Hippolyta, perhaps biased, interpreted his expression as amused tolerance. His attention was on his neighbours, Mr. and Mrs. Dinmore, though he tried to keep up with Georgina's conversation. She seemed to be behaving herself for now, so Hippolyta, a little bored, passed on.

Peter Middleton and his preferred young lady sat at the opposite end of the picnic area from Georgina Pullman, and Hippolyta noticed that by chance or design he had his back to Georgina. He and the lady, heads bent, were deep in some conversation, the food on their plates long forgotten, and by the look on the lady's face not everything had as yet been resolved to their mutual satisfaction. Peter Middleton had some work to do still, it appeared –and serve him right, thought Hippolyta. She had thought him a sensible young man, and not one to go running after someone like Georgina.

The other girls seemed to be enjoying themselves, their picnic an unusual treat, the place a novelty for them. The younger Hendry men were not above lingering with them, attending to their plates and glasses. Hippolyta wondered if there were other girls there from Tobago too, for whom the Hendrys would be old friends. Mrs. Kynoch kept careful watch over her charges and the men with whom they spoke, and Hippoltya saw her give a little nod to herself at the sight of Peter Middleton and his lady talking matters over.

The meal was eaten lazily, as befitted the day, but one by one they finished the fruit and cheese and creams, and began to discuss how to spend the afternoon.

'Who's for a walk around the lake?' asked Richard Hendry, rising with more energy than anyone should after a large meal. One or two stood to accompany him, while others objected.

'It's too hot. Can we not explore the woods instead?'

'Or do nothing at all?'

'I'd like to paint, if that's all right,' said one of the girls, and Mrs. Price grinned.

'I'd like to look at that rock formation again,' said Lennox Hendry.

'There's nothing to stop us all doing different things,' said Mrs. Strachan, taking on the role of peace maker. 'As long as we all meet back at the carriages at – what? Four o'clock?'

'Oh, no,' said Hippolyta, 'can't we make it a little longer?'

'What about five, then?' There was general approval. 'Five o'clock at the carriages, then.'

'And girls,' said Mrs. Kynoch quickly, 'don't anyone go off on their own! You don't know the area, and there could be – well, anybody – about. Stay in twos and threes, at least!'

'Do you think Johnnie Boy Jo would attack here?' Hippolyta asked Mr. Durris. 'Where there are so many of us?'

'Why not, if some of the girls stray?' asked Durris. 'But if they are sensible and stay together, he will not have the nerve.'

'I heard he had been seen at Tomnakeist,' said Patrick, his voice as low as the others'. 'And we passed there on the way here. He could easily have come this far.'

'Well, Mrs. Napier, you will be safe with us,' said Durris. 'What would you like to do?'

'Oh,' said Hippolyta, 'it's very pleasant just sitting here for now. Would you mind? You two can go off and circumambulate the loch if you want to – I'm sure I shall be quite safe!'

Patrick looked at Durris, and then around them. Lord Tresco did not seem likely to move too far, and nor did Mr. Hendry and his daughter, or the two little girls under the table. And the Strachans' servants were still about, tidying the picnic things. Mrs. Price and at least two of Mrs. Kynoch's girls already had sketchbooks out and were surveying the view to pick out likely subjects. Hippolyta was hardly going to be on her own.

'Well, we shall not be long,' said Patrick, 'if you are sure you do not want to come.'

'Quite sure,' she said, settling herself on her cushions and adjusting her parasol. It would be very good just to sit for a little and watch what people were doing. And there would be gossip to be had, no doubt, if she moved only a little in almost any direction. But movement, for the moment, seemed impossible. The air was thick and heavy, the sun too bright on the calm waters of the loch, and she had eaten a little more than was necessary. Patrick and Mr. Durris blurred in the heat as they walked together down towards the loch shore. Peter Middleton and his companion had disappeared, and so, she saw to her surprise, had Georgina. Mrs. Kynoch appeared to be asleep. Mabelle, Georgina's usual companion, sat dismal and alone on a cushion, watching the wanderings of the picnic guests with much less interest than Hippolyta felt. At the table, which the servants had already cleared of all but lemonade, Miss Hendry had brought out a book and was reading it aloud to her father, while the little girls, slaves or not, fanned them both. Hippolyta watched them. They were not quite what she had expected of slaves, if slaves they were: they were both neatly, if plainly, dressed and shod, and they seemed quite content in their work which was not particularly onerous. She tried to imagine a painting of them by Adelina Price, something to tug at the heart of those who might support the abolitionists. She closed her eyes.

When she opened them, her shadow had grown much longer in front of her. She glanced around quickly. Miss Hendry and her father were asleep in their chairs, the book folded neatly in Miss Hendry's lap. Mrs. Price had changed her position and was unobtrusively sketching the two little girls, while Mrs. Kynoch was chatting with Lord Tresco. Mabelle had left her perch on the cushion and was walking slowly arm in arm with Peter Middleton's girl, who seemed to be crying. Peter Middleton was nowhere to be seen.

As she very gently eased her legs and arms into movement, Hippolyta saw that Patrick and Mr. Durris were heading back from the loch: it must be nearly time to go. Miss Strong noticed her stirring, and winked at her broadly.

'Ah, back in the land of the living, eh, Mrs. Napier?'

'Yes, indeed, Miss Strong. What time is it?'

Miss Strong pulled out a pocket watch that was a little large for a lady's timepiece.

'It lacks only fifteen minutes to five o'clock. Time to be bestirring ourselves!'

Hippolyta stood, and others, sensing the course of movement, began to put away paints and embroideries and to gather themselves together. Hippolyta went to the table and gently laid a hand on Miss Hendry's arm.

'Time to go home, Miss Hendry!' she said.

'Oh, already? Pa, it's time to go back to the carriage!'

'Is it? Is it?' The old man's confusion cleared quickly. 'Oh, what a fine evening it is! Where are the boys?'

'I'm sure they'll be back soon,' said Hippolyta, glancing around but not seeing them. 'They may even be at the carriages already, if they came back through the woods. Will you need any help, Mr. Hendry?'

He nodded at her.

'We'll be grand, Rebecca and me. She's a strong lass.' The two girls were gathering up the rugs as Rebecca Hendry helped her father to stand, and then began their slow progress back up the hill to the road. Hippolyta folded the rug on which she had been sitting and returned it to a servant, then waited for Patrick and Mr. Durris to meet her.

'I'll be heading back now,' said Durris. 'It's been a very pleasant afternoon. Thank you for inviting me, Mrs. Napier.'

'Not at all, Mr. Durris: it was a pleasure to see you not on duty, for once!'

They were among the last to climb up to the road, and almost everyone was already there, waiting while the horses were harnessed. Hippolyta took their own pony to the trap, and tipped the servant that had had to bring the pony from the grazing: the creature cost them more in consolatory tips than in feed and stabling together, according to Patrick. Gradually people arranged themselves into the carriages again, and Mrs. Kynoch carefully counted her girls. Then she counted them again.

'Seven,' she said. 'There should be eight.'

'Are you sure?' asked Mr. Strachan, eager to be off home. 'We had four with us, didn't we, dear?' he asked his wife.

'We did,' said Mrs. Strachan, anxious. 'Who did we have?'

'Where's Mabelle?' asked Mrs. Kynoch.

'Here, Mrs. Kynoch,' said Mabelle, poking her head out of the Strachans' carriage.

'Oh, goodness, girl! Thank the Lord!'

'But Mrs. Kynoch – Georgina's not here.'

'What? Nonsense: she must be around somewhere. Is she in Mr. Hendry's carriage?'

But Georgina was not in Mr. Hendry's carriage, nor was she with the Strongs. In fact, as far as anyone could tell, Georgina Pullman had completely vanished.

Chapter Six

'Who saw her last?' asked Dod Durris, taking charge. Lord Tresco and the Dinmores, looking him up and down for a moment, conceded any superiority they might have felt. He could have that effect on people: no one was ever very certain of his social position, and it put them off guard. 'Well? Can anyone remember?'

There was some discussion amongst the girls, and Mrs. Kynoch said,

'Lord Tresco, you were sitting with her.'

'I was,' he agreed, genially concerned. 'But she wanted to take a stroll, and I fear my leg was hurting after the walk to the Vat thing so I suggested she should find another companion.' At present he was seated on a chair, retrieved by the servants to be set incongruously beside the carriages. The Strongs had an open carriage and had already perched in it, able to survey the conversation from above. Hippolyta stayed beside the pony, hoping that no one would venture too close to it.

'And did she?'

'I'm afraid I don't know,' said Lord Tresco. 'I turned to look at the view, and when I looked back she seemed to have gone. I assumed she had set off with some of her friends.'

'I saw her leave him,' put in Mr. Dinmore, 'but I didn't pay much attention to where she went.'

'Did she walk down to the loch?' Dod turned to the Hendry brothers. Richard looked the more anxious of the two. Mr. Hendry and his daughter had also been granted the use of chairs, and Mr. Hendry was wrapped in a rug.

'I don't think she followed us,' said Richard, frowning, 'but I went one way and Lennox another. The charm of the woods drew me in, and I abandoned the loch for the shade,' he explained.

There was a muttering amongst the girls, and suddenly one was pushed forward.

'Where's Peter Middleton?' she demanded, looking scared. Everyone stared around. Peter Middleton was not there, either.

'He – he was supposed to be here to see my friend,' said the girl, clearly elected spokeswoman for the girls. 'My friend Grace, he's been – well, you know, he'd been coming to visit her at Dinnet House.'

'He had, very properly,' put in Mrs. Kynoch, perhaps alarmed for the reputation of her establishment. 'He's a respectable lad, a farmer at Tarland.'

'Which is further up this road, is it not?' asked Lord Tresco.

'Yes, that's why he chose to meet us here rather than in Ballater,' said Mrs. Kynoch.

Grace's friend, though, had more to say.

'He was supposed to be here to meet Grace,' she emphasised, 'but Grace had heard that he'd been seen in the company of Georgina Pullman. And we all know what she is.'

'Margaret!' exclaimed Mrs. Kynoch, hushing the girl. Margaret was scarlet, but defiant.

'She gave him the eye and he fell for it, Mrs. Kynoch! You know what she's like! She always has to have her men around her, like – like hens at the kitchen door!'

'Margaret, dear, do calm down,' said Mrs. Kynoch, taking her by the arm.

'Well,' said Dod Durris with a sigh, 'who was the last one to see Peter Middleton?'

'Apart from Georgina Pullman,' Margaret muttered, as Mrs. Kynoch drew her to one side.

'It might have been me,' came a small voice. Hippolyta recognised Peter Middleton's erstwhile – or possibly present – sweetheart. 'We sat together at the picnic.'

'You're Grace, are you?' Durris asked, his voice more gentle. The girl was fair haired and fragile looking.

'Grace Spencer, sir.'

'Well, Miss Spencer, when did you and Mr. Middleton go your separate ways?'

'We had words, sir. Well, when he came to the picnic he

was all lovely again, just as he had been before – before she arrived. And he never looked at her for ages. And he said he hadn't seen her since … oh, since that day we were all in the garden together. Mrs. Napier, you were there, too, and Mrs. Price was painting Georgina's portrait. And then I heard he had met her yesterday on the road to Tullich, and he'd been lying to me again!'

'Dear me,' said Durris, encouragingly.

'And then I started to cry, and he said he could explain everything, and I said he needn't bother wasting his breath, and he said … oh, he said he'd go and get her and she would tell me what happened, and he went off to find her. And that's the last I saw of him!'

'Did you see which direction he went in?'

'I think – I think he went up the hill. Towards the woods, anyway, not towards the loch.'

'Thank you, Miss Spencer, that is very helpful.'

He might as well have treated her less kindly, for she immediately burst into tears again, and Margaret came back to lead her away into a nest of clucking fellow pupils. Only one of them was separate from the rest: Mabelle, Hippolyta noticed, had not yet left the Strachans' carriage, and was watching the proceedings with an odd air of anticipation. As Georgina's particular friend, surely she would want to be down in the midst of the questioning and searching?

'Well,' said Durris, surveying the company with something like dismay, 'we know that neither of them is hiding in any of the carriages – at least, we looked for Miss Pullman and I imagine that we would have noticed Mr. Middleton had we come across him instead. Dr. Napier, Mr. Strachan – you know the area quite well. Will you stay and help me to search?'

'Of course,' said Patrick, and Mr. Strachan nodded.

'May I be of assistance?' asked Mr. Dinmore. 'My manservant can help, too.' Mr. Dinmore's keen, intelligent face seemed set on solving a mystery. Hippolyta warmed to him, but Mrs. Dinmore, as if a divide had been made in the party, left her husband's side and came to stand near Hippolyta.

'You watch your knees,' she urged him, as she went. Hippolyta pretended not to have heard.

'It's good of him to volunteer,' she said.

'Oh, he's been all about the place since we came her,' said Mrs. Dinmore shortly. 'I thought perhaps on a holiday I should see more of him – we've come far enough from his precious banking house, after all – but no, off he goes. Tell me, Mrs. ... how do you amuse yourself in these parts?'

'Well,' said Hippolyta, 'there is the house, and there are friends, and of course I paint.'

'Oh! Painting. Are you any good?'

'Well …'

'I painted when I stayed here before at Braehead. I think I have exhausted the merits of any beauty spot within a ten mile scope.'

'I find the light and colours change so often there is always something new to be found.'

'Oh, no. When one has truly captured the essence of a place there is no sense in painting it again.'

Hippolyta blinked.

'Really?' The conversation had caught her up so swiftly she had to bite her lip to remind herself where they were and what they were doing. Mr. Durris was still selecting his search party.

'What about us?' asked Richard Hendry. 'Could we not help, too? I know the place is new to us, but we could at least walk around the loch, or something, where we wouldn't get lost and cause more confusion.'

Of course, thought Hippolyta, knowing Georgina as a childhood friend must make them feel responsible in some way. Lennox Hendry looked more reluctant, glancing at his father's comfortable carriage, but he shrugged and stood by his brother. Their father waved a hand from within his rugs.

'I'd help, too, of course, if I could.'

'Not at all, Mr. Hendry,' said Durris, bowing. 'You and Lord Tresco would both be better off resting. Mrs. Napier,' Hippolyta straightened, half-hoping she might be asked to join in the search too, 'would you kindly alert the constable when you reach Ballater, and tell him we need a search party? It may seem a little premature, but when she is unfamiliar with these parts and there are – individuals in the area who might take an interest in such as her, I should like to move quickly. Better safe than sorry.'

'Of course,' she said, disappointed but making do. 'Shall I

call at houses along the way?'

'Yes, please.' He nodded. Patrick slipped an arm discreetly about her waist and gave her a quick hug.

The girls were tidied into the various carriages and Mrs. Strachan and the Strongs prepared to lead the way back down to Ballater. But Hippolyta hesitated, still watching Mabelle.

'Mr. Durris!' she called, and he came over at once. 'That girl there – she is as close to a friend as I think Miss Pullman has here. She looks ... well, she might know something useful. Mabelle Ash, I believe her name is.'

'Indeed.' Durris strode over to the Strachans' carriage, and opened the door sharply. 'Miss Ash, may I have a word? Mrs. Napier will take you back, there is no need to detain Mrs. Strachan.'

White as a sheet, Mabelle stepped clumsily out of the carriage and landed on the dusty road with a thump. Durris waited until the Strongs, the Strachans and the Hendrys had driven off, taking the noise of iron wheels and iron-shod horses with them, leaving only the Strachans' servants with their cart and the beginnings of a search party. Patrick and Mr. Strachan kept the Hendrys and Dinmore at a distance for now, scouting about the roadway for any trace of the missing pair, debating a pattern for the search. Hippolyta felt very proud of Patrick taking his place like this.

'Now, Miss Ash,' Mr. Durris began, 'I believe you are friendly with Miss Pullman?'

'Yes, sir. I suppose I am, sir.'

'How was she today?'

'She was very well, sir. I believe the sea voyage from Tobago agreed with her, and she has had no fevers or anything since she came.'

Durris' lips pursed.

'I mean, was she in good spirits? Excited? Anxious?'

'Um, I'm not sure. She was looking forward to the picnic, I suppose – I mean, we all were, but I don't know that she was particularly excited about it.'

'And about anything that might happen after it?'

Mabelle squirmed.

'I don't know, sir.'

'I think you do, Miss Ash.'

'I don't *quite* know, sir,' Mabelle modified.

'And what you do know?'

For a long moment, Mabelle said nothing, but her eyes were like the face of a skeleton clock: you felt you could see the workings behind them.

'I wasn't supposed to know, that's the thing, sir. I only found out by accident.'

Hippolyta could see that Durris was manfully containing himself.

'It's quite important that you tell us, Miss Ash. Miss Pullman could be in some danger.'

'Oh! Really? Do you think so?'

'A girl on her own, here in an unfamiliar country? Of course she could be.'

'Oh!' Mabelle squeaked again. 'But if she isn't ... if she comes back, and finds out that I said ...'

'I think you should consider more how you would feel if she is, Miss Ash,' said Durris, an edge to his voice. She flinched.

'She was going to meet someone, after the picnic,' she said quickly, before she could stop herself again.

'A man?'

'Of course! Georgina would not put herself out to meet a woman!'

'No, I don't suppose she would,' Durris agreed. 'How did you find out?'

'I saw a note I wasn't supposed to see ... I went to borrow a book from her, and the note was in it – I stupidly picked up the wrong book, you see, it wasn't the one I thought it was at all and the note was in the book, you know, like a bookmark, and I saw it before I even realised what I was looking at – it was all my fault - and oh! she was cross!'

'I imagine she was,' said Durris, sympathetically. 'And the note was to arrange an assignation? For today?'

'It was, yes. She was to go into the woods at a certain point – over there, I think, but I'm not sure – when she was able to slip away from the company after the meal, and he would meet her there.'

'And was the note signed?'

'I don't know!' Mabelle suddenly seemed to grasp the gravity of the situation. 'I don't know who sent it! It was folded over, so I couldn't see the other half, and I wouldn't have looked anyway, but that was when she found me and she snatched it away!'

'Then how do you know it was a man?' asked Hippolyta, unable to help herself.

'Because she said – she swore me to secrecy, and she said she wasn't going to tell me his name, but he was going to take her away from this awful place to somewhere much more exciting, and she wouldn't have to live this dreary life any more, and her father would be pleased with her in the end.'

'Her father would be pleased with her? For eloping?'

'That's what she said!' Mabelle confirmed, miserably. 'And that's really, really all I know, sir!'

Durris looked at Hippolyta. She shrugged. It seemed unlikely that they would find out more just now.

'Mrs. Napier will take you home now,' Durris said. 'Thank you for telling me. It really is important.'

'Yes, sir,' said Mabelle, her face dismal. She went to the pony trap as if it were to take her to the gallows, and climbed in.

'It looks like an elopement, doesn't it?' Hippolyta said.

'It does. I'd like to find young Peter Middleton, all the same. It must be him.'

'I have to admit I'm surprised,' said Hippolyta.

'Why?'

'Georgina strikes me as a calculating girl. I don't think she would be romantic enough to throw away her reputation and hopes for the sake of a young farmer from Tarland. I'd have said her aims were much higher than that.'

'Would he have the means to take her somewhere more exciting?'

'I've no idea. I shouldn't have thought so, but I've only just met him.'

'What about Lord Tresco?'

'That would be the sort of level I would have expected, yes. But I'm not sure he was particularly interested in her.'

'Not for marriage, perhaps. But for a dalliance?'

'Goodness! Do you think?' Hippolyta was shocked, and

Durris looked apologetic.

'Forgive me, Mrs. Napier. But such things do happen: a handsome, wealthy man with a title, luring in a young and innocent girl without any thought of her respectability … well, I hope I am wrong. And certainly, the disappearance of Peter Middleton at the same time makes him much more likely to be the suitor in question, and that, in the end, might not be a bad thing. A farmer from Tarland cannot afford a dalliance: he would be looking for a wife.'

It took some time to reach Ballater. Mabelle sat in unhappy isolation in the trap while Hippolyta walked the pony between cottages, at each one stopping to ask if either a girl or a man had been seen, then, when that came to nothing, to ask if the menfolk of the house could go up the Tarland road and join the search party. Most did: she said nothing of the suspected circumstances and while several leapt to the conclusion that they were to prevent an elopement, others muttered the name 'Johnnie Boy Jo' and headed up the road with grim purpose. Hippolyta's lips tightened. She had not even thought of Johnnie Boy Jo. She asked Mabelle if the idea had crossed her mind.

'Johnnie Boy Jo? Isn't that the man that Mrs. Kynoch warned us about, after Mr. Durris came to visit?'

'Yes, that's the one.'

'But I thought he only … well, undid himself.'

Hippolyta tried not to smile at the odd image this presented.

'My husband has come across such creatures before,' she explained, 'and he says that while none of them ever stops what they are doing, many grow more aggressive and frightening in their behaviour. Since we don't know where Johnnie Boy Jo has been for the last few years, it is hard to know if he falls into this set, but it is sensible to be cautious.'

'You think Georgina may have met him in the woods?'

'If so, I'm sure it was an accident. It may be that …' She pictured a number of eventualities but thought that they would be much too distressing for Mabelle to hear: she seemed a delicate girl. 'It is indeed probable that she has arranged to meet Peter Middleton and has gone away with him.'

'To Gretna?' asked Mabelle, suddenly excited. 'Like Lydia

Bennet in Miss Austen's novel?'

'I think the point was that Lydia Bennet did not go to Gretna,' Hippolyta pointed out. 'But in any case, the purpose of going to Gretna was to cross into Scotland where the marriage laws were different.' Even Hippolyta's girlhood reading had been influenced by coming from a family of lawyers. 'In case you hadn't noticed, we are already in Scotland.'

'Oh. Oh, yes, of course.' Mabelle spent a moment taking that in, while Hippolyta walked on. They were almost at Tullich: no doubt Mrs. Price was already at home, having taken a place in the Strachans' carriage on the way back. 'But I'm almost sure she would not have run away with Peter Middleton, you know.'

'Really?' Hippolyta glanced back to show she was interested. 'Why do you say that?'

'Well, obviously Peter Middleton admired her, very much. And Grace Spencer was furious, because she and Mr. Middleton had an understanding, long before Georgina came here. You see?'

'Well, yes, but –'

'And Georgina, well, while Mr. Middleton was the only man who came to visit, apart from the minister and the doctor – I mean, Dr. Napier, Mrs. Napier,'

'Yes.'

'He was the only young man, you know, and without a wife as yet.'

'Georgina was prepared to flirt with him because he was the only available man around?'

'Mrs. Napier! You make Georgina sound … I hated it when Margaret said that we all know what kind of girl Georgina is. She's not! She's not one of those silly girls always falling in and out of love and reading ridiculous romances!'

'No, I'm sure she isn't,' said Hippolyta, who had Georgina Pullman down as quite a different kind of girl.

'She's very definite about who she wants to marry, and Mr. Middleton – well, he was very far from what she wanted, I'm quite sure.' Mabelle seemed to grow in confidence as they went along – and to be more comfortable talking to Hippolyta's back than to her face. 'And anyway, I was there when Mr. Middleton declared himself, and she turned him down.'

'You were what? Mr. Middleton actually proposed to Miss

Pullman?'

'He did! Yesterday morning. We were supposed to be in our Italian class, but Georgina can't abide languages and we'd gone for a walk in the garden instead, and Mr. Middleton came in the back gate.'

Hippolyta made a mental note to remind Mrs. Kynoch to lock it. If Mr. Middleton could come in, anyone could.

'Did he make a nuisance of himself?' she asked, remembering the scene she and Patrick had encountered on their way back from Tullich.

'No, he did not,' she said, after a moment's thought. 'He was perfectly polite. But there was something … I'm not sure. Something in their conversation I thought I was not hearing.'

'Something they did not want you to hear?'

'Perhaps. It was as if neither of them really meant the words they were saying, they just needed to be there and say them.' She sounded sad. Hippolyta wondered if Mabelle had been excluded from many conversations in her time, then remembered something.

'Mr. Middleton and Grace – Spencer? Miss Spencer had a quarrel at the picnic, didn't they? And you ended up comforting Miss Spencer.'

'Well, she was my friend before Georgina came and everything became awkward.' This time Hippolyta felt as if there were something she was not being told, but they had reached another cottage and she did not feel it was the place to pursue it. She drew the pony to a halt and as before knocked at the cottage door, asked her questions, gave her news and encouraged any male inhabitants to go to help the search party. Then they carried on.

'So if you don't think it was Peter Middleton she went to meet,' Hippolyta began, 'then who do you think it might have been? Who did she think it would be worth her while to meet?'

'I don't know. I wondered about Lord Tresco,' said Mabelle, her voice trembling even over the awesome name. 'But then I did wonder if he would bother with her, beautiful though she is. I mean, I'm sure he has a bride lined up somewhere already.'

'And you did say that Georgina was not romantic, so an assignation like that – secret messages, a clandestine meeting – surely none of that is in her character?'

'Well, true,' said Mabelle, then in a burst of realisation she added, 'unless she believed that that was the only way to get what she wanted.'

'To trap a man into marriage? Would she do that?'

'The right man,' said Mabelle, and took another deep breath. 'Yes, I believe she might.'

Hippolyta took Mabelle all the way back to Dinnet House before driving back down into the village to rouse the constable and give him Mr. Durris' message. Then she returned pony and trap to their stable at the inn, and walked slowly back up the main street to the green and their little high-browed house opposite the centrical church. It was not unknown for her to be returning home alone while Patrick was out somewhere: patients did not always wait for convenient hours to be sick or to injure themselves, but this evening she felt particularly lonely. It was already nearly nine o'clock, but in the Scottish midsummer it was still broad daylight outside. She went to tell Ishbel the cook what was happening, and asked for tea and something simple to eat. It seemed like a day and a night since their picnic meal.

On a bright night like this, the search party would be able to see quite clearly until maybe eleven o'clock, unless, by good luck, they had already found them by then.

By good luck, or maybe by bad.

She sighed, and drank her tea, and murmured to the cats, and wondered when Patrick would be home.

Lexie Conyngham

Chapter Seven

Patrick returned about midnight, scratched and grubby, having been given a welcome lift back on Mr. Strachan's servants' cart.

'No sign of either of them,' he muttered, exhausted, as he dropped into bed beside her.

'That might be a good thing,' she murmured, 'or at least not an awful thing.' But he was already asleep.

There were no patients urgently demanding his attention the next morning and though he normally played the piano for their church service at the inn, that took second place to the search for a missing girl. As soon as he was up and breakfasted he and Mr. Strachan set off again, this time on horseback. Hippolyta spent a frustrating half hour trying to teach Johanna the maid the virtues of cleaning dishes and pots between uses, before fetching her bonnet and parasol and setting off for the service herself. The visiting clergyman had been before and was used to dealing with a diverse congregation of visitors and locals, and cheered them through the unaccompanied singing with some skill, being, like many Episcopalian clergy, a musical man. She herself had her usual task of greeting the worshippers as they arrived and handing them hymnbooks, a humble position from which she was delighted to be able to see the whole congregation and watch them during the service. Old Mr. Hendry attended, with his daughter and the two little girls, and Lord Tresco also hobbled carefully to a seat in the midst of the room: Hippolyta was interested to see that he did not insist on a place at the front as would befit his status. Mrs. Dinmore stalked in and did sit at the front – was she really sitting as far from Lord Tresco as she could? It seemed unlikely, as they were friends. None of Mrs. Kynoch's girls came to the

Episcopalian service: it was expected of them throughout their stay that they should attend the kirk, with her. After all, the late Mr. Kynoch had been the minister there.

'No word yet?' Lord Tresco asked, as he handed back his hymnbook at the end of the service.

'Nothing last night. My husband and Mr. Strachan returned to the place this morning early.'

'My sons, too,' said Mr. Hendry, hearing her. Mrs. Dinmore, appearing behind them, added,

'My husband is already making his way there.'

'The pair must be far away by now,' said Lord Tresco, his tone lightly regretful. 'I saw the young man only in the garden last week and at the picnic, but he did seem the impulsive kind. I hope she does not regret allowing herself to be persuaded into such a course of action.'

They all nodded, sombre, though Hippolyta thought that that would be better than Patrick's theory of an attack by Johnnie Boy Jo. But then, if there had been an attack of that kind, surely they would have found her by now? And what had happened to Peter Middleton?

While the visitors to Ballater returned to their rooms at the inn, or waited for a ferry to take them back across the river to accommodation around Pannanich Wells, she strolled up towards the fine church that centrically served the three parishes of Tullich, Glenmuick and Glengairn. The congregation there was just beginning to emerge, shaking hands with the minister as they blinked in the bright sunlight. Hippolyta found Mrs. Kynoch and her subdued flock of girls after a moment of waiting, and they exchanged their lack of news together.

'Mr. Durris came to Dinnet House late last night,' said Mrs. Kynoch, her little face screwed up with anxiety. Hippolyta wanted to hug her. 'We discussed – possibilities. He is to make enquiries of the mail coaches, though of course they would have been too late to catch one last night, and there are none today. He might have hired a gig.'

'Had he no gig of his own?'

'Apparently not, or so Grace Spencer tells me, anyway. He always walked here from Tarland, or took a lift on the way.'

'And how is Grace Spencer?' Hippolyta looked about her

at the flock of girls, but could not see her.

'In her bed with a headache,' said Mrs. Kynoch. 'He has treated her very shabbily, I think: I had thought him a much more honourable young man than that, or I should never have let him near the place. I have let her down, I fear.'

'You weren't to know!' said Hippolyta at once. 'I blame Georgina Pullman for drawing him in. She certainly seems capable of working fast.'

'Then it is my fault for allowing her to behave like that. I feel I should never have accepted her at my little school. She has been nothing but a disruptive influence from the start.'

'But what else could you have done, Mrs. Kynoch? You were not to know truly what she was like until she arrived, and you could hardly then cast her out to fend for herself.'

'I was proud, that is what it was,' said Mrs. Kynoch, and Hippolyta was shocked to see tears in her eyes. 'My husband's old friend, who wrote to me about her, thought I could do some good with the girl, and I allowed myself to be flattered into believing it was indeed within my power. I should not have been so vain!'

Hippolyta fleetingly thought of her maid Johanna, and her own belief that she could improve her when Mrs. Strachan could not. She pursed her lips: was she too proud, too? She was certainly not as good a person as Mrs. Kynoch. She herself would happily have relied on Mrs. Kynoch to correct the faults in any spoilt young woman: she simply had not had Georgina Pullman under her wing for long enough.

'Mrs. Napier!'

Hippolyta turned to find the elegant figure of Mrs. Strachan approaching. The shop owner's wife as usual was dressed in the height of fashion but lacked some energy that would have made her seem entirely charming.

'Mrs. Napier, would you mind very much taking your pony and trap out? My husband intended this morning to take a hamper up to Burn o' Vat to feed the search party, and he has left it behind – and all the servants that could go with it are already up there.'

'I should be happy to,' said Hippolyta at once. At least it would mean she would see Patrick, and there might even be news. 'If you have it ready, I shall go and fetch the trap straight away. They started early: I should imagine they will be very grateful to receive it.'

She stopped at her own house nearby only to change her
gloves and boots: her Sunday gown would have to manage. Soon
she had the hamper snugly tucked into the back of the trap, and the
pony placated, and she was off along the flat highway that led back
towards Tullich and Loch Kinord. This time, with only one person
to pull, the pony was just about willing to climb the hill to Burn o'
Vat without having to be led, and to her satisfaction she arrived
where they had left the carriages the previous day to find that Mr.
Dinmore, Mr. Strachan, Patrick and Mr. Durris had just convened
there to compare notes. The Hendry brothers, too, appeared from
amongst the trees as she drew up, and Patrick came to greet her.

'I bring food,' she announced triumphantly. 'I'm sure you
are all ready for it.'

'I knew you were an angel,' said Patrick, with a grin.

'Is that the hamper I was meant to bring?' asked Mr.
Strachan. 'Excellent.'

The men gathered around. The hamper was generously
sized, and very full of all kinds of nourishing supplies: the servants
were as well fed as the others, and Hippolyta, too, who would have
taken it badly had she been left out, found herself well satisfied
with a meat pie and two jam tarts. She allowed the men to eat
before she asked any questions: it was clear they had had no
success.

Durris confirmed it.

'No sign,' he said. His eyes were tired. 'Of course in a way
…'

'That may be a good thing,' Hippolyta finished. 'He's a
respectable young man, if a little impulsive,' she added,
remembering what Lord Tresco had said. 'He'll stand by her, no
doubt.'

'I only wonder if she will treat him as kindly?' Patrick
murmured, only for Hippolyta and Durris to hear. But Lennox
Hendry evidently had very good hearing.

'I doubt it,' he said tightly. 'She'll never stick with him.
The moment a better opportunity comes up, she'll be off.'

Durris regarded him blandly.

'Have you some acquaintance with the young lady, then?'

'Our families knew each other back in Tobago,' said

Lennox, very much as if he wished they had not. 'Her mother was a wild one, too, but she died young. And the father – well, he indulged her, didn't he? Got everything she wanted – and nothing that she didn't,' he added, with a hint of bitterness. Presumably Mr. Hendry was not so weak as Mr. Pullman. 'And if you ask me, I think it's very odd that she went off with that Middleton lad,' Lennox went on, brushing pastry crumbs from the front of his plaid waistcoat. 'Now if it had been Lord Tresco she had managed to snare, that would be a different thing. But a farming lad, from nowhere anyone's heard of? Not likely – not for Miss Georgina Pullman.'

Durris looked at him for a moment, then removed a small black notebook from his pocket, and made some minuscule shape in it. Hippolyta was too far away to see what it was, to her disappointment. Did Durris believe Lennox Hendry? It was very much what Mabelle had told her on the way home last night. But there was something else: Lennox clearly disliked Georgina, with something a little more than just ordinary distaste for an old acquaintance whose character he found difficult. There was some story there, and Hippolyta wondered if Durris, like her, longed to know what it was. She glanced at Richard Hendry. He was watching his brother anxiously.

'Were you acquainted with Miss Pullman in Tobago too, Mr. Hendry?' she asked the younger brother.

'I was,' he said, turning to her in apparent gratitude. 'I never thought ... I mean, yes, she was a little sharp sometimes, but if she found a man she loved I'm sure ...' He tailed off, mouth open, as if all the words he could think of had trickled out and he had forgotten to close up after them.

'Well,' said Durris, folding away his notebook, 'I think it's time we changed tactics. Up to now I have been anxious to make sure that Miss Pullman – and indeed Mr. Middleton – were not injured or perhaps even attacked here somewhere, and awaiting help. Let us take it as good news that we have not found any signs of that, and now take more seriously the theory that they have in fact run away together. Dr. Napier, would you allow Mrs. Napier to drive us both to Tarland, and we shall see if there is news of them there?'

'Of course,' said Patrick, nodding at Hippolyta. He knew

she would be pleased to be involved, and the pony did very little for anyone else.

'Mr. Strachan, perhaps you and these gentlemen –' he nodded at the Hendry brothers and Mr. Dinmore, 'would care to return to Ballater? You can ask there again for news, and if you, Mr. Strachan, would be so good as to call on Mrs. Kynoch, you could tell her where we are going.'

'Of course,' said Strachan. 'If you really believe we can do nothing more here.'

'We could just stay and take one more turn around the loch,' suggested Richard Hendry.

'No, Dick, he's right,' said Lennox. 'There's nothing more to be done here. If she was here, we'd have found her.'

Richard shrugged, and together they joined Strachan in his carriage. The empty hamper was loaded in with them, and the Strachan servants organised themselves to walk or ride back as the space permitted. Durris and the Napiers waved them off, then climbed into the rather less splendid trap and continued up the road to Tarland.

'We even took boats out on to the loch,' Patrick told her. 'It's so shallow one would have been able to see … well, anyone down there, I think. Anything light coloured would show clearly. But there was nothing.'

'What do you think of Lennox Hendry?' She was keen to find out if they shared her curiosity.

'No love lost there,' Durris remarked shortly.

'I wonder who arrived here first? Were the Hendrys already here … yes, I believe they were, for Georgina has only come to Ballater in the last week. Did she know they were staying here, I wonder?'

'I think the Hendrys have been away from Tobago for some months,' said Patrick. 'When Mr. Hendry consulted me, he mentioned having been to stay with friends near Manchester before his health worsened, and a physician there recommended a visit to Ballater.'

'Georgina told me that society in Tobago is very restricted, and she complained that they had to associate with all kinds of people. Perhaps she saw the Hendrys as beneath her.'

'I think she saw most people as beneath her, from all I have heard,' said Patrick.

'Including Peter Middleton,' said Hippolyta. 'You know, yesterday on the way home Mabelle said much the same thing that Lennox Hendry did – she said Georgina was ruled by reason, not by romance, and would not be likely to run away with anyone who would not be advantageous to her.'

'Maybe her heart got the better of her for once,' suggested Durris, unexpectedly, and they drove on in silence.

The road they took quickly left the birch and conifer woodlands around Loch Kinord, and slipped blissfully down into the rich farmland of the Howe of Cromar, green even in this dry spell. Hippolyta was not sure whether it was just her imagination, but the cattle here seemed glossier, the sheep rounder, the air itself full of warm, earthy promise. Perhaps Peter Middleton was a prosperous farmer indeed, for this was fine country. The road was lined with dykes that were more hedge than stone, and full of flowers. Hippolyta reminded herself that she must come here to paint soon.

They drove into the long central square of Tarland village, sunny in the Sabbath quiet, and looked about them. Durris pointed out the inn, a respectable, clean-looking establishment.

'We can enquire there,' he suggested. 'I'll go in.'

Hippolyta took the precaution of stepping down to hold the pony's head and to distract it from the possibilities of nipping passersby, and Patrick stood with her. The square was lined with plain, respectable granite buildings: somehow in the Howe of Cromar she had expected something more splendid, but there was nothing out of the ordinary.

Durris was not long in the inn, and waved to them as he emerged.

'We passed it,' he announced, waiting until the Napiers had climbed back into the trap before joining them. 'The house is just outside the village, on a lane to the left – it would have been on our right.'

Hippolyta persuaded the pony to set off again and they turned back the way they had come. Durris confidently pointed out the lane end, and with care they manoeuvred the trap into the narrow entrance. Hippolyta wondered where and how they were going to turn it. But around four hundred yards along the track they came to a neat little farm house with a clean, swept yard and fresh-looking outhouses. The sound of the wheels must have been heard inside the house, for before they could stop a woman flung open the door, a smile on her face, and quickly frowned.

'Mrs. Middleton?' Durris tried, and she nodded, the frown deepening at once.

'Is this about Peter?' she asked. 'Has something happened to him?'

'We're not sure, Mrs. Middleton,' said Durris, hopping down lightly from the trap. 'Is he your son?'

'He is,' she said. She held her hand over her eyes to angle out the bright sunlight. 'And he didna come home last evening. Courting, he told me he was, and all pleased with himself, but where is he now? It wouldn't be like him to stay out all night with a lassie, not a respectable one he hoped to marry. The fines for antenuptial fornication are getting steep,' she added frankly.

'Well, we're trying to find out where he's gone, Mrs. Middleton. Do you think – did you suspect at all – that Peter might elope?'

'Elope? Peter? What for would he do that? If it's that Grace girl then he had no need – Mrs. Kynoch was away to write to her father and see it all done properly if they wanted to go through with it.'

'No, not Miss Spencer,' said Durris. 'Miss Spencer is safely at Mrs. Kynoch's still. But Peter was at a picnic at Loch Kinord yesterday with a number of us, and when we were ready to go both he and another girl were found to be missing. No one had seen them for an hour or so.'

'And they went off together?' Mrs. Middleton's eyes narrowed.

'No one really knows. But he had a quarrel with Miss Spencer – Grace – which we believe was connected with his interest in this other girl.'

'Oh, aye?' She reflected for a moment. 'Thought he'd get away with it, did he, but that Grace was too quick for him? Aye, he's like his father,' she said, chuckling fondly. 'Never as clever as he thought he was. Aye, I thought that Grace would be up to him: I like the lass.'

'Well, that's good,' said Durris, 'but it doesn't explain

where he is now. Has he been back here at all since he went out yesterday morning? Would he have collected anything from here – money, clothes, perhaps?'

'I didna see hide nor hair of him,' his mother acknowledged. 'I doubt there's clothes gone, but he would have had a wee bit of money with him, I suppose, he usually did.'

'Did he own a trap, or a gig?'

'No, he talked of it, and in my mind I thought he was putting it off till he married, till he could swan around showing off his new wifie. Aye, and bonnie enough she is, too. He's a fool if he's gone off with another.'

'Perhaps you have a riding horse?' Durris tried again. It seemed that Mrs. Middleton had a higher opinion of her daughter-in-law to be than of her own son.

'Aye, we do, but it's yonder in the stable. I fed it myself this morning and rode it to the kirk, for my feet arena what they used to be for the walking.'

Durris glanced back at Patrick, eyebrows raised. Patrick shrugged. What else was there to ask?

'If he does appear – or if you hear word from him – can you send me a message?' Durris explained how he could be reached. 'I'm the sheriff's officer in these parts.'

'Michty, are you? You never said! Then it's serious?'

'We'd very much like to speak to him, yes,' said Durris politely.

'Aye,' she said, 'aye.' The matter had clearly taken on a new significance for her, and she spoke absently. 'Aye, if I hear a'thing, I'll be sure to ...' She tailed off, retreating into the house and fumbling the door shut behind her.

'Interesting,' said Patrick, as Durris returned to the trap.

'I don't suppose they manage this place on their own, the two of them,' Durris said quietly. 'That looks to me like the farm bothy there, and it's as neat as the rest. There's probably a loon or two about.' He edged into the yard, one eye on the house in case Mrs. Middleton re-emerged, but all was peaceful. He glanced into the stable to which she had pointed, and a brown nose emerged for patting, the intelligent eye of a curious horse. The pony whickered, jealous of the attention. Then a door, already ajar, swung fully open next to the stable, and a man emerged, eyeing Durris up and down and then examining the trap.

'Good day to you,' said Durris. 'Are you the farm loon?'

'Och, I'm naught but the orra loon,' said the man, his voice squeaky. He coughed, and apologised. 'I heard you talking with the mistress there. You're looking for the master, eh?'

'That's right, for Peter Middleton.'

'Aye, he's away, right enough,' said the man, and coughed again. 'It's the dust, ken,' he explained. 'I had a news with a pal of mine this morn at the kirk, and he says that the master's away with his master's gig, and said he'd no be back this side of next Sabbath.'

'He took a gig? From Tarland?'

'He did an' all,' said the man, and wiped his mouth with the back of his hand, swallowing hard. 'From the next farm. Last night it would be, late.'

'On his own?'

'Aye, not a soul with him.'

'And luggage?'

'Not a scrap,' said the man, looking pleased to be the informant. 'Not a wee bittie bag nor nothing.'

'And did he say where he was going?'

'Well, he set off in the direction of Aberdeen, ken. But a road can take many turns,' said the orra loon, nodding in satisfaction at his philosophical tilt. 'He could be anywhere.'

Chapter Eight

'What am I to tell her father? There is a letter arrived from him this morning – I feel I should open it, but what if she returns?'

Mrs. Kynoch had never had a girl abscond before: Hippolyta knew that she would know exactly what to write to Mr. Pullman, but she needed a little while to think it through and arrange her words. Mrs. Kynoch always knew what to do, in the best and most charitable way there was.

'You could tell them that Mr. Durris is flying about the countryside trying to bring her back, couldn't you?'

'He only sent me a message last night,' said Mrs. Kynoch, without a hint of reprimand. 'And his writing is so tiny ...'

'Well,' said Hippolyta, thinking again of that tantalising notebook where Mr. Durris made his minuscule mnemonics, 'of course he did not take the orra loon at his word. He went back and spoke to Mrs. Middleton to ask if she knew where he might be going, and she said he has a sister in Aberdeen that he's fond of, but she had no idea why he should suddenly head off to visit her without even waiting for the mail coach. So then we drove to the friend – the one the orra loon's friend works for, on the next farm ...' The lane had grown even narrower, briars and gorse scraping the sides of the trap and the dykes so close Hippolyta could have reached out and lifted a stone from the one next to her. The pony, who might have been expected to refuse to tackle such a path, instead came as close to bolting as it ever did, presumably keen to leave the place as quickly as it could, and it was as much as Hippolyta could do to draw it up when they reached what was evidently the next farmhouse. A man had looked out of the window in alarm at the sound of clattering hooves, a slice of bread and butter still in his hand from the tea table.

'And what did he say?' Mrs. Kynoch wanted the whole story.

'He and his wife came out and invited us in, and gave us tea,' said Hippolyta, the memory a happy one. 'And they said that the orra loon was quite right: Peter Middleton had borrowed their gig and a horse, and headed off back through Tarland – that's to the north. But he could have gone that way to Aberdeen, or to Alford, or to all kinds of places. And so now Mr. Durris has borrowed a horse from the same farmer and he's off trying to find him. Tracking him across the countryside!'

'Such a good man, Mr. Durris,' said Mrs. Kynoch, with feeling. 'I believe he sent the note with you?'

'Yes, he did, and Wullie ran up here with it last night. I would have come here myself, but when we arrived home we found that Johanna the maid has been causing problems again. Tell me, is the minister preaching a series of sermons on slavery?'

'I believe he is, yes. There seem to be several visitors to the neighbourhood at present connected with plantations, and he appears to think they need admonishment.' Mrs. Kynoch looked down at her lap, and it struck Hippolyta that she was avoiding Hippolyta's eye. It was so unlike Mrs. Kynoch that Hippolyta blinked in surprise, forgetting for a moment her train of thought.

'But what has that to do with Johanna?' Mrs. Kynoch prompted her, and again, it felt like a deliberate change of subject.

'She has a theory that she is our slave, and that she has no freedom to make her own decisions or go her own way. It makes her reluctant to carry out any of the work that she should be doing, and unfortunately she refuses to help Ishbel, whose poor wrist is still not quite better.'

Mrs. Kynoch considered.

'Perhaps you should explain to her that she can leave at any time.'

'If this goes on much longer I shall be encouraging her to leave as soon as possible,' said Hippolyta, a little more sharply than she intended. Mrs. Kynoch nodded.

'But you did say you would teach her, didn't you? To help her find a situation in a bigger household?'

'I did,' said Hippolyta, and because Mrs. Kynoch

encouraged such things, she added, humbly, 'I was too proud, and took on more than I could manage. And she upsets Wullie.'

'Give her a little longer,' said Mrs. Kynoch. 'I'm sure you and Ishbel between you will be able to show her how to behave.'

Hippolyta lapsed into silence for a moment, considering how she might explain things better to Johanna. The pause helped Mrs. Kynoch to think over all Hippolyta had told her.

'Mr. Middleton left Tarland in a gig, with no luggage,' she said slowly.

'Yes, in the direction of Tornaveen and Echt and such places.'

'But on his own.'

'Yes, I know. The man who lent him the gig saw no one with him.'

'Could he have picked her up from somewhere? Could he perhaps have planned this in advance, taken luggage somewhere and left it and collected it and her?'

'Is there anything missing from her room?'

'I haven't looked. I'm not sure,' she went on, 'that I would know. But we can bring Mabelle, if you would like to look now.'

Hippolyta had been restless all morning at the thought of Mr. Durris cantering over the countryside hunting for Peter Middleton, while she sat at home fretting over her housemaid. The thought of being able to do something at least related to the hunt was irresistible, and she was already on her feet.

'Yes, let's!'

Mrs. Kynoch's school was arranged in such a way that the girls were allocated their rooms in pairs, in one case to accommodate a couple of sisters, and otherwise to encourage friendships and avert loneliness so far from home. Hippolyta was not surprised to find that Mabelle and Georgina had fallen together this way, and when they had drawn Mabelle out of an accountancy lesson – valuable for all young ladies with a household to manage but particularly useful for those intending to set up businesses as milliners and so forth – Mabelle led them upstairs to the first floor, to a pretty room facing the front of the house with its trees and lawn. The morning sunlight dazzled at the window, bringing out the colours in the bed clothes and the decorative shawls and small ornaments about the chamber. Mabelle stood back, looking about her, as if her care of the place was being judged, and allowed Mrs. Kynoch and Hippolyta to go further into the room.

'Which bed is yours?' Hippolyta asked. Mabelle pointed, nervous. Hippolyta nodded.

Both beds were made up with identical counterpanes, but she could almost have guessed which was Mabelle's and which Georgina's. The little chest of drawers that stood between the beds was littered with combs and fans to the extent of about two-thirds across. The final third held a plainly-framed miniature of a middle-aged woman and a brass candlestick, and nothing else. There were two chairs in the room, and two large kists: again, Mabelle's chair and kist were tidy and bare, set back against the wall, while Georgina's were littered with petticoats and bonnets and wound about with stockings, while boots and shoes tangled, far from their partners, amongst the tails of the curtains, as if that was where Georgina was accustomed to throwing them. Mrs. Kynoch looked about her in dismay.

'The maid sees to the beds,' she explained, 'but beyond that the girls are expected to look after their own rooms. I see you have your things in good order, Mabelle,' she added, and a small anxious smile wriggled across Mabelle's face.

'I don't have as many things as Georgina,' she said, 'so it's much easier for me.'

'Is there any chance at all,' said Hippolyta, 'that you could tell if some of Georgina's things are missing?'

Mabelle's eyes widened and she looked about obediently.

'It's a little hard to tell,' she admitted. She stepped cautiously forward past her own bed and into the mess. Hippolyta wondered if she had ever before been allowed into that half of the room. Certainly she looked as if she were venturing into forbidden territory. She stopped in the middle of a rug, and turned slowly.

'I don't see her favourite boots,' she said. 'Um … and there's a small kist missing. How did I not notice that?' She put a hand to her forehead. 'It sits beside the large one, just there.'

'How large? What colour?' Hippolyta thought she knew the kinds of questions Mr. Durris would ask.

'About this size?' Mabelle described a shape with her hands, around two feet long by a foot and a half deep, and a foot tall. 'And it is painted black, with a brass lock.'

'So it could contain the boots, easily enough, and perhaps a clean shift and night clothes?' Hippolyta suggested.

'Oh, yes, it could. But I wouldn't know if any of that was missing. But I don't see her blue bonnet, and she might have squeezed that in, if she was careful.'

'Was she carrying a reticule on Saturday?' Mrs. Kynoch screwed up her face, trying to remember.

'Yes, a deep bag one,' said Mabelle at once. 'I thought it a large one for a picnic, but it was very fashionable, of course.'

'And she could have carried all kinds of things in that,' said Hippolyta. 'A spare shawl, perhaps, and a change of gloves.'

'Easily,' agreed Mabelle.

'But how could she have taken the kist away?' asked Mrs. Kynoch.

'That's a good question,' said Hippolyta. 'Could Peter Middleton have taken it away? He was here during the week, wasn't he?'

'He hasn't been here since Tuesday, I believe,' said Mrs. Kynoch, and Mabelle went pink.

'He was here on Friday, Mrs. Kynoch,' she said in a small voice. 'And he made a proposal of marriage to Georgina, and she turned him down.' She glanced at Hippolyta. Hippolyta wondered if she would have told Mrs. Kynoch if Hippolyta had not been there, but decided she would. Mabelle was a sensible girl, who knew when secrets had to be kept and when they were best revealed. But Mrs. Kynoch's jaw had dropped.

'What? And you didn't think to tell me?'

'She made me promise not to!' cried Mabelle, on the verge of tears. 'And I thought, since she had turned him down and he went away all quietly, that there was no harm in it!'

'Oh, what am I to tell her father? All my pupils will be taken from me. I shall never be sent any girls again!'

'I think anyone who has met Georgina would know you had a challenge on your hands, Mrs. Kynoch,' said Hippolyta, taking her hand and squeezing it gently. 'But Mabelle, didn't you say you thought there was something else about the conversation? Something odd?'

Mabelle nodded.

'But I don't really know what.' She pulled out a handkerchief and blew her nose thoroughly. 'I just felt they were saying things I wasn't hearing.'

Mrs. Kynoch met Hippolyta's eye.

'You think he might have taken the box then?' she asked. She had already recovered some of her composure.

'I think he might have,' said Hippolyta. 'It sounds as if they might have been play acting for you, Mabelle: the proposal was a cover for other things.'

'But why?' said Mrs. Kynoch. 'It doesn't make sense. If they wanted to elope, then why did she turn him down? If he proposed, why did she not accept and come and tell me? He's a decent young man, if not quite of the rank that I believed Georgina would aim for, and there would be nothing against the marriage, I'm sure. I should happily have written to her father in support of the match, only that poor Grace would have been so disappointed. But better to lose a suitor than to lose a husband,' she added sensibly. 'So why did they not go about it in the normal way?'

'Romance?' suggested Hippolyta.

'Mrs. Napier, I think I said to you that she is not a romantic,' said Mabelle. She wrung her hands. This business, Hippolyta thought, was drawing out a much stronger Mabelle than she had previously seen. Perhaps Georgina's shadow had been a heavy one. 'Mrs. Kynoch, I'm sorry, but I cannot believe she has any intention of marrying Peter Middleton, secretly or not.'

'Then what?'

All three of them looked at one another, Mabelle baffled, Hippolyta and Mrs. Kynoch, knowing a little more of the world and its failings, with concern. Then a thought struck Hippolyta.

'I saw them together on Friday evening,' she said. 'On the road to Tullich.'

'But what on earth was she doing out there? Friday evening … did she not say she intended to retire early that evening, in advance of the picnic?'

'She did,' said Mabelle, 'and I believed she had done so, though I did not come up here until late.'

'She could have slipped out, I suppose. Oh, really, she has been a most disappointing pupil in every respect!'

'When we saw them, Patrick and I, we thought they were

quarrelling. At first, in fact, because we saw them from a distance, we thought it was someone encountering Johnnie Boy Jo, and Patrick ran to interrupt.'

'But they were quarrelling?'

'That's what I thought had happened, when we caught up. But if they were presenting a deceptive front, for some reason, then I am not so sure.'

'But what would they be doing out there?'

'Hiding her box? And perhaps a box of his own, too?'

Mrs. Kynoch looked at her, and then at Mabelle.

'You know, my dear, you could be right! That makes sense. And in weather like this, for only a night, if they tucked it into a ditch it would take no harm from the damp.'

'They were next to that little wood by the corner, you know?'

'Do you think there might still be some trace, if we went to look?' Mrs. Kynoch was eager now, and even Mabelle had a hint of excitement in her expression.

'There might! Though in a way,' Hippolyta continued, thoughtful, 'it doesn't quite make sense. Peter Middleton drove away from Tarland to the north, and the kist, if it is there, is to the south, back towards Ballater.'

'He could have doubled back later,' said Mrs. Kynoch.

'But then he would have run into the search parties ... but there must be some lane somewhere he could have used, some other road, I'm sure. Let's go and look. We can stop at the inn and collect the pony and trap.'

To Hippolyta's surprise, by the time Mrs. Kynoch had found her bonnet and shawl and gloves, Mabelle too had equipped herself and was waiting for them in the hall. Hippolyta would not have thought her quite so decisive. Mrs. Kynoch looked at her but said nothing, and Mabelle followed them down into the village and to the inn, where Hippolyta quickly arranged pony and trap and they set off, more slowly than Hippolyta would have liked. The pony apparently felt it was being overworked. Even Richard Hendry, walking briskly as he waved them a greeting, was able to pass them as he headed out along the road, and soon left them behind.

It was pleasant to be out in the sunshine today, though: the air was lighter, there was a soft breeze brushing over the road carrying the scents of the woods across the river, and last night's dew had been heavy enough to damp down the worst of the dust under their wheels.

They were hardly outside Ballater proper when Hippolyta drew the pony to a halt. Mrs. Price was marching towards the village, her painting gear arranged about her like a pedlar.

'Good morning, Mrs. Price! Who will be your subject today?' she called.

'Is there any news?' Mrs. Price responded at once, an arm across her forehead to shield her eyes from the sun as she looked up at them. 'Has she been found?'

'No, not yet,' said Mrs. Kynoch gently. 'The search continues. Mr. Durris is hunting for Mr. Middleton, too, in the hope that he can answer some questions.'

'Silly girl,' said Mrs. Price. 'Silly, silly girl.' She turned, and tramped off towards the village without another word.

'She's very artistic, isn't she?' said Mabelle.

'Hm,' said Hippolyta. She was about to set the pony going again when it shied at the sight of a handcart approaching, and jerked them about a bit. By the time they had righted themselves, the handcart was level with them, and to their surprise they saw it contained no market goods, but Mr. Dinmore, of Dinmore's Banking House, seated on some straw.

'Good morning, ladies,' he said, bowing his head as best he could. The carter, seeing the chance of a rest, set the cart legs down and rubbed his hands together.

'Good morning, Mr. Dinmore. Have you been with the search party this morning?'

'Ah … yes, yes, Mrs. Napier,' he said, 'until my ridiculous knee gave way. I shall have to consult Dr. Napier, I fear.'

'If you like I shall pass a message along,' said Hippolyta. 'Is it an old injury?'

Mr. Dinmore sighed.

'Yes, it is, and a most annoying one. Every few years, just when I believe all is well, my knee simply gives way again. The last time it happened I was crossing a busy street in London, and was nearly run over by a carriage. Fortunately, Lord Tresco saw me and was able to carry me off to his house nearby, where I was able to stay until the knee was quite better again.'

'Fortunate indeed,' Hippolyta agreed, noting the details for Patrick. 'I shall tell my husband when I next see him.'

'Thank you, thank you! I hope we shall have good news of Miss Pullman soon, Mrs. Kynoch, but I fear I shall be searching no more just now.'

'Not at all, Mr. Dinmore: please concentrate on your own recovery,' said Mrs. Kynoch, clearly touched. Mr. Dinmore waved to the carter, and nodded farewell, and once the handcart was clear Hippolyta managed to persuade the pony to start again.

Thereafter they made good time to the little woodland where Hippolyta and Patrick had seen Georgina speaking with, if not quarrelling with, Peter Middleton. There was some undergrowth between the trees, of a brambly, rough kind. It would be an ideal place to hide a box for a day or two. Hippolyta was delighted that it had not rained: the ground under the trees was sheltered, but even so rain might well have wiped away any traces of something heavy set on it.

She jumped from the seat and turned to help Mrs. Kynoch down. Mabelle scrambled down on the other side and came round to them, careful not to stray within teeth reach of the pony. Hippolyta wound up the reins, and they turned to contemplate the wood.

'It won't take us long to search,' she said, 'but we need to be careful that we don't trample over any traces.'

'Yes, indeed,' said Mrs. Kynoch. 'They won't be that obvious.' They paused for another moment, then without speaking they began to circle the little wood, examining the ground before each step, heads down. Hippolyta tried to imagine what she was looking for – a mark on the earth where a sharp corner had dug in? Trampled grasses, or broken brambles? A mark on the bark of a tree where a careless step had caused the box hider to stumble? Could the box, in fact, have been hidden in a tree? But when she looked around at eye level she realised that none of the trees was really strong enough or broad enough to take the weight of a kist of the size Mabelle had indicated, and that anyway, if one had been perched there it would have been obvious to anyone walking past on the road.

She met Mrs. Kynoch and Mabelle on the other side of the woodland, and they all shook their heads at each other. It was worth continuing, though, for though they would now be passing the same places the others had already passed, they would be looking from a different angle. Hippolyta put out a hand to squeeze Mrs. Kynoch's arm, and they carried on.

And in a few steps, she had found it.

Not a mark in the earth, or a scrap on the tree trunk, but the box itself, tucked under a bramble bush, with a broken branch artfully arranged to disguise it. It was the pale wood of the branch that had caught Hippolyta's eye and drawn it to notice the upturned leaves.

'Is this it?' she called, as if the local population were in the habit of leaving black-painted kists with brass locks, approximately two feet by one foot by one and a half, under trees in the summer time. Mabelle was quicker than Mrs. Kynoch to hurry back.

'That's the one!' she exclaimed. 'That's Georgina's kist!'

Mrs. Kynoch was just behind her, and stopped to stare at it.

'But what's it doing here?'

'Maybe they didn't come back this way after all,' suggested Hippolyta. 'Maybe they decided it would be better to run north while no one had noticed they had gone, and they would come back for it another time. Or simply buy what they needed.'

'But then where did he pick her up?' Mrs. Kynoch had clearly linked the missing girl and the missing luggage in her head.

'She didn't have to be hiding in the same place as the kist, Mrs. Kynoch,' said Hippolyta.

'I suppose that's true ...' But Mrs. Kynoch did not seem to be convinced.

'Should we see what is in it?' asked Mabelle, quivering slightly. She was not the kind of girl who would poke about in other people's luggage, normally. The strangeness of the occasion was affecting her. Hippolyta knelt beside the kist, and tried the latch.

'It's locked, of course,' she said. 'Who would leave an unlocked box unattended? And presumably she has the key with her.'

'In that enormous reticule,' added Mabelle, nodding.

'Should we take it back with us?' Mrs. Kynoch asked. 'I think it should be kept with the rest of her things, don't you?'

'But what if she comes back for it?' asked Mabelle.

'Then she will have to come and explain herself,' said Mrs. Kynoch.

'She won't if she thinks it's been stolen,' Hippolyta pointed out. 'She'll just go away again.'

'Perhaps we could leave a note?' suggested Mrs. Kynoch.

'We could,' said Hippolyta. 'It might be rained on.'

'We can tuck it under here, where the box is,' said Mrs. Kynoch, now determined on this idea. 'I have some paper, and a pencil.' She usually did, and began fishing about in her own generously-sized reticule. Hippolyta, since she was still crouched beside it anyway, tested the weight of the box and found she could just lift it. She pulled it free of the brambles, and Mabelle took one end as they stood and waited for Mrs. Kynoch to word her note, fold it, and tuck it into the brambles' shelter with a stone on top. Then she detached herself from the clinging thorns, and they set off back to the trap.

'I hope she does come for it, and then comes up to Dinnet House,' said Mrs. Kynoch, helping them to lift the kist into the trap to rest at their feet. 'I should like to see that she was well, and happy. To say nothing of asking her what on earth she thinks she's doing, running off like that!'

'And then she can pack her own things,' said Hippolyta. There was a small noise from Mabelle, as though she would be very happy to have her room tidied up.

'But she is usually quite nice to me,' Mabelle said suddenly, as if she had been following the same train of thought. 'She made me laugh sometimes.'

'Did she?' asked Hippolyta, surprised.

'Yes, but I suppose I shouldn't have. She said things about the other girls, and ... and people, and they weren't very nice, but they were funny.'

'Then I should think you will benefit from losing her influence, my dear,' said Mrs. Kynoch sadly.

Hippolyta went to the pony and began to turn the trap on the road, not an easy manoeuvre. By the time the trap was facing in the right direction, and the pony had been placated, Hippolyta noticed two men approaching from the Tullich direction along the road, walking slowly, as if they had already come some distance. She peered more closely. Was one of them Mr. Durris?

'Look,' said Mabelle, 'there's Mr. Middleton! And he's with that man – gentleman – um, Mr. Durris!'

'Goodness!' cried Mrs. Kynoch. 'Isn't Mr. Durris wonderful? He's found him!'

'Well, yes,' said Hippolyta, still staring at the two approaching men. 'But where is Georgina Pullman?'

Chapter Nine

Yet none of them asked the direct question when Durris and Peter Middleton caught up with them. Durris met Hippolyta's eye and gave the least shake of his head.

'Mrs. Kynoch, could we impose upon your hospitality at Dinnet House?' he asked. 'I think we should all like to hear what Mr. Middleton here has to say.'

'I have no idea –' began Peter Middleton, but Durris nudged him on and waved to Hippolyta to drive the trap forward.

'We'll see you up there shortly,' he said, allowing them to go ahead. The pony was always eager to make for its own stable, and set off at a trot, only slowing when it realised they were passing the inn and continuing up through the village to Dinnet House. Hippolyta and Mabelle brought Georgina's kist into the hall and tucked it for now under the stairs, where no one coming through the front door was likely to notice it. Hippolyta did note, however, that Mrs. Price's painting of Georgina had disappeared from the same hiding place.

'Come on, come on!' Mrs. Kynoch had popped into the kitchen to call for tea, but now hurried them into the parlour. 'I want to be ready when they arrive. Where on earth do you think Mr. Durris found him? Could they have left Georgina there, for whatever reason? But why? Did she refuse to come with them?'

'I have no idea, Mrs. Kynoch, and we shall not find out until they arrive!' Hippolyta found that Mrs. Kynoch's anxiety made her patient by contrast – though what was keeping them? The pony had barely put one foot past the other on the way up the hill. The men could surely have caught up, if they had been walking normally and taking no detours.

It turned out that they had taken a detour: when Durris and Peter Middleton finally arrived, just after the tea tray, Patrick was with them. Hippolyta was delighted to see him, and he came at once to sit by her on the sopha, taking her hand discreetly in his. Durris gestured to Peter Middleton to place himself on a central chair where all five of them could see him. Hippolyta noticed that Mabelle was sitting up very straight, as if to persuade herself that she was going to cope with whatever was about to happen in this unexpectedly adult world she had suddenly entered.

'Right, Mr. Middleton. Please be so good as to tell us, from your own perspective, what happened at the picnic on Saturday?'

'At the picnic?' Peter Middleton assumed a surprised look. 'But that's days ago!'

'Yes,' said Durris patiently, 'Saturday.'

'Well,' said Middleton, as if his mind had been on something else entirely and he had to resort things in his head. 'I waited with you for the others to arrive, just on the road at Loch Kinord. I walked up from Tarland, of course. And then, as you know, the others did arrive, and they arranged the carriages just there by the side of the road. And then some of us went to see the Burn o' Vat. Some people didn't, but I did. I mean, I'd been there before, many times, all my life: I've known it since I was a lad, but it's always nice to show other people around it.'

'Who were you showing around it? Was there anyone in particular there who had not seen it before?'

Middleton's shoulders moved uncomfortably as he thought.

'Well, those Hendry lads hadn't seen it, of course. And I don't think any of the girls from here had been up there before, had they?' He glanced, briefly, towards Mrs. Kynoch, as though she might see more in his face than he would like. She opened her mouth, but said nothing and shut it again. Durris gave Middleton a moment to add to his remarks, but nothing was forthcoming.

'Then what?'

'We all decided we'd seen enough and it was time to walk down to the loch for our picnic. I walked with Miss Spencer – Grace Spencer,' he added, with a degree of emphasis.

'Where did you sit?'

'Well, you were there yourself. We scattered ourselves a bit, didn't we? Those who needed the tables stayed at the tables, and we younger ones sat about. I sat with Miss Spencer,' he added.

'Did you happen to notice where anyone else sat?'

'I was conversing with Miss Spencer,' said Middleton. 'I wasn't paying much attention to anyone else.'

'Not even to Miss Georgina Pullman?'

Middleton paused, thoughtful, as if he was searching his memory. Hippolyta was quite sure he knew exactly where Georgina had been sitting.

'I believe she was somewhere behind me. A little nearer the tables. But I could be mistaken. Miss Spencer might know,' he added, with a hint of asperity. 'She was facing that direction.'

'And after the meal,' said Durris, just when Hippolyta was hoping he would ask Middleton about his apparent quarrel with Grace Spencer. 'What did you do then?'

'Well, that's all a little more vague. Miss Spencer and I continued our conversation for a little, and then we went our separate ways – I believe she spoke to you, Miss Ash?'

Mabelle, startled at this direct question, jumped and nodded frantically. Mrs. Kynoch put a calming hand on her arm.

'And what did you do?' Durris pursued.

'I … um … you know, it's three days ago. I can't remember every detail!'

Durris gave him a moment, but Middleton was stubborn.

'Perhaps then if we work from the other direction. Would you mind explaining where I found you this morning?'

Middleton turned sulky.

'Must I? I shall look foolish.'

Durris' eyebrows rose as he kept a steady gaze on Middleton's face. Middleton sighed, and rubbed his eyes with his fists.

'Sorry, I haven't slept much. I was at the harbour in Aberdeen.'

'Doing what?'

'Looking for a passage,' said Middelton, his voice low.

'To where?'

'To anywhere! All right? Happy now, Mr. Durris? I just wanted to go away! I've made a mess of everything!'

'What about the horse you borrowed?' Hippolyta could not help asking, thinking of the poor horse abandoned in a strange stable. Middleton stared at her as though it were the last thing on his mind.

'She's at the New Inn in Aberdeen, with a message saying my neighbour will call for her. I've paid for her stabling and the message. She's very happy.' He glared at her, clearly feeling that his own condition was much more in question. Durris glanced at her, and she contained her response.

'Going back to this mess, Mr. Middleton – would you care to expand on that? I think we need some clarification.'

'Why? All this is my own business – and the horse's, of course,' he added pointedly to Hippolyta. 'I made a bad decision, all right? And things were going badly, and I wanted to get away for a bit.'

'On your farm?' asked Durris innocently. 'Your harvest looked in danger?'

'No! The farm is grand. And my mother can look after it.'

'You didn't think to tell your mother where you were going?'

'I went in a hurry,' he said shortly. There was silence for a moment.

'You went pretty much straight from the picnic,' said Durris, almost gently. 'Could one conclude that whatever went wrong happened there? Perhaps that will help you to remember what you did after the meal?'

Middleton glowered.

'I still don't see what business it is of yours.'

'Mr. Middleton, where is Georgina?' Mrs. Kynoch could hold it in no longer. 'Please, please tell us!'

'Georgina? Georgina Pullman? I haven't the remotest idea!'

'But you arranged to elope with her?'

'I did not! Why would I do that? It's Grace Spencer I have – well, I had – an understanding with. And that's all gone to the devil now, too! I just needed to get away for a while, see some new things, get away from this place and forget about them both for a bit.'

'Them both?' queried Durris. Middleton, who had been muttering almost to himself, blinked and swallowed hard.

'Miss Spencer and my mother, of course. My mother would

rather have Grace than me, I think. If she finds out Miss Spencer has broken with me, she'll be furious. And you don't want to meet my mother when she's furious!' He tried to make a joke of it, but his face told another story. Hippolyta remembered how much Mrs. Middleton had indeed favoured Grace Spencer, but somehow she was not convinced that Peter Middleton had really included his mother when he said 'both of them'.

'And why did Miss Spencer break with you?' Durris persisted.

'Oh, can a man not be broken with without having to explain it all to the world? I suppose I had displeased her in some way. How is one supposed to know? And even when one apologises – I don't know, girls can never forget that kind of thing. It's like being on trial forever, without ever reaching a proper verdict. How can a man live like that? I should be pleased to be thrown over. I should be on a ship to who knows or cares where, and forget about all of it.'

He slumped down with his face on his hands, elbows propped on his knees. Durris and Patrick exchanged looks.

'Do you realise that Miss Pullman is missing?' Durris asked. Middleton pulled himself up sharply.

'Missing? How do you mean?'

'I mean no one knows where she is,' said Durris with care.

'Well, I know nothing about it,' he said firmly. 'I saw nothing of her after I left the picnic place. And you thought we'd absconded together?'

'It seemed likely,' Durris admitted. 'You both disappeared at the same time.'

'She never came with me. I never saw her after the picnic,' he repeated. 'You can ask anywhere I went – I was alone. Ask them at the New Inn,' he insisted.

'I already have,' said Durris. 'No one saw you in the company of anyone else from the moment you left Tarland to the moment I found you at the harbour. And I'm aware you were asking for a passage for one. But that is no proof that you did not both intend to meet somewhere, even somewhere some distance away.'

Middleton reflected.

'You're right there. Miss Georgina would have no fear of

travelling on her own. But she did not arrange anything like that with me, I promise you. If it helps,' he drew a deep breath, 'if it helps, I'll just go straight home from here, and not try to leave again. I suppose I might as well face reality.'

'Yes, you'd better,' said Durris. 'I should much prefer it if you stay within your own parish until this matter is resolved.'

'And not even venture as far as Ballater?'

'I think that might be wise for now, don't you? And I shall expect to find you at Tarland when I come looking for you.' Durris spoke quietly, but it would have been a bolder man than Peter Middleton who would be likely to defy him. Durris sat back on his own chair, and Middleton took it as a signal.

'Should I go home now, then?'

'Yes,' said Durris, 'I think you should.'

Middleton stood uncertainly, as if he suspected some kind of trap, and looked around them all. Then he stepped towards the door, and opened it.

He gasped.

'What's that?'

Durris was on his feet in an instant: Hippolyta was not far behind. From this angle, Georgina Pullman's kist was visible, a dark square under the shadowy stairs.

'We believe it's Georgina's kist,' said Hippolyta. 'What do you think?'

'What's it doing here?' Middleton hissed. His eyes seemed fixed on it.

Durris looked at Hippolyta for an explanation.

'We found it, amongst some trees on the road near Tullich. Where you met us a little while ago.'

'It was still there?' Middleton looked as if he could not take it in. 'Why was it still there?'

'I think,' said Durris, moving in front of him and closing the parlour door firmly, 'you need to come back in and sit down again, and tell us a little more of what you know.'

'She was going to come away with me,' Middleton began in a low voice. Mrs. Kynoch, with trembling hands, had refilled the teacups, and Middleton had resumed his seat, huddled around his cup and saucer. 'She promised me.'

'But why?' asked Hippolyta, attracting a black look from him. 'No, I mean, why should she abscond with you? Didn't you make her an offer of marriage? And didn't she turn you down?'

The black look was turned on Mabelle.

'I thought you at least would keep a secret.'

'I couldn't,' said Mabelle, close to tears. 'Not when she went missing.'

Middleton thought about it, then nodded.

'And anyway, you were deceiving Miss Ash,' Hippolyta nodded at Mabelle. 'You had some other plot in hand, didn't you?'

'I was to collect her kist,' Middleton jerked his head towards the door, 'and help her to hide it so that we could pick it up later. We hid it down in those trees – you know, where you found it.'

'Where we saw you both on Friday evening,' said Patrick, suddenly realising what had happened.

'That's right. I would have hidden it on my own, but she wanted to make sure it was safe.'

'And what were your arrangements for departing?' asked Durris, who had drawn out his notebook. Hippolyta could not possibly see the contents from here.

'We were to leave the picnic early, she said, and take one of the traps back to collect the kist, then back to Ballater and drive towards Braemar. She said that was the clever bit: no one would look for us that way. They would all assume we had gone to Aberdeen.'

'And what would happen once you reached Braemar?'

'We would wait until the dust had settled, then take the mail coach back to Aberdeen and south to Edinburgh or London. That's where she wanted to go, really.'

At that, everyone nodded. Georgina would not be happy until she was settled in some fashionable city.

'Yet you left on your own, and she is missing. What happened?'

'She ignored me through the whole picnic. I thought that was her being clever, throwing any hounds off the scent. She spent most of her time with that Lord Tresco, all romantic with his injured leg.' Only a jealous lover, Hippolyta thought, could resent someone's disability in that way.

'And you spent the time with Miss Spencer.'

'Yes … well, I should have done that anyway, I suppose.'

'But you quarrelled.'

'We did. She accused me of still paying more attention to Georgina than to her, and she walked off. So I went up a bit early to where Georgina and I had arranged to meet, near the carriages.'

'Mr. Middleton, why did you try to make up with Grace if you intended to elope with Georgina?'

Peter Middleton flushed red.

'I like Grace,' he muttered. 'I want to marry Grace. But when Georgina tells you to do something, well, that gets the blood racing. And anyway, she told me not to talk to her during the picnic. And Grace was being nice to me, at first.'

Heavens, thought Hippolyta, this young man's mother needs to take him in hand!

'And where was Georgina?' asked Durris.

Middleton's face screwed up.

'I have no idea. She never appeared. Not a sign of her. I realised she wasn't coming, and I couldn't bear to wait there until everyone else appeared to drive home, so I walked back to Tarland. And on the way I realised what had happened: she had tricked me. Used me.'

'How was that?' asked Durris.

'She must have gone off with Lord Tresco. That's what she was planning all along. If she was going off with me, we could have gone by Tarland. I could have hidden the kist along the road on Friday night, and we wouldn't have had to go back towards Ballater at all. It would have been much easier. But if she was going off with Tresco –'

'But Lord Tresco has not gone anywhere,' said Patrick. 'I saw him this morning.'

'Well, that's the thing,' said Peter Middleton, serious. 'Whether it was him – and I did think it was him – or whether it was someone else, why didn't she collect her kist?'

'What is in it?' asked Durris, with a glance at the door.

'I've no idea, but it was heavy enough,' said Middleton with feeling. Hippolyta and Mabelle looked at each other and nodded.

'And it's locked,' added Hippolyta. Durris met her eye.

'Let's take a look,' he said. He stepped outside, and in a moment brought back the kist. He laid it on the floor by the tea table.

'But it's locked,' said Hippolyta again. Patrick grinned at her. Durris took out his pocket knife, did something quick about the lock, and opened the kist. Hippolyta blinked.

'Perhaps, Mrs. Kynoch, you would prefer to do this,' said Durris, rising and stepping back. Mrs. Kynoch knelt beside it, and fingered through the contents.

'A clean shift, as we suspected, and stockings,' she said quietly. 'And the boots you mentioned, I think, Mabelle.'

'That can't be that heavy,' said Patrick, as Mrs. Kynoch pulled the boots clear.

'And money,' she added. Something clinked, and she lifted out a small cloth bag, opening it. 'Sovereigns! I had no idea she had so much with her!'

'Just the one bag?' asked Durris.

'By no means – there are …' she counted quickly, shifting bags, 'six, altogether. It's a small fortune!'

'Enough that she would be unlikely to leave it behind,' Durris murmured. 'Not of her own freewill, anyway.'

Mrs. Kynoch sat back, her face pale. No one spoke.

'Right,' said Durris at last, bending and closing the lid of the kist. 'I shall lock this in the cell at the kirk. I think you would be happier not to have so much money in the house, would you not, Mrs. Kynoch?'

She nodded.

'Georgina …'

'We'll do our best, Mrs. Kynoch,' he said firmly. 'She may yet come to claim it, if she does not think it stolen.'

'We left a note,' said Hippolyta, and he gave her an odd look.

'If she had planned to lie low for a few days, she might yet come for it,' he repeated. 'But it would be more than helpful if we could discover who her companion was.'

'Is there any chance,' said Patrick, 'that she is conspiring with Lord Tresco and they still plan to meet and leave together? In which case,' he added, a little sheepishly, 'she might not need the money. I believe he is a very wealthy man.'

'He would never intend to marry her,' said Mrs. Kynoch, forlorn.

'But at least she would be safe,' said Hippolyta. Mabelle gulped back a sob.

'I could challenge him to a duel,' said Peter Middleton, not sounding at all sure about the idea. 'For her honour, you know.'

'You'll do nothing of the sort!' said Mrs. Kynoch at once. 'We've had enough of duels around here!'

'And I should be forced to arrest you,' added Durris. Peter Middleton opened his mouth as if to protest, then decided that he should err on the safe side.

'All right, then. I just thought, you know, it might be expected of me.'

'If she really has gone, Mr. Middleton, and you can no longer fall for her charms,' said Mrs. Kynoch earnestly, 'I suggest you work hard to win back Miss Spencer's favour. You and she are very well suited, if you only have a little more sense next time you meet a – a more than run-of-the-mill young woman.'

'I shall, Mrs. Kynoch, I promise. I wish I had never set eyes on Georgina Pullman, you know. I was perfectly happy before I met her.'

'Mr. Middleton, you have walked a long way today,' said Hippolyta suddenly. 'How would it be if my husband and I set you on your way home in our trap?'

Patrick and Durris both favoured Hippolyta with suspicious glances, but Peter Middleton did not appear to notice.

'If you would I should consider it a very great favour, Mrs. Napier. I feel I have been walking for days, and my sleep has not been good these last few nights.'

'Then if Mr. Durris has finished with you, perhaps you would like to come along? Mr. Durris, if you were to walk with us as far as the kirk, we can carry the kist in the trap, too.'

'Hippolyta, if you think the pony is going to agree to pulling two grown men and a kist of sovereigns …' said Patrick. His tone was clear: he felt he should be warning her against some course of action, but unfortunately for him he could not yet work out which action she intended to take. It did not bode well.

'You know I can persuade the pony,' she said as sweetly as she could. He met her eye, and sighed.

'All right then, go ahead and try it, but I shall not be surprised if it refuses to move!'

But Hippolyta, walking beside Mr. Durris, led the pony and trap back into the village with Patrick and Peter Middleton ensconced on top, their feet on the kist.

'What are you doing, Mrs. Napier?' Durris asked quietly, when they were clear of Dinnet House.

'I'm not quite sure,' she replied honestly. 'I want to see the picnic site again. If Georgina waited a long time, if she had an alternative kist hidden somewhere, if she was taken away by the wrong man – surely there would be some trace?'

'We looked everywhere, and for as many eventualities as you can think of,' Durris objected.

'Well, I should like you to come back with us to search again, too, but if you feel like that about it there's no point, is there? And besides, the pony would definitely renege at three grown men, not to mention me.'

They arrived in silence at the kirk, and Durris reached into the trap to lift out the kist. He turned away from the trap so that Middleton should not hear.

'Take care, Mrs. Napier. You have a great tendency to take one more step than is either wise or safe, to the constant consternation of those who are concerned for you.'

'Patrick and I shall be together, Mr. Durris. You have no need to fear!' She climbed into the trap and settled beside Patrick, who had clearly heard the exchange and was looking at her with resignation.

'What am I to do with her, Durris?' he asked, trying a laugh.

The pony, relieved of the sovereigns at least, trotted back down the hill and once again reluctantly passed its stable at the inn, heading out along the flat road towards Muir of Dinnet. When they turned in to the Tarland road, she and Patrick both climbed down to relieve the pony of the load, allowing Peter Middleton to continue to ride as their guest. At the place where the carriages had gathered, however, they stopped, and Middleton hopped down.

'Thank you for your courtesy,' he said politely. 'I hope you find something here that will help us to find her. I mean, I don't want her back in Ballater, not if I ever want to settle down with Grace – and I do, I really do – but I don't want her not to be safe, either.'

'I understand, Mr. Middleton,' said Hippolyta graciously. 'And I hope you find it an easy walk from here.'

'Time to think, that's the thing,' said Middleton, though it was unclear whether he considered that a good thing or a bad thing. 'Time to think. Good day to you!' He bowed, and headed off up the road. Patrick and Hippolyta waited until he had vanished from sight.

'Now, what do you want to do?' Patrick asked. 'Durris is right: we covered every inch round here between us, three times over.'

'I just wanted to look again,' said Hippolyta. 'I've only been here three or four times, and I don't know it intimately. I wanted to see where she might have waited for her beau, whomsoever he might be. After all, she had never been here before. If we're talking about Lord Tresco, he could hardly have been familiar with the place either. Would they have risked an assignation when they had no idea what the place was going to be like? Where would you go to meet a girl – well, where would you have gone in the past, before you found me?' She grinned at him, and he took her hand, drawing her close to him as he turned to survey the place.

'Let's see, then, shall we? What might people have told her about the place before she came here? The loch, and the open ground around it – lovely for picnics, but not much good for secrecy. The woods – birch trees, rather open, really, particularly down by the loch itself. Up here, around the road, they are a little more dense. Or,' he added, turning around and looking up the road, 'or, of course, there's Burn o' Vat itself. What about that?'

'Perfect!' said Hippolyta. 'I know, I know before you tell me, you all searched it a dozen times up and down. But I just want to picture what might have happened.'

'Come on, then: let's see what scope there is for our assignation in there!'

Patrick led the way once more up into the glen, amongst the mossy rocks. The sunlight glittered through the leaves, illuminating the pale trunks of the trees, making the dead trunks stark in golden green. They stepped through the tunnel into the body of the Vat, hand in hand, excited almost, a young couple enjoying their exploration for its own sake and for the sake of each other's company.

The hollow was as bare as it had been before, the gravel floor soggy with the spreading burn. Ahead was the rocky climb out of the Vat again, one steep surface black where pine needles had gathered and rotted in the pool above, and a crystal-white cascade foaming bright to one side of it. Patrick handed Hippolyta up into the green glade beyond, and she stood for a moment, drawing in the balmy air, dazzled by the coin-bright birch leaves sprinkled over the trees. Then something pale caught her eye, something out of place, and she gasped.

Chapter Ten

'Oh,' she said, and took an uncertain step back to press hard against a tree. 'Oh.'

'Oh, my dear,' said Patrick, holding her hand tightly. 'You'd best …'

'No, it's all right,' she said, breathing heavily. 'It's the shock. It's – oh, my.'

Georgina Pullman lay flat on her back on a little beach of pinkish gravel, arms crossed, legs straight, as though arranged for burial, her fine shift tumbled around her. Where the rest of her clothing had gone was anyone's guess: apart from one stocking and one boot, incongruous on the left foot, she looked like an abandoned angel fallen to earth. If fallen angels have bruises about their throats. Hippolyta felt the smooth bark of the tree cold through her gloved fingertips, through her clothing, and shuddered. Georgina would be cold, in only her shift. But she would be cold anyway.

Patrick was scrutinising the body even as he still held her hand, taking in as much as he could before he touched anything.

'It looks very much, my dear, as though she has been strangled, but there might be something else. Can you – could you bear to go on your own for Mr. Durris? I don't think I should leave her, and I cannot leave you here with her on your own.'

'No, indeed. I'll go, of course. Oh, my.' She eased herself sideways, preparing to clamber up and down back to the best climb down into the Vat. 'Be – be careful, my love!' she whispered.'

'Of course. You too.' They kissed, briefly, needing the contact but not feeling quite right in present company. Then she turned, and hurried back through the Vat and down the path to the poor pony, who would not like to have to come out here again today. She herself was very much looking forward to her dinner, then considered poor Georgina. No more dinners for her.

Hippolyta hardly noticed the drive back to Ballater, but before she had a chance to do more than pause outside the inn and wonder where Mr. Durris might be, he appeared from the stable yard.

'Mr. Durris,' she gasped, and found that she was shivering. To hide it, she made a business of climbing down from the trap, which also meant she could give her news more quietly. The stable yard was a busy place. Durris came over, a frown already on his face as if he had guessed what she had to say. 'We've found her.'

'At the Muir of Dinnet?' he asked at once.

'In the Burn o' Vat,' she explained.

He looked closely at her face.

'You need a brandy,' he said, and before she could blink he was at the back door of the inn, calling for service. She closed her eyes and stood for a moment, clutching the pony's reins, feeling its warmth against her side. Warmth, and life, not like those cold, damp rocks and squelching gravel where Georgina lay. In her mind's eye she saw again the rumpled shift, the bare legs, the feet brushed by the running burn, the sunken face, grey about the mouth and eyes, and tried her hardest to banish the vision. She was not sure how long it was before she heard a footstep close to her, and opened her eyes. Mr. Durris had a glass of brandy ready.

'Thank you,' she whispered, feeling it burn her throat. More heat, and with it the vision faded, just a little.

'I shan't ask you any questions but this one,' he said, gently, 'which I barely need to ask anyway, I think. Is she dead?'

Hippolyta nodded, and her eyes filled with tears. She blinked furiously, praying that no one would see apart from Durris. She could not hide it from him, so close.

'Patrick stayed with her,' she managed to choke out the words, then found it was easier to speak. 'And I am to take you back there.'

'Does the pony agree with that?' asked Durris with a slight smile. 'I doubt it. I shall hire a horse.'

There were some more minutes of flurried activity before Durris returned with a sigh.

'All their horses are out at the moment,' he said, tossing a bag into the trap. 'I've arranged a cart for – for later, but I'm afraid that for now I shall have to impose …'

'I'd rather be there to bring Patrick home, anyway,' she said, pushing reluctantly away from the pony's support. 'I'm sure I shan't have to – to look, again.' She was conscious of his eyes on her before she was able to shift herself to climb back into the trap. He joined her, and they set off.

The journey back seemed longer, the pony justifiably tired now, and Hippolyta torn between distress and hunger. Mr. Durris sat quietly, true to his word, yet Hippolyta thought she might almost rather speak about it. She cleared her throat.

'I wanted to go back up there,' she said at last, 'just because I couldn't picture where she might have wanted to wait for her – for a man. She wouldn't know the place. And if it were Lord Tresco, he wouldn't know it either. So how did they make arrangements?'

'That's a very good point,' Durris agreed. She was pleased, then wondered if he were just being nice to her because she had had a shock. He had certainly seen the tears in her eyes. She was annoyed at herself. But he solemnly took out his notebook and despite the jerking of the trap, he made the least little note in it, just at an angle that Hippolyta could not see. One day, she thought, one day, I shall see what is in that little notebook of yours, Mr. Durris! But she knew the thought was unworthy, and, confused as to where to let her mind wander, she concentrated instead on the broad grey back of the pony as it tramped back towards the Tarland road.

To her delight, though it caused her pangs of guilt for not having thought of it for herself, the bag that Durris had flung into the trap at the last minute had been food for the pony. Where the carriages had been arranged at the picnic she unharnessed the poor beast, led it to the grass opposite through the birch trees, and made sure it had some of the oats and a draught of water from a clean-looking stream. It took her mind off the business-like way Durris had drawn himself up and disappeared towards the Burn o' Vat, and what he and Patrick would be doing there.

It was definitely wearing towards dinner time. She should have taken a moment to go home and explain to Ishbel and Johanna that they might both be late: Ishbel was used to keeping food hot for Patrick, called out to some medical case, but Johanna would undoubtedly be less forgiving. What was she to do about Johanna? If the girl found the Napier household strict, and akin to slavery, she would never manage in most other households. If she had complained about the lack of regular hours and difficulties with animals, now, though, she might have had a case. Hippolyta grinned to herself, still unsure what to do, and found a comfortable rock to perch on. Her mind danced from thought to thought, buzzing like a summer grasshopper. The pony munched rhythmically, tearing at the grass, while she sat and gazed out at the loch lying shallow and bright. The birds were silent in the afternoon heat, but insects hummed. She hoped she was not to be midge-bitten.

She always carried with her, in her reticule, a small drawing pad and a pencil. Knowing that all she could really do now was wait, she extracted it from the depths of the bag and looked about her. The pony was still shredding grass, standing peaceably in a way it rarely did. She studied it for a long moment, then took up her pencil and began to sketch.

She was more than capable of spending hours that way, if the light was good, so she had no idea how long she had been there when a slight sound to her right, amongst the trees, brought her to her senses. A deer, perhaps? She turned to see.

A startlingly handsome young man stood there, his hair bright gold in the sunlight, a little tousled – the way Patrick's often was when he had just removed his hat. This man seemed to have no hat, nor indeed coat, but his waistcoat was that of a reasonably placed farmer, or successful minor tradesman. It was hard to see his eyes where he stood in the mottled shade, but his face was friendly, smiling straight at her as though he knew her well and had expected to find her here. As far as she knew, she had never seen him before in her life.

'Hello,' she said, tentatively.

'Hello,' he replied. His voice had a pleasant timbre, in that one word, and seemed as youthful as he looked – around her own age, she thought. He nodded, and stepped forward a little way, not close enough to cause concern. The pony took no notice, being intent on the decent meal it felt it deserved. The handsome young man cast it a glance, then looked back at Hippolyta.

'Hello, Miss,' he said again, as if he had not quite done the job the first time. 'Is that one yours, then?'

'That's right.' He stepped again, a little closer, and she saw that he was older than she had first thought: there were webs of fine lines near his bright blue eyes. And the eyes themselves – was there something not quite there? His breeches were smeared and dusted with glour, as were the sleeves of his shirt. Her mind, still dealing with the challenges of portraying the varying textures of the pony's coat, was slow to catch up. She glanced at his hands. One could always tell a good deal from someone's hands, she remembered. No gloves, of course, somewhat grubby fingers, nails outlined in black. Probably not a tradesman, then, she thought.

'He's a fine looking beast,' the man remarked. His accent was local: why had she never seen him before? 'You'll be a wealthy quine, then, lass?'

'What?' She had not been called a lass for a few years, now. Suddenly, her mind cleared. 'Oh!' she said. 'Why, are you looking for a rich wife?'

It was not, on reflection, the brightest thing to say in the circumstances. She waved her hands, her drawing pad and pencil still gripped in them, and tried to recover the conversation.

'I mean,' she said, 'I mean … are you Johnnie Boy Jo, by any chance?'

'Aye, my name's Johnnie.' It was his turn to look confused. 'I've no seen you afore, though, have I? I'd have minded a bonnie quinie like you.'

'You're very kind, and you're right, we haven't met,' she said, speaking quickly, more quickly than her mind would work. Not quickly enough, perhaps, for her gaze dropped once again to his hands. They were making their way, as though of their own volition, towards the buttons of his breeches. The smile on his face stayed the same. 'No, listen,' she said. 'I'm not a lass, and I'm not rich. I'm a married woman, and my husband's just up there.' Johnnie Boy Jo paused, but did not withdraw his fingers. Desperate, she added, 'With Mr. Durris, the sheriff's man.'

That stopped him.

'Oh,' he said slowly. 'Mr. Durris disna like me much. He's no kind to me, ken.'

'Oh, that's a shame, Johnnie,' she said, trying to keep his sympathy. Her heart was running like a deer. 'He's usually a nice man.'

'If Mr. Durris is up the hill, I'd better be off,' he murmured. His fingers were still making something like unbuttoning movements, but his hands were now spread out at his sides, as if he were considering the possibility of flying. 'I'd be better away out of here.'

'Oh!' she said, before she could stop herself, 'don't go! I mean … this is a lovely spot,' she galloped on. 'Is it somewhere you often walk?'

'Why,' he asked, his smile turning mischievous, 'do you want to meet me here again, bonnie quinie?'

'I was just wondering if you had been here much before,' she clarified, not daring to answer him directly.

'Aye, I come walking here times,' he said. 'Bonnie lassies come here, see, and I can take a look and see if I can find myself a rich wife.'

'Yes, very sensible. You don't want to hurry these things: you need to give the matter some thought.' She tried not to rush her words, either. 'Were you here last Saturday, do you remember?'

'Saturday?' His smile stayed but his eyes were blank.

'The day before the Sabbath,' she tried. For a moment she thought it had been no help, then his face cleared.

'Oh, aye,' he said, 'my sister goes to the kirk on the Sabbath. That's right: I ken now what you're speaking of.'

'So were you here? The day before your sister went to the kirk?'

'I believe I was an' all,' he agreed. 'There was lots of bonnie lassies that day, all eating and drinking and walking about in fine dresses. I could have had my choice of rich wives!'

'Maybe you could, Johnnie.' She smiled: it would do no harm now for him to think about them. 'Did you maybe see a lassie with green feathers in her bonnet? And a white dress with green ribbons to match?'

He considered, and he seemed to be going through a list of the girls he had seen in his head, rejecting each one as they did not fit her description. Then he nodded.

'Aye, I seen her. She was sitting with a man, and then off she went. I thought maybe she would come to see me, but she didna. I was a bit sad, but then I thought maybe I was better off without her. She was a fine rich quinie, but she didna look as if she'd be awful kind.'

Hippolyta refrained from comment.

'Did you see where she did go?'

He shrugged.

'Away up the hill,' he said, as if that was further than he cared to consider. 'Up among the trees there.'

'Was she on her own?'

'I think so,' he said, but he was frowning. 'Aye, I think she was. There was no other lassie with her, and I dinna think there was a man at all. I dinna think so.'

'And you didn't follow her yourself, then, Johnnie?'

'Me?' His face clouded over, the smile left forgotten on his lips. 'Me?'

'Did you follow her?' she asked gently. She had no wish to alarm him, but that hand was wandering again to the front of his breeches, fumbling at the buttons. His eyes were glazing over. 'Johnnie, did you follow her?' He had the top button undone, and both hands now joined to work together, faster. 'Oh!' she cried, and slapped her hand over her eyes. That was no use, though: she needed to see to flee. Grabbing sketchbook, pencil and skirts in one hand she seized the pony's reins with the other, and ran, never looking back, through the trees and up to the road. Praying that Johnnie lacked the focus to follow her she plunged off the road again and along the winding path to the Vat, dragging the pony behind her. At the rocks she hurled the reins over a nearby branch and scrambled inside, bouncing off mossy walls and slithering on the rounded rocks. Panting, she stopped, and listened. There was no sound from the path outside. And, she reflected, she had never heard stories of Johnnie giving chase, once the objects of his interest had fled. She sucked in a deep breath, straightened, and tried to stop her shoulders from shaking. She turned to peer through the narrow opening she had just come through – the pony looked bored outside already - and it was then that she noticed something white to the side of the opening, where a cleft in the rocks provided just a little shelter for a collection of white and green cloth ...

'Are you all right?'

She blinked up at the rocky face upstream. Patrick was standing at the top, waving to her.

'Yes,' she called, 'yes, I'm fine. I … I just met Johnnie Boy Jo.'

'You did?' Patrick's voice was anxious, so she hurried over and began to climb the rocks to speak with him close by, rather than shouting across the hollow. He reached out an arm to help her up the last few steps.

'Yes, I met him over in the woods,' she explained. 'I asked him if he had been here on Saturday and he said he had, and I think he remembered Georgina, but he told me he saw her heading up into the woods and he didn't follow her. He wasn't very clear, though, about whether or not she was alone.'

'Johnnie's never been great managing more than one person at a time, man or woman,' said Mr. Durris, appearing behind Patrick. The thick greenery of the little glen stifled their words into murmurs. 'It seems to confuse him more than usual. Did he understand the idea of Saturday?'

'I think he did,' said Hippolyta. 'He said it was the day before the Sabbath, and he knew the Sabbath because that was the day his sister goes to the kirk.'

'He has a sister?' Mr. Durris' eyebrows rose. 'I had no idea he had kin hereabouts. Perhaps that is why he has come back. But he did you no harm, Mrs. Napier?'

'He never touched me, nor threatened to,' she said firmly, then added, 'He admired the pony, though.'

'It's a very fine pony,' said Patrick stoutly, despite having been bitten by it on numerous occasions. 'Perhaps Johnnie Boy Jo is not so peculiar, after all.'

'Have you – have you found anything new?' she asked, eager to change the subject. She felt like a fool for running so fast: on reflection, Johnnie had seemed harmless. She had just lost her nerve.

'I don't think so,' said Patrick, glancing at Durris for confirmation. 'She has been dead since we first missed her, or thereabouts, but of course she has not lain here all that time. We searched through the Vat and up here and beyond, any number of us, on Saturday evening and yesterday. She has been moved from somewhere else.'

'And no sign of her clothes up here, anyway,' added Durris.

'Ah,' said Hippolyta, 'there I may be able to help you.' She turned and pointed back across the hollow to the cleft she had spotted. 'We would not have seen them as we came in, but they are very clear to anyone leaving, I think.'

'Yes, indeed.' Durris was off and down the rocks in a moment, and they could hear his footsteps crunching through the soggy gravel of the hollow's floor. Hippolyta watched him pull out a gown, the stuffed sleeves sagging, some petticoats, and a very crushed bonnet with its pale green feathers damp and dejected. Tears pricked her eyes at the sight: the bonnet, so proud at the picnic, was now almost more pitiable than Georgina's dead body. From where she stood, she knew, it would take only a little turn of her head to see at least Georgina's pale leg trailing in the brown stream, but she could not do it, not now. Whatever she had thought she was coming up here for, whatever delights or benefits she believed she would gain, this undignified end could not have been her intention. And to be carried about the place from where she had been killed to this public place, in only her shift! Georgina Pullman had not been a pleasant girl, but who could have disliked her so much that they would do all that to her? And if she had been stripped to her shift ... well, what else might have been done?

Mr. Durris had made a neat pile of the garments he had found on a dryish part of the Vat's floor, and was now standing near the entrance as if listening.

'I hope Johnnie Boy Jo has not followed you,' Patrick remarked, watching him.

'I hope no one is stealing the pony,' she responded, not wanting him to see how the thought of Johnnie Boy's attentions had upset her earlier. But instead, two men emerged, sideways, from the narrow tunnel, and straightened when they saw Durris ready to greet them. They were in shirt sleeves, with waistcoats of tough tweed and dun-coloured breeches tucked into heavy boots. One carried a folded blanket. Durris pointed up to where Patrick and Hippolyta were standing, and the men nodded. Durris began to lead them towards the rocks.

'My dear, perhaps you had better go down before they begin. It will not be easy for them to carry her through the entrance, I should think.'

'Oh, of course,' she said. As soon as the men had climbed up to their level, nodding a sombre greeting to her, she slid herself back down into the Vat, skipped across the deeper runs of water, and wriggled back through the entrance again. The pony looked at her disparagingly. A hurdle was propped against the rock face. Otherwise the place was deserted.

She led the pony slowly back down to the road and made a long job of harnessing it again to the trap. Even at that she was ready and waiting to leave when the two men, led by Durris with the pile of clothes and with Patrick bringing up the rear, processed down the path towards her, the hurdle between them with its light burden wrapped in the blanket. Hippolyta held the pony's head as they passed to lay Georgina's body in the cart they had brought, and Durris laid the clothing alongside the hurdle. There was a pause as they all stood in silence for a moment, heads bowed, taking stock. Then it was time to go.

Chapter Eleven

For the sake of the pony, Durris rode in the cart with Georgina Pullman's body and her pile of clothing. The body was laid on a bier under a thick sheet, with a blanket spread on top, yet it was still so obviously what it was that Hippolyta almost wept again, thinking how Georgina would have hated parading through Ballater in this awful way. Before they set off she went once more to the back of the cart to make sure every scrap was tucked in and covered, not a hand nor a foot bare, not a hair, loosened from the elaborate style she had affected at the picnic, snaking out from under the sheet.

Then Patrick helped her up into the trap, and they set off, in slow procession after the cart. The view in front of them did not promote much in the way of conversation for a while: sombre thoughts filled both their heads, and the pony was content with the pace.

'So what was he like, then?' asked Patrick at last. 'Johnnie Boy Jo, I mean?'

'He's very handsome,' said Hippolyta, 'until you see his eyes, and until he starts talking about his hunt for a rich wife. He called me 'lass'!' She laughed, hoping to make light of the encounter. 'And anyway, it's fairly clear what he's going to do, if you know, so there was plenty of time to distract him or to leave. He didn't come very close, you know. He was almost harmless.'

'He might be harmless,' said Patrick, solemnly. 'But there is a girl dead, and possibly meddled with, and he is in the area. If you see him again, be very, very careful, my dearest.'

'I was – I would be,' she assured him, smiling to reinforce it. 'I just meant that if you didn't know, he seems harmless – a nice young man, even, wandering in from his farm work. His fingernails were filthy! And he had neither coat nor hat.'

'Clear signs of an unstable character!' Patrick told her, a laugh in his voice. He hid his smile as they approached the houses of Tullich: it would not be seemly to be seen laughing behind a cart bearing a corpse. At the nearest house, Hippolyta saw a figure, a woman, standing in the little garden, watching them approach.

'There's Adelina Price,' she remarked. 'I wonder does she guess?'

Mrs. Price came to the gate as they neared her, her eyes fixed on the cart.

'Good afternoon, Mrs. Price,' Hippolyta called, keeping her voice subdued, a warning.

'Is that – who is that?' Mrs. Price stared at the cart. Hippolyta stopped the trap, and jumped quickly down, hurrying to the gate.

'It's – I'm afraid it's Georgina Pullman,' she said. Mrs. Price's eyes widened white in her narrow face, and as if she would try to hold back the cart her hands gestured after it.

'She's dead?' she whispered. 'Dead?'

'I'm afraid so. It's awful, isn't it?'

'But I thought,' Mrs. Price seemed to mumble her words. 'I thought she had eloped. With that Mr. Middleton, or someone.'

'She – she was dead on Saturday. Patrick says – my husband says – she was killed very quickly after she went missing, probably.'

'Killed?' Mrs. Price at last tore her gaze from the departing cart, cast a glance at Patrick as he stood silent behind Hippolyta, and turned to Hippolyta as though she had never heard the word before. 'An accident?'

'Not an accident, I'm afraid.' Hippolyta took a quick look at Patrick, too, then reached for Mrs. Price's hands, folding them into her own, noting the paint and charcoal smeared over her fingers. 'Someone killed her, Mrs. Price.' She hesitated. 'Mrs. Price, are you quite all right?'

Mrs. Price seemed to have frozen to the spot. Hippolyta looked back at Patrick again, and he hurried forward. The pair of them had to squeeze through the half-opened gate before they could take each side of Mrs. Price, an elbow each, and work her gently towards the cottage. Patrick pushed open the door, calling out to the landlady. A plump body appeared at the strange voice and Patrick issued rapid instructions. The woman ran for brandy, hot tea, and a blanket, and the Napiers manoeuvred Mrs. Price into a chair by the empty fireplace. Hippolyta crouched to try to make something of the fire, as the landlady rolled back in with brandy and blanket.

'Kettle's on the boil,' she announced, and immediately went to tend Mrs. Price. Patrick nodded approval.

'She's had a shock,' he said. 'Bad news. Keep her warm and make her drink plenty of hot tea, and she should be all right.' He whipped off his gloves and tested Mrs. Price's forehead, throat and wrist, and stared for a moment into her eyes. 'Yes, she should be all right. Do you understand what to do?' he asked the landlady, without hostility.

'Aye, sir, I ken well. Keep her warm, hot tea, keep an eye to her. I'll do all that.'

'Good, thank you,' said Patrick, helping Hippolyta up from the hearth where the fire was now catching. 'We'd better be going, but if you need me –'

'Aye, I ken your face, Dr. Napier. I'll know fine where to find you.'

Mrs. Price had barely moved, had not acknowledged her landlady. Patrick frowned at her, assessing once again to be sure, then he included both women in a professionally bright smile.

'Excellent. Mrs. Price, take care of yourself.'

The pony had not bothered to wander away – too lazy, Hippolyta thought.

'I hope it's not her heart,' Patrick was muttering, half to himself, as he helped her up into the trap. 'It doesn't look like it.'

'She did take it badly, though, didn't she?' said Hippolyta. 'Perhaps it was because she had only just painted her. Or because they had not come to terms over it.'

'Really?' Patrick turned to her. 'You didn't mention it.'

'I heard it by accident,' said Hippolyta. Patrick made a tutting noise. 'I was not eavesdropping!' she cried. 'It really was an accident!' She glared at him. 'Do you want to know what happened, or not?'

'Well, I suppose you want to tell me, so I shall indulge you as a loving husband should.'

'I don't have to tell you. I can keep a secret.'

'I know you can! It's most alarming. But on this occasion …'

'Well, no doubt Mrs. Price will be able to tell you. And Georgina probably told Mabelle. Georgina detested the portrait, and refused to take it.'

'So what did Mrs. Price do with it?'

'We were all about to go to the picnic, so she left it at Dinnet House, I believe. She may have gone back for it since, for all I know. It was not there when we hid Georgina's kist under the stairs.'

They passed the small wood where Georgina had made Peter Middleton hide that kist of money.

'This road is growing crowded at present,' said Patrick. 'Too many people and events along it: I should be glad not to see it for a day or two.'

'And it's dinner time,' said Hippolyta. 'I should be glad to see nothing but that for an hour or two.'

'I know,' said Patrick, 'but Mrs. Kynoch will need someone with her, will she not?'

'Oh, poor Mrs. Kynoch! She did not deserve this.' Hippolyta was torn. Mrs. Kynoch was a good friend, and a friend in need of help had to be helped, if at all possible. Besides, there might be things to be learned, in observing the girls at Dinnet House when they first heard the news of Georgina's death. But dinner was also an important point in Hippolyta's day, and all her rushing about the place had made changing her clothes a welcome thought, too. She sighed heavily.

'Will you go home and tell Ishbel?' she asked, pleading. 'You can eat yours if you wish, but will you ask her to set some aside for me? For later?'

'I don't want to eat on my own,' said Patrick, 'but I'll do my best to delay dinner.'

They left the pony and trap, much to the pony's obvious relief, at its stables at the inn, then walked on up the hill. The cart, not moving fast, was still visible ahead, with one or two passersby casting it curious glances. When they arrived at the green in front of the kirk, it was only at the top of the green. Patrick turned and squeezed her hand in farewell.

'Be careful, my dear,' he reminded her. 'And don't be too late! If it is quiet, please ask Mr. Durris to see you home.'

She opened her mouth to tell him she could manage perfectly well on her own, then thought of how she had felt with Johnnie Boy Jo that afternoon. And he could easily have reached Ballater before them. She shut her mouth again, and nodded.

'I'll be careful,' she almost promised, and as he disappeared through their gate she hurried after the cart. After all, on these long days it would scarcely be dark even if she stayed late. And surely Johnnie Boy Jo would not reveal himself in the middle of the village.

She arrived at Dinnet House at the same time as the cart, and almost ran along the drive so that she would be there when Mr. Durris broke the news to Mrs. Kynoch. She was sure he would do it kindly enough, but there was nothing like having a friend nearby at moments like that. Panting, she came to the door beside him, and as a consequence of their shocked, urgent look, Mrs. Kynoch probably guessed their tidings straightaway. She looked past them at the cart, and turned white. Hippolyta seized her hand.

'We'll bring her inside, Mrs. Kynoch,' said Durris, and his voice was gentle. 'Where would you like us to lay her?'

'The – oh, where? The dining room would be best. Oh my. Oh my. Oh, Mrs. Napier! What am I to do? Oh, the poor, poor girl!'

The men with Durris lifted the bier from the cart with its sheet and blanket still draped over it, like a mortcloth. Durris, his hat in his hands, led the little procession at an even pace through the hall and into the dining room on the right. Mrs. Kynoch gripped Hippolyta's arm so hard it almost hurt, and watched the men lay their burden down with great care on the dining table, hardly making a sound. Then they withdrew discreetly, with a tip from Durris in their hands, and he remained as the last one out shut the front door.

'You'll want to see her, no doubt,' he said, and Mrs. Kynoch, not looking at all eager, entered the dining room. Hippolyta guided her up to the head end of the bier, and helped her to draw back the blanket and the sheet. The smell was not pretty, and Hippolyta was for once glad she had not yet had her dinner.

'Dr. Napier is sure she has been dead since about the time she went missing,' said Durris, standing a little to one side. 'She cannot have suffered for long.'

'She was strangled?' Mrs. Kynoch's fingers lightly touched the bruises on Georgina's throat. 'Where are her clothes?'

'Here.'

'She was left – with nothing?'

'She was in her shift, Mrs. Kynoch,' said Hippolyta. 'She'd been brought into the glen above the Burn o'Vat, and laid on a little beach by the burn.'

'But she wasn't there on Sunday, was she?' Mrs. Kynoch turned to Durris with a sharp look.

'Dr. Napier and I believe she was killed somewhere else. There was grass on her shift, and some seed heads – we shall do our best to work out exactly what happened.'

'Oh,' said Mrs. Kynoch, 'he has even taken her little necklace.'

'She had a necklace?' Durris had his notebook out already. 'What did it look like?'

'It was a chain of agates, I believe: she wore it always. I don't think it was particularly expensive,' she said, frowning, for most of Georgina's things had been expensive. 'but it had belonged to her mother, I think.'

'And she was wearing it on Saturday?'

'She was certainly wearing it at breakfast. I happened to overhear Mabelle asking her about it. I cannot see why she would have taken it off before the picnic.'

'Perhaps it became caught in her clothing,' said Durris. 'Mrs. Napier, would you mind very much …'

She met his eye, puzzled, then realised he did not want to go through the girl's clothes in front of Mrs. Kynoch. She knelt by the bundle of silk and lace, and began to sort through it. Fortunately the clothing was all pale: the agates, even if caught on a loop or a thread, would show up.

'No, no sign of them,' she said. 'Was her reticule found?'

'Not yet,' Durris admitted. He looked more ashamed of himself than Hippolyta had ever seen. 'After all, we could not find her: how much more difficult to find a reticule?'

But Mrs. Kynoch did not seem to blame him.

'She was not a likeable girl,' she sighed. 'But she certainly did not deserve an end like this.' She tilted her chin, and stood small but determined. 'I must tell the other girls, and then I must write to her father. And then there will be the funeral to arrange – as soon as possible, I think, in this weather.'

She stepped to the fireplace and pulled the bell for the maid.

'Did you notice anything in particular about her clothes?' Durris asked. 'Anything at all useful?'

'Well ...' Hippolyta poked through them again. 'They are expensive, and very light and summery – pretty, but perhaps not practical for running away in.'

'That is true,' said Durris, to her immense gratification.

'But then she could hardly turn up to the picnic in any old thing, not Miss Pullman. And they are in a terrible mess. But look here.' She held out part of the bodice of Georgina's gown. He knelt opposite her to see more clearly. 'This tape has not been untied. It has been cut – and all the others are the same.'

'Her clothes were removed in a hurry? All of them?'

'Apart from her shift, of course, yes,' said Hippolyta thoughtfully, examining every other place where the clothes had been fastened. All had been cut, and the one stocking that had not been removed was almost shredded. 'Yes, it looks as if someone was in great haste.'

Durris sat back on to his heels. The maid appeared, and gave a little squeal, though Hippolyta thought she had already some idea of what had happened. Mrs. Kynoch issued instructions for the girls to be gathered in the parlour, for Mabelle to wait for her in the hall, for brown paper and herbs to be brought in against the smell, and for the woman Martha Considine to be brought from the village, as well as the carpenter who made coffins. The maid nodded at each instruction, and promised not to spread gossip – Hippolyta's mouth twisted a little in disbelief – and vanished. Mrs. Kynoch came to join them.

'Her clothes have been removed in a hurry?' she asked, confirming what she must have overheard. She took a deep breath. 'Mr. Durris, do you believe that she was assaulted?'

Durris looked at the clothes again, then up at Hippolyta.

'Martha Considine will be able to tell us, or Dr. Napier. The light was not good at the place. But yes, that is certainly what it looks like.'

'And do you have any suspicions as to who might have done it?' Mrs. Kynoch was over her shock now, incisive and organised, just as she usually was. Hippolyta was relieved to see it. 'Peter Middleton?'

Durris let out a breath.

'I'm inclined to say no. I found him very plausible this morning – a little centred on what directly affected him, certainly, but not necessarily guilty of assault and murder.'

Mrs. Kynoch nodded, her lace cap jerking back and forth.

'I would say I agree,' she said. 'Then do you think it was someone else she had agreed to meet, or was this an unfortunate coincidence?'

Durris hesitated.

'Mrs. Napier, when we were looking in the Burn o' Vat just now, met Johnnie Boy Jo.'

'You didn't!' exclaimed Mrs. Kynoch, staring at Hippolyta.

'I did,' said Hippolyta, 'but don't worry, I'm unharmed. But I did ask him if he was there on Saturday, when the picnic was happening. He's a bit muddled – only really knew Saturday because it's the day before his sister goes to the kirk –'

'He has a sister?' asked Mrs. Kynoch at once. 'Now that I did not know.'

'But it did sound as if he was there on Saturday,' she finished. 'But he did seem harmless, and slow. And at the same time, there was something odd enough about him that I'm sure Georgina would have known to stay clear of him.'

'But as your husband said, Mrs. Napier,' Durris said, 'people like Johnnie Boy Jo can grow worse. They do what he is known for doing, sometimes for years, and then one day they perhaps turn violent, or commit some more disturbing offence. You can never tell.'

'But if he had turned violent, would he not have attacked me? Is it like … I don't know, rabies? Once they are violent, they cannot be not violent?'

She fell silent, and neither Mrs. Kynoch nor Durris seemed to know how to reply. They all looked down at Georgina's violated clothing, and across at her body. If only she could tell them, thought Hippolyta. Was it Johnnie Boy Jo, taking her by surprise, or was it some suitor she thought she could trust?

The maid appeared at the door carrying herbs and brown paper. Mrs. Kynoch, snatched once again from her worse thoughts, hurried to arrange them around the room and light them.

'Miss Ash is in the hall, ma'am,' said the maid as they finished.

'Have you said anything to her?'

'No, ma'am, not a word. And I've sent for Martha Considine, and the other girls are all in the parlour.'

'Thank you. I'll speak to Mabelle just now. Mrs. Napier ...' She turned to Hippolyta, and her eyes were still a little lost. 'Would you mind?'

'I'll tidy the clothes away,' said Durris.

Hippolyta followed Mrs. Kynoch into the hall. Mabelle was standing, confused, by the open parlour door, and the other girls could be seen inside. Mrs. Kynoch gestured to her to close it. She did so, and stepped over Mrs. Kynoch.

'Mabelle, I'm afraid we have some very bad news,' said Mrs. Kynoch, her voice low. 'Would you prefer to sit down?'

Mabelle shook her head sharply, eyes on Mrs. Kynoch's face.

'Please, just tell me.'

'Georgina has been found, and I regret to say, my dear, that she is dead.'

Mabelle gave a little gasp, and shook, but she steadied herself in the next moment.

'How? How did she die?'

'Someone killed her – just after the picnic, it appears. Her body was found near the picnic site today.'

'But – but they searched and searched!' Mabelle seemed to find this more shocking than the fact that her friend had been murdered, but it was perhaps difficult to take everything in. Mrs. Kynoch nodded.

'They did, my dear, but she seems to have been moved later.' She cleared her throat. 'She is back here now, in the dining room. She has not been laid out yet. Would you like to see her?'

Now Mabelle shook her head even more urgently.

'No, no,' she said at once. 'No, I cannot.'

'That's all right, Mabelle, that's quite all right,' said Mrs. Kynoch, a hand on her arm. 'You don't have to.'

'Maybe later,' said Mabelle desperately.

'It's quite all right. But I believe that Mr. Durris has a question or two for you, if you feel you can manage.'

'A question? But I've said everything about her! I have.' She was shivering, shuddering, almost. The maid was lingering in the hallway.

'Brandy, and tea – and plenty of it for the parlour, too,' said Mrs. Kynoch. Hippolyta put an arm around Mabelle, to support and warm her. Mr. Durris emerged from the dining room, where he had evidently heard the exchange so far.

'Miss Ash,' he said, 'I only want to know one thing. Do you remember the necklace Miss Pullman used to wear?'

'The agates? Yes, it belonged to her mother, she said. Her mother died when she was small, she said,' said Mabelle, chattering out the words as though they were a rope she could cling to.

'Was she wearing them on the day of the picnic?'

'Of course,' said Mabelle. 'She almost always wore them. I noticed them that morning at breakfast particularly. That was when I asked her why she wore them, and she said they had been her mother's. Her mother died when she was small, she said,' she repeated, not listening to her own words.

'Thank you,' said Durris, with a gentle smile. The maid appeared with the brandy.

'Here,' said Mrs. Kynoch, making her take a large sip. 'Go and lie down. I'll send tea up for you in a moment or two. I shall have to break the news to the others, but stay in your room for as long as you want to be left in peace. Come down when you are ready.'

Mabelle, still shaking, pulled herself up the stairs by the banister rail as if she did not quite trust her feet. Mrs. Kynoch watched her go, as far as the landing, then straightened her shoulders again, a soldier facing the battle.

'Now for the rest of them,' she said. Durris made sure that the dining room door was firmly shut, and followed the two ladies as they entered the parlour. Several sets of wide eyes greeted them, particularly focussing on Durris as he came and stood just inside the parlour door. Mrs. Kynoch made her announcement, to gasps and cries, and one faint, but as all the girls were seated no one was injured. Hippolyta tried to watch all their faces as they took in the news, but the one that really stood out was Grace Spencer. While all the others turned pale, jaws dropping, eyes wide, Grace went quite pink, and bit her lips hard. It was almost as if she were trying her hardest not to smile.

Chapter Twelve

'I don't think Grace Spencer was any great enthusiast for Georgina Pullman,' Hippolyta remarked, as Mr. Durris politely escorted her back into the village. 'Did you notice?'

'I did indeed,' said Durris thoughtfully. 'But then, Miss Pullman had more influence than she should have over Peter Middleton.'

'More influence?' said Hippolyta. 'She seemed to be teasing him like a kitten, making him sort everything out so that she could elope with someone else! Not that that was not probably a blessed release for Mr. Middleton, in the end.'

'There,' said Durris with a smile. 'You are as bad as Grace Spencer, and without anything like the excuse.'

'Well ... Georgina was scarcely honourable, was she?'

'No, indeed she seems not to have been. But we do not know much about her upbringing. It might not have been entirely her fault: if her mother died and her father spoiled her.'

'Ah, there! Men are always ready to find an excuse for a pretty girl!'

'A reason, perhaps,' Durris returned calmly. 'Miss Pullman was beautiful, certainly, but she was not very likeable. But she is dead, and I must try to find out why, regardless of what I thought of her.'

'That is true,' said Hippolyta, as they reached the gate. 'Come in, will you? Patrick will be pleased to see you and hear what has been happening, no doubt.'

Hippolyta liked the fact that they knew Mr. Durris well enough to have him stay to dinner – even if the dinner was now cold – at the last minute. Though, on reflection, she thought, as she quickly changed, they really did not know Mr. Durris at all, or at least they knew nothing of the facts that one normally gathered about one's friends: information on their parents, their siblings, their home life, their education. Mr. Durris was a discreet man, to the point of secrecy. Really, sometimes it was quite ridiculous.

Ishbel, used to cooking for a physician who might or might not be called out to a patient even as the meal was being brought to the table, had produced today her veal pie, a dish which was perhaps even better cold than hot, and the creamed potatoes had survived their prolonged stay in the oven. Hippolyta sat happily with Mr. Durris and Patrick over the dinner table, hoping that Patrick would not expect her to go off to the parlour on her own too soon – or that they would join her almost straightaway. What gentlemen talked about when the ladies had departed was probably much less exciting than she had imagined it to be when she was younger, but still, it pricked her curiosity, and she had no wish to miss anything if it pertained to the mystery of Georgina's death.

'Do you think,' she asked now, when Johanna had taken away the pudding dishes, 'that the same person killed Miss Pullman and arranged her body like that afterwards?'

'It's worth considering,' said Durris. 'If it is the same person, I should say that rules out Miss Grace Spencer. She could hardly be strong enough to remove Georgina from some hiding place we could not find, and bring her down – or worse, up – to where she was found. Georgina might have been a girl but she was no lightweight.'

'No, indeed,' said Patrick with some feeling. 'And of course whoever it was must have been quite wet by the time they had finished. It would have been noticed when they went home, if they had a home to go to.'

'You're thinking of Johnnie Boy Jo still, aren't you?' asked Hippolyta.

'I am,' said Durris. 'If the same person killed Miss Pullman, and moved the body then there are two points over the last few days when they would have had to be on their own, unaccounted for. Even if it is two separate people, we now have two points to examine, instead of one. And we have a body.'

'You're quite pleased she's been found, even dead, aren't you?' Hippolyta accused him lightly, but he took it seriously.

'Of course I am, Mrs. Napier. A girl missing is a far greater mystery than a girl killed, and in many ways more concerning for her friends. At least we know now that she is dead, that she is no longer suffering, and that there is no sense in hoping any more. Part of the story is definitely over – it is kinder by far to dash false hopes as quickly as possible.' Hippolyta was surprised to note a bleakness in his voice, and she met Patrick's eye. He seemed taken aback, too.

'I'll – I'll go through now,' said Hippolyta, not quite sure of herself. She rose, and the men stood as she left the dining room and made her way, frowning, to the parlour.

A fire had been lit, cheery though the evening was mild, and she sat close to it and held out her fingers, as if she were going to be expected to play for the company. Alive, and feeling the warmth, not like Georgina, not any more.

She examined her hands, a little shabby, always with some paint around the nails no matter how much she scrubbed, a little worn from tending to cats and hens and pigs and helping, on busy days, with baking and laundry. Nearly everyone worked, according to their station, she thought. Her mother, grander than she, worked hard with her needle, not always the fine work associated with a wealthy lawyer's wife but the tougher, workaday sewing for the gowns and underclothing of the women in the charities she helped. Ishbel cooked and baked and laboured in the kitchen, but Hippolyta knew well that she loved the work – so was it work? The two little girls Mrs. Price thought might be slaves – they seemed content, too, well cared for, well fed. And then there was Johanna, cross and resentful, even though she was paid on time and had a room to herself and a warm kitchen and, most importantly, the freedom to leave whenever she wanted – at a month's notice for preference. Who was the slave, and who the free woman? Hippolyta's eyebrows rose high at the thought. Who was ever entirely free? Johnnie Boy Jo?

Her mind had wandered so far that she jumped when the parlour door opened and Patrick ushered Mr. Durris in.

'We had no intention of staying away so long, my dear,' said Patrick, heading for the piano out of habit. 'There was no brandy, and Johanna took a while to fetch more.'

'No, no, I was thinking,' said Hippolyta with a smile.

'To a useful end?' asked Durris, but he meant it well.

'Not for the present circumstances. I was thinking about slavery.'

'She will read my newspapers,' said Patrick, in mock complaint. 'No matter how much I encourage her to resort to novels.'

Durris smiled. Neither man, Hippolyta thought, preferred women of no information.

The men settled and the cats arranged themselves about the company, indulging their humans for an hour or so before heading out into the promising evening air. The humans, too, relaxed, easy again in each other's company. Johanna brought in the tea tray and retired, and they were once more ready to talk.

'Well,' said Durris, perhaps conscious that he had drawn the conversation to a close earlier, 'the body is discovered, and that was clearly the intention. Why would that be?'

'The answer must depend,' said Patrick, unable to resist a twiddle on the piano keys, 'on whether it was the murderer who moved her, or someone else.'

Durris nodded.

'Could the murderer have asked someone to move it?' asked Hippolyta, returning to thoughts of Miss Grace Spencer.

'That doesn't seem very likely,' said Patrick. 'Imagine going up to someone and saying look, I've killed someone and hidden their body up the hill – would you mind shifting it to somewhere a bit more visible?'

'That may be the key,' said Durris. 'A missing person is just missing: a body is definitely dead. The murderer may have needed everyone to know that Georgina was dead, and not perhaps absconded.'

'Oh, perhaps for legal reasons!' cried Hippolyta.

'Or for other reasons of their own: some kind of recognition that he had really destroyed her, or proof to himself that he was brave enough ... who knows?'

'But that must mean the murderer moved her, or arranged her removal,' said Hippolyta. 'Who in their right mind would find a dead body, particularly one that everyone has been searching for, and just rearrange it somewhere more visible, without telling anyone?'

'Ah, well,' said Patrick, 'you may have something there.'

'Perhaps someone, though,' said Durris, 'who guessed from where the body was found who the murderer was, and wanted to protect them? I'm not saying it was, but if you were, say, Mrs. Middleton, and you found Georgina's body in your stable, wouldn't you think that suspicion might fall on your boy, and move the body somewhere else not connected with them?'

'Oh, Mr. Durris, you are far too imaginative!' Hippolyta complained. 'I cannot see old Mrs. Middleton shouldering Georgina's corpse and marching across the Howe of Cromar to the Vat!'

'It was just an example,' said Durris mildly. 'It could have happened anywhere, to anyone.'

'Well, I think we need to find her reticule,' said Hippolyta, with the air of one returning to practicalities.

'Perhaps we should look in Mrs. Middleton's stable,' Patrick suggested with a grin. She glared at him.

'But Mrs. Napier is right,' said Durris. 'That may indeed point to the place of death, and that in turn may point to the murderer. We need to find the reticule. But I need to spend tomorrow arranging a search for Johnnie Boy Jo.'

'And I have patients to see,' said Patrick. 'But no, Hippolyta, you are not going to go looking for it yourself. Not alone.'

'I thought perhaps I should ask Mabelle to go with me,' said Hippolyta, all innocence. 'I think she might be more sensible than I at first thought her.'

'You'll need to take more than Mabelle,' said Patrick sternly.

'I'll see who I can find!'

But her morning adventures were to be severely curtailed when a note arrived at breakfast: Mrs. Kynoch, fearful of infection and alarmed by the smell of the corpse in this warm weather, had managed to arrange the funeral for that day at eleven. Patrick sighed, and promised to go up to Dinnet House when he had seen his patients, but Hippolyta, feeling a little guilty that she had so enthusiastically planned her reticule hunt without thinking of supporting her friend, wound herself into her second best mourning gown – the best one was far too thick and warm for a hot day – and hurried up the road to Dinnet House.

The whole house smelled so thickly of smoke that for a moment she thought it had taken fire again. Then in a moment she realised the smoke was cold, mostly issuing from the open but curtained windows of the dining room. Mrs. Kynoch, her eyes red either from tears or from the fumes, blinked at her as she opened the door.

'Oh, my dear Mrs. Napier! Come in, come in if you can bear it. The herbs we had to burn were all a bitty green, I'm afraid. Do you – do you really want to pay your respects to her?' Her head jerked towards the dining room, and Hippolyta had the impression that Georgina was causing just as many problems in death as she had done in life.

'I'll just go to the door,' said Hippolyta bravely. Two girls were there, seated in the hallway, not actually in the room, and inside a carpenter and his apprentice, rags tied tightly about their red faces, were kisting Georgina, lifting the body with slightly more haste than was proper into its coffin. The minister, who seemed to be mercifully inflicted with a summer cold, was praying in a stuffy murmur right beside a window. A fire oozed smoke in the hearth. Hippolyta bowed her head and stood by the door as the carpenters fastened the lid over Georgina's shrouded corpse and stepped back. The minister drew his prayer to its Amen, which everyone present repeated. Then the senior carpenter gave an awkward little bow and marched out, followed by his apprentice, and the minister followed, wiping sweat from his forehead.

'I dinna think a'body should stay in that chamber,' he remarked hoarsely as he emerged. 'It's no healthy. I'd say we'd get her away earlier than eleven, but that the gravediggers are having to come down fae Braemar, for our lad has racked his back.'

'We'll just have to be patient,' said Mrs. Kynoch, nodding. 'Will you take a cup of ale?'

'Aye, aye, I will,' agreed the minister, and with the dining room door now closed as near as was proper, and the girls stationed opposite it rather than right beside it, the minister, Mrs. Kynoch and Hippolyta all retreated to the parlour.

So far only Mrs. Kynoch's girls were there, including Mabelle, her eyes redder than most, and Grace Spencer, as prettily dressed as black could make her. But with the interment intended so early, it was not long before other mourners began to arrive: in fact, Hippolyta started to think that Mrs. Kynoch must have sent out a notice to all three parishes. She had certainly included the hotels at Pannanich, for among the earliest to arrive, perhaps anxious not to make a mistake at an unfamiliar Scottish funeral, were the Hendrys, closely followed by the Dinmores and Lord Tresco, both the latter men leaning heavily on sticks. Ah, thought Hippolyta, how gratified Georgina would have been to think that Lord Tresco would attend her funeral! Unless, of course, he had been the one to murder her. Her mind took off along that alley for a moment: if he had killed her, he would probably have needed someone else to place her as she had been found at Burn o' Vat. On the other hand, he was probably the person in the whole of Ballater best able to afford to pay someone enough to do that and keep quiet about it. Patrick had said he had no physician with him, but he must surely have a manservant, at least, mustn't he? Whereas how could Grace possibly have persuaded anyone to move a body without talking about it? She frowned.

'Mrs. Napier, isn't it?'

Hippolyta jumped, and looked up, then across. Old Mr. Hendry had settled himself on the other end of the sopha on which she was sitting, and he was examining her apologetically.

'I startled you, ma'am,' he said. 'My apologies. My strength is not what it used to be, and sometimes when I go to sit I land faster than I intended!'

'It's quite all right,' said Hippolyta with a smile. 'I should not have been allowing my thoughts to wander in company. You knew Miss Pullman in Tobago, I believe? It will be reassuring for her father to know that someone from home was able to be here at the last.'

'Aye, we've known the family since ... oh, before old man Pullman married, I reckon. A fair long time. He and I would have been out there thirty years or more, and neighbours, as it happens, though that don't mean our dwelling houses are close together, you understand. We don't live in each other's pockets there.'

'Someone told me that society was a little limited, but perhaps I have misunderstood?'

'Well, plenty folk, not so many families, if you take my

meaning. Not so many you'd actually be dining with and what have you. And even at that, there are them that are choosy enough where they'll let their womenfolk stop for tea.'

'People can be strange,' Hippolyta agreed, not wishing to commit herself to more than that with someone she did not know. 'I hope you find everyone friendly in Ballater?'

'Oh, very obliging, I must say. And our fellow visitors, too. That Tresco, for all he's a Lordship, he's a decent man. Understands the ways of the world.'

'I suppose – does he sit in the House of Lords?' Hippolyta asked.

'Not when he's injured, no. But he'll be going back soon and I daresay he'll put his three halfpenceworth in for the debate.'

'The emancipation debate?' asked Hippolyta. 'Goodness, yes, I hope he does! I look forward to seeing it all go through!'

Mr. Hendry laughed, a crackly laugh that for a moment she took for a cough.

'Go through! I doubt he'll do that, lass! No more should he. Go through!' He nudged Miss Hendry, whom Hippolyta had barely noticed on his other side. 'Mrs. Napier knows nothing of it, does she, Rebecca? If she lived out there where we live, she'd have more idea of what's going on in the world. Go through? The Government knows well enough it could never afford it! Ha!'

'Father, a funeral, remember?' murmured Miss Hendry, aware of the quiet room around them. Mr. Hendry looked unabashed, but at least reduced the volume of his chuckle. Hippolyta was praying that no one noticed her own red face. How could she have forgotten that he was a plantation owner, a slave owner, possibly even a man who had, perhaps unwittingly, brought slaves into this country? Of course he would not be in favour of emancipation. How could she have opened her mouth so wide, so stupidly?

She changed the subject quickly to ask them how long they planned to stay in the area, and while Mr. Hendry outlined their plans, most of which seemed, by necessity, to revolve around his medical requirements, she glanced quickly around the room. Most of the girls here came from plantation families. Most had grown up in slave-owning families, without a doubt. Lord Tresco himself, if he was, as Mr. Hendry had suggested, sympathetic to the anti-abolitionists, may have interests in plantations – many rich people did. Perhaps Mr. Dinmore's bank had investments there. Only Mrs. Kynoch, whose school, though, depended mostly on the girls' fees, and Mrs. Price, sitting bleak by the empty fireplace, might be thought to be on Hippolyta's side of the argument. And the minister, of course, whose anti-slavery sermons were so stirring up her maid Johanna. She wished Patrick would arrive.

'Is Father telling you all about his illness?' came a new voice, and she looked up to see both the young Mr. Hendrys, Lennox and Richard, standing before them. 'I'm sure you're used to that, as a physician's wife!'

'Oh, yes,' said Hippolyta, trying a smile again. 'People do tend to try their ailments on me, first. But in this case Mr. Hendry was kindly telling me about your travel plans. You seem intent on visiting some of the loveliest places in the country!'

'If it has a spa, we're going there!' said Richard Hendry cheerfully.

'At the rate of one a week, it seems,' added Lennox, returning her smile with an oleaginous one of his own. He probably thinks it charming, she thought.

'But surely there is enough entertainment in such places to satisfy anyone?' she asked. 'You must enjoy the travel, too.'

'Oh, yes,' said Miss Hendry quickly. 'My brothers are too flippant, Mrs. Napier. We are very lucky to be visiting, as you say, such lovely places.'

'Harrogate was my favourite,' said Mr. Hendry with satisfaction. 'Now, that's a town with a bit of class! There's not a peer in the House of Lords that would turn up his nose at a fortnight in Harrogate!'

'I have heard that it is very charming,' Hippolyta agreed. 'Have you tried Peterhead?'

'Aye,' Mr. Hendry's face turned sour. 'Smells of fish.'

'I imagine so. I have not been, myself,' she said.

'We liked Brighton,' put in Richard, his smile a good deal less unpleasant than his brother's. 'It's a lively town.'

'With bonnie lasses - begging your pardon, Mrs. Napier,' added Lennox. Hippolyta thought she detected a slight tut from Rebecca Hendry, but she might have been wrong. 'Ballater's not quite so lively. I mean, there are girls here, of course,' he gestured about the parlour as if Hippolyta might not have noticed the pupils there, 'but it's different when you know one of them from home, anyway.'

'Is it?' asked Hippolyta faintly. This did not seem a suitable conversation for a funeral, still less the funeral of the girl they knew from home anyway, but Mr. Hendry was nodding as if he quite agreed. Then he seemed to notice Hippolyta's discomfort, and draw his thin shoulders up.

'It's a great loss, though: she'll be sorely missed at home. And her poor father.'

'I gather her mother died when she was young,' said Hippolyta, recovering at this more conventional response. 'Was she an only child?'

'Oh aye, aye, she was. Apple of her father's eye, you know? And a fine-looking girl, when all's said.'

'She was indeed,' Hippolyta was able to agree. 'I believe she had already made friends here.'

'And –' Mr. Hendry leaned in close to Hippolyta, a little too close, though the smell of his eau-de-cologne made a welcome change from the smoke '- they tell me she was murdered! Can that be true?'

'I'm afraid it can, Mr. Hendry.' The Hendry family members all exchanged glances, eyebrows raised. 'Does that seem particularly surprising to you? Do you think – is there anything you knew about her, perhaps from her home life, that would have caused such a thing to happen?'

'What,' said Mr. Hendry after a second, 'something from Tobago? Here, in Ballater? That don't seem very likely to me, Mrs. Napier. Maybe in a big city, like, where there are all sorts about and people from Tobago in every street, more than likely, but here, miles from anywhere?' He gave another short laugh.

'No, Mrs. Napier,' said Lennox, his smile comfortably oily. 'It'll be some local, no doubt, excited by all the rich visitors come to stay. He'll have seen her fine dress and gone to rob her, as like as not, and knowing Miss Georgina Pullman she would have given him as good as she got, and he whacked her one. Father's right, as always. Robbery gone wrong.'

The Hendry family, appearing to find some comfort in this analysis, smiled and nodded at one another.

Chapter Thirteen

When the men had gone off to the interment – the Hendry sons taking a share in bearing the coffin at least for the start of the long walk to Tullich kirkyard – Hippolyta was left with the women, the less able men, and the minister, as usual. Missing Patrick, she looked about for someone to talk to: her aims were somewhere between social and a desire to find out more about Georgina and anyone with whom she might have arranged an assignation. Mrs. Kynoch was deep in conversation with the minister and his wife, and Hippolyta was intrigued to note an air of conspiracy about the three of them. Not that she had the least suspicion that any of the three was up to no good: the minister was a decent, if simple, man, and his wife was far too mousy to do anything daring, and she trusted Mrs. Kynoch completely. She smiled to herself, and continued to scan the room

Mrs. Price was there, seated near the window, and Hippolyta wondered if she were perhaps unwell. After all, she was a visitor to Ballater in the summer time: one almost assumed that any strangers were there because their health was in need of repair. Adelina Price had closed her eyes and leaned back in her chair – her stiffness was more likely due to corsetry than to any injury, surely – and she seemed paler than usual. Hippolyta watched her face for a moment, but it was motionless. Then she noticed the woman's fingers, twitching apparently randomly, as if she were going over a conversation in her mind and the imagined accompanying gestures tickled her hands into action. Hippolyta hoped that that was all. A nervous complaint that caused hands to move like that, of their own accord, could be no friend to an artist. Her mind drifted to wonder whose portrait Mrs. Price was working on at present – and what had become of the one of Georgina?

She had left old Mr. Hendry and his daughter on the sopha when Patrick had arrived, and when some other mourners had come to speak with them. Glancing towards them now she noticed, for the first time, that the two little dark-skinned girls were standing in the corner of the room, where Hippolyta would not have seen them before. Dressed very properly in black they kept to the shadows, presumably waiting until they were summoned to serve. She studied them for a moment: they seemed quiet and sombre today, as befitted the occasion. She glanced around the room again, looking for the Misses Strong or some other local friend to speak to, and saw that Adelina Price had opened her eyes and noticed the girls, too – in fact, she was watching them with some intensity. It struck Hippolyta that she herself had better stick to landscapes and animals: she did not have quite the nerve to stare at a person as ferociously as that.

'Mrs. Napier! If you have nothing better to do, perhaps you would be kind enough to keep an old cripple company?'

She blinked, and looked down at the seat next to her. Lord Tresco, unable to accompany the other men to the interment, had been temporarily abandoned to his own thoughts, and if he had invited one of the girls to sit with him – which would probably have been his preference, and at which no doubt most of them would have run to accept – the gossips would have had them married off in a week. Not averse to the conversation of a charming man herself, even protected by her marital status, Hippolyta smiled and sat down on an adjacent chair.

'I'm afraid this is not much of a welcome to Ballater, my lord,' she said. 'Picnics are all very well, but funerals are not happy occasions for visitors.'

'I daresay with all the sickly people visiting it is not an unknown occurrence – and perhaps a timely reminder to some,' said Lord Tresco, unusually solemn. 'And when the dead person is a pretty young girl, the reminder is all the more tragic.'

'Were you much acquainted with Miss Pullman?' Hippolyta asked, trying to make her tone more sympathetic than nosy.

'I met her for the first time here last week,' said Lord Tresco. 'In the garden – I believe you were there too.'

'Oh yes! So I was. She had not been here long, of course.'

'Nor have I, so there was little opportunity to form an acquaintance, unfortunately.'

'I think that when I saw you sit together at the picnic I may have drawn the conclusion that you were perhaps a friend.'

'Oh! As to that,' said Lord Tresco, 'it is not up to me to decide, at the moment, who sits next to me! Unless they are kind enough to accept my invitation to sit, of course.' He bowed his head in acknowledgement that he had asked her. 'No, that sounds ungracious. I was sitting alone, and she and Miss Ash –' he nodded at Mabelle '- kindly came to bear me company. But after a little Miss Ash had to see to a friend who was in some kind of distress, and I thought Miss Pullman would very properly accompany her, rather than stay with me without a chaperone. But I suppose we were in full view of everyone, and we were – at least I was – enjoying an entertaining conversation, so I should have been unfriendly indeed to bid her leave me.'

Though it would indeed have been more proper, more protective of Georgina's already rather marked reputation, Hippolyta thought. But young men were young men, whatever their title.

'Did she, by any chance, remark on any plans she might have had for the day? I believe you were among the last to speak to her. At the picnic, anyway.'

Lord Tresco raised his eyebrows, and sat back to survey the room. His gaze lingered for a moment on his friend's wife, Mrs. Dinmore, but his thoughts seemed to be elsewhere.

'Would you do the job of the parish constable, Mrs. Napier?' he said at last.

'If you'd met our parish constable you might not feel the need to ask, my lord,' said Hippolyta. 'But it is the sheriff's officer who is investigating Miss Pullman's death. No, I feel very strongly that the ladies in the village may run the same risk as Miss Pullman, if we are not fully warned of the circumstances of her last hours – not of her death, you understand,' she added hurriedly, feeling he needed a little reassurance. 'That would be far too indelicate. But if she had intended to walk in a particular place, or meet a particular person ...'

'I see,' said Lord Tresco, after a moment's consideration. 'It is true that the ladies in the area should be warned to take particular care. I thought it was believed that she had intended to meet that Peter Middleton, but she said nothing of that to me.'

'Nor of any other plans?'

'When she left me,' he said, frowning, 'she excused herself by saying that she and some friends had hoped to take a turn in the woods, perhaps to go back up to the Burn o' Vat. But I didn't see her meet anyone else. Naturally I watched her for a little, but she set off on her own at least. Then someone – oh! The Misses Strong, it was – kindly came to see if I was all right, and I did not see her further.'

He spoke with some regret. But perhaps there had been nothing to stop him saying to Georgina,

'Go ahead and wait for me in the woods, and I shall join you later!'

But was his leg up to such adventures? She would have to ask Patrick.

'Ah, and here they are again to tend to me! Miss Strong, Miss Ada – delighted, ladies.' He struggled from his seat as the Strong sisters, broad and decisive, strode into the conversation. Hippolyta left them to it, thinking hard about the picnic and its aftermath. If only they could find Georgina's reticule! Surely that would help. The clothes and the body had been arranged for discovery, but if the reticule had been overlooked it must surely tell a story.

The men returned from the interment, dusty and sweaty in their black, and the mourning party began to disperse. Patrick apologised to Hippolyta and returned to his patients, but Hippolyta had other plans.

'Mabelle,' she said, 'listen. Georgina's reticule is still missing, and I think it must still be up there on the hillside near the loch. Will you accompany me to find it?'

'Oh!' Mabelle, who had just risen to leave the room, was wide-eyed with surprise. 'What, now?'

'Well, yes. The sooner someone finds it – someone reliable – the better, wouldn't you think?'

'Oh, yes, but … I don't think I ever want to go back up there, Mrs. Napier!'

'I'll go, then,' came another voice, and Grace Spencer stood next to them. 'Whatever killed Georgina is not going to kill me – or you, Mabelle. Or Mrs. Napier,' she added as an afterthought. 'You know what type of girl comes to that kind of end.'

Hippolyta was about to protest that Georgina's funeral was hardly the place for remarks like that, but no one else was listening and she wanted Grace to go on. Grace, however, had made her point. Mabelle was white.

'I can't!' she cried, and left the parlour. Grace watched her go.

'Have I time to change my boots and gloves?' she asked Hippolyta briskly.

'Oh, oh yes of course,' said Hippolyta. 'I'll wait.'

It was not long until Grace appeared in the hall where Hippolyta stood, enjoying its cool shade. Mrs. Kynoch had seemed happy enough that Hippolyta was taking one or two of her girls out for a post-funeral airing, and had not (to Hippolyta's guilty satisfaction) asked where they intended to go. Grace had assumed a sensible bonnet with a brim that was not outrageously wide, and a practical pair of boots. Hippolyta could see why Mrs. Middleton might think she would make a good wife for Peter – if Peter ever again won her favour.

'The pony and trap are at the inn,' Hippolyta was explaining, when there came a cry from the top of the stairs.

'Mrs. Napier! Wait!' Mabelle, similarly reshod and in a bonnet that had seen better days, hurried down to them. 'I shall come, after all. Even if – even if there is danger, we shall be together, shall we not? And Mrs. Napier, you are quite right. That reticule needs to be found, and I am perhaps the one who knows best what it looks like.'

'Good girl, Mabelle!' said Hippolyta. 'And we'll be quicker with three of us!' Though it would be harder for her to have a confidential conversation with either of them, but still, who knew what she might learn? And if they found the reticule, then it would all be worthwhile.

They set off away from Dinnet House, and began the walk down through the village. Grace looked about her.

'Mrs. Napier, have you no attendant who could accompany us?'

'Well, no,' said Hippolyta, surprised.

'But I thought … you see, my father would not normally allow me out without a sl – a servant to escort me.' She turned a little pink, and Mabelle had an embarrassed look as of one in the presence of a social misstep that was not of her making. 'I know at Mrs. Kynoch's school we don't have such things, but I thought perhaps you, as the physician's wife, would …'

'Well,' Hippolyta sighed, 'I suppose I could ask Wullie if he wants to go.'

It was fortunate that they were only on the green. Hippolyta darted across to her own front gate, and hurried inside. In the kitchen, Wullie was happily rinsing lettuce leaves while Ishbel sang and worked dough. Both broke off when Hippolyta appeared at the door.

'I'm glad to hear a happier kitchen!' she remarked. 'But where is Johanna?'

'She went out, ma'am,' said Ishbel.

'And we're in no great rush for her to come back,' added Wullie with a grin.

'This isn't her day off, is it?' Hippolyta screwed up her face to try to work it out.

'No, ma'am. She said there was a problem with her brother, and she had to go. A message came for her.'

'A message? Well, I suppose, if there's something wrong … after all, she is not a slave, whatever she thinks.'

Ishbel grinned down at her dough, and Wullie smothered a small giggle.

'Can you spare Wullie, though, Ishbel?' Hippolyta asked. 'If dinner's late it's quite all right.' She hoped she was correct: it would just be her luck that she and Patrick were both ready and starving on a day when the dinner was not on the table on time.

'What's your will, ma'am?' Wullie asked. 'Do I need my boots on?'

'That's up to you, Wullie.' She knew how averse Wullie was to footwear, and in this hot weather it was even more understandable. 'I need you to come with me – and two of Mrs. Kynoch's young ladies – up to the Burn o' Vat to look for the dead girl's reticule.'

Wullie sucked in air in a long assessment of the task.

'Aye, ma'am, I'm your man,' he conceded, drawing

himself up to his full three and a half feet. 'Can I bring the dog?'

'Essential, I should think,' Hippolyta agreed, and with a farewell to Ishbel they left her. She was already singing again before they reached the hall.

There was no room for Wullie in the trap, but he was content to walk. The dog, however, preferred to squirrel under the ladies' skirts and rest its paws, and the pony seemed resigned to this new routine of almost daily trips to the borders of the parish. The girls may not have known that they were passing their companion's burial place, the churchyard at the ruin of the old Tullich kirk, but they were subdued by the events of the morning, nevertheless, and spoke little until they had joined the commutation road and were well on their way to the junction with the Tarland road. By that time Hippolyta had mostly recovered herself, and was eager to talk, but she did not want to question either girl closely in the company of the other, not yet.

'Tell me,' she said, as the pony slowed on a hill, 'what is it like to live with slaves?'

There was an unexpected but distinct yelp from Mabelle, and both girls stared at each other. The dog stirred at their feet, and poked a wary nose out to assess the danger, then settled again. Mabelle cleared her throat.

'What should it be like?'

'Well ...' said Hippolyta, not quite sure. 'How is it different from just having servants? In feel, I mean: I know what the legal position is.'

Both girls looked a little anxious at the mention of a legal position. The question obviously taxed them.

'Servants are more alarming to have in the house,' said Grace slowly. 'Because they can do anything they like, and you can't have them whipped if they disobey you.'

Hippolyta frowned. In fact she was sure you could give a servant a beating, but it was certainly a last resort and not something one would boast of in decent company.

'But how does it feel to own someone? Like owning ... this pony?'

'Slaves don't bite you!' said Grace with feeling. The pony had not taken to her.

'It will be difficult to work the plantations without the slaves,' said Mabelle, who had been silent up to this point. 'But it must be attempted. It is true that a well-cared-for slave can live in good conditions and be well fed, but slavery allows much mistreatment and overwork. Emancipation is essential.'

To her surprise, Hippolyta noticed that Grace was nodding through this remarkable little speech, probably the longest she had heard Mabelle give. Mabelle suddenly seemed conscious of this, and shut her mouth like a fish, eyes swivelling towards Hippolyta.

'I quite agree,' said Hippolyta firmly. 'But I thought the people on the plantations, people like your fathers, presumably, were against it.'

'Before we came here, we … I think we were,' said Grace. 'But now … Mrs. Kynoch has spoken so movingly on the subject. She has told us many stories of mistreated slaves, of freed slaves actually surviving and working hard even when they weren't forced to. We are told that they need to be driven because they are naturally lazy.'

'No more than any other person, I should think,' said Hippolyta. 'Some of us work hard and some of us would rather let others do the work.' She eased the pony in to the side of the road where they had all stopped before. She was thoughtful – was this what her old friend was up to with her school for plantation owners' daughters? Some form of education, however small, for them to take home to Jamaica and Tobago and Nevis? She wanted to laugh: Mrs. Kynoch had only reluctantly taken the money left her by her cousin, but she clearly had plans for it.

'Where shall we start?' asked Grace, back to practicalities. Wullie hauled the dog out of the trap, and saw to the pony. Hippolyta looked about her.

'I think,' she said, 'we should walk back up to the Burn o' Vat, and work out from there. That is where she was found – does that concern either of you?' She gave them a severe look, hoping to stop any missishness in its tracks. Both girls assumed solemn expressions, and shook their heads. Hippolyta nodded, and led the way up the path towards the rocks once again. They had been walking for only a minute or two when they heard a shout from up ahead.

'Mrs. Napier!'

Hippolyta's heart sank. Mr. Durris was striding down the path towards them, not looking at all pleased.

'Mr. Durris! I had thought you were … um, well, elsewhere, today.'

'So you believed you could slip up here undetected and into all kinds of danger? Mrs. Napier, I should march you back straightaway to your husband!' At least, she thought, he had the courtesy to keep his voice down: the girls had withdrawn a little distance – possibly from fright at the look on his face.

'Miss Ash and Miss Spencer both wished to help,' she said, somewhat disingenuously. 'And on the day of their friend's funeral, they wished to visit, and pay their respects to, the place where she was found. Surely you would not bar them from laying some flowers down on the spot where she was abandoned?'

Durris' mouth twitched.

'I see no flowers,' he remarked.

'In this weather they would not keep for long. They would be better picked fresh, as you no doubt know.' She raised her eyebrows innocently. 'May we proceed, Mr. Durris?'

'If you will permit me to accompany you,' he said, stiffly.

'But of course! If you have nothing more urgent to do? I should hate to pull you away from your work.'

She had intended to tease him with the words, annoyed at his annoyance, but as he waved the girls to follow them and began to lead the way back up the little glen, she thought more about what he might have been doing here. The dog snuffled past them on one side and Wullie on the other as she asked, quietly,

'Are you here looking for Johnnie Boy Jo?'

'I am, and with no good fortune whatsoever.' A lesser man would have kicked in his frustration at some stone on the path, but he paced on steadily. 'For all it would appear, Johnnie Boy Jo makes his occasional appearances and then returns to the land of the faerie until the next time.'

'It is rough country about here,' said Hippolyta in consolation. 'It would be easy enough for a man to hide, surely.'

'But where is he eating? Who is feeding him? You said he mentioned a sister, but I have no information about her. I've heard at least three possibilities for his surname, none like the others, and no trace of anyone else in the three parishes with any of them. I have ridden miles already today, and can find no one who has seen him. So I returned here to where I know he was last seen ... much, as I think, you have done too. It is the missing reticule you seek, I suppose?'

Hippolyta sighed.

'Yes, of course it is. Mabelle knows what it looks like, and only when Miss Spencer shamed her into coming, against, to be fair, her better judgement, did she come along. And Wullie came because Miss Spencer wondered that I had no attendant, and the dog came because – because Wullie came. Though it did sit in the trap.'

'Well,' said Mr. Durris, 'I feel I have been fully informed now.' She looked sideways at him but he seemed at last to be smiling, just a little. 'And here we are. Allow me to assist you, Mrs. Napier.' He held out a hand and she took it, just for a moment, before she was steady on the rough rocks and could make her way step by step, holding her skirts tight to her sides, through the narrow gap and into the echoing well of the Vat. Wullie was already scrambling up the facing rock wall, while the dog, less enthusiastic, sniffed around in the water pooling in the open cavern. In a moment the girls had joined her, followed by Mr. Durris. Hippolyta drew the girls together, not wanting to allow any vestige of drama about the place to distract them from being useful.

'Now,' she said, 'Georgina's – belongings – were mostly found there.' She pointed to the sharp little recess to the right, as they looked back at it, of the entrance. 'Of course we would see it if the reticule were there. And she herself –'

'But it is there, Mrs. Napier,' said Mabelle.

Hippolyta, who had turned to point up towards the incoming stream, spun back impatiently.

'How could it possibly be there?'

But it was. The bag reticule lay, half propped against the side of the recess, and half on the gritty floor of the Vat, just out of reach of the water.

'We could not have missed that before, could we?' asked Hippolyta, breathlessly.

'No,' said Durris. He stepped carefully across, and with a glance upwards to the cliffs above, which she did not quite understand, he stooped and picked up the reticule. He held it at arm's length. 'Is it hers?' he asked generally.

'It is,' Mabelle agreed. Her face was white, but her mouth was firm.

'Then someone, somewhere,' said Mr. Durris grimly, 'is working us like puppets.'

Chapter Fourteen

'It definitely was not there before,' said Hippolyta, slightly shaken. Was someone watching their every move? But why?

'No,' agreed Durris. He sighed. 'Is this enough for you now, ladies? Will you go home?'

Mabelle shuffled, and looked to Hippolyta and to Grace, before saying,

'I would actually like to see where she was found, please, sir.'

Durris, too, looked at Hippolyta, as if this were all her fault.

'Can you climb up there, Miss Ash? Did you manage it the other day, at the picnic?'

'Up there? Oh, no!' Mabelle looked as if she might be about to faint, but turned to face the tumble of rocks with purpose. 'But I said I would do it, didn't I?' she added, half to herself. 'Grace, will you come too?'

'Of course.' Grace took Mabelle's hand with unexpected sympathy.

'If you'll permit me, I'll go ahead,' said Durris, 'so that I may help you if necessary.' And, no doubt, thought Hippolyta, so that he could see their faces when he pointed out the spot where the body had been found. But she let him carry on, taking up the rear as they picked their way across the watery gravel of the Vat's floor, over to the easiest point to scramble up the rocks. Mabelle had to let go of Grace's hand to grab the best holds, and at one point squeaked and seized Mr. Durris' hand as she swayed on an unsteady step, but it was not long before she was securely at the top, with Grace and Hippolyta close behind. Durris led them a step or two down to the right towards the river, and, making sure both the girls were stable, he pointed out the little pebble beach where

Georgina's body had been found. Hippolyta blinked, half-expecting still to see the water playing with the hem of her shift, the hair spread out and mingled with the damp gravel, a bright point under the dark cliff. But there was nothing there now, of course. The girls clung to each other, and Mabelle appeared to be praying, though her eyes were fixed on the little beach.

'Where's Wullie gone?' Hippolyta asked, after a respectful moment. She was not too concerned: they could hear the dog's rough progress through the bracken-bright undergrowth. 'Wullie!' There was no immediate answer, but there was a kind of cry of alarm. 'Wullie!'

'I'm here, ma'am! Mrs. Napier!'

She and Durris strained to see him – the voice had come from somewhere upstream, but high in the woods to the side of the burn. There was more crashing and they could hear running footsteps. Durris started towards the sound, and Hippolyta stood firm between the girls and whatever was approaching. Then Wullie and the dog, almost one body, burst from the bracken and tumbled down into the green glen amongst the birch trees. The dog had something in its mouth, but the boy had other concerns.

'Johnnie Boy Jo! Mr. Durris, I saw Johnnie Boy Jo!'

'Up there?' Durris snapped, pointing back to where Wullie had been.

'That's right. In a wee kind of a clearing, sir. He's a bothy and all.'

'Show me,' Durris shouted, and the pair of them half-ran, half crawled back up the steep green side of the glen and into the woods, suddenly moving much more quietly. The dog watched them go, looked at Hippolyta and thought better of the whole business. It dropped whatever it had in its mouth, lay down with it between its paws, and began to chew thoughtfully. The girls, temporarily frozen, stared at each other.

'What should we do?' Grace asked. 'Should we go home? If that man – that Johnnie Boy Jo – is here, surely we're in danger?'

'Johnnie Boy Jo will not attack us if we stay together. I'm not really sure he'll attack us at all,' said Hippolyta, thinking. 'And I cannot abandon Wullie. Would you rather we went back and waited in the trap, or would you rather stay here? I would choose here,' she added, 'in case either Mr. Durris or Wullie needs any help when they return.'

'You mean they might be injured?' asked Mabelle, her eyes wide.

'They might. All that dashing about in woodland can easily lead to a sprained ankle, at the very least.'

Evidently consoled at the thought of this rather more workaday injury than whatever drama she had been imagining, Mabelle considered a nearby rock, and then sat carefully on it. Grace joined her. Hippolyta smiled.

Silence fell about them: the air was left to the flutter of the burn below, and the occasional sleepy bird sheltering from the heat of the day. Mabelle stared again down at the gritty bay where her friend had lain, and Grace seemed lost in her own thoughts, whether of Georgina or of Peter Middleton or of both, no one could say. Hippolyta still clutched the damp reticule, almost forgotten in the climb up here and the alarum of Wullie's discovery. Yet it did not seem entirely right to examine its contents – it was quite heavy – here and now. She would have to be patient, and wait until at least they were back in the trap. The dog, slightly too far away for her to see what it was it had, yawned and sighed. Hippolyta squinted at the prize, then frowned.

'Fetch!' she commanded, making both the girls jump. 'Fetch!'

The dog tilted its head at her, ears mildly enthusiastic, then as if it were doing her a great favour it picked up whatever it had been chewing, and brought it over to Hippolyta, dropping it at her feet. Hippolyta crouched down.

'Oh!' she said.

'What is it, Mrs. Napier?' Grace asked at once.

'It's a boot,' said Hippolyta. She poked it with one finger: the dog had caused it to be extremely slimy. Mabelle leaned in for a closer look.

'It's Georgina's boot,' she said, just as Hippolyta turned it over and pulled from the depths a silk stocking.

'The one that was missing,' she said, as if it were not obvious. 'Hm. Where did you find this, you clever dog?' She rubbed the dog's ears. 'I hope Wullie was watching where the dog went. Oh, but what if the dog found it where Wullie found Johnnie

Boy Jo?' She scowled. She was so sure that Johnnie Boy Jo had done no physical harm to Georgina or anyone else, though she could not quite say why.

'Then that would prove that Johnnie Boy Jo killed her, wouldn't it?' asked Grace, a little sharply.

'Not necessarily,' said Hippolyta, though she hesitated to say more. After all, Peter Middleton was still under suspicion, and Grace could not be said to be disinterested. But if Johnnie Boy Jo had come upon Georgina's body, Hippolyta could see that he might indeed have taken her to the Vat, either to be found or for some purpose of his own – perhaps even tidying her out of where he wanted to camp. And the boot and stocking could have gone missing at any point in that. Could it not? It could not have pulled off by accident, she thought, examining the loosened laces. These had been deliberately untied, by the look of them. And would Johnnie Boy Jo be the person Mr. Durris suspected of playing with them, hiding clothes and keeping back the reticule, or again would Johnnie see the Vat as some kind of midden for the disposal of things he no longer wanted, or things he found in his wanderings? Would Johnnie Boy Jo even be able to explain? She was far from sure.

But it seemed to make an examination of the reticule much more urgent, and she was just about to lift it and open it when there was a rush of footsteps upstream, and Wullie appeared.

'He's off!' he cried, before he even reached them. 'Johnnie Boy Jo's off like a racing horse, and Mr. Durris after him. Michty, the man can run!' He was panting with excitement himself, and when he reached them he sank to lean with his hands on his knees. 'He says, Mrs. Napier, that you've to take the young ladies away home and keep the reticule safe against him coming back and he'll see you later if it's convenient.'

'He said all that as he ran off?'

'Aye, well,' said Wullie, catching his breath at last and standing up, 'That was the gist, like. I'd like fine to work for Mr. Durris, ken: I think that man could teach you all sorts.'

'He probably could,' agreed Hippolyta. 'Look, Wullie, see what the dog's found? Did you see where he found it?'

'Fit's that – a boot? Och, he's always picking things up.'

'But where did he find this?'

Wullie considered.

'I wasna watching close, but I think it was up by where we found Johnnie Boy Jo. Ken, he has his own wee camp up there, but I dinna think he's been there for long. It was just like a wee burrow under the bracken, and a few stones for a fire.'

'And you think the boot was there?'

'I ken the dog found something while I was looking at the stones, and then Johnnie Boy Jo came out from under a tree and I near died from the fright!'

'What is he like?' Grace was clearly bursting to ask. Wullie considered.

'He's gey bonnie, ken. Yellow hair and blue een. And he's no starved, I'd say, by the look of him. But he's clarted with dirt.'

Grace shuddered at the thought.

'Come on, let's do as Mr. Durris says and go home,' said Hippolyta. 'Wullie, would you mind carrying that boot? And don't lose the stocking that's inside it, either.'

They made their way slowly back down into the Vat, Wullie sure-footed in his bare feet and careless of walking through the shallow stream, while the women tried to save their boots from a soaking. Hippolyta carried the reticule carefully, not sure what might be inside it, and argued silently with herself about whether or not to open it before Mr. Durris came to examine it. When they reached the trap she had made up her mind: it would be best to open it in Mabelle's presence, so that she could say whether or not there was anything out of place. She therefore laid the reticule in the footwell of the trap, and pulled it open. It formed a large bag, silk on the outside and lined in dark green cotton.

'More coins, in a purse,' she said, poking amongst the contents. 'She was not short of money, even leaving behind the kist. A clean handkerchief. Some keys – is this one for the kist, Mabelle?'

'Yes, and the other is for the trunk that is still in our room – the large one.'

'A comb, and a spare pair of stockings – one does not usually carry those to a picnic. And a spare pair of gloves, too. What a size of a reticule!'

'Is her notebook there? It's a gold one.'

'Yes, here it is,' said Hippolyta, 'with a pencil. What kind of thing did she write in it?'

'It was private,' said Mabelle firmly, and Hippolyta, who had been about to open it, checked herself. She would wait until later.

'Well, let us go, then,' she said. Wullie had the pony ready. 'No doubt Ishbel will be keen to see you back in the kitchen, Wullie, particularly if Johanna is not returned.'

Wullie made a face, and helped the dog up into the trap. The girls followed, and Hippolyta carefully placed the soggy boot behind the dog so that it would be less likely to resume its chewing to pass the time on the journey. Wullie cautiously patted the pony, and they set off at Wullie's walking pace back to Ballater.

The girls were willing enough to walk up the hill to Dinnet House unaccompanied, particularly as they knew Johnnie Boy Jo was racing across the countryside some distance away, with the reliable Mr. Durris in hot pursuit. Hippolyta rather wondered how long such a pursuit could be kept up, on such a warm day. She found herself sending up a swift prayer for both of them.

Until dinner time, she kept herself busy catching up on domestic chores, particularly as Johanna seemed still to be absent. Hippolyta, stitching quietly at Patrick's pocket edges, which had a tendency to fray from the pressure of constant use, wondered if she had decided to make a bid for freedom, and hoped that she would not run into any kind of danger. She toyed with the idea of reporting her absence to Mr. Durris, especially when another young woman had been killed in the neighbourhood, but she had not even been missing for a whole day and a night yet. Durris might be concerned, courteous as he was, but he would hardly have the time at the moment to run around looking for Johanna.

Patrick arrived back from his round of patients about half an hour before dinner time, for a wonder, and they were both washed and changed and seated at the dinner table before the meal was served. Just as they were leaving for the parlour together afterwards, attendant cats flowing across the flagged hall, there came a knock on the door and Patrick, who was not above such things, opened it himself. It was Durris.

'Dr. Napier, good evening. I apologise for intruding once

more upon your hospitality, but I believe Mrs. Napier may still have the item she found this afternoon.'

'Oh, the reticule! Come in, Durris, please, and make yourself at home. Our maid is missing, but no doubt Ishbel or Wullie will bring some tea in a moment, and would you care for a glass of brandy?'

'Your maid is missing?' Durris queried, as they processed into the parlour.

'Only since this morning,' said Hippolyta. 'And she has been thrawn recently, resenting her employment here, so we are not too worried: she might only be taking a little time to herself, to make a point.'

'What does she look like?' Durris took out that elusive notebook of his. 'Just in case I should happen to come across her – no doubt there is no reason to worry as yet.'

'Small – about this height,' said Hippolyta, waving a hand. 'Flat black hair, that will not stay up when it is pinned. A pale face – surly, I was about to say, but that may only be when she is in this house. Outside she might be perfectly cheerful.'

'Her name?'

'Johanna Murdoch.'

Durris nodded.

'I don't know anyone of that name locally. Has she family anywhere?'

'She has not mentioned any. She came to us from the Strachans, for they were having great difficulty with her. She is not really cut out for service, I think, but at the moment she has no other option if she wants to better herself, and she does.'

Durris made his tiny note, and folded the book away again. Hippolyta sighed.

'What have you written, Mr. Durris?'

'Her name and description, Mrs. Napier,' he replied blandly. 'As an aide-memoire.'

'What on earth would you expect him to write, Hippolyta?' Patrick asked with a laugh.

'I just wondered,' said Hipplyta, trying not to pout. She had hoped it would be simpler just to show her.

'Hippolyta told me of your pursuit of Johnnie Boy Jo,' said Patrick, more seriously. 'Was it really him, just hiding in the woods?'

'It was, though I think he had not been in that exact spot for long.' Just what Wullie had said, the clever boy, Hippolyta thought. Perhaps he would go and work for Mr. Durris.

'And did you catch up with him?'

'As it happens, I did,' said Durris. 'Though we made a fair distance before I made him stop. He ran like a frightened hare.'

'I suppose he was frightened,' said Hippolyta. 'Did he even understand why you wanted to talk to him?'

Durris looked, for once, a little uncomfortable.

'I have him in the cell behind the kirk,' he said. 'But I'd sooner not. I spoke to him about Georgina, and he seemed to have no idea who I was talking about. He remembered the picnic – that might be because you had already stirred it up in his mind, Mrs. Napier.'

'Oh, yes.' She was not sure from his tone if that had been good or bad.

'Then I asked him about the Vat, how often he went there, what he thought about it. He likes to go there when it's quiet, he says, and sometimes he hides and watches the visitors when it's busy.'

'That's not surprising,' said Patrick.

'No. I asked if he had ever hidden anything there, and he was a bit more circumspect. But when I said was it clothes, maybe a girl's clothes, he said no, it was a bag – the reticule. He had found it somewhere I could not recognise by his description – something about where the witchy lived long ago? And he thought it better in the Vat because it clearly belonged to a girl, and that's where the girls came. He was ... he was quite convincing, in his own way.'

'I have the reticule,' said Hippolyta, 'over here. And something else – something that Wullie's dog found. Look!' She brought the reticule over from the dresser, along with the boot which she had wrapped in a cloth. 'Mabelle says it's Georgina's.'

'It certainly matches the one she was wearing.' Durris took the boot gently, revolving it in his hands. 'And the stocking, a fine one ... The boot laces are untied, rather than cut, I see. Perhaps he had more time, or perhaps she removed it herself?' He seemed to be turning over the possibilities to himself, and Patrick and

Hippolyta did not interrupt. 'Where did the dog find it?' he asked at last.

'Wullie's not absolutely sure – the dog was wandering around on its own – but he thought he heard it chewing on something when he was investigating the clearing, just before he met Johnnie Boy Jo.'

'In the clearing?' Durris' face was blank. He had just been trying to accept the idea that Johnnie Boy Jo was innocent, and now here was something that seemed to point in the opposite direction again. 'It has certainly been chewed.' He placed the boot back on the cloth, and wiped his fingers on a corner of it. 'Johnnie Boy Jo has not been sleeping at that place since as long ago as Saturday – I doubt he has been there longer than a night. And he has no things – why would he carry her boot around with him? But I must show it to him, anyway, and see what he says. And then, unless something extraordinary happens, I should like to let him go. No one has reported any unpleasant happenings around him all the time he has been here, unless we count his conversation with you, Mrs. Napier.'

'I'm not even sure what he intended, but I did not feel under any physical threat,' she said – perhaps not with complete accuracy, but one could feel more secure about such things in the comfort of one's own parlour, with the evening sun across the windows and one's husband a hand's length from one's side. Durris nodded.

'Well, the reticule, then,' he said.

'It's on the table,' said Hippolyta. They rose, and went to sit around it, waiting only while Ishbel brought in tea and brandy.

'No sign of Johanna yet?' Hippolyta asked.

'Not a hair of her,' Ishbel acknowledged.

'She's definitely not in her room?'

'I've checked three times, in case she came back hurt or something and went in past me. But no, she's no there.'

'Very well. Thank you, Ishbel.'

She turned back to the table to find that Durris had once again taken out his notebook. The reticule was laid flat on the table, or as flat as its contents would permit. Durris flicked back the flap-like mouth, and drew out the comb, the stockings, the gloves, the notebook, the purse, just as Hippolyta had done earlier.

'Ready for some eventuality, anyway,' Patrick remarked.

'Not the one that befell her,' said Durris, grimly. 'I take it you've already looked at this, Mrs. Napier?'

Hippolyta opened her mouth to protest, but they both knew her far too well to accept any excuse. She nodded.

'But I haven't looked in the notebook,' she added, making it sound as if she had managed to resist the temptation through sheer willpower.

'It's a wonder,' Patrick remarked. Durris opened the little gold rectangle, and they noted a pencil on a chain, but nothing written on the topmost sheet of paper.

'Perhaps she was not a natural note taker,' Hippolyta suggested, disappointed.

'She has taken some notes before,' said Durris, tilting the pad to the slanting sunlight. 'There are some impressions on the paper. Let me see …' He drew out the little pencil, laid it almost on its side, and brushed quickly back and forth across the paper. He squinted at the result. 'I think we'll need better light than this. Daylight, not candlelight or lamplight. We'll have to wait till tomorrow.'

Hippolyta, frustrated, fiddled with the reticule as it lay splayed on the table, and something within it rustled.

'What was that?' asked Durris.

'It sounded like paper.' She tried to make the sound happen again, to work out where precisely in the layers of cloth it had come from. 'There! Oh, there's a pocket, look, between the outer bag and the lining!'

'Let me see,' said Durris, but Hippolyta's fingers were already finding their way inside. She drew out a fold of paper, and across it were the words, 'Miss Georgina Pullman – by hand'.

'Mabelle mentioned a note …' she said, and allowed Durris to pull it towards him. Durris unfolded and flattened the paper in the centre of the table, so that they could all see it.

'Dear Lady,' it said, and the handwriting was broad and confident, the ink black as night, 'My life will not be worth living if it is not lived by your side. You know, or you must know, that I am captivated by your beauty, by every curve of your lips or flash of your eyes. If you feel as I do, as I am persuaded you do, let us be together. Meet me after the picnic, in the woods. There is an abandoned cottage upstream from the Vat where we can make our plans. Be prepared to leave at a moment's notice!

'With all my heart,

'Tresco'.

Chapter Fifteen

'Well, you can't speak to Lord Tresco just now,' said Patrick, after a moment's silence.

Durris looked at him in surprise.

'I think I need to,' he said mildly.

'The thing is, he was the last patient I saw before dinner, and I gave him sleeping powders – his leg was causing him some pain after the strain of the funeral. He was to take a bowl of broth and the powders. He'll be asleep by now.'

'Oh, Patrick!' Hippolyta was disappointed, but at the same time relieved. She was not sure how she would manage to hear what Lord Tresco had to say for himself if Mr. Durris interviewed him alone, and this delay might give her the chance to work out a way.

Durris shrugged.

'I shall have to speak to Johnnie Boy Jo in the morning about the boot,' he said, 'and then if I can I shall let him go. He is not the kind of man who likes to be cooped up.'

'I don't suppose anyone does,' said Hippolyta.

'More so in his case, though. It seems to make him nervous even being indoors.'

'Poor man.'

Durris nodded, and Patrick said,

'Do you know, it's a strange thing: I have read of cases before where a girl has been assaulted or killed, and there has been someone like Johnnie Boy Jo in the neighbourhood, and the locals have turned on him, whether innocent or not. No one in Ballater seems to consider Johnnie Boy Jo had anything to do with Georgina's death.'

'You mean amongst your patients?'

'Anyone I have spoken to over the last few days. The townspeople think it likely to be a visitor, and the visitors consider it a local matter, but no one seems to have picked on the oddity, the one they might perhaps agree on.'

Durris considered.

'I am inclined to think him innocent, myself. And with a pointer to Lord Tresco – to someone else, visitor or local, and no harm likely to come to him outside, I don't want to keep him in the cell longer than I have to.' He frowned down again at the note from the reticule. Hippolyta studied it upside down. Did the writing really look arrogant, whatever it said? She felt as if it did: confident of being obeyed, assured of escaping the consequences of its actions. Perhaps she was reading too much into those black downstrokes and flourishes.

'This abandoned cottage,' said Durris after a moment, 'does either of you know it?'

'Upstream from the Vat? I thought we had gone quite a way in that direction when we were searching, but I suppose several of us concentrated more around the roads and the loch, believing she had eloped or begun to.'

'But we didn't see such a thing, did we? Could it be what Johnnie Boy Jo called the place where the witchy lived?'

'I didn't see anything of the sort, no,' Patrick agreed. 'And I hadn't heard of such a place till I read that note.'

'I suppose you're not a local, either,' said Durris thoughtfully. 'But then nor is Lord Tresco.'

'No,' said Hippolyta, 'and he's lame. How was he supposed to climb up that glen? And alone, presumably.'

'I suppose there really is something wrong with his leg?' Durris asked Patrick.

'Very much so,' said Patrick. 'You can easily see where the break has healed badly. He has to be in constant pain.'

'Could he have intended to send Georgina up there without meaning to go to meet her? For a joke, perhaps? Or to meet someone else, either for that other person's benefit – I mean, that he was perhaps playing Cupid for some man, knowing that she would jump at Lord Tresco's summons but might not agree to see whoever this man was –'

'In that case he can tell us on whose behalf he was acting,' said Patrick, with satisfaction. 'Could it be Mr. Dinmore? After all, they seem to know each other well.'

'Or he intended her to be killed, and sent her there to meet some person he had bribed to kill her?'

Durris and Patrick looked at each other.

'It would be harder to have him admit to that,' Patrick acknowledged.

'But that would argue, would it not, some prior association with her?' said Durris, thinking it through. 'Even a man who was insane would not arrange the death of someone he had only just met, for no personal gain.'

'Could he have interests in Tobago, somehow? Be acquainted with the family? Be related to the family, even – what about her dead mother?' Hippolyta's imagination was building spider's webs of associations. 'Could it be revenge?'

'Steady,' said Patrick, a hand on her arm. 'You're rushing ahead.'

'I shall write to some acquaintances in London and see what I can find out,' said Durris. 'If he has lands in Tobago it should be quite well known – in fact, presumably Mr. Hendry would know. He says it's a small society there: everyone is bound to know everyone else's business.'

'I'd very much like to see this abandoned cottage,' said Hippolyta, allowing a little wistfulness into her voice while keeping her eyes on the table in front of her. Durris sighed.

'I daresay you would, Mrs. Napier. Dr. Napier, would you do me the great service of coming with me to examine this cottage later tomorrow, if you have time?'

'I should be happy to be of use,' said Patrick. 'Perhaps I might bring my wife?'

Durris exchanged looks with him.

'Aye,' he said, 'you might.'

Wednesday morning dawned in a haze, but anyone who hoped it might turn to rain was disappointed. It burned off quickly, leaving a day as hot and dry as any that had preceded it. Hippolyta bathed herself in cold water and regarded her petticoats with regret: just today she would give a great deal to go back thirty years to her mother's youth and wear an Empire muslin, airy and thin – not usually a dress to long for in the Scottish climate.

But the hot day was going to be a mercy in another way, she was sure. The house where Lord Tresco was staying had a garden, in which Patrick had told her he was encouraging his patient to sit out in the fine weather to benefit from the Deeside air. Surely he would be there this morning, and he would not wish to cause himself pain by moving indoors just to be interviewed by Mr. Durris? All through breakfast she kept at least one pair of fingers crossed under the table, and even after Patrick had gone out to work she made herself wait just a little, as if rushing to the place would jinx her plans. She went instead to the kitchen, as a good mistress should, to see how the servants were and what they required of the day.

Johanna was not yet back.

'She's never stopped out overnight before,' said Ishbel, who was beginning to allow her worry to show. Even Wullie looked more concerned than pleased at Johanna's continued absence.'

'You're sure her bed has not been slept in?' Hippolyta asked. She would tell Durris later.

'If it has, she made it up again awful neat afterwards,' said Ishbel.

'Is there anything missing?'

Ishbel blushed.

'Only a veal pie,' she confessed. 'She should not have taken it: it was for your table, not for us.'

'I don't suppose she minded the distinction,' said Hippolyta, 'and that's the least of our worries. I've told Mr. Durris that she's gone, and I'll send word to Constable Morrisson, too, in case he or his men see her anywhere. I don't doubt she's gone off on affairs of her own, but I should like to know she was safe.'

Ishbel and Wullie nodded darkly.

'Wullie, will you go and see the constable? I'll write you a note for him.'

It was tricky to write the note with crossed fingers, but she managed, and sent Wullie off. Then, and only then, did she allow herself to tie on her smallest bonnet and pull her gloves on – crossing and uncrossing fingers carefully so that at no point had she no fingers crossed – and leave the house for a visit to her friend Mrs. Strachan.

Mrs. Strachan lived in a fine new house on the Braemar road, almost outside the village, a house indicative of the success of her husband's general emporium in the main street. It was decorated in the latest styles, and in the loveliest taste, a reflection of its mistress. One or two other houses of similar scale stood nearby, and in common with many houses in the village were known to take paying guests in the season. The Strachans' house took no guests, even though it had two very elegant parlours and a drawing room, but on this fine, hot day Hippolyta asked if they might perhaps walk in the garden.

'I so enjoy a visit to your garden, Mrs. Strachan,' she said. 'Though on a day like this it is perhaps best admired from the shade.'

'Yes,' said Mrs. Strachan, a little dazed by Hippolyta's unaccustomed enthusiasm for her policies. 'We have some chairs set about a table in the shade of this tree here.'

'Oh! Yes,' said Hippolyta, 'but surely the view is better if we sit over here, by the wall? Here, let me help you move the chairs.'

She bustled Mrs. Strachan into a general removal of furniture to a point from which they had an unimpeded vista of the kitchen garden. Mrs. Strachan looked bewildered. Hippolyta, never quite sure about the state of Mrs. Strachan's health, had a pang of guilt, but settled down with every appearance of satisfaction.

'Aren't your fruit bushes doing well this year?' she said with enthusiasm. Then she paused at the sound of voices from the other side of the wall. She nodded to herself. 'And your hens – how plump! I do love to watch hens as they poke about a garden, don't you? Just sit in silence and watch them – lovely!'

It was worth a try, she thought, eyes on the hens, as she strained to hear what was being said next door. Her crossed fingers must have worked, for after a moment, with her silence apparently driving Mrs. Strachan to distraction, her hostess rose and murmured something about seeing what was happening with the tea. Hippolyta held her breath.

'I assure you I have sent no note to any female during my stay here,' she heard Lord Tresco say. 'I would certainly not have insulted Miss Pullman – or any other of Mrs. Kynoch's ladies – by suggesting an assignation of the kind you seem to be hinting at. And even had I been so inclined, I fear that my current state of health does not permit any such ramblings about the countryside. You may ask my physician, Dr. Napier, if you do not believe me.'

'Thank you, I shall do so, my lord,' came Durris' voice. 'Perhaps the note has been misinterpreted.'

'To be honest,' said Lord Tresco, 'I am struggling to think of any note I have written since I came here. The invitation to the picnic was an informal, verbal one and was accepted in the same way. I have not needed to contact any tradesmen, as my landlady here does all that for me. I should be very interested to see this note in my name, should you be willing to show it me.'

'Perfectly willing, my lord,' said Durris. There was a pause. Hippolyta could picture the note being withdrawn from the folds of Mr. Durris' mysterious notebook, and handed over with care. She waited.

'Well,' said Lord Tresco at last, 'I do not see how that could be misinterpreted, really, do you?'

'Not really, my lord.'

'And the writing is – well, you could almost say it is a cousin to my own. I could have my landlady fetch a sample of my own from my rooms, if you wish, or perhaps the letter I wrote her to make the arrangements in the first place would do?'

'Thank you, I shall attend to that. You did not, my lord, have your secretary write her?'

'No, I cannot be bothered waiting for servants when it is something I can do myself in half the time,' said Lord Tresco. 'I hate all these trappings. I like to travel on my own, quickly, and go where I wish without having to take consideration for the movements of others or tell them where I am. I have a factor for my estates and he has staff, of course, and there are servants about the houses when I am there – one has responsibilities, unavoidable in an old family, to provide employment for the families on the estate, of course. But when I travel I like to be free of all that.'

Hippolyta raised her eyebrows. That was a new interpretation of freedom for young Johanna, if she saw her again to tell her.

'Do your estates include any land in the West Indies?'

Durris asked, quite as if it were a casual interest.

'Not now, they don't. They used to, but my father sold them off. The factors were always dying of fever and the like, and he had no wish to send any more good men out there to waste them on that enterprise.'

'Yes, it's tragic,' Durris agreed. 'Whereabouts were they?'

'Jamaica, if the old ledgers tell me true,' said Lord Tresco. 'I've never been, have you?'

'No, my lord.'

'No. Damn' sight too unhealthy – I say, stuck here with my leg all wrong in my own country.' There was a silence: Lord Tresco's injury was clearly impeding that freedom he valued so much. 'So what are you again, then, a sheriff's officer?'

'That's right, my lord.'

'What's your background, then? You're not my idea of the parish constable.'

Hippolyta could feel her ears straining to hear. What would he say?

'There we are, Mrs. Napier – tea at last!' said Mrs. Strachan, hurrying over followed by a servant with a clanking tea tray. 'I'm so sorry you had to wait.'

'Not at all, not at all, Mrs. Strachan,' said Hippolyta, swallowing her disappointment. 'I could watch those hens all day.' She gestured towards the kitchen garden but as she and Mrs. Strachan looked, she saw that the hens had long moved away. She felt herself blush, and sat up in her chair. 'Mrs. Strachan, remember Johanna Murdoch, who worked here?'

Mrs. Strachan blinked at the change of subject.

'Of course.'

'Do you know of any family she has? Or anywhere she might go? She has left us, I'm afraid, with only a veal pie to her name!'

'Mercy!' cried Mrs. Strachan. 'That's terrible! How long has she been gone?'

'Since yesterday morning.'

'Oh, Mrs. Napier – you don't think that whoever killed that poor girl of Mrs. Kynoch's – could the same man have found her?'

'It's possible,' agreed Hippolyta, not inclined to cushion the truth in a case like this. 'I did not think so at first, but to have her missing all night … Mrs. Kynoch, who do you think might have killed Georgina Pullman? You know the people around here better than I do.'

Mrs. Strachan's still pretty face creased on long-worn lines.

'I think we'll probably find that it was someone visiting Ballater, wouldn't you say?'

'Not, perhaps, Johnnie Boy Jo?'

'Is Johnnie Boy Jo back?' Mrs. Strachan must be further behind on the claik than Hippolyta had thought. 'Are you sure? I haven't heard of him for – oh, it must be three or four years. He could be dead for all I know, for he has the kind of face where it would be hard to tell his age.'

'He's back,' said Hippolyta, 'I've seen him myself.'

'I'm – I'm sort of glad to hear he's alive,' said Mrs. Strachan, 'though he could be an awful bother when the girls were younger.' Mrs. Strachan's daughters were married and away. 'But there's no harm in him. He's just confused.'

'So if someone told you that Johnnie Boy Jo had been arrested for Georgina Pullman's murder –'

'Oh, no! Never that. Has he?'

Hippolyta shook her head at once.

'Mr. Durris brought him in to talk to him last night, but I think he's going to let him go today.'

'He was in the cell at the kirk?'

'I believe so, yes.'

Mrs. Strachan sighed.

'Oh, poor Johnnie! That won't have pleased him. He cannot stand a roof over his head, the poor soul.'

Hippolyta could not help smiling. To hear such sympathy for a murder suspect was almost refreshing.

She made sure that she left Mrs. Strachan's after Mr. Durris had left the house next door, and resisted the urge to go and speak to Lord Tresco herself: that would certainly not have been proper, and in any case Mr. Durris had asked all the questions she wanted to ask for now. Later, perhaps, if she could speak to him at some social event, she might take her chance. And she hoped that any other suspects or witnesses also lived conveniently close to her friends and acquaintances: Mr. Durris did not approve of eavesdropping, when he found out about it. It made things so much more pleasant if he never knew.

Out of consideration for the pony, which was growing more ill-tempered every day, they had agreed to hire horses from the inn, meeting there at noon. The day might be at its warmest, but they would have time to reach the cottage, they hoped, and still be home before the deceptive summer dusk.

Mr. Durris assessed his offered mount quickly, as a man well used to hiring horses and acquainted with most of the nags for hire in the county. Patrick regarded his with less suspicion, and Hippolyta hers with a friendly greeting: as a regular visitor to the stables to see to their own pony, she knew all the horses and had befriended them. She led hers to the mounting block and with a little help from Patrick clambered up and around the fixings of the side saddle, arranging her skirts about her. At least the thick petticoats that she had so loathed in the morning padded her nicely now.

As they rode without unseemly haste out of the village and back towards Tullich, Durris told them that he had released Johnnie Boy Jo at first light when he had denied all knowledge of the chewed boot. Johnnie had skipped out of the village like a confused deer, running this way and that as if he could not decide his quickest way to freedom. They all fell silent for a moment, reflecting on Johnnie and his behaviour, and Hippolyta remembered the fondness with which Mrs. Strachan had spoken of him.

Then Durris, clearing his throat firmly, outlined Lord Tresco's reaction to the news of the note they had found. Hippolyta managed to respond quite as if it were all new to her.

'And did you believe him?' she demanded.

'I saw the letter he had sent his landlady making the arrangements for his stay,' he said. 'The hand writing is of the same type, I should say, but several of the letters are formed quite differently. If you told me the two hands were those of two brothers who had been brought up together and then sent to different schools, I should not have been surprised. But then apparently he has no brothers.'

'Has he any connexion with the West Indies?' Patrick asked, nodding up at the view of Pannanich Wells high in the woods on the other side of the river. 'So many of these wealthy families have a plantation or two.'

'Apparently his father had, but sold it. And it was in Jamaica, not Tobago.'

'I still wonder about revenge,' said Hippolyta, half to herself. 'I wonder who Georgina's mother was. Perhaps Mrs. Kynoch knows, or has a name, at least.'

'I think you're stretching your imagination out of shape, my dear!' said Patrick, teasing.

'You'll see! There's more to Tobago and its close society than you think!'

But she was only joking. In truth, she could find no sure answer to Georgina Pullman's death at all.

Back once more at the Burn o' Vat, and without the encumbrance of carriages or even traps, they could ride directly up the path from the road to the mouth of the Vat itself. A slippery, steeper path led up to the right hand side of the rocks, and with Hippolyta's encouragement all three horses (horses, generally, went out of their way to be obliging to Hippolyta) climbed the path and they were able to lead them through the trees and follow the burn upstream. Here the woodland was striped black and white with birch and pine, and the thick, bright bracken cushioned the ground: Hippolyta could see easily how a body, or a sleeping Johnnie Boy Jo, might lie undiscovered.

It was a good fifteen minutes since they had passed the Vat when Patrick exclaimed, and pointed. Up ahead was a cottage, not so much abandoned as ruined almost beyond repair. One gable wall, taller than one would expect in such a dwelling, still stood, the stones picked clean by the wind and rain, but to this side of it they could see nothing but the trace of the outline, no more than two or three feet tall even in the best preserved places.

'A strange place to meet,' said Patrick. 'It does not provide much by way of shelter. I suppose the roof was thatch of some sort, for there seems to be not a scrap left.'

'I wonder who lived here,' said Hippolyta. The place had a melancholy air, stale with neglect. 'And I wonder how we are supposed to believe that Lord Tresco knew about it. I have lived in Ballater for four years and I have never even heard of it.'

'And I for longer, and I knew nothing of it,' Mr. Durris agreed. 'But we should look and see if there is anything remotely connected with Georgina Pullman – or any recent visitor – here.'

'We still have not found her agate necklace,' Hippolyta reminded them.

'Dark brown: that will not be easy to find,' Patrick complained. He tied the horses' reins to a tree, and patted his own mount. 'They don't seem too happy here.'

'Perhaps there is someone about.' Durris glanced around, not pleased with the idea. 'I'll check quickly around the other side of that gable before we concentrate on the inside of the cottage. Just in case.'

'Does the ground fall away on that side?' asked Hippolyta. 'Or does it rise? Why is the wall so high, and so well preserved?' She followed him as he approached the corner and stopped.

'What is it?' she asked, peering round the corner past him.

'Oh, no,' said Durris, his voice strangely hoarse. 'Mrs. Napier, don't look.'

But of course she did.

Dangling from some odd piece of wood that protruded from the wall was the limp, pale body of Johnnie Boy Jo.

Chapter Sixteen

Hippolyta could not stop crying.

Mr. Durris marched her back to meet Patrick, and they sat her down, and Patrick administered warm embraces and smelling salts and handkerchiefs, but the tears kept flowing as if her eyes would never be dry again. Every time she thought she had her breath under control, and her mind calmed, she thought of that pathetic, dangling figure, and began all over again.

She sat there by the horses while Patrick and Mr. Durris left her briefly to work out how to cut Johnnie Boy Jo's body down. She could hear them, though no doubt they hoped to be inaudible:

'He must have climbed up the wall – how else could he reach that pole?'

'No one climbed up there with him, that's for certain. Unless they lifted him some other way ...'

'No, it must be suicide, surely?'

A weighty pause, then an awful scraping.

'Steady!'

A bump, then silence.

'I blame myself, if it is self-killing.'

'No! Why would you?'

'Locking him up like that, last night. He was miserable. You never saw a man so low.'

'But then you let him out. Why would he kill himself once he was free again?'

'Perhaps the harm had been done. You would not call him a man with a normal mind, would you?'

Hippolyta could picture, could not avoid picturing, Patrick's gentle examination of the body. Her throat hurt and her eyes stung, but her face was still running with tears. Her horse nuzzled at her shoulder, and she rubbed its nose, and bawled like a baby with colic.

In the end all they could do was take her home so she could cry in comfort. Durris elected to stay with the body, while Patrick escorted his wife and promised to send carriers back to help to bring the body – where? Johnnie had no home. But to bring it away from this desolate spot, at any rate.

For once she was glad of the broad wings of her bonnet on the way home, hiding her stained face from public scrutiny, though if anyone had seen how her shoulder shuddered they might have guessed she was crying. She waited in a corner of the stableyard at the inn while Patrick returned the horses, then he took her arm and walked her home, going the back way so that fewer people were likely to meet them. Once he had settled her in the parlour, he rang for tea and brandy, and sat beside her on the sopha, rubbing her hands in his.

'My dear,' he said, 'you must calm yourself: you're doing yourself no good at all.'

'But it's just so sad!' she sobbed. 'I'm sorry. I just keep seeing him there.'

'Hippolyta, are you sure he did you no harm the day you met him?'

She blinked at him, able for a moment to draw breath.

'Of course he didn't. He didn't even touch me. And I have spoken to people who have known him here for a lot longer than we have, and they are convinced that he is innocent. As am I.'

'But my dearest,' said Patrick, 'I think we must face that he may have committed this final act in remorse for what he had done to Miss Pullman.'

'I cannot believe it,' she said stubbornly. 'Are you sure he even killed himself? Was he not murdered, too? No one more likely than he to have seen something he should not have, to have been around when the murderer – the real murderer – was going about his horrible business.'

'I saw no evidence of his dying at any hand but his own, Hippolyta. I'm sorry, but I still think his guilt killed him.'

She scowled, and pursed her lips. She knew very well she looked and sounded like a child in a tantrum, but she could not seem to help it. She felt completely miserable, completely convinced that Johnnie Boy Jo had not killed Georgina Pullman, and, suddenly, completely exhausted.

'I think I'll go and lie down for a while,' she said. He helped her up, and took her in his arms for a long moment. She felt his lips on her hair, but she was still cross with him and with the world. She slipped away from him, and with an attempt at a sideways smile, she headed up to their room, removed her cumbersome outer clothes, and huddled herself into the eiderdown that still lay at the foot of their bed, despite the hot weather. It was very comforting. The sobs gradually subsided: she poked at the wound, as it were, by making herself think again about Johnnie Boy Jo's death, but the worst seemed to be over. She laid her aching head on the pillow, closed her eyes, and fell sound asleep.

She woke to a different angle of light and shade, and familiar voices downstairs. She sat up, feeling clumsy and stupid. The clock on the mantelpiece declared that it was eight o'clock. She could hear it ticking so she could not be mistaken: but she had missed dinner, which was not at all like her. She wondered briefly if she were ill, and put the back of her hand to her forehead, but she had been scrunched under the quilt and everything was hot anyway. She sighed, contemplated lying back down again, then thought that she would never sleep properly later if she allowed herself to stay in bed now. She rose, and began to make herself presentable. There might even be some dinner left, though strange to say she did not feel particularly hungry.

Downstairs, as she had thought from the voices, Mr. Durris was in a chair in the parlour. He and Patrick both rose as she came in, and Patrick went to take her hand, examining her face closely. He did not seem entirely reassured by what he saw, but led her nevertheless to a chair by the fireplace.

'Are you warm enough? Too warm? Would you like something sent in? You missed dinner – surely you must be ill!' He was trying to make light of it, but Hippolyta could see that she had worried him. He was always over anxious about her. She squeezed his hand.

'I am perfectly well! All this hot weather – we are not used to it, are we? I think I overheated and now I feel perfectly rested. I should not last ten minutes in the West Indies, I should think!'

'One doesn't arrive there all at once, though,' said Durris, as though he had been considering the matter for some time. 'In sailing there, one must gradually become accustomed to the climate. It is not so much the heat, as the fever and the insects, that are harmful. Is that not so, Napier?'

Patrick hesitated.

'The heat weakens those who are not used to it, and that makes the fevers all the more virulent,' he suggested, handing Hippolyta a cup of tea. It was most welcome. 'And now, my dear, I know you must be sickening for something, for you have been in the parlour fully five minutes and you have not yet asked for any information from Mr. Durris!'

Hippolyta, spun back once more to the awful ruin where they had found Johnnie Boy Jo, feigned a smile.

'I was only waiting for a pause in the conversation,' she said pointedly. 'Mr. Durris, I hope you were not left there on your own in that desolate place for too long. I know Patrick went almost immediately to send the carriers to help you.'

'I was there long enough to make an uninterrupted investigation of that ruin,' he said, 'which was what I desired. I found this, which if it had rained would no doubt have been reduced to an unrecognisable scrap, but we have been fortunate in the weather.'

'This', as he laid it on his hand and showed it to Hippolyta, was a feather – small, light, its tendrils shivering in some unknown draught. It was dyed a familiar shade of pale green.

'It's from Miss Pullman's bonnet! Or something very similar,' said Hippolyta in triumph.

'It is at least an indication that she went that far,' said Durris, nodding. 'But there was nothing else.'

'No manly footprints? No marks of a splendid horse come to whisk her away?' Patrick echoed the romances of a popular novel, but Hippolyta turned to him.

'Mabelle says she was not romantic. He needed money, not splendour, to satisfy her.'

'In any case,' said Durris practically, 'it is too dry for much trace of prints.'

'Mr. Durris, you must still believe Johnnie Boy Jo to be innocent – don't you?'

Durris glanced at Patrick.

'I don't know now what to believe.'

'Oh! You have been listening to Patrick. I cannot believe that Johnnie Boy Jo killed himself out of guilt. He would have needed to have some knowledge of what he had done wrong, surely? Do you really think he was capable of that?'

Patrick and Durris exchanged another look. This time they seemed puzzled.

'Perhaps not,' said Patrick at last. 'Perhaps you are right.'

'He was always smiling,' said Durris quietly. 'Always. Until I locked him in that cell.'

'My dear Mr. Durris,' said Hippolyta, aghast. 'You cannot blame yourself! You must not!'

'My wife is quite right,' said Patrick, just as quickly. 'With a man like Johnnie Boy Jo, nothing is entirely predictable. He could as easily have seen something, met someone, who upset him. He was free for hours before we found him.'

Durris opened his mouth to reply, but at that moment someone pounded on the door. They heard running footsteps in the hallway. None of them so much as breathed before Ishbel flung open the parlour door.

'Ma'am, it's a Mr. Hendry, down from Pannanich, looking for Mr. Durris.'

'Then show him in,' urged Patrick at once. Ishbel turned, then paused in the doorway.

'Ma'am, just to let you know: Johanna's just back.'

'She's back? Then why didn't she answer the door?' asked Hippolyta, confused.

'Och, she's that upset, ma'am! But I'll fetch Mr. Hendry.'

Hippolyta did not know which Mr. Hendry to expect, but was pleased to find that it was Mr. Richard Hendry when he arrived, a little breathless, in the parlour.

'Forgive me, Mrs. Napier, Dr. Napier,' he said, clinging on to his hat and gloves despite Ishbel's agitated hovering. 'It was Mr. Durris I sought. The landlord at the Wells said that if you were anywhere in the village, it would be here.'

'Well, you've found me,' said Durris, rising to meet him. 'How may I be of service, sir?'

Richard Hendry's eyebrows wriggled, as though he were

not quite sure how to address this sheriff's man. He almost shrugged to himself.

'It's my sister's maids, Hannah and Ruth,' he said. 'You've maybe seen them? Two little native girls.'

'Native to Tobago, I suppose, sir,' remarked Durris, humbly.

'Of course. You've seen them.'

'Yes, sir. What appears to be the problem?''

Hippolyta watched them both, wondering if Durris were about to accuse the Hendrys of keeping slaves. But the opportunity hardly arose.

'They've vanished, Mr. Durris. Completely disappeared – and taken nothing with them,' he added, as though that in itself were completely unnatural.

'When were they last seen?' Durris asked. Richard Hendry danced on his toes, expecting action before questions.

'I don't know. You'd better ask my sister.'

'At Pannanich, though? You're staying at the wells, aren't you?'

'Aye, we are. I imagine they were there. We haven't been far today: Father's been taking the waters, and we've just sat around gossiping. There would be no reason for the lasses to have gone anywhere else.'

'So Miss Hendry did not expect them to have left the hotel at all?' Durris made sure. 'She sent them on no errand?'

'I shouldn't think so. Where would she send them?'

Durris had produced his notebook. He made a mark in it.

'Mrs. Napier,' he said, making her jump, 'perhaps I might have a word with your maid?'

'What?' Richard Hendry was red in the face. Durris hastened to explain.

'Mrs. Napier's maid has been missing since yesterday and is just now returned, and in some distress. Is that correct, Ishbel?' he asked.

'Yes, sir,' said Ishbel, surprised to find herself part of the conversation.

'Then we should speak with her. It is possible,' Durris explained, as though to someone of very little brain, 'that where one maid has been absent, she might give information that would prove useful to find other maids who are absent.'

Richard Hendry took a moment or two to work his way through this argument. He frowned weightily, then nodded.

'I believe I see what you mean,' he said. 'By all means let us question this maid.'

'No, sir,' said Durris gently. 'I think it best if you rest for a little and recover yourself. I shall speak with the maid, in Mrs. Napier's presence, if she will permit.'

Hendry was taken aback, but Patrick encouraged him to rest himself and partake of some tea, for his constitution.

'You have come here at some speed, I see,' he said, 'and one must rest a little before engaging in further activity. Leave it to Mr. Durris: he will see the maid is asked all the right questions.'

Durris and Hippolyta rose and left the parlour, with Ishbel, a little bewildered, leading the way.

In the kitchen, Johanna sat in what Hippolyta thought of as the cook's chair by the fire, a privileged position, awarded, it seemed, because she was clearly upset. Even Wullie looked anxious as he handed her a cup of very black tea.

'Johanna, I am glad to see you back,' said Hippolyta, going to sit on a stool opposite her, 'but what has distressed you? Has someone hurt you?'

Johanna, who had been crying almost as much as Hippolyta herself earlier, looked at her in confusion.

'What?' she asked. Hippolyta resisted the urge to respond 'What, *ma'am*?'.

'Johanna, you have been missing for over a day. If you needed to visit family you should have asked.'

'You said I wasna a slave!' said Johanna, distracted from her upset for a moment. Hippolyta sighed, conscious of Mr. Durris waiting beside her.

'You're not a slave. It is common courtesy to let others in the household know when you expect to be away. And when you are being paid to work here, it is usual to ask permission of your employer to be absent from work.' She was beginning to sound like her mother, she thought. 'Heavens, Johanna, we were worried about you!'

'Aye, well,' said Johanna, sulkily, 'I was grand.'

'Then what is the matter?'

'My brother's dead.'

'Oh, Johanna, I'm sorry to hear that. Had he been ill? Was he seeing a doctor?'

'A doctor? Naw, not him! I doubt he'd ken fit that was at all.' She drew a breath, composing herself. 'Naw, he was hangit.'

'Hanged?' Hippolyta stood suddenly, staring at Mr. Durris.

'Johanna,' he said after a moment, his voice kind, 'was your brother Johnnie Boy Jo?'

'Aye, he was.' She sniffed. 'And dinna give me a'thing about that. You'd never have taken me on at all if I'd said.'

'Oh, Johanna!' Hippolyta's head was spinning.

'Did you see him yesterday? Or today?' Durris asked.

'Why, what he supposed to have done now?' Johanna snapped back. 'It canna be much, for you had him locked up in that wee cell the back of the kirk all last night. And he could never stand a roof over his head.'

Hippolyta remembered Mrs. Strachan saying the same thing.

'Did you see him after he came out? Was he – was he all right?' Durris' voice was uncharacteristically uncertain.

'Was he all right, the man asks?' said Johanna to the room in general. Wullie, Hippolyta noticed, was once again under the kitchen table, his refuge from all disturbance. 'He went and hangit himself. What do you think, eh?'

Durris held any direct response in check.

'Has he spoken to you at all over the last week? Have you talked with him?'

'That's my business.'

'Johanna! This is the sheriff's officer!'

'I ken fine who he is. It's no business of his to go asking questions about what me and my brother said to each other. Or didna say.'

'Well, it is, actually, if your brother is suspected of murder,' said Hippolyta, trying to be accurate.

'Aye, right, there it is, out in the fresh air!' said Johanna. 'Now we all ken fit we're talking about. Suspected of murder – there it is. Always blame our Johnnie.'

'I'm trying not to,' said Durris tightly. 'But it's not easy when he's in the right place at the right time and cannot answer a straight question. I was hoping you might be able to help.'

But at this Johanna folded her arms firmly across her chest, pressed her lips tight together, and looked away. The message was clear. No help was coming from this quarter. Durris looked at her for a moment, then turned away.

'By any chance,' he said to Ishbel and Wullie – or to Wullie's feet, anyway, 'has either of you seen two little West Indian maids anywhere today?'

Ishbel shook her head, and there was a muttered negative from under the table. Durris looked at Hippolyta.

'Back to Mr. Hendry, then.'

Patrick wanted Hippolyta to stay at home, but she insisted on accompanying them to Pannanich with Richard Hendry, saying that the walk in the cooler evening air would do her good and help her to sleep. Patrick insisted she take a warm shawl, and indeed it was a little chilly as the ferryman took them over the river where the old bridge had been.

'Anyway, perhaps Miss Hendry would appreciate some female company, if she is in distress,' Hippolyta said. Durris made a small sound.

'We know you would find some way of discovering all that happened if we didn't let you go,' said Patrick, keeping his voice low. It was one thing not being able to control his wife's boundless curiosity, and another to make it obvious to a stranger like Richard Hendry. Hendry was marching ahead up the road between the trees, as if he could hurry them along.

Old Mr. Hendry and his daughter were waiting in one of the small parlours at the inn at Pannanich Wells. A fire was lit, and the window firmly closed: Hippolyta at once pulled off her thick shawl, feeling the hot air wrap about her. Miss Hendry was pale, though, and clasped her hands together tightly amongst her skirts on her lap.

'It is very good of you to come, Durris,' said old Mr. Hendry. 'No doubt you have other worries on your mind – the death of that poor girl, of course.'

'When did you last see the maids? What are their names – Hannah and Ruth?'

'Hannah and Ruth, that's right,' said Mr. Hendry.

'Hannah's the elder. Well, I don't know, when did we see them last, Rebecca?'

'At dinner,' whispered his daughter. 'They attended us at dinner, which we took in the dining room here. Then I sent them to have their own meal in the kitchens.'

'Who else was at dinner?' Durris asked.

'Let me see,' said Mr. Hendry. 'The four of us, of course – Lennox is out looking for the lasses now and I sent Richard for you, but we were all there then. That painter woman, Mrs. Price, who's done the boys. I wanted to talk to her about doing Rebecca too, see if she would give me a good price for doing all of them. Funny thing, she wanted to paint the maids as well. I think I'll get a good bargain there!'

'Anyone else?' prompted Durris.

'Lord Tresco was here – it's that kind of an establishment,' said Mr. Hendry with a hint of pride. 'He had been asked to dine by some acquaintance or other – they sent a trap down to the ferry to pick him up, of course. Poor fellow – it's a bad deal, in one so young and active. Me, now, I've had my life and made the most of it.'

'And other guests?' It seemed difficult to keep Mr. Hendry entirely focussed, but he was quite frail, Hippolyta thought.

'The usual crowd. All the rooms are full, the proprietor tells me, and some people who don't stay here spend the day at the bath and then come here for their dinner before going back to their lodgings down in the village.'

'Have the girls ever run away at all?'

'Run away? Why would they do that? They're well treated, given decent clothes and food: they know they're lucky.'

'Mr. Hendry,' said Durris, 'before you brought them to these shores, were these girls slaves?'

'Aye, paid for fair and square,' said Mr. Hendry. 'Buy them young and cheap then you can train them up in the household, they haven't learned dirty ways. Some breed their own but I like to buy in, fresh blood, and take them away from their mother's influence. Works better.'

Hippolyta felt her jaw drop. He spoke of the girls as if they were no more than cattle. Mr. Hendry caught her expression, and laughed.

'Oh, aye, I mind now – this lady thinks emancipation is a good idea! I'd keep her away from the newspapers, Dr. Napier: she's finding opinions for herself!'

'To which she is entitled,' said Patrick, without rancour. Mr. Hendry laughed again, but made no further comment.

'Mr. Durris, can you find my girls?' asked Miss Hendry. 'I'm fond of them, and they know so little of life here. They cannot be safe!'

'I'll do my best, Miss Hendry. Have you noticed anyone taking a particular interest in them?'

'Apart from Mrs. Price wanting to paint them, no, not at all. People stare a little, you know, but that is all.'

'And have they displayed any interests in anyone, or anywhere, near here? Is there anything they might have wanted to go and see on their own, and perhaps lost their way?'

'They would never stray. They never go anywhere unless I tell them to,' said Miss Hendry, not quite able to believe that two small girls might have any initiative of their own.

'Father!'

The door burst open behind them, and Hippolyta spun round to find Lennox Hendry standing dramatically in the doorway.

'Have you found them?'

'I know where they are!'

'Where, then, son? Spit it out!'

'Mrs. Price has taken them!'

Chapter Seventeen

'Don't be ridiculous, boy! What kind of stupid story is that?' Mr. Hendry demanded, striking his stick on the floor for emphasis. Miss Hendry gave a cry of alarm, though whether at the news or at her father's outburst it was hard to say.

'Where did you hear that?' Durris asked quickly.

'The ferryman,' said Lennox more quietly, looking not at Durris but at his father. Hippolyta averted her eyes from him, almost embarrassed at his anxiety, and noticed that his brother Richard was white as the walls, mouth opening and shutting like an overheated hen. 'That's what he said, honest, Father. He said they'd crossed over a while back, and he'd noticed because the woman was very careful of the girls, making sure they were secure in the boat and all.'

'That's enough of that nonsense,' old Mr. Hendry snapped, and Lennox subsided like a kicked dog. 'What would Mrs. Price be wanting with our girls? It makes no sense!' The old man was more angry than Hippolyta felt he had the right to be. Surely Mrs. Price could not mean anything bad by this?

'Nevertheless, sir,' said Durris, 'the ferryman is not a fool. I shall go and question him further, and continue the search on the north side of the river.'

'Which you should have done,' Mr. Hendry snapped at Lennox, 'if you were so sure of yourself. They could be miles away by now. When's the next mail coach?'

'Not till tomorrow,' said Durris.

'So you've still time. That is, if you're right,' said Mr. Hendry to Lennox. Lennox was not the over-confident, pushy young man Hippolyta had seen before. Here, in confrontation with his father, he was pleading.

197

'I thought I should come back and tell you before I went off back to Ballater in search of her,' he said, with something of a whine in his voice. 'I thought you'd want to know ...'

'You follow that woman if you want to, Lennox. Richard, you keep looking about the hotel and the wells. The girls can't have gone far, and if they did no doubt some man has taken them. I want them back. They might have been cheap enough to buy, but I've invested in them since, and I'm not throwing my money away. Understand? Richard?'

'Yes, father,' said Richard, his voice a little shaky. 'I'll go at once.' He met Lennox' eye so briefly Hippolyta was sure he was scared of his father noticing even that little communication. Then he picked up his hat and stick, and left the parlour, making for the front door. Even before the parlour door had shut, they heard the front door slam.

'Aye, action, that's what's required,' said Mr. Hendry with satisfaction. 'Well, off you go: if some fellow did take them he might as well be going back to the ferry as anywhere else. He was probably on the ferry with that woman and the girls, and you didn't even ask. Get off after them, boy!'

Lennox looked at Durris. They were about to make for the door, too, when old Mr. Hendry called them back.

'What about that fellow that's showing himself off to the local girls? He could have been around here, couldn't he? Should have thought of that, boy, shouldn't you? Mr. Durris, I'm surprised at you, not speaking of him.'

'I might have,' said Durris, 'only that he's dead.' He nodded Lennox Hendry and the Napiers through the door in front of him. 'Miss Hendry,' he added with a short bow, and closed the door.

'So, off to talk to the ferryman, eh?' asked Lennox, once they were outside the hotel. A few minutes away from his father and his mood already seemed better.

'As I say, he's a reliable man,' said Durris. Hippolyta wondered if Lennox were as reliable, but no doubt they would see. And at least poor Johnnie Boy Jo could not be suspected of this.

'What a family, eh?' Patrick remarked quietly to her, as they dropped back a little from Durris and Lennox.

'Are they always like that? Is it his illness that makes Mr.

Hendry so irascible?'

'I don't think he enjoys being dependent on anyone,' Patrick said. 'Though the brunt of that work falls on Miss Hendry, I suppose. The sons seem chiefly bored, when I meet them.'

'Perhaps he should have left them at home to oversee the plantations,' said Hippolyta. 'And all those slaves! Those poor little girls. Do you think they might just have run away?'

'No, I don't,' said Patrick. 'Why would they? They know nothing of this place, and they are well treated - better than they would be if they came back as runaways. No, I think they have gone only at someone else's suggestion, and with someone else's help.'

'And do you think that someone could really be Mrs. Price?'

'She is against slavery, isn't she? She told us so herself. Actively campaigning against it, not just disapproving.'

'Yet ... it seems such a dramatic act, don't you think? Perhaps,' said Hippolyta, trying to find an excuse for someone she admired, 'perhaps she simply wanted to paint them.'

'But she had already begun to arrange that, didn't Hendry say? And this way she loses a commission, too, for if she has stolen the girls Mr. Hendry will hardly employ her to paint his daughter. And I have the impression,' he lowered his voice still further, 'that Mrs. Price cannot afford to reject commissions, don't you think?'

They broke off their discussion: just ahead were Durris and Lennox, and the ferryman was just pulling his boat up to the shore. Lennox, it seemed, had not waited for him to touch land before he was asking him questions.

'You said you saw them with the artist woman,' he was saying, and the boatman was nodding, though his face was indistinct in the evening light.

'It was Mrs. Price, and she had two little black girls with her,' he said, quite sure of himself.

'I told you so!' cried Lennox Hendry, raising his joined fists like a boxer.

'Just the three of them?' Durris paid him no attention. 'Was there anyone else on that crossing?'

'Oh, aye ... that high heidyin. What's he cried? Lord

Tresco. Him.'

'Lord Tresco was on the same boat crossing?' Hippolyta had to interrupt.

'Oh, aye,' said the boatman, 'I'll take a'body.'

'Then did you see which way the lady and the children went? Did they, for example, leave with Lord Tresco?' Durris asked.

'Naw,' said the boatman, 'they never. His lordship had a trap waiting to take him away up where he's staying, and I helped him get into it. When I'd finished doing that and he was away, the lady and the twa quinies were gone. Not that I was really looking for them, ken. I just dinna mind where they went.'

'That's a shame,' said Durris. 'Would there be anything that would help you remember, by any chance?'

The boatman shook his head, well knowing what Durris meant.

'I canna remember what I didna see,' he said reasonably. 'It's not like she gave me money to forget and you can give me more to remember.'

'All right, then,' said Durris with a smile.

'Aye, it was worth a try, right enough, Mr. Durris!' said the boatman. 'But I wouldna deceive you! Now, are you wanting across the river or no?'

'Yes, we'll cross,' said Durris, and the boatman helped all of them into his boat with the ease of long practice. Hippolyta held both Patrick and the boat's edge tight, only happy when they were once again abutting the shore on the north side. She closed her eyes while the boatman sorted out his ropes, and was surprised to find herself sleepy still. She was helped to disembark, and walked slowly up to where the inn stood, by the ruins of the old bridge. The village was quiet, the evening late, with lamps in a number of windows hinting at cosy rooms inside. She shivered: her thick shawl was somehow not quite thick enough.

'We should visit her lodging first,' said Durris to Patrick. 'She's out at Tullich, isn't she? But I'll ask at the inn first, in case they stopped there or took some transport.'

'The girls are very small,' said Patrick. 'It would be a long walk for them.'

'Let's see,' said Durris, and led the way to the inn's front door. Inside the place had the air of clearing up for the night. Durris disappeared into the depths, and Lennox Hendry looked disposed to wait in the hall. Hippolyta wanted badly to sit down, and made her way into the nearest parlour.

'Are you all right, my dear?' Patrick asked.

'I'm perfectly all right, thank you.' She smiled at him. 'But if you are off to Tullich this evening, I believe I shall wait here for you to come back.'

Patrick crouched beside her, frowning.

'Then you are not all right, are you? If you were, you would be fighting for a place on the expedition, not declining it before it is offered! You should go home.'

'No, I shall be perfectly all right here,' she said, made worried herself by her lack of energy – and lack of curiosity. She wanted to know, of course, where Mrs. Price was and whether or not the little girls were all right, but just at the moment it seemed more than she could manage. Patrick was right: that was not like her. 'If I stay here,' she said, almost as much to convince herself as anything else, 'you can come straight away and tell me what you have found.'

'If you insist on staying, I should stay with you,' said Patrick. 'Or you should go home.'

'Then I'll go home,' she said, pushing herself wearily to her feet. How could she be so tired? 'Mr. Durris will need you, no doubt.' Again she made herself smile at him, trying to reassure him. 'I'll be in no danger walking home from here: it's not as if poor Johnnie Boy Jo can attack anyone now.'

'True,' said Patrick, 'but what about whoever attacked Georgina?'

'Oh,' said Hippolyta, unable to suppress a huge yawn, 'that was Georgina. I'm sure it doesn't apply to me.' She rearranged her shawl about her shoulders, and wondered if the parlour fire was lit at home. 'Oh, Mr. Durris! I hope Patrick will bring you back to tell me what has happened! Otherwise, good night. Good night, Mr. Hendry.'

She felt Mr. Durris' look of astonishment follow her to the door as she left the inn. Her feet seemed confused by the path, but she made them go on, step after step, until she reached her own gate, where she had promised herself a rest. She counted to ten, then pushed on along the path to the front door.

Inside, the parlour fireplace was cold. She rang for Johanna, but Ishbel appeared, and hurried to light the fire and bring tea, explaining that Johanna had taken to her bed. Johanna, Johnnie Boy Jo's sister, Hippolyta remembered as she sank on to the sopha. Poor Johanna, so defiant. She had every right to take to her bed. It was an appealing idea anyway. Should she take to her own? But she wanted to hear what Patrick and Durris would have to say for themselves. Heavens, she hadn't even stopped to find out whether or not Mrs. Price had taken a trap or something from the inn! She must be sickening for something – but what?

Ishbel brought the tea, and, with a cautious look at her mistress, a rug, as well, tucking it around her legs. The cats considered this a suitable attraction, and two of them settled about her, quiet and watchful, just as they would for a sick person, Hippolyta thought. Then, her tea only half drunk, she slept.

She was beginning to stir at a clatter at the doorway when a cool hand touched her cheek, then her forehead. She opened her eyes: it was Patrick, his blue eyes full of concern.

'Here you are, asleep again!' he said, his voice as light as he could make it. 'If I didn't know better I might think you had taken once again to wandering in the night, chasing mysteries!'

'I promise you I have not!' she assured him. 'Not this time. I am just so sleepy: and the cats appreciated it, anyway.' She roused herself: Mr. Durris was standing at the parlour table, effacing himself from the room until they had finished. 'Have you called for tea? Or brandy?'

'For both,' said Patrick, 'though it is late, but Ishbel seemed happy to oblige.'

'Did you find her? Did you find them?' Hippolyta was beginning to call everything to mind.

'No.' Mr. Durris came forward, and took a seat across from them. 'Only the landlady was at the cottage. There was no sign that she had even been back there, and the landlady denied seeing her.'

'So you have nothing? But where could she have gone with them? She would not have walked far, not with two little ones.'

'No one said we have nothing,' said Patrick, taking her hand. She had thought his words half-joking, but his face was serious. 'The landlady allowed us to search Mrs. Price's rooms –

the parlour we saw, and a bedchamber, simple enough but lined with more paintings. Including, I may say, the one she painted of Georgina. Her luggage was not extensive: she had a box for her paints and easel and so on – all things whose appearance you know well, for you have a box very much like it yourself – and another kist for her clothes, which were few enough. And what there was was not new.'

'As you said, my dear,' Hippolyta put in. 'Not so much money that she could afford to turn down a commission. Did the landlady believe she had taken anything with her?'

'She thought not. She remembered that when Mrs. Price arrived, she had wondered at a lady having so little luggage.'

'So then what did you find? Had she begun the painting of the two little girls? Is that it?'

She was rather proud of this deduction, particularly in her sleepy state, but Durris was shaking his head. Hippolyta did not like the expression on his face. What was he trying to say?

'Is – was there some clue? Is she in some kind of danger?' She looked from Mr. Durris to Patrick and back. 'Tell me, Mr. Durris! What did you find?'

'This,' he said, reaching into his pocket, and drawing forth a handful of what looked like dark shining caramels, glinting with gold.

'What is that? No, it can't be!'

'It is,' said Mr. Durris. 'It is Miss Pullman's agate necklace.'

'How can you be sure?' Hippolyta gasped out. 'One agate necklace is surely much like another!'

'Look,' said Durris. He stood, and held the clasp of the necklace towards her between his fingers and thumbs. There, on the gold clasp, was engraved 'Georgina'.

'But how? How?' Hippolyta's mind would not work. It fixed on the scar on Georgina's greying throat, the bruises, the scrape of something snatched off, broken away. 'You can't possibly imagine that Adelina Price murdered Georgina? Can you?' Again her eyes flicked from one to the other man, desperate for some response. 'Can you? Answer me!'

'It's not conclusive, obviously,' said Durris at last. He gathered the necklace into his fist, and dropped it once again into his pocket. 'But I'd certainly like to ask her a few questions. Particularly since she has now taken two more girls, albeit somewhat younger.' He returned to his seat. Ishbel arrived with the tea tray, allowing Hippolyta a chance to breathe again. Could Adelina Prince have murdered Georgina? She remembered hearing Georgina's response to her portrait: it seemed almost deliberately hurtful, and if Mrs. Price had risen to that … Hippolyta could imagine how she herself would have felt in that situation. But to kill? And anyway, why then would the little black girls be in any danger from her? Why would she have taken them?

'Can you think of anywhere she might have taken them?' Good heavens, Mr. Durris was asking her, now, as if she were a witness. 'Do you know if she had friends anywhere nearby?'

'No. No, I can't think of anywhere. She was new to Ballater, as far as I know. I don't know that she had been any further than Pannanich, and Loch Kinord on the picnic. Why are you asking me?'

'You probably spoke with her as much as anyone else here. But I shall ask all around the village. A woman with two small black girls will not be able to hide for long.'

'What made her come here?' asked Patrick. 'I don't know that she ever said, do you?'

'No … I had the impression that it was simply to find people to paint, people who could afford to pay her, and would be at ease enough to give her the time.'

'Who did she paint?' Durris asked.

'I saw her paint both the young Mr. Hendrys,' said Hippolyta. 'Old Mr. Hendry said she was to paint Miss Hendry. And of course she painted Georgina. There were probably others.'

'And she wanted to paint the little slaves?'

'She did. She was watching them during the picnic. But not in a disturbing way,' she added hastily. 'Just the way an artist looks – trying to work out what colours show up where, how to give a sense of shape, what the best position might be … I could see what she was thinking, then.' She shrugged, awkward. Then they all jumped.

'Mr. Durris, sir?' came a voice at the window. 'Mr. Durris!'

'Good heavens,' said Durris, rising suddenly. 'Excuse me.'

He went to the front door, and for a moment they heard him conversing with someone – a man – outside. Then he reappeared, already pulling on his gloves.

'I am sorry for the disturbance,' he began.

'Is that the night watchman?' asked Patrick, rising and going to the window. He waved to the man who was still standing in their garden.

'It is. There is a prowler around Dinnet House: as he passed the house he made his usual detour to the front door, and Mrs. Kynoch attracted his attention. There has been a strange figure seen at the back of the house, about the kitchen door. Of course,' he added, 'they believed it was Johnnie Boy Jo, and when the night watchman told them he was dead, some of the girls decided it must be his ghost, and now they are in a worse state than ever. I must go.'

'Let us come with you,' said Hippolyta, feeling a surge of energy. 'I have not seen Mrs. Kynoch today and I may perhaps be of assistance in calming the girls.'

'Napier?' asked Durris. Patrick looked at Hippolyta, and shrugged.

'My dear, if you are feeling up to it I hardly want to prevent you.'

She had hoped he might feel that way. She hurried into her shawl and bonnet once more, and they were ready to follow the night watchman up through the village and along the road to the familiar gateway. As they stepped on to the gravel, Durris paused and listened.

'Try to walk on the grass,' he suggested, low-voiced. 'It will be quieter. I shall go round the back. Malkie, do you go about the house clockwise, and I'll meet you.'

The night watchman nodded and was off, happy for a little excitement in his rounds.

'We'll go inside,' said Patrick, 'and to the back of the house. Cry out if you need us.'

Durris slipped away, unexpectedly quiet, into a shrubbery to the right of them. The Napiers tiptoed to the front door, which opened with unnerving suddenness as they approached.

'I saw you outside with Mr. Durris,' Mrs. Kynoch whispered. 'Where has he gone?'

'Close the door, Mrs. Kynoch,' said Patrick, 'and lock it for now. Mr. Durris has gone round the back of the house. Can we go into the old study?'

'Of course,' said Mrs. Kynoch at once. 'It's still a study, you know.' She gestured to them to precede her to the room at the back of the hallway. Patrick opened the door, and the women followed him in. He closed the door quickly behind them so that the study was in darkness, and they could see something of what was happening outside the windows. Hippolyta squinted through the nearer one, and held her breath. It was open: they had to be silent.

Before them, shadowy and mysterious, was the garden where they had sat under parasols, only last week, while Mrs. Price had sketched Georgina. To their right were the kitchen quarters, and to their left, inconveniently, were the kitchen gardens, with the usual sheds and glass houses. Hippolyta wondered who could be out there, hiding in the dark.

'Is it true that Johnnie Boy Jo is dead?' murmured Mrs. Kynoch.

'It is, by his own hand. Up by the Burn o' Vat,' Hippolyta added.

'Then it really cannot be him out there,' said Mrs. Kynoch, as if she were echoing Hippolyta's thoughts. 'Who could it be? Really, it is not good for anyone's nerves, running a girls' school.'

'Hush,' said Patrick gently. Mrs. Kynoch strained to see through the window.

There was a movement in the dark, a brief fluttering, almost to be mistaken for a bat only that there was the least scrunch of gravel with it. No bat made that sound. The flutter eased off in the direction of what seemed to be a low shed of some kind, and stopped. But at once, from the other direction came a quicker, urgent rhythm of movement. There was a heavy step, a cry, and a loud creak.

'Napier!' came Durris' voice. 'A light!'

Patrick jumped back from the window and made a dash for the hallway, lighting a candle at one of the lamps. He was back in an instant, and leaning out through the window.

'Here!'

'What have you found?' Hippolyta and Mrs. Kynoch cried

out almost as one.

Durris seemed to shuffle in the dark, manoeuvring something out of the little shed, edging it towards the waiting group at the window. There seemed to be too much of it for one person. Durris pushed it forward, and in the sharp candlelight they saw.

Three faces, two dark as mahogany, one white.

Mrs. Price had brought the slave girls to Dinnet House.

.

Chapter Eighteen

'Where did the Hendrys go?' asked Hippolyta, finding herself now wide awake when it was long past her usual bed time. The parlour at Dinnet House was chilly and she paced up and down, rubbing her arms under her shawl. The action was not so comforting when one was wearing summer sleeve shapes: she kept poking the frames into herself.

'I managed to send them home after we left Tullich. We parted at the inn. I suppose the ferryman was still up and about,' said Durris innocently.

The hall door was open, for propriety's sake: Patrick was upstairs checking to see that neither the little girls nor Adelina Price had suffered any kind of injury. Pale figures of anxious pupils flitted occasionally past the doorway, nightgowns wreathed in shawls, presumably watching out for the ghost of Johnnie Boy Jo. Hippolyta wished that they would all go off to their beds, for they were extremely unsettling. Then a scratching at the door preceded the arrival of Mabelle, with Grace Spencer close behind her.

'Mrs. Napier, is it true that they have caught Georgina's murderer?' Mabelle gasped.

'And that he was hiding in our coal shed?' Grace added, sounding a little less convinced.

'No,' said Hippolyta. 'This is something else entirely, and has nothing at all to do with Georgina. There was someone hiding in the coal shed, or whatever that place is, but they are only in a state of distress, and will not cause any of you any harm. You'd be best to go off to your beds.'

There she was, sounding like her mother again. She was only a few years older than these girls, but at the moment she felt ancient.

'Mrs. Napier, is it true that Johnnie Boy Jo is dead?'

'Yes, that is true, sadly.'

'Why sadly?' demanded Grace. 'Could he not have killed Georgina?'

'Johnnie Boy Jo was not a violent man,' said Durris. His voice was at its most reassuring, for two girls wandering about at night in their nightgowns worrying about a stranger in their coal shed. 'Poor fellow, he took his own life, but I do not think it was out of remorse.'

'But Mrs. Kynoch warned us about him!'

'So that you would not be embarrassed or shocked, yes,' said Hippolyta quickly. 'Mrs. Kynoch was quite right. But Johnnie Boy Jo was not a killer. And he is certainly no threat to anyone now.'

'Betty Hopkins swears she saw his ghost. Hovering outside her bedroom window, it was!' said Mabelle.

'Betty Hopkins may have been eating too much cheese,' Hippolyta suggested severely.

'Besides, Betty Hopkins is always looking for men outside her bedroom window,' added Grace.

'Grace! You make it sound as if ... Betty's not like that, really, Mrs. Napier. She's just – well, nosy.'

'She likes a gossip. More than is good for her,' added Grace. 'And sometimes,' she went on thoughtfully, 'if she hasn't anything to gossip about, she'll make something up.'

'Like Johnnie Boy Jo's ghost,' said Mabelle, nodding.

'Girls!' Mrs. Kynoch appeared behind them. 'Why aren't you off to your beds?'

'We're going now, Mrs. Kynoch,' said Mabelle at once.

'Sorry, Mrs. Kynoch,' said Grace, and seemed to mean it. The two girls trooped off quietly, passing Patrick as he came down the stairs.

'Well?' asked Durris when the parlour door was shut on the four of them. 'How are they?'

'Physically they are all in good health,' said Patrick, relieved when the ladies sat down and he could fling himself into an armchair. 'The little girls are tired and sleepy, and seemed pleased to be given a warm drink, too. They have settled well, though they have not spoken a word to me.'

'And Mrs. Price?' asked Hippolyta. 'What does she say?'

'Mrs. Price is very much overwrought,' said Patrick. 'It was hard to prise the girls from her, but we have her in a separate room – and locked in, for now, as much for her own safety as anything else.'

Durris nodded his approval.

'Is the window secure?' he asked. 'I should not like anything untoward to happen to her.'

Hippolyta drew breath sharply when she realised what he meant. Surely Adelina Price would not commit self-destruction?

'It is an attic room: there are bars at that level,' said Patrick, nodding his understanding. 'And for now I have given her something to make her sleep. She was almost hysterical.'

'What did she say?' asked Hippolyta. Mrs. Kynoch shook her head.

'Nothing that made any sense,' she said. 'Apart from not wishing to lose her children.'

'She thinks they are her children? The little girls?'

'It sounded that way,' Patrick agreed. 'I wonder if she has been out in the sun for a little too long? The weather has been so hot: perhaps it could be heatstroke?'

They looked at each other, wondering. Then Durris fished in his pocket, pulling out once again the agate necklace.

'We found this at Mrs. Price's lodgings, Mrs. Kynoch. Do you know it?'

Mrs. Kynoch snatched a surprised breath.

'It looks very much like Georgina's,' she said. 'But how could it have come to be at Mrs. Price's lodgings?'

'We don't yet know,' said Durris. 'I hope she might be able to tell us soon.'

'In the morning, though,' said Patrick, immediately protective of his patient.

'Of course.'

'But I thought,' said Mrs. Kynoch, frowning deeply, 'that you believed that necklace had been snatched by Georgina's murderer? Is that not what you said?'

'That, or something very much like it,' Durris admitted. His face was bland, but there was something about his hands that looked uncomfortable. Mrs. Kynoch gave him a sharp look.

'Then do you believe that Adelina Price killed Georgina?'

Durris breathed out lengthily.

'A woman?' he said at last. 'That was not what I had thought, no. But Martha Considine assured me that Georgina had not been assaulted. It could be that her body was left as it was in order to make us assume that she had been.'

'They quarrelled – well, no,' Hippolyta corrected herself. 'Georgina rejected Mrs. Price's painting of her. She was not kind about it.'

'No,' Mrs. Kynoch sighed, 'Georgina would not be. She was not a kind girl. Perhaps she would have learned, if she had been given the chance.'

They sat in silence for a moment, perhaps considering how improved Georgina might have been if she had been granted a few more years. Hippolyta, uncharitably, thought it unlikely. Georgina had not shown much promise in that direction. But then, if she had stayed under Mrs. Kynoch's tutelage, perhaps …

'Well, there is nothing more we can do here tonight,' said Durris at last. 'Unless you need me, Mrs. Kynoch, I think we should allow you to settle your household for the night. I shall be back in the morning.'

'Thank you, Mr. Durris, and thank you for coming so promptly. When I think that we summoned you to tackle the threat of a woman and two little girls, I am almost ashamed! But then, she needed help, so it worked out well in the end. As it does,' she added, with a little smile.

'We may pray that that is so,' said Durris, bowing slightly. 'Good night, Mrs. Kynoch.'

Hippolyta woke the next morning late, and dazed. In her workaday gown, she wandered through the kitchen, greeted Ishbel and Wullie and the dog, and found that Johanna was still locked firmly in her room, refusing to listen to anyone. Ishbel expected that she would show some interest when it came to breakfast. Hippolyta nodded, briefly worried about Johanna and how she had managed with such a brother, and carried on into the garden. The hens, released from their coop, murmured around her, fluffing out their feathers in the fresh sunlight. She fed them, and collected eggs in a basket, then carried on to look at the pig in its sty. The pig looked back. She emptied the kitchen scraps out for it, and scratched its back absently as it ate.

The dew had burned off the leaves and grass already, and the sun illuminated raspberries like rubies in the canes along the wall. There would be more jam to be made for the winter, if Mr. Strachan had enough sugar – enough sugar from plantations where slaves were not used. Goodness, how was one ever to tell? She imagined the sugar would taste much the same. She would ask Mrs. Price – if Mrs. Price were fit to tell anyone. Could it have been the sun? Had she had some kind of stroke? And if so, could that have made her attack Georgina? Hippolyta's head felt woolly. It had been a late night.

She pushed herself away from the pigsty and waded back through the hens to the kitchen door. The dog had come out to investigate, following her, and three or four of the cats watched the hens with interest. It was soothing, she thought. She could just stay out here today, amongst the various animals, and draw, or paint. Or just sleep.

Patrick was unnecessarily bright and awake at breakfast.

'This summer light rouses me early,' he said, helping himself to more bacon. 'I see you've been out already. The hens seem to be laying well.'

'Yes, yes,' she said, toying with an egg. She could not quite summon up her usual appetite. She felt Patrick look at her, and pulled herself together.

'Are you going to see Mrs. Price this morning?'

'I hope to,' said Patrick, his attention back on his bacon. 'I am quite concerned about her.'

'Do you think that heatstroke would have allowed her to kill Georgina? In a rage, perhaps?'

Patrick considered.

'I should not have thought so, but there are strange things in the mind. Do you think, if she had killed her, that she would have been strong enough to move Georgina's body?'

It was Hippolyta's turn to consider. She forced her rubbery mind to work.

'She's used to hauling round her easel and stool and painting things,' she said. 'I'd have said she was quite a strong woman. Wiry, you know? And Georgina was not particularly heavy, was she?'

'No, she wasn't.' She could tell that Patrick was remembering the task of carrying Georgina out of the Burn o' Vat, and regretted her words. 'And perhaps that is even why her clothes were removed. They would have been heavy and unwieldy. Say, for example, that she was killed up at the ruined cottage where – where we were yesterday. She seems to have been there, to judge by the feather that Durris found. Say she was killed there, and for whatever reason the murderer, or someone else, wanted her to be down in the Vat where she was found. What better way to lighten the load than to remove all those petticoats and padded sleeves?'

Hippolyta tried to picture carrying a fully-clothed body down through the woodland to the glen and the river. The skirts would catch on every twig, and the petticoats would make every narrow gap a squeeze – and yes, they would add considerably to the weight.

'Perhaps you are right. It would certainly make things easier. But why move her in the first place?'

'Because whoever it was wanted her to be found?'

Hippolyta looked at Patrick.

'That makes sense. Left in that ruined cottage, the only one likely to find her would be Johnnie Boy Jo, wandering the woods. Who else knew about it? I think you're right!'

'Wait,' said Patrick, suddenly doubtful. 'At least two other people knew about the cottage.'

'Who?'

'Well, Georgina knew. She went there because of the note – and there may be someone, someone Durris hasn't spoken to yet – or even someone who is hiding the fact - that she told about it. And of course, the writer of the note knew – and I think we can be fairly sure that that was not Johnnie Boy Jo. I never heard of him being able to read or write. Not even his name.'

'Oh, goodness,' said Hippolyta, 'I cannot see how we shall ever be able to tell who did anything in this matter. It makes less sense to me every day!'

When Hippolyta had changed into a more respectable gown, they made their way up to Dinnet House, to find that Mr.

Durris had already been there for half an hour or so.

'He's been quizzing me about the girls,' Mrs. Kynoch admitted with a smile, 'and anyone who ever came to visit Georgina Pullman. It was not difficult to answer that, though: she had barely arrived in Ballater. No one had come specifically to visit her except for the Hendrys, who had known her family in Tobago.'

'Did she talk much about her family?' Hippolyta asked.

'Not really,' said Mrs. Kynoch, leading the way out into the garden. 'The girls are out here again, the day is so lovely. She did say that this would be the wet season in Tobago. Her mother died, of course, when she was very small, and she lived with her father. I gather their house was quite remote, and they did not entertain much, but from time to time they went to stay in ... oh, what is the name of the chief town? I believe she would have met the Hendrys there, and any other prominent families.'

The girls were about the lawn, some working at books or at needlework, a few contentedly playing with the two little black girls. Hannah and Ruth sat a little stiffly amongst them, but seemed happy enough to be decorated with flowers like dolls, and learn simple clapping games. Neither seemed stupid, but they were both watchful, as if afraid that they would break some rule.

Mrs. Kynoch led the way to a table and chairs a little distance from the others, but keeping the girls in view. Hippolyta sat gratefully.

'Are any of your other girls from Tobago?'

'No, indeed. They are from all over the place: I confess that before I began this school, I had thought the West Indies a small, neighbourly place, but the names we hear of are much spread about. My late husband's old friend, who recommends girls to me – and indeed me to the girls – had never met Georgina Pullman directly, but knew her minister in Tobago.'

'Did Lord Tresco come to visit her, or pay her particular attention?'

Mrs. Kynoch raised her eyebrows in despair.

'Oh, handsome young noblemen should never be allowed near a girls' school! No, I did not think he did, no more than any young man in the presence of a pretty young woman. Yet you tell me there was a note to her, apparently from him, in her reticule! I have not yet written to her father, my dear Mrs. Napier: I cannot think what to say. Yet it must be done forthwith, before he hears in any other way.'

'Lord Tresco denies the note is in his hand,' said Durris. 'And indeed it is hard to see how he could have come by the local information that is in it.'

'He could ask someone.'

'He has had very little contact with the village since he came here,' said Patrick, 'or so he assures me. A visit here, the picnic – dinner yesterday at Pannanich Wells – he hardly has a wide local circle.'

'He could not have climbed to the place where we think she died,' said Hippolyta, 'that ruined cottage, and even if he had done he could not have carried her body down to the Vat.'

'Not without more pain than a reasonable man would bear,' added Patrick.

'But he has money,' said Mrs. Kynoch. 'Could he not have paid someone to help him? Or could he have asked Mr. Dinmore?'

'He could, but why would he?' asked Durris simply. 'It seems to make no sense. And Mr. Dinmore seems to be no more fit to carry loads around woodland than Lord Tresco himself.'

'Then who, oh, who, is the murderer?' Mrs. Kynoch sighed. 'Will we ever know?'

'I think we shall,' said Durris. 'I believe it has to be someone who was at the picnic.'

There was a moment of silence. Hippolyta, at least, was running through the names of the guests in her mind. Lord Tresco, the Dinmores, the Hendrys, Peter Middleton, the girls, Adelina Price …

'Not some passing stranger?'

'No. Someone had to persuade her to climb to that ruined cottage. Why would she do that for a stranger? And someone brought her body back down to the Vat. Why would a stranger do that? Better to have her lost than found. And whoever killed her did not rob her. I should say that robbery would be the motive for most attacks on strangers.'

Mrs. Kynoch nodded.

'Someone, then, that she knew and trusted.'

'Yes,' said Hippolyta, 'but it strikes me that that is a broad field.'

'What's that?'

Hippolyta frowned.

'I don't mean that Georgina was a trusting soul. I mean that she considered herself somewhat superior to most of us. She would have trusted any of us to the extent that she would be confident we would mean her no harm – that we would not dare to mean her harm.'

'Ha!' said Patrick, but he nodded.

'Ma'am,' said the maid, appearing suddenly from the house, 'Mrs. Price is awake, ma'am.'

'Is she out of her room?'

'No, ma'am, but she's calling out.'

Durris looked at Patrick, then, almost reluctantly, at Hippolyta. They rose, and went indoors.

'Is there someone there? Please, the door is jammed!' Adelina Price was calling, perfectly reasonably, from the room where she had been imprisoned. Patrick stood to one side of the doorway, nodding to Hippolyta to stay back, and Durris applied the key.

'Mrs. Price,' he called, 'I've unlocked the door. When you're ready, please open it.'

The wait seemed interminable, yet it must have lasted only a moment or two. Hippolyta felt her heart beating faster as the door handle turned, and the door slowly opened.

Adelina Price, looking ten years older than she had a week ago, peered around the door, blinking as she took in each person waiting on the landing outside.

'Mrs. Price, may we speak with you?' Durris asked.

'If you are feeling quite well,' added Patrick.

She stared at him, then glanced back into the room, as if assessing its facilities.

'Is there maybe somewhere else?' she asked, a little plaintively.

Durris looked at Hippolyta.

'There won't be anyone in the parlour,' Hippolyta suggested. 'They're all in the garden.'

'Where are the girls?' asked Mrs. Price, suddenly anxious.

'The girls are all in the garden,' said Durris, his voice soothing.

'No, my girls,' said Mrs. Price, insistent. 'My girls. Hannah and Ruth. They're only small, they'll be frightened! Where are they?'

'They're in the garden too, Mrs Price,' said Hippolyta. 'They're being looked after. They have flowers in their hair, and they're playing games ...'

'But they're well? They're safe?'

'Yes, of course.' She stepped forward. 'Come along, Mrs. Price, come to the parlour. We'll all be comfortable there, and when Mr. Durris has had a little chat with you, we'll go and see Hannah and Ruth. All right?'

She reached out, and hesitantly Mrs. Price took her hand. Patrick frowned at Durris, and hurried to go down the stairs just in front of Hippolyta: she was sure he was convinced that Mrs. Price was about to pull her into a tumbling fall to the bottom of the staircase. Just for a moment, she almost thought he was right: her head reeled, and she clutched at the banister. But she steadied herself, and continued, holding Mrs. Price's hand, until the two of them were settled on the sopha in the dim parlour, with Patrick attentive on one side and Durris standing with his back to the dark fireplace.

'Mrs. Price,' he began, half an eye on Patrick for his consent to continue, 'tell me what happened yesterday.'

'Yesterday?' Adelina Price seemed puzzled.

'You went up to Pannanich Wells – you were there for dinner, I believe?'

'Oh, yes. Up across the river. I went to paint someone – well, to draw them. I paint them afterwards, in peace.'

'Who were you painting?'

She thought for a moment.

'A man named Howard. Interesting face, quite old.'

'The innkeeper mentioned him,' Durris murmured. 'Did you speak to anyone else while you were there?'

'Mr. Hendry waved me over in the dining room, wanted me to paint his daughter. But I wanted to paint the girls – the daughter is a pale, thin thing, of no interest to anyone.'

'Did you talk to the girls?'

'I saw them sent to the kitchens for their food. They had to stand at the table while the Hendrys ate, then go and find what they could. But they are so small!' She reached out a hand as if she were touching the top of Hannah's curly brown head, then found it was not there. The hand dropped, forgotten. 'So I went to look for them, to make sure they had enough to eat. And then ... and then I brought them here.'

'Why here, Mrs. Price?'

'I thought – I think – that Mrs. Kynoch is a good woman.'

'In that at least you were correct,' said Hippolyta warmly, squeezing Mrs. Price's hand.

'But why did you take them away from the Hendrys?' Durris persisted. 'Did you perhaps see them mistreated?'

'No, no,' said Mrs. Price, 'but it's only a matter of time. Only a matter of time, and then the pretty house slave is cast out to be an outdoor slave, and the babies! The babies are always slaves, too. And then the whole thing begins again.' She nodded, her eyes ominous, meeting each of them in turn.

'The babies of slaves are always slaves,' Durris repeated, making sure he had it right. Mrs. Price shuddered.

'But the babies of white men, they're free. My first baby was free, you know, my girl. As free as anyone ever is.'

'Your first baby?' Hippolyta was confused: Mrs. Price had never mentioned a child before.

'My girl, much good did it do her.'

'Mrs. Price,' A cold fear seized Hippolyta. She held Mrs. Price's hand close. 'Mrs. Price, was Georgina your daughter?'

'She was, the proud fool. She was my first baby.'

Chapter Nineteen

'But we were told that Georgina's mother was dead,' said Durris. 'How can it be?'

Mrs. Price gave a little snort of laughter. She did not seem entirely settled.

'I should have expected him to do that, but I didn't think of it. No wonder she didn't realise!'

'You mean you told Georgina? You told her you were her mother?'

'Not in quite so many words. I hinted, you know? I suppose I wanted her to recognise me, somehow, the same way that I had recognised her.' She shivered. 'But it didn't happen.'

'Mrs. Price,' said Durris, 'perhaps you had better explain from the beginning.' He crossed to an armchair, and sat neatly in it. Then, too far away for Hippolyta to see it clearly, he drew out his notebook and pencil. Adelina Price was silent for a moment, then took a long, shuddering breath.

'I was very young,' she began. 'George Pullman was wealthy, and rather exciting, to me. He was home on a visit to London, and I was there for my first season – he was older, and tall and handsome and a little distant, though quite charming, really. He had a plantation on Tobago, which sounded like paradise, as he described it. The British had not long secured the island from the French after the wars, and it was a new society, peaceful and industrious. And I was very innocent. I suppose I thought that the sugar leapt from the ground already in loaves, all on its own. There would be servants, of course, as there were servants at home, and a farm manager and tenants – I thought it would all be much as it was in Berkshire, only with bright birds, and lush foliage, and a warm sun all year round.' She stopped again, her eyes far away, remembering that innocence.

'Mrs. Price, are you sure you are able to tell us all this now? You have been much disturbed in the last few days, and –'

She raised a hand to stall Patrick's concerns.

'I have been disturbed, indeed, but now I need to tell someone. I have held this in for too long, and Georgina has gone to her grave without knowing her mother. It must be told.'

Patrick sat back, though his expression was still anxious. He exchanged looks with Durris, but Durris nodded slightly.

'Please go on, Mrs. Price.'

'We married, and set sail for Tobago almost at once. I had only my maid with me, and she was not a good traveller. I spent much of the journey looking after her. We were eight weeks at sea, and my husband whiled away his time on business papers, legal documents and so on, for he had returned to England to see his agents and his bankers and suchlike people – perhaps collecting a wife was also part of his plan, for I heard him say afterwards that Tobago was a closed society and needed new blood.

'Tobago was almost as extraordinary as I had hoped, and yet in some ways it was too extraordinary, too strange. There were hardly any real people there. There were the whites, the foreign owners like my husband, for whom the heat and disease meant that it was never really home – and there were the slaves.

'I could not cope with the slaves. I had come from a small household, where we knew each of our servants and treated them like members of the family. When they grew elderly or infirm they were pensioned, and continued to live nearby and were taken soup and vegetables from the garden, not just out of duty but because they were our household. To buy and sell them, to walk past them as if they were not there, something less than the cattle in the fields – I could not do it. And that did not please my husband.

'I had soon discovered that if Tobago was warm, he was not. I was to be useful to him, a society hostess up to a limited point, and a bearer of children. Plenty of children, for the climate there is harsh and one must expect to lose some, at least. I bore him Georgina, and he was pleased enough with her, though he wanted a son, of course. But somehow that did not happen.

'My maid died of a fever. I was riddled with sorrow and with guilt – guilt for taking her there from our little Berkshire town, so far from home, and sorrow because she had become my only friend. The island is not huge, but my husband had somehow contrived a house that was remote, cut off from society. It suited him. We would travel into the town, Scarborough, from time to time, and meet other plantation owners, other white people like the Hendrys, but not often. For the rest of the time it was just my husband and me, and the baby, and the slaves.

'I'm not even sure he could tell them apart, you know. They were not even as interesting as cattle to him. One or two of the house slaves, perhaps, he would know if he met them about the house, but if he should come across them outside he would not recognise them. He simply didn't care at all. He was not actively cruel, I believe: what his foreman did out in the fields I don't know, but the workers were reasonably fed or they could not have worked as they did.

'I painted, of course, when I could: he considered that harmless enough, even when I painted the slaves. And then one day I painted a slave ... a man ...'

She broke off, her words lost. Hippolyta wrapped her hand in hers, then put her arm about Mrs. Price's shoulders. She was terribly thin.

'Mrs. Price, if you need to stop –' Patrick, anxious again. She shook her head, but her eyes were tight closed, her lips too, as if she could not quite allow the next part of the story to leave her. At last she gave a little nod, and opened her eyes again, though the scowl remained.

'You will wish you had not become – I think friends – with me, Mrs. Napier,' she said, her mouth still tight. 'I did not behave as a good wife should.'

'You mean you and this man – this slave –'

'Yes.' The word came out a little more loudly than she had intended, and they all jumped slightly. 'Yes. I loved him. And in due course, I gave birth. To a daughter, another daughter. And when my husband saw what the child looked like – so pretty, so plump and healthy, with her toffee skin and her black hair – he took her away from me, and he locked me in my room. And I do not know what happened to her, or to my lover. My Joshua.'

The silence was bleak. Hippolyta, shocked, found tears pricking her eyes. What on earth would Patrick do in that situation

– not that it would ever arise? Would he be so harsh? But a man had to protect his wife … sometimes from herself.

'And then?' asked Durris, as gentle as she had heard him.

'And then I ran away.'

'Leaving your daughter behind?'

'Leaving both my daughters behind,' she corrected, bitterly. 'I fled: I sold jewellery to buy a passage back to England under an assumed name.'

'And returned to your family?'

'I was too ashamed to return to my family. What could I tell them? I had been unfaithful to my husband. I had borne a child out of wedlock. And if they could forgive that, could they forgive my other crimes? When I escaped, I did not bring my daughter with me. I did not look for my other daughter. I did not look for my lover. I was too frightened, and I ran. Could they forgive my cowardice? I could not.' She drew breath again. 'I had some other jewels, and I had my skills as a painter. And that is how I have lived since then. Until I came here, by chance, following the fashion for Pannanich and the clear air of Deeside, and found my first baby, my daughter.'

'Mrs. Price,' said Patrick again, and this time she nodded. He had taken the precaution of fetching a jug of water and a glass: now he added a few drops from a little bottle to the glass and poured water into it, and handed it to her. She drank, and began to cry.

It took some time for her to recover, but at last she wiped her eyes and without apology looked over at Durris.

'Will you find who killed her?'

'I shall do my best, ma'am,' said Durris. He reached once again into his pocket. 'Do you know these?'

She knew even by the sound of the beads, Hippolyta thought, before she saw it in his hand.

'My agate necklace,' she said. 'My husband must have thought it would look strange if I had left nothing to my daughter, and allowed her to have this. When I saw her wearing it – then I was certain.'

'We found it in your lodgings,' Durris said, without expression.

'Ah, yes.' She bit her lip. 'Yes, you would have.'

'We were looking for you. And the little girls.'

'May I see them?'

'In a moment. How did Georgina's necklace – your necklace – come to be back in your possession? You say that Georgina had not realised she was your daughter.'

'No ... we had harsh words. Or ... Well, I suppose she was the one with the harsh words. She was my daughter, but the more I saw of her the more I recognised that she was my husband's daughter, too – and remembered that he had had the bringing up of her. She was not a kind girl.'

'Was it the painting?' asked Hippolyta, earning herself a fleeting look of annoyance from Durris.

'Yes, it was the painting. The morning of the picnic,' said Mrs. Price, rubbing her free hand over her face. 'It was not the meeting I had hoped it would be. She did not find my portrait of her flattering enough. I paint as I find, as I see, even when it is my own daughter – perhaps particularly then. With customers, paying customers, I can bring myself to flatten out the wrinkles, ease away the foolish expression, soothe the harsh mouth, melt the overgenerous lines. But I wanted her to see what she really looked like, however beautiful she was – and she was, wasn't she?'

'Very,' agreed Durris. 'She would not take it?'

'No ... but at least now I have something to remember her by. Even if our last proper conversation was an unfriendly one. After all, I have been lucky:' she said bitterly. 'I might not have had that conversation at all.'

'And the necklace?'

'It came off in my hand when I reached out to her,' said Mrs. Price. Hippolyta, her arm still about Mrs. Price's shoulders, could feel her back tensing as she said the words. 'Look, the link is broken between those two beads.'

Durris watched her for a moment, then sat back in his chair.

'Tell me, Mrs. Price, have you done much walking or riding about during your time in Ballater? The countryside is very fine around here.'

'It is, isn't it?' Mrs. Price agreed, and her shoulders relaxed again. Perhaps whatever Patrick had dosed her with was beginning to work. 'But I have had little opportunity to look at it more closely. Mrs. Napier and I have been discussing painting, and agree that while I might be able to turn out portraits, she is the master of landscape. I have had to busy myself in my chosen field, and have no excuses to go out and paint trees and rivers, unfortunately.'

It seemed more than likely, if she were as poor as Hippolyta suspected. And she was no more local than Lord Tresco: how would she have known about the ruined cottage? And ... Hippolyta's imagination wandered a little – how could a mother leave her daughter lying like that in only her shift and one boot, with her feet in the cold water? She could never do that. Tears rose to her eyes at the very thought.

'But you have been to Loch Kinord,' said Durris, careful not to mention Burn o' Vat with its more directly tragic connexions. 'Tell me what you did at the picnic?'

'Avoided Georgina,' said Mrs. Price promptly. 'I did not want to annoy her. But I did watch her flirting with Lord Tresco: I was surprised how anxious it made me, for he could not have honourable intentions in that direction, I should think. Though he seems a decent man.'

'Did you think her in any danger from him?'

'No, only from herself,' she said, after a moment's thought. 'If I thought her in any danger, and I don't believe I did, at the time, or I should have done something about it – but afterwards, you know, one thinks back. I wondered if that man Middleton might have had something to do with it. He did not seem to know what to do between Georgina and his old sweetheart, and Georgina seemed to have him properly ensnared, the silly girl. He could have been driven to do something harmful. But I barely know him, or anybody else around here.'

'Except for the Hendrys,' said Hippolyta. Mrs. Price turned to her in surprise.

'Oh, yes, the Hendrys! But they did not even recognise me. I suppose one does not expect to meet a dead woman in a strange place – and I have changed, no doubt, in my life since.'

She would have been a beauty once, like Georgina, Hippolyta thought suddenly, looking sideways at her oversharp cheekbones and finely shaped, weary eyes. Mr. Pullman had taken a prize back to Tobago, and poverty and loneliness and shame had destroyed it.

'Did you see Georgina leave Lord Tresco at the party?'

'No, I did not. I was intrigued by the little girls, by Hannah and Ruth, and I thought I would disconcert Georgina if she found me watching her all afternoon. I made myself look away, and look to other people, too, seeing whose face interested me, who might be a good subject. I prefer, on the whole, to paint people who are at least amusing to paint.' She shrugged, as if she had acknowledged a failing on her part. 'Please may I see the girls now?'

'Why did you take them, Mrs. Price?'

'Why?' She rubbed her nose, considering. 'Because they are slaves – you know they are slaves, or were until they reached these shores; because the Hendrys have them bound by more than just a voucher for their purchase, for they are completely dependent on the Hendrys for everything they have ever known, and it would not even occur to them to run away. Because they are little girls that perhaps I might, had I had the courage once more to flee properly with them, have been able to care for and bring up to a state of useful and happy womanhood, fully people in their own rights, not passive dolls. They did not resist, you know. They did not even cry out when they realised we were leaving the inn. They simply did as they were told, without question. They are – and now I think of what I said of my husband and his cattle – they are hardly human at all, as if all humanity has been bred out of them.' She heaved a sigh so deep Hippolyta thought she might break one of her delicate ribs. 'We cannot allow this to go on, gentlemen. It must be stopped.'

Durris watched her for a moment, and she looked back at him, head high, recovered in her spirits from whatever downturn had afflicted her last night. She had relinquished Hippolyta's hand, and Hippolyta let her supporting arm slide from Mrs. Price's back. The death of her daughter, and whatever might befall her now as repercussion for what she had done, were simply more burdens to be borne, quietly and alone. She would manage, as she had done for so long.

Durris snapped his notebook shut.

'You may go to them now,' he said. 'They are, I believe, still in the garden. But you must not take them anywhere. They may not be Mr. Hendry's property, but they are his responsibility, and he should be consulted if they are to leave his service.'

Mrs. Price rose and straightened her skirts.

'I daresay you'll want to come and see if they flee from me,' she said, almost with a smile.

'I shall certainly accompany you,' said Durris, with the shadow of a bow. Mrs. Price left the parlour, followed by Hippolyta, with the men trailing behind, no doubt comparing notes, Hippolyta thought. She hoped they would tell her later.

The sunlight was high and dazzling when they entered the garden, and the girls were huddled under the large parasols, trying to keep their complexions pale. Hannah and Ruth were now at one of the tables, Ruth seated on Grace Spencer's lap, solemnly eating a slice of cake each. Mrs. Price made a small sound, as if she suppressed a cry, and hurried over to them. Mrs. Kynoch, seeing Hippolyta approach, stood and waylaid her.

'I have questioned the little ones – oh! Gently, you know, so as not to alarm them. They are curious girls, in fact they do not speak, but I do not think she intended them any harm. Do you? What did she say about them?'

'That she was concerned at how they were being treated and brought up,' said Hippolyta briefly. Mrs. Kynoch would have to know the whole story at some point, but in private and in comfort and at length. 'I agree that she intended them no harm. As to what the Hendrys will say, that is another matter.'

'But they do not belong to the Hendrys, not on these shores,' said Mrs. Kynoch firmly. 'And they are so young! If they were in a factory they would not be allowed to work. Surely neither of them is over nine years old? They should be at school.'

'They seem well fed and well dressed,' said Hippolyta, hesitantly. She watched as the girls made room for Adelina Price at the table, and she took a napkin to wipe crumbs from little Ruth's mouth, smiling hard at her as though she could make the child smile back. Patrick and Mr. Durris observed from a little distance, and seemed, in Patrick's case at least, well satisfied with the scene for now. 'They might not wish to leave the Hendrys – the family must be the only home they have ever known.' Mrs. Price's words about their upbringing. 'It might not even have occurred to them that there were other ways to live.'

'Do you think,' said Mrs. Kynoch, also watching, 'that the Hendrys might be prepared to give them up? In return, perhaps, for

– informal compensation?'

'Mrs. Kynoch! Do you mean to buy the children?'

'Hush, hush! No, of course not. They are not slaves. But if Mr. Hendry feels he would be at a loss without them …'

'I think you should talk to Mr. Durris about what you can and cannot do,' said Hippolyta, anxious for her friend.

'Well, my dear Mrs. Napier, you know: sometimes the last thing you should do is find out what is the legal way. Sometimes ignorance is best, both for the sheriff's officer and for oneself.'

'Mrs. Kynoch!'

'Oh, I am only playing with words, my dear,' said Mrs. Kynoch, her eyes still on the party at the table. 'Pay me no heed. I need my sleep, and last night was not conducive to it, I'm afraid. Will you take a cup of tea, now that they seem settled? You'll be tired too, no doubt.'

Hippolyta had to admit that she was. Now that the children were safe, and she had heard Mrs. Price's story, she really wanted only to go home and rest.

'I'd love one,' she said, and Mrs. Kynoch turned to summon the maid from the house. But even as she did so, the maid appeared at the kitchen door, looking uncertain. Mrs. Kynoch and Hippolyta hurried over.

'Ma'am, see, it's Mrs. Considine from the village.'

'Martha Considine? What does she want? I'm sure I paid her for tending to Miss Pullman,' said Mrs. Kynoch, frowning.

'No, ma'am, it's no you she's wanting. It's thon Mr. Durris, and the doctor.'

'Oh! I'll fetch them, shall I?' said Hippolyta at once, forgetting her weariness. What could Martha Considine want? Hippolyta thought hard, then stopped short. Martha Considine had been summoned to lay out the body of Johnnie Boy Jo. What had she found?

Mr. Durris had seen Hippolyta hurrying towards them and gestured to Patrick to go with him to join her.

'It's Martha Considine. She's here to speak to both of you,' said Hippolyta.

'So I see,' said Durris, nodding towards the side of the house. Mrs. Considine had clearly decided not to waste her time waiting.

Her trade required her to be respectably dressed, but there was always something about Mrs. Considine that made Hippolyta think she was only teetering on the edge of respectable dressing, a carelessness or an eccentricity not quite held in. But she was a kind and sensible woman, and good at her twin tasks of midwifery and layings out, and Patrick respected her skills and her manner with the patients. Which was just as well, because a malicious midwife could ruin a doctor's practice with a few well-chosen words.

'I'm right glad to find you both here together, gentlemen, for I want to get back: there's only my niece with the body, ken.'

'What is it, Mrs. Considine?' Durris prompted her.

'It's yon Johnnie Boy Jo, of course,' she said, wriggling her fingers to demonstrate her uneasiness. 'You say he hangit himself, aye?'

'That's right. That's what it looked like.'

'Aye, well, someone gave him a dunt on the heid to be getting on with.'

'A head injury? Could it not have happened as he climbed up the wall? Or as he fell?'

'Aye, mebbe. Only I doubt he'd have had time to wash at the hair afterwards, for it would have bled like the Muckle Spate. And the traces are still there, but someone's done their best to hide them. And I doubt it was Johnnie Boy Jo.'

Chapter Twenty

'I'll need to look at the wound,' said Durris at once.

'How could they have done it?' Patrick asked. 'It was a hard enough scramble up that wall ... sorry, my love,' he added, with a glance at Hippolyta. 'I know you found it very distressing.'

'Perhaps they used a rope to pull him up, then secured him,' suggested Durris. 'The question is, why?'

'And the obvious answer,' said Hippolyta, annoyed at having been so weak when Johnnie Boy Jo was found – surely if she had been strong enough to look at the body, she would have seen the head injury, when Patrick and Mr. Durris missed it? 'The obvious answer is that he saw something, or someone, that he was not supposed to. Who more likely to have seen the murderer, or the person moving the body, than Johnnie Boy Jo, hanging around up there and sleeping in the bracken?'

Durris looked thoughtfully at her, then at Patrick.

'She's probably right, you know.'

'Yes, I think so.'

Hippolyta nodded. Of course she was.

'Will you excuse us, Mrs. Kynoch?' said Durris. 'And,' he added, his voice sinking, 'will you please keep the little girls here? If you can keep Mrs. Price, too, that would be very much appreciated, but I cannot ask you to lock her up. I don't think she will flee if the children stay.'

'I'll do my best, Mr. Durris,' said Mrs. Kynoch, tilted her little head at him. 'The girls like looking after the children, anyway. They seem so sweet.'

'Have they spoken at all?' asked Patrick, concerned.

'Not that I have heard, Dr. Napier. But they do not seem to

be harmed or in any way upset. Will the Hendrys be calling for them?'

Durris breathed in and out again, weightily.

'If they do – forgive me, Mrs. Kynoch – but if they do, can you try to keep them here, too? And send for me at once.'

Mrs. Kynoch frowned.

'I'm beginning to think that perhaps you should take the children with you, Mr. Durris. Am I to guard them against half the county?'

'I'm sure you could do it, if you had to, Mrs. Kynoch!' said Mr. Durris, surprising them all. 'But just for now, I'd be very grateful if you would try.'

'Very well. But come back soon, eh? As soon as you can!'

Durris bowed. Martha Considine was jiggling, ready to go, halfway back through the kitchen door. Patrick went to follow her, with Durris close behind. Hippolyta turned quickly and bent close to Mrs. Kynoch's ear.

'Mrs. Price has a story to tell you, concerning Georgina. You need to hear it – and it will keep her here with you for a while.' She straightened, nodding, and Mrs. Kynoch, her eyes wide, glanced back at Mrs. Price. Hippolyta hurried after her husband.

'Mr. Durris,' she began, as she caught up with them, 'what are you going to do about the children? What can you do?'

'That is a very good question, Mrs. Napier,' said Durris, pausing briefly as Patrick took her arm. Martha Considine trotted a few paces ahead, as if leading reluctant donkeys on a long rein. 'The case is not completely clear.'

'They are not slaves here, whatever they might have been in Tobago,' Hippolyta persisted.

'Of that I am well aware,' said Durris. 'But they are still the responsibility of the Hendrys, and Mrs. Price has no rights in the case at all.'

'But they are servants, then, are they not? They have a right to leave their employer if they wish to.'

'Well, Mrs. Napier, to answer the second point first, we do not know if they wish to. To the best of my knowledge, they have not said a word nor indicated an opinion or objection at any time that I have seen them. And as to the first point, what if they are apprentices?'

'You mean that they may have an apprenticeship agreement, signed and sealed? An indenture?' As a child, Hippolyta had been fascinated by indentures, fitting the two halves of jagged parchment together in her father's office to see if they matched. 'But who would have been the other party?' she asked. 'Surely the parents of those children would not have been in a position to enter into such an agreement, even if the Hendrys were prepared to?'

'All avenues need to be explored, Mrs. Napier.'

'But what if the Hendrys come to Dinnet House and demand them back?'

'Hippolyta ...' Patrick seemed to think she was going too far, but she needed to know. There had to be some way to protect the children. 'The Hendrys seem to have looked after them very well up to now.'

'I need to talk to Mr. Hendry about the girls,' Durris said. 'I don't know enough about this particular situation to be able to judge for the moment.'

'And what about Mrs. Price?'

'They will not go with her, not for now at least. If the Hendrys come to some arrangement with her ...'

'You mean if she buys them from the Hendrys? But does that not make them slaves again?'

Durris sighed.

'I mean no more than the arrangement that might happen if your cook wished to leave you, for example, and go to work for the Strachans.'

Hippolyta felt a jolt of anxiety.

'She won't, will she?'

Durris blinked.

'I was inventing the situation, as an example. I have heard nothing about your cook.' He made a sound that seemed to hint at exasperation. 'Look, your maid ... Johanna, isn't it? Wasn't she with the Strachans before she came to you? And you did not buy her, and you did not pay the Strachans, and she is not a slave, is that not correct?'

Hippolyta considered.

'Can you come and tell her that, Mr. Durris? I think she needs convincing, even if I do not.'

They all grinned, and stopped for a moment. They were at the green: the kirk, where Johnnie Boy Jo's body was laid out, was just beside them. Martha Considine skipped off to the door, expecting them to follow imminently.

'Look, what about leaving things as they are for now?' asked Durris. 'If Mrs. Kynoch is willing, I shall ask her to let the children stay at Dinnet House for now. The Hendrys may visit, and so may Mrs. Price, but none can see them except under Mrs. Kynoch's supervision. Then I can assure both sides that the children will be well cared for, that the other party is not able to take them from Ballater until the matter is settled, and that all will be agreed in accordance with the law and, beyond that, with the welfare of the children in mind. How does that sound?'

Hippolyta thought it through, though as she had a great deal of faith in Mrs. Kynoch it was an easy decision.

'Yes,' she said. 'I cannot see that either side could object to that, as long as the situation is resolved quickly. Otherwise I'm sure Mr. Hendry would start demanding his staff back.'

'I'm not even sure what they do for the family,' said Patrick. 'I have never even seen them fetch a book, or take a message.'

'An ornament, perhaps,' suggested Durris. 'Like the right kind of dog. I am speculating, Mrs. Napier.'

'Indeed,' said Hippolyta, a little disturbed at the thought. 'Shall we go and see Johnnie Boy Jo? I believe we have kept Mrs. Considine waiting long enough.'

'No,' said Patrick. Hippolyta blinked at him. 'Mr. Durris and I shall go and inspect this wound. You will go home and rest. You are pale, and still tired, and if you take some infection from the corpse who knows what might happen?'

'But Patrick!'

'No,' said Patrick. 'Home.'

It crossed Hippolyta's mind to defy him, to run across to the church and see the body before they could stop her. Then, for once, the image of a physician's wife running across the green with her husband chasing after her, protesting, struck her as a bad thing. It would not add to Patrick's dignity, nor help his practice, she knew well. She swallowed, and turned in the direction of her home.

It was true, she was tired. She did not even call for Ishbel or Johanna, but went to the parlour and sagged, as much as corsetry would permit, on the sopha, eyes closed. What was wrong with her? She felt stupid and clumsy. At any other time no doubt she would have been able to win Patrick over, to persuade him to let her see Johnnie Boy Jo's mysterious head wound, but just now she almost did not care. It must be the heat: they were not used to it, and all those petticoats ... so heavy ...

'Ma'am? Ma'am, are you well?'

With the words came a strange damp snuffling about the hands on her lap. She opened her eyes – her eyelids felt unnaturally heavy. Wullie's dog was anxiously poking its nose at her fingers, and Ishbel stood over her.

'Oh, Ishbel – I was just nodding off. It's the heat.'

'Aye, it's rare,' Ishbel agreed. 'I thought I heard the door but then nothing happened. Do you need a cup of tea, ma'am?'

'I believe I do, Ishbel, thank you.' Ishbel spun on her heel to go, but Hippolyta called her back.

'Is Johanna still keeping to her room?'

'Yes, ma'am. She's no come out for food, even.'

'I think I'll go and see if she'll speak to me. Yes, in fact, can you bring the tea there instead? And two cups?'

'Ma'am ...'

'I know, but she has had a bad shock, and she's upset. Let's see if we can win her round. For her benefit, of course,' she added quickly, thinking that she had sounded a little callous. 'If she is going to stay here I would rather she were happy.' She caught Ishbel's eye. 'And if she is not, it would be better if we made the decision and let her go on her way, so that we can find a replacement.'

'Aye, indeed, ma'am.' A tiny smile tweaked at the corner of Ishbel's mouth as she bobbed a curtsey and departed again for the kitchen. Hippolyta gave her a moment to arrange the tea tray – and to gather her own strength – then made for the servants' quarters herself. Patrick might have made her stay at home, but there were questions she could ask without even leaving the house.

The corridor of servants' rooms lay to the right of the kitchen. Each room was small and rather dark, but comfortable enough, with a small window high in the wall allowing in a block of light from the garden. The two at the far end of the corridor were unoccupied, but Ishbel and Johanna each used one near the kitchen end of the passage, Wullie preferring a blanket on the kitchen floor next to the stove, where, he claimed, he and the dog could guard the kitchen door. The door to Ishbel's room was ajar and Hippolyta could see that her window, too, was open, so she had set the room to air. The next door was firmly shut. Ishbel, following Hippolyta into the corridor, rattled the tea tray slightly, and at Hippolyta's silent direction set it down on the floor by the closed door. Hippolyta knocked.

'Johanna?' Silence. 'Johanna, may we talk?'

A slight sound indicated that Johanna was there, but there was still no reply. Hippolyta sighed, but quietly.

'Johanna, I'm on my own – the sheriff's officer isn't here. And there's a cup of tea for you. You must be hungry, surely.' She waited, but clearly Johanna was able to tolerate hunger more than she herself was. 'Johanna, please? I met your brother the other day. I know he couldn't have hurt anyone. Please, will you tell me about him?'

Again, a small movement could be heard in the room, then silence. Hippolyta sank down beside the tea tray, eyeing it longingly.

'I'll pour your tea, shall I? We'll just take it here.'

The door handle gave a tiny squeak by her ear, and turned slowly. Johanna peeped round the doorpost, then her eyes widened when she saw her mistress sitting on the flag floor. Hippolyta, as if it were all perfectly natural, waved at the tea tray. Johanna frowned, but nodded, and knelt down in the doorway. Hippolyta poured the tea, and handed her a cup. Johanna took a long, scalding draught, and sighed.

'My, that was fine.'

'Nothing like it, is there?' Hippolyta agreed, sipping hers with more restraint. 'There's shortbread there, if you're hungry.'

Johanna glanced at her as if to check that it was not a test, then snatched two pieces of shortbread and devoured them. Hippolyta refilled her teacup.

'How are you, Johanna?'

Johanna swallowed the last of the crumbs.

'Och, I'll do,' she said. 'But I've no seen his body, the wee lamb, nor do I ken where they've taken him.'

'He's over at the kirk. Mrs. Considine has laid him out: I'm sure she's done a good job. You know she always does.'

'So I've heard.' Johanna nodded, absorbing the information. 'Can I go and see him?'

'Of course you can.'

Relieved, Johanna settled back with her second cup of tea.

'Thank you, ma'am.'

'Will you tell me a bit about him? I only met him once.'

Johanna blew out a long breath, settled her cup back on the saucer.

'What can I say? He was my wee brother. We dinna ken what went wrong with him. Our mother aye said that he must have hit his head when he was a babbie – she blamed a lassie that used to keep an eye on us both if she had to work, but I dinna ken. My faither tried to beat it out of him but that never worked. Johnnie would just smile, smile at everything and everyone. It would drive you mad, sometimes.'

'It can't have been easy, having him as a brother,' Hippolyta prompted.

'Well, no, not always,' Johanna agreed. 'The other children – and then when we were older, brothers and fathers coming round to complain, or sometimes taking him and giving him a kicking, and they all knew Johnnie just couldna help it, and he wouldna do a'body any harm. He didna think a'thing wrong with what he was doing, even when we told him to keep it in his breeches ... He didna show himself to you, ma'am, did he?'

'No! No, he didn't,' said Hippolyta quickly, not wanting to wonder what might have happened had she not run away. She had a sudden awful urge to giggle like a schoolgirl, and had to make herself take a long sip of tea to calm down.

'And there was no one would give me a job back in Torphins, so I came up here, to try where no one knew me – well, I'd been here a while ago, when I had a wee job in the summer twa three months, but that was with strangers. I thought Johnnie would probably have been here some time – he wanders all over the place

– but no one would have any idea of the connexion. But he must have heard I'd come here, and he followed me back. I think he'd been up Grantown direction.'

'Grantown! But that's nearly forty miles away!'

'Aye, I tellt you he wandered. Always on the move, aye. He never liked a roof over his head: he slept where he could find shelter, and ate what he could find or was given – and maybe whiles he stole, but I doubt he would even have known it was stealing. Anyway, I hadna seen him for months, and I needed to meet him and see he was all right and somehow get word to my mother, for she still worries about him. Her heart'll be wrecked now,' she finished, her eyes wide with sorrow. Hippolyta could feel her own tears welling again.

'And did you see him, and talk to him?'

'I did, aye,' said Johanna. 'He was all full of this quine that was murdered, the lassie from the school. He said there'd been men in the woods, marching up and down, and he was half-excited and half-frightened.'

'Had they accused him of anything? Questioned him?'

'No, no, Johnnie Boy knew how to hide when he wanted to. He said there was a ruined cottage – broken, he said it was – up in the woods, and the men didn't go near it. He watched them from somewhere behind it. But they'd disturbed him, right enough, beating back the bracken and looking in all the kind of places he would usually curl himself into. He didna like it at all.'

'Apart from that, did he say anything about the murder? Or about the girl?'

'He didna do it!'

'I know, but you know he was around at the time, and could hide. Would he have seen anything? Something that might – might be dangerous for the murderer?'

Johanna looked at her sharply.

'What do you mean, dangerous for the murderer?'

'I mean that if Johnnie told someone what he had seen, the murderer might be caught.'

'Och, nobody would believe a'thing Johnnie said! All the murderer would have to do is laugh and say no, and that would be that.' There was bitterness in her tone. Hippolyta wondered if there had been other times when Johnnie had not been believed, when perhaps Johanna had suffered as a result. There was a long and unhappy history here, of which she had known nothing.

Johanna tilted her head back, pressing it against the corner of the doorpost.

'I canna bear to think on it,' she said, almost too low to be heard. 'I canna bear to think of him so unhappy that he hangit himself, and he couldna talk to me about it. I seen him when he came out of that wee cell, and he was as light as a fairy away down the road. I followed him, see, and he tellt me he'd been locked up overnight, so he was so happy to be out again in the fresh air. And that was all he would talk about, said he wanted to get back to the woods and his wee hidey-holes and all his wanderings. He was going too fast for me, though I kept up for a whiley. I wanted to make sure he was all right before I'd let him go. And then I stopped him and I gave him a big bosie, and I let him go. And what did he go and do then?'

A sob shook her, as Hippolyta in her mind's eye saw the brother and sister embrace for the last time, somewhere on the road to Tullich.

'Listen, Johanna, there's something you ought to know,' she said quickly, before she succumbed to sobs herself.

'Aye, that thon sheriff's man thinks Johnnie killed the quine.'

'He doesn't, he really doesn't. And he's sorry he locked Johnnie up for the night. But listen: there's some evidence – I mean there's something that maybe shows us – that Johnnie didn't hang himself.'

'Then what?' Johanna jerked back, suspicious.

'It's not much better, I'm afraid, but it might be something. It looks, a bit, anyway, as if he might have been murdered.'

'Murdered? Like the quine?'

'A bit like Georgina Pullman, yes, and probably by the same person. Somebody may have thought, even if it wasn't true, that Johnnie saw them kill her, or saw them move the body – her body was left later in the Burn o' Vat.'

'Aye, aye, I heard the claik. With all her claes ripped off, like an animal had attacked her.'

Hippolyta's eyes widened.

'What?'

'Well, that's what they were saying, ken.'

'Well, it's not true. I saw her myself.' She grew stern, cross at such ridiculous gossip. 'Her clothes weren't ripped off, and she was still in her shift.'

'I'm only saying what they said.'

'Yes, yes, I know,' said Hippolyta, 'but it wasn't true. Just so you know. Do you think that there's any chance that Johnnie moved her there? She wasn't killed there,' she added hastily, a hand on Johanna's arm. 'I'm only saying that maybe if Johnnie found her dead, he might have moved her – maybe because he didn't want her where he found her? Or because he wanted people to find her?'

Johanna, tight-lipped at the idea, still managed to give it some thought. Eventually she shrugged.

'I dinna ken. See, I could see Johnnie might not have wanted her somewhere he wanted to be. But he wasna that strong. I never saw the quine to my knowledge, but if she was any size at all he'd no be able to lug her around the woods. Was it far?'

'We don't know where she was killed – maybe in the ruined cottage. If it was there, then yes, it's a bit of a distance down to the Vat. I wouldn't do it myself.'

There was silence for a moment, and they both sipped their tea, lost in thought.

'Did Johnnie say much about the men he saw searching?' Hippolyta asked at last, determined to find out something. 'Would he have recognised any of them?'

'Men, he said,' Johanna shrugged again. Then she frowned. 'I wonder why they didna go as far as this ruined cottage?'

'I suppose they had to stop somewhere.'

'Aye, but ma'am, think about it. If you're walking in the woods, or wherever, with your sweetheart, even.' Hippolyta was taken aback, and rather pleased, to see Johanna blush. 'You say to each other aye, we'd best turn back soon. But then you dinna just turn back then and there, do you? You say Och, we'll just go so far as that gate, or just up to that funny tree, or, aye, just as far as that ruined cottage and see if there's anything there. Do you think?'

Hippolyta nodded slowly.

'Do you know, I think you're right? It is odd.'

'And the thing is,' said Johanna, growing more excited,

'I've remembered – he did say. The men he saw: he said they were strangers.'

'But what would Johnnie count as a stranger? Who would he know, locally?'

'He kent Dr. Napier,' said Johanna, 'for he knew I worked here. And,' she added with a dark look, 'he kent Mr. Durris fine, and all, and the local constable. But a'body else could be a stranger, well enough.'

Chapter Twenty-One

'No more tea,' said Hippolyta after some thought, weighing the pot in her hand. 'I suppose we'd better take the tray back to the kitchen.' She looked at Johanna, then deliberately looked away. 'Do you want to stay here, Johanna? Or do you want to leave? It's up to you, but if you do stay, you have to do your work and help Ishbel.'

Johanna sighed, but not with irritation.

'I dinna ken,' she said. 'Can I bury my brother, ma'am, and then decide?'

'Of course you can. And if you want to tidy yourself up now, you'd better get off and see him, and talk to the minister. If you want Ishbel to help with the funeral you can ask her – and if there's anything we can do, of course, ask.'

'Thank you, ma'am.'

Her face was still sour, but Hippolyta thought it was probably more force of habit than anything else. She scrambled up awkwardly from the floor, and took the tea tray as Johanna reached it up to her, and headed back to the kitchen.

In the parlour, there was still no sign of Patrick or indeed Mr. Durris. It would not be long to dinner, as Ishbel had reassured her on her way through the kitchen. She folded her arms and drummed her fingers on her elbow, pursing her lips. Strangers, strange men, she thought. Had Johnnie Boy Jo really seen the murderers as they pretended to search for Georgina, or was there some other reason why he was killed? If indeed Patrick and Mr. Durris decided that he had been killed.

She had not bothered to sit down, fearing the effort of having to stand up again. Standing by the window she could just see a slice of the village green through and over the gate, and after a few minutes she caught a glimpse of Johanna, black woollen shawl over her head, hurrying from the back of the house towards the church. She slipped up a little prayer for her and for her future, then thought it would be best if she herself went and changed for dinner.

Her summer dinner dress was a compromise: the lace about the breast was not quite as deep as the fashion plates dictated, an economy she was rather proud of. The sleeves were not quite as wide, which was less a matter of economy and more a matter of Hippolyta deciding that she would be forced, in their little house, to approach every doorway sideways, which would look more ridiculous than failing to meet the fashion standards. Finally, the colour: Hippolyta loved to wear green, which she felt produced the best effect with her fair hair and complexion, but she had discovered rapidly when she had moved to Ballater that green was not considered a lucky colour – no doubt this would be reinforced by Georgina Pullman's death in a green and white ensemble. This gown of Hippolyta's was as close to green as blue could come and not be green, a colour that Patrick took amusement in calling, not eau de nil, but eau de Forth. He did, however, confess that he liked it better on Hippolyta than any other colour he had seen, so in the end they were both pleased.

The waist was narrow, and today it seemed over-snug under her ribs, not quite as if she had overeaten, but rather as if she had breathed in too deeply and could not exhale. But as she was considering whether or not she could perhaps benefit from one fewer petticoat, she heard a noise in the hall downstairs. Patrick was back. In a moment he popped his head around the bedroom door, cast an admiring glance at his wife, and asked,

'All right if Durris stays to dinner? Ishbel says there's plenty.'

'Of course!'

Patrick vanished again, and in a moment returned to change his own clothes.

'You look brighter, my dear. Johanna said you'd had a word with her.'

'Yes, we shared a pot of tea on the floor of the servants' passage! Oh, Patrick, she has not had a happy life.'

'Does that mean we're keeping her?' Patrick asked, a hint

of wariness in his voice.

'It's up to her for now: she wanted to bury her brother first. But not as a charity case, Patrick, I promise. She has to do her work, and I think she accepts that now. She thought she would be thrown out when we found she was Johnnie Boy Jo's sister, you know.'

Patrick shrugged.

'Some would not like it. But Johnnie's strangeness originated in an injury: there is no reason why Johanna should be peculiar in any way. Though she is a little.'

'That is because she has not been treated well, I think,' said Hippolyta. 'Did you call for hot water for Mr. Durris? Is he in the guest room?'

'Yes, as usual. I hope you don't mind?'

'Not at all. If you are going to stop me accompanying you then the next best thing is to hear all your news afterwards!'

'Hippolyta, you were tired …'

'It's all right, my dear: I was tired, I agree. I was glad of the rest, even if it was on the floor with the tea tray.'

Patrick set aside his neck cloth and came over to her at the dressing table. He took the hair brush from her hand, and touched her forehead gently. Then he put his fingers to her wrist, and paused, counting quietly.

'You have no fever, and your pulse seems close to normal – a little quick.' He gave her a quizzical look.

'It is the heat, my love.'

'Is it, indeed?' He contemplated her for a moment. 'Well, it is hardly the time to consider this further now, when we have a dinner guest. Are you almost ready?'

'Almost!' She tried to put his look from her mind as she pinned her twisted braids into place on either side of her head, and added a flower to each arrangement. Patrick took her necklace and fastened it for her, then held out a hand to lift her from the stool, bowing as if they were in a ballroom. She smiled, and kissed him as if they were not in a ballroom, then led the way downstairs.

'It is certain that he was hit on the back of the head,' said Durris solemnly, as they began to eat. 'And certain that some attempt was made to wash the blood away. His hair is extremely thick and the attempt was not entirely successful, but the wound is also not that obvious.'

'Could it have happened earlier in the day?' asked Hippolyta. 'Perhaps he slipped and fell, and tried to wash it himself?'

Durris and Patrick looked at each other.

'Yes, it's possible,' said Patrick.

'I should go up there tomorrow and start a search for a possible weapon,' said Durris. 'If I find nothing it is not conclusive, of course, but if I do find something then we have a better idea as to where and when it happened.'

'There might be light enough after dinner,' Patrick suggested.

'After dinner I must go and speak to the Hendrys. I sent them a brief message saying that the children had been found safe and well and I would contact them, but I have not yet done so. They must be puzzled as to the delay.'

'Would you rather I did that?' asked Patrick. 'I have to go to Pannanich anyway for my evening patients. I shall be calling on the Hendrys in any case.'

Durris considered.

'That is a generous offer, and I have to say it is tempting,' he admitted. 'But it is my duty to go and explain my actions to them. I shall pray that it does not rain tonight, and look for the murder weapon – if it exists – tomorrow. I made a good study of the wound: I think I should know what kind of thing to look for.'

'Yes,' said Patrick, 'and remember the bark. It must have been a birch branch, to judge by that.'

Durris nodded. Hippolyta, watching their conversation, felt left out, and a little irritated.

'Well,' she said, slicing into a slab of beef, 'if it adds any weight to your arguments, I think it's quite possible that Johnnie Boy Jo saw the murderer.'

Durris set his cutlery down on his plate.

'She's been talking with Johanna – you know, the maid. Johnnie's sister.'

'I remember. I presume she was more forthcoming with you, Mrs. Napier, than she was with me?' he asked, stiffly.

'She didn't suspect me of wanting to have her brother

arrested. For murder, or for anything else that might have happened.'

Durris let that one pass, and Hippolyta was glad: she had not meant to sound quite so accusatory, when she had defended Durris to Johanna anyway.

'Then what did she tell you?'

'She said that Johnnie watched the search, from somewhere behind the ruined cottage. And that the men who were searching up there didn't go as far as the cottage, although they must have seen it. And she thought that was strange.'

Durris took this in and thought about it.

'I agree,' he said. 'Natural curiosity, if nothing else, would draw you on. And he saw them there?'

'Yes, that's what he told her.'

'Did she ask him if he recognised them?'

'He didn't: apparently he said they were strangers.'

'Strangers to the village?' She could see Durris' hopes rise: that would at least eliminate one or two people.

'Just strangers to Johnnie, apparently. And she said that he would know you, and he would know the doctor,' she nodded to Patrick, 'but aside from the two of you, almost anybody could have been a stranger to him.'

Durris sighed.

'Well, it could certainly explain why he was murdered, if he really was.'

'But I was thinking,' said Hippolyta, 'that it was interesting that he said there were men searching, and none of them went near the cottage. Do you think,' she went on, 'that the men he saw searching might both, or all, have known that she had been killed there – probably was still hidden there – and were working together for some reason?'

Both men looked at her.

'You mean the Hendrys, don't you?' asked Durris.

'Well,' said Hippolyta, who thought perhaps she did, 'it might fit. But there could be others, too.'

'We might be able to find out who was searching up in that direction,' said Patrick after a moment. 'Men, and not Lord Tresco, of course. Nor old Mr. Hendry. Peter Middleton and a friend?'

'Mr. Dinmore and a friend?' Durris suggested. 'He would

be more likely to be called a stranger.'

'I think perhaps someone of a strong enough character could persuade any other man with him not to search somewhere he did not want searched. They did not have to be friends, or conspirators: the murderer might just say "Oh, she is not likely to be hiding there, I think. It is too ruinous." We still thought they were looking for a runaway at that point, or that she had met with an accident. We were not really looking for a body – not that we were admitting to. And of course we were calling out as we went along, too: we would have expected an answer.'

'I believe Dr. Napier is correct,' said Durris. 'And it would work particularly well with a servant, I should think. Mr. Dinmore's man was helping with the search, too.'

'The trouble is,' said Patrick, 'I think several men went up in that general direction. The woods seemed the most likely place for her to be hiding, or to be lost – though it's true there was enthusiasm for searching the loch. And they went up in waves, too, so at any time almost anyone could have been up there. And I don't suppose Johnnie gave a specific time for his sighting?'

'No,' Hippolyta sighed. 'He did not, of course.'

'I'll test the idea on the Hendrys this evening,' Durris conceded, 'and see what reaction I have.'

'Before or after you tell them you aren't returning their slaves just yet?' asked Hippolyta, wondering how he would handle the conversation.

'I shall have to think about that,' said Durris, with a smile. 'I can't see that either conversation will make them sympathetically disposed to the other one.'

Hippolyta smiled too, and set her cutlery on her plate. Her beef was only half-finished, but her appetite had gone, and she felt tired again. Ishbel came to clear the plates and Hippolyta could sense her surprise: Hippolyta's plate was usually wiped clean.

'There's a fruit sponge, ma'am, with sugar cream.'

'Excellent, Ishbel, thank you.' But she really had no interest in it. What was wrong with her? 'I wish I could be there when you talk to the Hendrys,' she said, but even her voice lacked the energy to fight her corner. Patrick put a hand over hers, looked her in the eye and shook his head firmly. She nodded.

'And no eavesdropping, please, Mrs. Napier!' said Durris,

smiling again.

'No, no eavesdropping. I promise. It feels like a long way to Pannanich at the moment.'

Durris paused, as if taken aback at this reaction.

'And I promise I shall do my best to extract any possible information from them, Mrs. Napier, while causing them the least distress – in both the murder investigation and the matter of the little girls!'

'Oh, good,' she said. 'And you'll tell me all about it later?'

'Hippolyta!' said Patrick. 'Mr. Durris is under no obligation to tell you anything at all about either of his investigations!'

'On the other hand,' said Durris, 'if I tell her, then she will not confuse matters by trying to find out for herself. Sometimes it is easier that way.'

Hippolyta opened her mouth to reply, but at that Ishbel returned with the fruit sponge, and she was distracted.

Patrick had gone as promised to Pannanich with Mr. Durris, to see his patients before their bedtimes. Hippolyta often waited up for him but this evening she could not keep her eyes open, and after a last cup of tea she dragged herself up the stairs to bed. The effort of undoing her braided hair, unpinning her lace, untying her corsets and her petticoats, seemed mountainous, and it must have taken her an hour at least to prepare for bed. She sank blissfully against the pillows, and almost forgot to blow out the candle.

Nevertheless she woke sharply when Patrick tiptoed into the room later.

'All well?' he asked, when he realised she was awake.

'Yes, yes. What happened? Did you go to see the Hendrys with Mr. Durris?'

'I did,' said Patrick, 'chiefly because I wanted to help reassure Miss Hendry that the little girls are in good hands and unharmed.' He had sat on the edge of the bed to greet her but now rose to begin his own process of undressing, talking sideways to her. 'Miss Hendry was really quite concerned about them: I believe she misses them.'

'Much?' asked Hippolyta. She was not sure how she felt

about Miss Hendry: the girl seemed a nonentity, hidden behind her father and brothers. If she really cared for the children, valued their companionship, then Hippolyta was sorry that the girls had been taken away. But the girls themselves did not seem like children who had been treated as valued companions. Surely children who were loved spoke and laughed and played, even with strangers?

'I could not say how much,' Patrick said. 'Admittedly, old Mr. Hendry seemed more cross than anything. I did not envy Durris the task of explaining where the children were and why. Mr. Hendry is determined to have them back, and have Mrs. Price arrested.'

'Did Mr. Durris start with the children or with the murder?' Hippolyta was curious. In the little while she had sat downstairs drinking her tea she had toyed with imagining how she would have done it herself.

'He had no choice,' said Patrick. 'As soon as we appeared they demanded to know about the girls.'

'Were they all there? The sons as well?'

'Yes: I have seen more of them in their father's company since all this started than I ever did before that cursed picnic. Before that they were never there: they were always out and about trying to stave off their boredom.'

'Do you think they wandered about the countryside at all? Could they have found that ruined cottage?'

'I have no idea. I had the impression that they would have preferred some card games and perhaps a theatre or two to anything Deeside had to offer by way of scenery and fresh air.'

'I knew there was something wrong with them!'

They laughed.

'But they freely admitted they had wandered up through the woods at a couple of points during the search. They said they did not remember seeing Johnnie Boy Jo, or anything like a ruined cottage, and by this stage old Mr. Hendry was growing impatient – well, angry, really – and I had to ask Durris to call a halt before the old man injured himself in some way. I can't say I much take to Lennox Hendry: he is not a man I should trust with my sister, if I had one, but Richard Hendry seems a decent young man. He seemed more concerned to answer Durris' questions with care and courtesy, even when his father began to shout at all of us.'

'And Miss Hendry?'

'Well, when the shouting began she started to cry. Not a full-blown wail, you understand: just a persistent low, squeaky greeting. I should not care to appear ungallant, but it was not a sound I took any pleasure in at all.'

'It must have been a delightful assembly altogether,' Hippolyta nodded. 'I cannot imagine how you were able to drag yourself away to come home.'

'No, indeed: I fancy Durris hoped the old man would adopt him on the spot and take him into the bosom of the happy family!'

'But you don't think they will try to steal the little girls away again, do you? Back to the bosom of the happy family?' She spoke lightly but it was a genuine concern. Patrick, recognising it, frowned.

'The sons, I believe, would do anything their father bade them do, you know. But I think old Mr. Hendry recognises that patience would be more likely to be rewarded here. He calmed down eventually, and acknowledged at least that Durris had to question anyone who had been up in the woods about who or what they might have seen. And we left soon after: enough for one day.'

'And you saw all your patients?'

'Yes, and more besides!'

'More patients?'

'Well, one more. The landlord called me aside and asked if I would visit an elderly gentleman, a Mr. Ravenscroft, who was suffering from a stiffness in his joints and wondered if I might have something for it, as he had not brought his usual pills.'

'Well, that's scarcely out of the ordinary.'

'Except,' said Patrick, a glint in his eye, 'he is the man who summoned Lord Tresco to dine with him last night!'

'But we only wished to speak to him because we wondered if Lord Tresco might have had a hand in stealing the children – well, that is, we were making a list of who had been at the hotel.'

'Yes, but listen, my dearest.' Hippolyta, taken aback at his enthusiasm, sat back on the pillows with her hands folded in front of her like a dutiful wife. 'He is some distant cousin of Lord Tresco, an elderly relative who might expect to have the right to summon a young kinsman staying nearby to dinner. He only realised after he had issued the invitation that Tresco is here for his

251

health: he had not known about the injury. Anyway, he gave me some minor account of their meal together. He does not seem to think highly of his cousin's mental powers, dismissing him as a foolish young thing –' Patrick's voice thinned into a waspish imitation. 'I should say this gentleman is as sharp as a tack, whatever his age. And I made some remark along the lines of this Mr. Ravenscroft, who has been here a couple of months, I believe, but has never needed to summon a physician before, being able to recommend places of interest to Lord Tresco as a relative newcomer, to visit as his health improves. And what did Mr. Ravenscroft say?'

'My dear,' said Hippolyta, who was growing drowsy again at this long account, 'I have absolutely no idea.'

'He said that it was quite the reverse: that Lord Tresco had indicated to him that he had been in Ballater before, and that not long ago, and knew the area quite well!'

'But we assumed –'

'Yes, we assumed. I had never heard of him visiting before, and it is usual if someone of the least importance turns up here that the news is all around the village before they have unpacked their first valise. But I don't think anyone has asked him directly.'

'Though if he told his cousin last night, then presumably he feels he has nothing to hide. He might not even know – why should he? – that we have been wondering how familiar people are with the area.'

'Indeed.' Patrick pulled his night shirt over his head, and his tousled golden hair fountained from the top as his face reappeared. 'But here's the thing, though. I called in on Lord Tresco on the way back – I know he retires late, and I really did want to make sure he had not overdone himself yesterday with two ferry crossings and a rough cart ride. And in the course of conversation, of course, I mentioned my chat with his cousin Mr. Ravenscroft. And I said how surprised I had been to hear that Lord Tresco had been in Ballater before, expressing my admiration at his managing to avoid the village gossips. I was trying to make it sound as little as possible as if I were investigating him,' he added humbly, knowing that Hippolyta was better at such things than he was.

'Well done!' Hippolyta was encouraging. 'And what did he

say? When was he here?'

'Well, according to Lord Tresco,' said Patrick, 'never before in his life.'

Chapter Twenty-Two

Hippolyta woke feeling refreshed in the morning, for the first time in days. Patrick was, as always, already up. She dressed in her pig-feeding clothes and trotted downstairs, and rapped on the study door. Patrick was indeed at his desk. The hen that had chosen his hearth as her preferred roost saw Hippolyta and was put in mind of breakfast.

'Good morning, my love!' said Hippolyta – to Patrick, rather than to the hen. 'Did I fall asleep while you were talking last night?'

'You did, I'm afraid!' said Patrick, standing to kiss her. 'My patients are much more attentive to me than you are. How do you feel this morning?'

'Much better! I must be on the road to recovery.'

He made an odd face at her.

'I shouldn't think so,' he said.

'What do you mean?' Her heart skipped a beat, then another, seeing the look in his eyes.

'Well, my dear, I know I'm only a doctor and know little of these things, but I should say that if all goes well, in a few months – probably seven - we may have an interesting addition to our household.'

'What? Oh!' Hippolyta's head spun. True, there had been signs, but she had felt so under the weather lately … 'Are you sure?'

Patrick laughed.

'It's one of the things they teach us about, you know! Oh, come here, my lovely Hippolyta, and let me hug you.'

Some minutes later, she pulled back from his embrace.

'You won't write to my parents, will you? Or tell any

member of my family?'

'If you'd rather I didn't …'

'Of course I'd rather you didn't! Not until the child is safely here. I could not bear my mother … She would tell me I had failed again.'

'Oh, my love,' said Patrick, 'she is not as harsh as all that. But of course I shall not write, or if I have to I shall not mention this. Now, in return: you are going to take care of yourself, aren't you? No galloping about the place – literally, in fact: no riding at all. Pony trap at walking pace. No taking risks – I know what you are like, so don't protest!'

'I don't really take risks,' Hippolyta objected. 'They just happen sometimes.'

'Because you put yourself in the way of them. Now, will you promise?'

Hippolyta considered.

'I promise to try,' she said demurely.

Patrick sighed.

'I suppose that is the best I will get from you. And I know you keep your promises. Oh, my dear – a child!'

The embrace was resumed, and in the end only the impatient clucking of the hungry hen roused them to their duties.

It was as much as Hippolyta could do to walk along the street without wrapping her hands about her stomach. A child in there? It seemed a very peculiar idea. How had her own mother felt? Well, by the time it came to Hippolyta, she was probably thoroughly accustomed to the feeling: Hippolyta was the youngest, and Mrs. Fettes would not have allowed a small thing like pregnancy to interrupt her blistering rounds of charitable works. Hippolyta glanced around. Could other people tell? Some of the women in this town could spot an expectant mother from fifty paces, long before the mother herself had any idea. Had people been talking about it behind her back? She shrugged: that was village life.

And of course she would be careful, as careful as could be. She already felt as if she were walking on glass. Patrick should have no anxieties on her account, or no more than would be normal with a pregnancy. But he would worry. Some people worried because they did not know enough, but Patrick would worry because he knew too much, because he would have seen ... things going wrong. But they wouldn't go wrong for her, would they? Or would they?

She hardly noticed anything or anyone that she passed as she climbed the gentle hill up to the gates of Dinnet House. She would not tell Mrs. Kynoch yet, she decided. Mrs. Kynoch had plenty of things to be thinking about, without worrying over her, too.

It was early yet, too early to be sitting out in the garden, and most of the girls, she discovered when she entered the house, were at their lessons. Accountancy, history, geography, spelling (some had come from very uneducated backgrounds), music, French and German for the more advanced, even a little Latin – Mrs. Kynoch would teach anything the girls took an interest in, and delight in some cases in learning along with them. The house hummed with quiet activity, as Mrs. Kynoch led Hippolyta into the parlour.

'Here we are!' she said. 'Our two youngest pupils!'

The two little black girls, Hannah and Ruth, sat plump on the floor, with Mabelle kneeling beside them. All three girls began to stand when Hippolyta came in, but she waved them down.

'I don't want to interrupt!' she said. 'How are you all?'

The two little sisters stared at her in silence. Mabelle sat back.

'They still don't say anything, Mrs. Napier. I don't know if they can even speak, but Dr. Napier said they were both all right so maybe they just don't want to. They don't seem unhappy: they just sit.'

'Mabelle has great patience with them,' said Mrs. Kynoch, and Mabelle glowed at the praise. 'She is showing them games of cat's cradle.'

'They seem amazed by it,' Mabelle said. 'Just like ordinary girls. But they still don't say anything. Now I'm trying paper cutting. Hannah's very neat, but Ruth is a bit young and fumbly with the scissors. Aren't you, sweetheart?' She lifted Ruth's little hand gently, and turned it over to tickle her palm, smiling. Ruth gave a tiny gasp, wide-eyed, but still said nothing. Hannah looked on in silence, and Mabelle, perhaps sensing some curiosity there, took Hannah's hand and tickled it, too. Hannah's eyes flashed from Mabelle to Ruth and back, mouth open.

'Well, that is progress! Well done, Mabelle!' Mrs. Kynoch murmured. 'I should like her to take them out for a walk, but Mr. Durris made me anxious with his talk of the Hendrys wanting them back.' She lowered her voice at that and turned away from the girls. 'He wants me to keep the little ones here until he has worked out what is best for them. If we had any idea what the girls themselves want, it would help tremendously.'

'Mr. Durris was here last night?'

'Yes, quite late. He had been up to Pannanich to tell the Hendrys, but he told me they were not too pleased.'

'Goodness.' If Mr. Durris had come here around the time that Patrick had arrived home – oh, but Patrick had gone to see Lord Tresco, too. She had been so sleepy when he came home, but at least now she knew why. Part of her wanted to share the news, and part wanted to hug it to herself, at least for now, a secret between her and Patrick – and the baby.

'Shall we take a little walk in the garden?' Mrs. Kynoch asked. 'The air is lovely and fresh just now, before the heat of the day.'

'That sounds very good,' said Hippolyta, and followed her hostess outside.

'My dear Mrs. Napier,' said Mrs. Kynoch, as soon as they were clear of any possible listeners, 'it will be a week tomorrow since Georgina was lost to us. Please, can you tell me if Mr. Durris is making any progress at all in finding her killer? Mabelle is distraught – it's a mercy that she is so good with those girls, for they are the only ones who can distract her. She feels she should have been close enough to Georgina to be able to do something to prevent it, whether it was Georgina intending to run away or Georgina being attacked for some other reason. Of course it was very far from Mabelle's fault, but she is a kind, responsible girl: I should perhaps not have put them in the same room, but after my friend's letter I thought Mabelle might be a calming influence – and Georgina was not here long enough for me to make any changes, in her or in the sleeping arrangements. And I still have not written properly to her father. And how can I, with the murderer still not caught? The other girls are scared to go out and will not settle at night unless I reassure them personally that all the doors are locked and the downstairs windows secured. Of course it is early days yet, but it is only a matter of time before questions are asked, and fathers and guardians begin to think about withdrawing their girls and sending them somewhere safer. But where is safer than Ballater? Usually, anyway.'

She stopped, breathless, and stood for a moment. The orange feather in her bonnet blazed in the sunlight against her purple ribbons. Hippolyta had never quite grown used to Mrs. Kynoch's individual fashion.

'It looks as if Peter Middleton is out of the question,' she said slowly. Whatever she said would be a balance between encouraging news of progress, obscuring their lack of it, and keeping to herself what she should not tell. 'I think so, anyway. And Johnnie Boy Jo seems unlikely to have done it.'

'So Mr. Durris really is convinced of that? That Johnnie was harmless, poor lad?'

'I believe he is, yes.'

'And ... what Martha Considine came here to tell him yesterday ...'

'It seems – it's not definite, but it seems that Johnnie was perhaps murdered, too.'

'Oh, the poor, poor boy. He never deserved such a thing.' Tears came to Mrs. Kynoch's eyes.

'He's laid out in the church,' Hippolyta told her. 'I believe the interment is to be tomorrow. And, Mrs. Kynoch ... our maid Johanna, remember? That used to work for Mrs. Strachan?' And for someone else, too, Hippolyta remembered briefly, a little while ago. 'As it happens, she is Johnnie's sister.'

'His sister? I never knew he had kin about here!'

'They were from Torphins, I believe. Anyway, of course we have given her leave to sit with him and attend the funeral and whatever she needs. I believe she would appreciate it if there were more than just her at the prayers. Her mother is not well enough to attend, and the father is long dead.'

'Of course she would. Of course, the poor lass. I'll tell Mrs. Strachan, and the Misses Strong. Aye, he had his wee ways, did Johnnie, but in a fashion we were all fond of the loon. He was an innocent.'

'I believe he was.' Hippolyta would never forget her conversation with him, sorry she had run away and relieved at the same time. Mrs. Kynoch dabbed at her eyes with her handkerchief.

'But Mr. Durris is no nearer to finding out who is really responsible? I don't like to push: I know it is extremely difficult, especially with so many strangers in the town. But I suppose we rely so much on him, it is hard to think that he might be struggling with this.'

'He knows how important it is,' Hippolyta reassured her, though she knew Mrs. Kynoch would not doubt it. 'He is doing his best. There are just so many possibilities.'

'And I know Dr. Napier will help him, too,' said Mrs. Kynoch. 'And no doubt you will have the advising of your husband.' Her eyes twinkled again for a moment, despite her worries. No doubt she too had advised her late husband when he was minister of the three parishes.

'I'll do my best, too,' said Hippolyta with a smile. 'I'll try to keep them both on the right track!'

Mr. Durris was in the study when she arrived home. She could hear both his and Patrick's voices, and sure of her welcome chapped the door.

'Shall I send for some tea?' she asked. 'You look as if your discussion is thirsty work, and I could manage a cup myself.'

'I hope you are quite well today, Mrs. Napier?' asked Durris, on his feet as soon as she came in. 'It is perhaps cooler this morning.'

'I think it is, Mr. Durris, and I am heartily thankful for it. One moment.'

She stepped to the kitchen, and found Ishbel on her own.

'Wullie's helping Johanna over at the kirk, ma'am,' she announced. 'He'll no be long.'

'That's perfectly all right. Tea for three of us in the study, though, please, when you have a moment?'

'Aye, ma'am.'

Ishbel was a perfectly reasonable servant, happy to act and be treated as a human being. Hippolyta wondered if Johanna could ever be brought to such a state of blissful servitude, and went back to the study.

'I am absolutely adamant that Lord Tresco's knee injury is such that he could not manage the climb up to that ruined cottage, much less a return carrying a dead body,' Patrick was saying as she came in again. He glanced up at her with a look that echoed her own, a brief intimate sharing of their secret knowledge, a silent question as to how she was, and an equally silent reassurance. She shivered with delight.

'Aye, I'll take your word on that, of course,' Mr. Durris was saying. 'But I still wonder if he had an accomplice, paid or otherwise. He has no servants here – which I still think is strange, for a gentleman in his position – but he could have paid someone else's. Or –'

'I still think anyone he employed around here to kill a girl, or even to move her body, would have said something about it by now!' said Hippolyta, taking her usual seat on the stool by the empty hearth.

'I agree, I find it hard to believe that he could have found someone willing to do such a thing,' Durris nodded. 'But what about an unpaid accomplice? Someone who acts out of friendship, or some personal debt of which we as yet know nothing?'

'You have someone in mind?' Patrick sat back in his desk chair, interested.

'Mr. Dinmore,' said Durris. Patrick and Hippolyta looked at one another, assessing the idea. 'If there is indeed an accomplice, he must be the most likely. After all, they knew each other before they came here. Perhaps, even, there is some reason for them both to wish her dead, though I cannot think what it might be.'

'Nor are they likely to tell you,' said Hippolyta. 'How on earth are you to prove such a thing?'

'There must be witnesses who saw Mr. Dinmore at or near the Burn o' Vat on Sunday or Monday, if he moved the body.'

'He could have done it in the middle of the night,' said Hippolyta, determined to make things awkward for no good reason.

'I'd like to see him try!' said Patrick. 'There was no moon, and though the sun set late there is little light in those woods at dusk. That is why we called off the search each night. And trying to hold a lantern and a dead body as you scramble through those trees would not be easy. Imagine it!'

She tried, but it was true: Mr. Dinmore looked strong, but he did not have three arms and an inch-by-inch familiarity with what was underfoot. Even if he had tried it, they would have found, or Durris would for he was unexpectedly good at tracking, some evidence of his inevitably clumsy progress. She shrugged.

'All right, then, not at night. Well, on Sunday morning Mrs. Dinmore said her husband was on his way to join the search.'

'And he did join us. It would be good to have a closer idea of when Miss Pullman's body was moved. I think I'll put the word out for anyone who was anywhere near the Vat on Sunday afternoon or Monday morning, either to tell me who they might have seen, or to say how late that spot under the cliff was empty, with no dead body there.

'Then,' said Hippolyta with unaccustomed humility, 'might I go and speak with Mrs. Dinmore?' Both men looked at her, but neither said no straight away. She took encouragement from their silence. 'After all, how likely is it that Mrs. Dinmore is part of whatever the matter might be between her husband and Lord Tresco and Georgina Pullman? And if I put some questions, no doubt she will put it down to the foolish locals prattling on, and not pay much attention to what she says in reply. Would that be all right?'

Mr. Durris glanced at Patrick. Hippolyta saw, rather to her shame, that the sheriff's man was taken aback at her wifely humility, and was clearly wondering whether or not Patrick had given her a good telling off. But Patrick's smile was not the smile of an angry husband, and Hippolyta felt her insides turn over – or was that the baby? Surely not so soon! How long would it be, she thought, before Mr. Durris guessed their secret? He was an intelligent and observant man.

'Um, yes, of course,' said Patrick, 'if Mr. Durris thinks it would be of use. Does that make sense, Durris? And I'll put some word out amongst my patients, in case any of them knows of or saw anything. The visitors amongst them probably did not go to Burn o' Vat for a few days after the picnic, when the search was still on and they would have good reason to be anxious, but the local patients might have animals there, or take shortcuts past it, or have been going to and from Tarland. I think you're right, Durris:

someone really should have seen something.'

'Well, Mrs. Napier, as always I urge you to be careful. Mrs. Dinmore seems an intelligent and sharp woman: if there is something going on as you say between her husband and Lord Tresco concerning Georgina Pullman, she might well be a part of it. So word your questions wisely, eh?'

'I'll do my best,' said Hippolyta, as Patrick came round the desk to help her up from the low stool. 'I believe she will be at the Strachans just now, with a few other people. I have a standing invitation and can easily slip in and make conversation.'

Mrs. Strachan's Friday morning teas were very pleasant affairs, to which a number of visitors to Ballater were often invited to leaven the usual gathering of local ladies. Mrs. Kynoch was not there this morning, being busy with her girls, but the Misses Strong, that pair of unclaimed treasures and sisters to the local man of law, were already quarrelling on a sopha, and the minister's wife who was no more than a mouse in a bonnet sat with her tiny feet dangling on an armchair.

'I invited that Miss Hendry,' said Mrs. Strachan quietly to Hippolyta. 'I thought perhaps it would do her good to have an hour or so away from her father and brothers and enjoy some feminine society, but she said she could not leave her father for so long. Poor girl!'

'But you have Mrs. Price,' Hippolyta observed, scanning the elegant parlour.

'My husband is to have her paint me,' said Mrs. Strachan with a gentle smile. 'I confess I am a little nervous at the result! I have not been painted since I was a girl.'

Hippolyta smiled back. Mrs. Strachan's faded beauty was still charming, but who knew what Mrs. Price might draw out of her secretive eyes? It would be interesting.

'She is an excellent artist,' she said, 'and a most interesting person. I am glad to see her well employed in Ballater.'

'Yet there was a rumour,' said Mrs. Strachan, even more quietly, 'something to do with two little girls who were staying with the Hendrys?'

'I believe there is some disagreement over a couple of young servants,' said Hippolyta blandly. 'The little girls are to stay with Mrs. Kynoch until everything is settled. They are of course in the best of hands there.'

'The very best,' Mrs. Strachan agreed. 'Mrs Price seems to me an unlikely person to have much to do with small children, do you think?'

'I haven't really considered it,' said Hippolyta. Her mind immediately flew elsewhere. Would she manage a small child? What does one do with one? She had never had much to do with her nieces and nephews when they were tiny. Goodness, where would she turn for help?

'Mrs. Napier, would you mind sitting with Mrs. Dinmore?' She dragged herself back from a terrifying future to the present. 'Mrs. Dinmore, it was so good of you to come. You know Mrs. Napier, I believe? Our doctor's wife?'

'Of course.' Mrs. Dinmore pulled in her skirts to allow Hippolyta to settle near her. 'I don't believe we have met since the church service on Sunday. I hope you are well.'

'Quite well, thank you,' said Hippolyta. 'Are you still enjoying your stay?'

'I am, very much,' said Mrs. Dinmore firmly.

'And what do you find to amuse yourself? I am always interested in hearing of new things so that we can pass them on to other visitors! Do you take the waters at Pannanich?'

'I have done, once or twice,' Mrs. Dinmore admitted, 'though I think such things overrated. I do a great deal of reading, and writing. I painted, as I told you, when I was here before, otherwise of course I should do that.'

'You write? How interesting! What have you written?'

'A short devotional text, for which I studied extensively. Then a novel in three volumes. Now I am composing a collection of poems, some of which I intend to set to music.'

'Such talent!' Hippolyta felt daunted. 'And what inspires your poetry? There are some lovely scenes around here.' And perhaps poetry was as good an excuse as painting landscapes for exploring the countryside, she thought to herself.

'The landscape is certainly picturesque,' said Mrs. Dinmore. 'And in this weather, which I believe is exceptional, it could almost pass for Italy or the south of France.'

'Have you ventured far to look for subjects?'

'I have mainly confined myself to what we can see from the garden of our house,' said Mrs. Dinmore, 'and drawn on the riches of my imagination and experience. My husband prefers to wander, though he does not paint nor write.'

'A geologist, perhaps?'

'Perhaps,' she said. 'He is a man of many interests, no doubt.'

'Which presumably he shares with Lord Tresco?'

'I suppose so,' she said. 'Men talk of such things.'

'It must be disappointing for him that Lord Tresco finds getting about so difficult at present,' said Hippolyta vaguely. 'He will miss having a companion in his adventures.'

'Adventures is doubtless a strong word for his meanderings,' said Mrs. Dinmore sharply. 'And anyway, he has a companion. A young man by the name of Peter Middleton, I believe.'

Chapter Twenty-Three

'I didn't realise he was acquainted with Peter Middleton,' Hippolyta said lightly, frantically trying to remember where they had left Peter Middleton as a suspect.

'He only met him here,' said Mrs. Dinmore. Her dismissive tone said all there was to be said of a local. 'Apparently he's some kind of farm worker: my husband has been employing him to show him the sights of the area, such as they are. I told him I had become the expert in the antiquities of the area when I was last here, but he prefers to find them out for himself. He has been to any number of no doubt fascinating places since we arrived. Either that, or Middleton has a list of Ballater lovelies with too much time on their hands and a willingness to please a foolish old man.'

'Goodness!' Hippolyta could think of nothing else to say — or nothing that fell within the range of good manners, anyway. She stared ahead of her for a moment, trying to come up with a suitable response, and failing. But questions were bubbling in her head: was Peter Middleton really so dishonourable? Could Georgina Pullman have been identified as one such Ballater lovely? Or was Mrs. Dinmore simply tired of her marriage, and happy to malign her husband at any opportunity? And if Peter Middleton were truly engaged in such an activity, she thought, coming full circle in her head, had he also helped Lord Tresco to find Ballater lovelies? Part of her was also reviewing rapidly in her head any local girls who might fall into such a category. 'Is Mr. Dinmore here this morning?' she asked at last, looking around.

'Oh, no! His knees, you know: still far too unreliable. He's stuck in the house and reading endless books. Though this is the kind of dull gathering that would usually appeal to him, if we were in London. He would be about everybody, promoting the interests of his banking house, the most beloved child he owns.'

'Goodness,' said Hippolyta again, and earned herself a look of mild pity from Mrs. Dinmore, who presumably thought her as empty-headed as her conversation might indicate. She pulled herself together.

'I thought I saw him along the Craigendarroch road last Sunday, after church,' she said. 'I had wondered at the time if he had any acquaintance in that direction, but of course if he likes to wander that would explain it.'

'Craigendarroch?' Mrs. Dinmore raised an eyebrow. 'No, he exhausted the charms of that road on the first week. I believe on Sunday evening he announced he had been in the direction of a place called – Tarpit, was it? Or some equally unpromising name. Or is that in a similar direction?'

'No, no, that would be Tarland. Quite the opposite direction,' said Hippolyta. 'Or, well, not the same, anyway.'

Mrs. Dinmore sighed the sigh of one forced to spend time with those of a significantly lower intellect than herself, and drummed her fingers on her lap. Her gown was trimmed with deep lace in a very fetching shade of green, which Hippolyta spent a moment silently envying before trying to think of another useful question to ask.

'How charming to meet an old friend here when you have expected to be amongst strangers,' she ventured.

'Who?'

'Lord Tresco. I had thought him an old friend of yours? Perhaps I was mistaken.'

Mrs. Dinmore had gone a slightly odd colour, her cheeks flushed.

'Of my husband's, yes,' she said stiffly.

'Oh, I must apologise! I meant a friend of your family, of both of you – not specifically your friend!' To judge by Mrs. Dinmore's expression Hippolyta had just accused her of the grossest of improprieties. Hippolyta felt that she was expected to fall to her knees at once and beg forgiveness, and she might even have been tempted to do it, such was the force of Mrs. Dinmore's look, but that she found she was bracing her hands hard against the sides of her chair to stop herself.

'Mrs. Napier!' came a summons from across the parlour.

She jumped, partly with relief. It was Miss Ada, the younger Strong sister, grinning at her, while her more properly behaved sister was uttering her usual sharp 'Ada!' in a futile attempt to restrain her.

'Please excuse me, Mrs. Dinmore,' said Hippolyta. 'I fear I must attend to our elderly neighbour.' No doubt Mrs. Dinmore would rather sit on her own anyway, and would not miss Hippolyta's company at all, particularly after that last exchange. Hippolyta rose and joined the Misses Strong, who had now established themselves at a table laden with cakes and sweet biscuits. Along with them were their brother the lawyer and another man, a stranger to Hippolyta. Mr. Strong and the stranger rose at Hippolyta's approach, and as soon as she was seated returned to the question of food. Mr. Strong had a more than healthy appetite, but the stranger, a desiccated creature who tilted his head at her like one of her hens, clawed at crumbs and did not tackle larger slices of cake.

'This is Mr. Ravenscroft, a visitor to the town,' Miss Strong explained. 'Mr. Ravenscroft, our physician's wife, Mrs. Napier.'

'Dr. Napier's a lovely young man,' put in Ada Strong, emphatically dreamy.

'Ada!' snapped her sister.

'I believe I had the pleasure of meeting him only last night,' said Mr. Ravenscroft, his words thin peelings of sound.

'Mr. Ravenscroft is a colleague,' explained Mr. Strong, pausing for breath in his consumption of cake.

'And he is staying at the Wells, so no doubt he saw Dr. Napier as he made his rounds,' added Miss Strong.

'He did mention you, yes, Mr. Ravenscroft,' said Hippolyta. 'He was very pleased to have been permitted to make your acquaintance, particularly as I believe another acquaintance of ours is a distant relative?'

Mr. Ravenscroft regarded her down the length of his thin nose.

'Really?'

'Yes, I believe so. Lord Tresco is the gentleman in question.'

One of Mr. Ravenscroft's fine white nostrils flexed just a

little.

'It is extraordinary,' Hippolyta went on, permitting herself to babble. 'There seem to be so many connexions between the visitors to our little town this season. The Hendrys knew Miss Pullman, and Lord Tresco has met both you and the Dinmores, who I understand are old friends. And I think I heard that Lord Tresco had family links with the West Indies? Is that right? Tobago, I think I heard.' She fixed her gaze brightly on Mr. Ravenscroft's grey-white face. There was almost no colour in it at all: the irises of his eyes were so pale it was hard to tell if they were faded hazel or faded blue, and his lips were thin to the point of invisibility. He had paused, finger tips pursed about a cake crumb, observing her.

'The West Indies?' he enunciated. 'Many do, I am sure.'

'Specifically Tobago, then,' said Hippolyta, persistent into the rough verges of good manners. 'I'm sure I heard he had a plantation there, or was related to someone who had lived there … Goodness, I am sure my head is full of nothing but feathers, for I cannot remember who told me!'

Mr. Ravenscroft stared at her for another moment, as though his mind were somewhere else, flicking through the pages of some family record.

'No,' he said at last. 'There is no connexion with Tobago in this family. His father owned a plantation, but that was many miles away, in Jamaica. And it is long sold.'

'Oh! Then I must be mistaken. Perhaps I even imagined it. How silly!' Hippolyta jumped as someone kicked her under the table. But it was only Miss Ada, struggling to control her chortles at Hippolyta's awful act. Miss Ada choked on her tea, and had to smother her mouth in her handkerchief, while Miss Strong whacked her with unsisterly force on the shoulder blades. Something about the wild look in Miss Ada's eyes provoked Hippolyta to push on. 'I really must strive to be more accurate – particularly with someone who has been interested enough in Ballater to return for a second visit. I am right there, am I not, Mr. Ravenscroft? Please correct me if I am being foolish again! But this is Lord Tresco's second stay in Ballater, isn't it?'

'I cannot see how it possibly matters, madam,' said Mr. Ravenscroft. 'But if it is any consolation to you he certainly indicated as much to me. The phrase he used, I believe, was "The last time I was here". Would you care to make a note of it? That might assist you in remembering.'

'Oh, what a clever idea!' cried Hippolyta. Miss Ada shoved her chair back and, napkin to her mouth, rumbled rapidly to the door.

'Oh, I do apologise for my sister, Mr. Ravenscroft!' wailed Miss Strong, with a sideways glare at Hippolyta. 'I think something must have gone down the wrong way!'

'Not at all, dear lady,' said Mr. Ravenscroft with a smile like a papercut. 'Whatever it is, it would be far from the only confused thing in this town.' He returned his attention to his cake crumbs.

'I should attend to Miss Ada,' said Hippolyta, unable to sit there any longer. 'Excuse me.'

Out in the hallway she found Miss Ada sagging in a hall chair, gasping. At the sight of Hippolyta she waved her hands frantically, chasing her away.

'You're a danger to society, Mrs. Napier! Dinna come near me!'

'Between him and Mrs. Dinmore I feel very stupid,' said Hippolyta humbly. 'I am trying to remember my place.'

'You're not at all,' said Miss Ada. 'I'd say you're trying to find out about Miss Pullman, aren't you? Connexions to Tobago, indeed!' She brushed crumbs from the expansive front of her morning gown. 'That was a fine cup of tea, and now I doubt there's more of it in my nose than in my stomach.' She sighed. 'Is that you away home?'

'I think I've done all I can here,' she said.

'Your friend, that fine fellow Mr. Durris, was away in next door when we were arriving. He'll be questioning Lord Tresco. Do you reckon the bonny peer was the one that did it, then?'

'You'd have to ask Mr. Durris,' said Hippolyta at once. 'But think about poor Lord Tresco's condition: you can't suspect him of rambling about on the hills by Loch Kinord, can you?'

'Aye, no doubt you can fake a limp,' said Miss Ada thoughtfully. 'But I'd no like to think of a fine young man like that – with a title and money to boot – wasted on being a criminal. It'd be disappointing, to say the least. Just when I thought he might be about to make me an interesting proposition!' She winked outrageously at Hippolyta, who tried to restrain her own laughter at the thought of Lord Tresco proposing marriage to little round Miss Ada, half his height and twice his age. And probably three times as intelligent. Stranger things might have happened.

'Well, anyway,' she said, 'I don't think I've found out anything new, but I've made things more certain in my own head. And now I had better find our hostess and make my thanks, and see if Patrick is home.'

'You're not still looking at young Peter Middleton, are you?' asked Miss Ada, wriggling off the chair to stand. Most chairs were a little tall for her.

'Well ... why?'

'Och, nothing. Only he has been asking things around the town, about old times here, old buildings, that kind of thing. A kind of antiquarian pursuit.'

'Maybe it's an interest of his.'

'Maybe, though I dinna remember it before. And he's been seen around with that Dinmore gentleman,' the emphasis she placed on the word rather took away from the courtesy the title suggested.

'Yes, I'd heard ... looking for old buildings? Interesting.'

'Aye, that's what I thought,' said Miss Ada. She smoothed down her skirts, turning this way and that briefly to shake them into shape. 'Well, you'd better find Mrs. Strachan and go off to your husband. In your condition you can't be doing with too much excitement.'

Hippolyta's jaw dropped, but Miss Ada had waddled back to the harbour like a duck that was rather pleased with itself, and all she could do was follow.

She was glad enough of a rest when she returned home, and a more relaxing cup of tea than anything she had consumed in Mrs. Strachan's parlour. Patrick was out on his rounds, and there was no sign of Mr. Durris – not that he had any responsibility to report to them, but Hippolyta liked to think that she and Patrick were of value to him in his review of the information he had gathered each day. Occasionally he stayed overnight with them, usually at short notice, and at other times he stayed elsewhere in Ballater –

sometimes at the inn, sometimes ... she did not quite know where. How could she not know, in a town the size of Ballater? It irked her, but she was too proud to make enquiries. People would expect her to know already.

Ishbel came in to talk over the provision for Johnnie Boy Jo's funeral on Saturday, the meals for Saturday and Sunday and arrangements for Monday's laundry. Wullie then appeared, concerned about a confrontation between one of the cats and an over-confident hen. She sat at her desk for a little and saw to a couple of letters she should have dealt with after breakfast, then dozed, roused only a little later by the sound of the front door opening. It was Patrick, tired from seeing a series of patients scattered distantly round the three parishes. For a little while they slumped together on the sopha, speculating on parenthood. When Mr. Durris did appear, it took the pair of them a moment to waken up to more immediate concerns.

'Lord Tresco has no idea why his relative should have thought Lord Tresco had visited the area before,' Durris said with a sigh. 'He denies ever having been here, insisting that the farthest north he had been up to now was Edinburgh. Nor, he says, had he any previous connexion with Georgina Pullman.'

'Have you spoken to anyone else this morning?' asked Hippolyta.

'Hippolyta!' objected Patrick.

'I'm just interested!' She felt herself going pink. 'Miss Ada Strong saw you going in to visit Lord Tresco, Mr. Durris, and that was some time ago. I was just surprised that you'd spent all that time there, if you did, for not very much information ... I mean, if he'd told you his life history and the tale of his long connexion with Georgina and her family then I wouldn't have wondered so much.'

'I was not all that time with Lord Tresco,' Durris agreed mildly. 'I have been sitting in the church, too, with Johanna and with Johnnie Boy Jo's body.' He sipped his tea. 'She was kind enough to talk to me, but she had no more information than she told you, Mrs. Napier.'

'I didn't think she would,' said Hippolyta.

'No, but I like to hear it for myself.'

'Well, in the same vein,' said Hippolyta, 'I had a

conversation with Mr. Ravenscroft this morning.'

'Did you?' asked Patrick. 'Where was that?'

'He has made the acquaintance of Mr. Strong, and was taking tea at the Strachans',' Hippolyta explained. 'I spoke to Mrs. Dinmore there, too. She says that Peter Middleton has been spending a good deal of time with her husband, and wonders if he is helping him to find local girls.' She had reddened again, she knew it. 'But Miss Ada confirms that it is antiquarian interests they are pursuing.'

'I had no idea Peter Middleton was an antiquarian,' said Patrick in surprise. He was inclined to interests of that kind himself.

'It would mean that Mr. Dinmore has a source of local knowledge,' Durris remarked thoughtfully. He drew out his notebook and made a mark in it. 'If we had such a thing as a motive for him, that would be useful.'

'Anyway, Mr. Ravenscroft was very definite that Lord Tresco had indicated he had been here before. He said that I should write down the phrase, "The last time I was here", as that was what Lord Tresco said to him.'

'Maybe he meant "in North Britain",' Patrick suggested.

'Perhaps. It would be useful to know the context,' said Durris.

'Mr. Ravenscroft was quite adamant,' said Hippolyta. 'He seemed to think I was foolish to doubt his word.'

'A little doubt does no harm,' said Durris, making another shape in his notebook.

'We should ask him,' said Patrick, but Hippolyta was drifting into thoughts of her own. If Mr. Ravenscroft was right, she thought … if Mr. Ravenscroft was right, but Lord Tresco was intent on denying it …

'I wonder,' she said aloud, 'if this could be right?'

The men broke off and looked at her.

'What?' asked Patrick.

'Mr. Ravenscroft says Lord Tresco let it slip that he had been here before. Mrs. Dinmore has been here before. Mr. Dinmore has not. Lord Tresco has been, but denies it. What if,' she said, the idea bubbling up inside her, 'what if Lord Tresco was here before, with Mrs. Dinmore?'

She could see both men thinking it through. She let her mind wander back through her brief acquaintance with the Dinmores and with Lord Tresco, remembering their responses and actions.

'It's not impossible,' Durris was saying, slowly.

'And I don't think either of them knew the other was coming this time. I was there when they met, and they all looked surprised, but Lord Tresco looked much more shocked than the Dinmores did, as if it was a less welcome surprise for him. If they came here together before, as a couple, I'd say it is a connexion they have put behind them now. But that does not mean that Mrs. Dinmore is any fonder of her husband: she is really quite rude about him.'

'He is a busy man with his banking house,' said Patrick, 'or so he told me when I saw him about his knee, and she, I should say, is a woman easily bored if left to her own devices.'

'And full of her own cleverness,' added Hippolyta.

'Did you ask her where he was on Sunday or Monday?' Durris asked, clearly just resigned to Hippolyta questioning his suspects. Patrick's mouth twitched.

'Just a little,' Hippolyta admitted. 'He was in Tarland direction on Sunday after church. They and Lord Tresco worshipped with us at the inn,' she added. 'The English visitors really increase our gatherings so dramatically.'

'What was he doing going to Tarland?' asked Patrick.

'Presumably Peter Middleton took him there, or arranged to meet him there.'

'But Peter Middleton was still in Aberdeen on Sunday, remember?'

'Goodness, so he was!' said Hippolyta. 'He left before Georgina's absence was noticed, and he didn't come back until Monday, did he? So what was Mr. Dinmore up to?'

'You'll have to allow me to question him this time, Mrs. Napier,' said Durris firmly. 'I have a feeling we are nearing our answer, and if you come close to cornering him he might take fright – or become violent.'

'Yes, Hippolyta, please leave him alone and let Mr. Durris speak to him. He does not strike me as a man who might flee, and if he killed Georgina, for whatever reason, then we know that he has the potential to be violent. Will you promise?'

Hippolyta sighed, suddenly conscious of the child inside her.

'I promise. I promise I shan't approach him, but if he comes up to speak to me I shall just be careful. I can hardly walk away.'

Patrick and Durris exchanged long looks.

'It is perhaps the best we are going to get,' Patrick admitted at last. 'And I agree, it would be difficult to ignore him at, for example, a social occasion. Or church on Sunday.'

Durris nodded.

'No talk of marriage or wives, or alibis or Tarland,' he listed. She nodded. When were they going to tell Mr. Durris about the baby, she wondered? He would be more restrictive than ever, then. And she knew she should be careful, but it was so hard to stand back when she knew she had questions to ask and there was no guarantee that Mr. Durris would remember to ask them, or tell her the answers if he did. And even if he did, she would miss hearing the tone of voice, seeing the expression on the face, of the person being asked.

'So anyway,' she said, 'if Mr. Dinmore moved Georgina's body, he did so without Peter Middleton's help. But that doesn't mean that he didn't do it, or didn't kill her. Peter Middleton could have shown him the ruined cottage, then realising Georgina was missing maybe even put two and two together, and fled to Aberdeen, realising he had helped a murderer!'

'Too far ahead,' Patrick sighed, shaking his head. 'I don't think Peter Middleton had any idea when we found him that Georgina Pullman had been murdered, or was missing. We don't even know if Peter Middleton knew about the cottage. It does not seem to have been common knowledge, even amongst those who have lived all their lives here.'

'In fact,' Durris added, 'even when Peter Middleton found out that Georgina Pullman was missing, there was not that sudden suspicion in his eyes as of one who realised who might have taken her. I can talk to him about Mr. Dinmore's movements, and anything he said or did that might be regarded as suspicious, but as yet we have no evidence that Peter Middleton even allowed it to cross his mind that Mr. Dinmore murdered Miss Pullman. And as I said before, we still have no hint that Mr. Dinmore had any reason whatsoever to kill her. We don't know whether or not they were acquainted before, we don't have a link between Mr. Dinmore and Tobago, and all evidence points to the fact that Mr. Dinmore had never been to Ballater before. I need more, Mrs. Napier – more information.'

'Lord Tresco had no link with Tobago,' said Hippolyta, after a moment. They stared at her. 'Well, it's information, isn't it? Another piece of negative information, it's true, but information, all the same. We don't know about Mr. Dinmore, but Lord Tresco seems unlikely to have had any previous connexion with Georgina Pullman.'

'What about Mrs. Dinmore?' asked Patrick. Now it was his turn to be stared at. He shrugged, self-deprecating. 'She doesn't even need a connexion with Tobago. What if you're right, Hippolyta, about Mrs. Dinmore and Lord Tresco? And how does he spend his time at the picnic? In intimate conversation with Georgina Pullman. She looks like a strong woman to me – what if jealousy drove her to kill Georgina?'

Chapter Twenty-Four

Durris heaved a weighty sigh.

'We need to speak to both the Dinmores. I agree, Mrs. Napier, your theory seems sound, but there could be other reasons for Lord Tresco to keep quiet about a previous visit – and of course we only have Mr. Ravenscroft's word that he even had the impression that Lord Tresco had stayed here. Mr. Ravenscroft is unknown to us and could easily be completely unreliable – I confess he does not give that impression, but age or infirmity could have rendered him more confused than he seems. Or he could have misunderstood what Lord Tresco was saying, or Lord Tresco may have misled him for reasons of his own. We need more information, when Lord Tresco himself denies it utterly.'

'No, you're quite right, Mr. Durris,' Hippolyta admitted. 'It was such a tempting conclusion that I leapt to it at once, but it does need substantiation, I know. And as Patrick points out, it doesn't tell us anything about who might have killed Georgina Pullman, except to hint at a couple of motives. It could be Mrs. Dinmore, it could be a conspiracy between Mr. Dinmore and Lord Tresco, or it could be something unconnected with any relationship between the three of them.'

'Where are they staying?' asked Durris.

'In the village – well, only a little outside it,' said Patrick. 'On the Braemar road, just this side of Dinnet House. You know the place? I think it's called Braehead, though I don't know to whom it belongs. It has been let out or lying vacant since I came here, and I don't believe I have ever had cause to visit it or been invited as a guest. But I think you can approach it along the main road, or take a shorter route by turning off the road at the Strachans' house, passing the house where Lord Tresco is staying and taking a path that runs along its far boundary, where there is a gate leading into the policies of Braehead.'

'Ah, yes, that might be quicker on foot,' said Durris, 'I have heard Braehead talked of as a place where visitors might stay if they seek more privacy. The drive is quite some length, if I remember right, so that the house is set back a good distance from the road. Do you know if the staff stay there, or do visitors bring their own?'

'I think they bring their own,' said Hippolyta, more aware of domestic matters like that than the men. 'I have never heard of anyone local working there.'

'A shame: local staff might have been more willing to talk about a local problem,' Durris remarked.

'And the Dinmores might still be at Mrs. Strachan's,' said Hippolyta, glancing at the mantle clock. 'They would be staying late, but if the conversation were flowing perhaps they would have continued there – oh, no! I am mistaken. Only Mrs. Dinmore was there. Mr. Dinmore is still suffering with his knees, apparently. It must be curtailing his walks severely.'

'What is his purpose in these walks, did she say?'

'I don't think she knows. Hunting for antiquities, perhaps, or the picturesque? That's what Miss Ada believes. Whatever it is, if he shares his discoveries with her she did not tell me, and seemed not to be interested. On the other hand,' she said with a smile, 'she thinks me a fool, and perhaps thought I would not understand any explanation she cared to give!'

'An easy mistake to make,' said Patrick, and winked at her. She made a face at him, and Durris cleared his throat.

'I should go and see what I can find out from Mrs. Dinmore, then. It may well be no bad thing to question them separately, for the impression I have is that they are very happy to malign each other in the other's absence. If I go now I should be clear of them before dinner time.'

'Oh, will you dine with us, Mr. Durris?'

'Thank you, Mrs. Napier, but I am honoured to have an invitation elsewhere this evening.' He rose and bowed. 'But no doubt I shall share with you both at some stage anything I learn this afternoon.'

'That would be very good of you, Durris,' said Patrick.

'Though I have no pretensions to the levels of curiosity demonstrated by my wife, I confess I should very much like to know who is telling the truth, Lord Tresco or his cousin Mr. Ravenscroft.'

'As would we all, I believe,' said Durris, and made his farewells.

Patrick had more patients to see, the ones for whom the morning was too early or the evening too late. It was fortunate, Hippolyta often thought, that the visitors and his heavy season came during the summer, when the days were longer and he could travel safely for a greater part of the day, but it did mean that he was often tired by all his duties. He was beginning to speak of hiring an assistant, at least for the busy months: with some care, he thought, they could afford it. Though Hippolyta regretted his weariness, she was often grateful for the time on her own to go out and investigate matters that had aroused that curiosity of hers, and find answers to the questions that nagged at her. She wondered, as she set her summer bonnet on now and tied the ribbons, what she might do when the baby came. But that was ages away, in the winter when Patrick would not be so busy anyway: she allowed herself a brief, idyllic vision of curling up in their cosy cottage, the snow thick outside, the animals and the baby safely snuggled with them ... and then the pig to be dug out with numb hands on the shovel, and Patrick summoned to some distant accident, bundled in three coats, and Wullie refusing to wear boots until his toes turned blue, and the baby crying and the cats irritated at the indignity of wet paws and stomachs, and she snorted at herself and her imagination. Better to apply her mind to this mystery of Georgina Pullman's death, for if that lingered into the winter the village would not rest easy on the long dark nights.

She left her departure late enough, she hoped, to avoid catching up with either Patrick or Mr. Durris: Patrick, she knew, had headed down towards the river to take a ferry to Pannanich, and would therefore be easy to avoid, but Mr. Durris was going exactly the way she wanted to go herself. She toyed with the idea of allowing him to take the shortcut path while she herself walked up the main road and along the drive to Braehead house, but she was more likely to meet someone she knew on the more widely-used route – notably Mrs. Kynoch – and would either be distracted and delayed or have to explain herself, which she had no wish to do. Also that was the longer way, and she was beginning to feel tiredness creeping over her again. She hoped this was not going to be the way she felt for nine whole months, but at least just now it was not too bad. She set off, trying not to hurry too much through the village itself, and slowing considerably when she reached the Strachans' house on the corner of the main road and the side road. She took a moment to survey her path, making sure that Mr. Durris was at least not immediately obvious. There was no one in sight. The road curved very slightly to the right, and she assumed he was already beyond that point, perhaps even on the little track. She stepped forward slowly, not quite ready to commit herself to taking the road in case someone should chance to see her.

She passed the Strachans' front gate, with its neatly symmetrical rosebeds and front door. She hardly dared look at it in case her glance attracted the attention of anyone inside. Beyond that the road was edged with a hedge, just high enough that she could see nothing over it, but in places thin so that the garden and house beyond were just about visible. This was the house where Lord Tresco was staying, the garden where he and Mr. Durris had sat while she imposed on Mrs. Strachan's hospitality in her garden and overheard their conversation. She had the grace to blush just a little at the memory, but not to regret it. She could already see the corner of the hedge where the path led off to Braehead – beyond were dry stone dykes on either side of the road – but she could see nothing around the corner, and once again proceeded with extreme caution, wary of catching up with Mr. Durris. She tiptoed forward, aware that the dry sandy road sounded almost hollow under her boots, then was struck by a sudden fear that her bonnet, both broad and tall, was large enough to be seen beyond the hedge. She hunched into an awkward lurch, bending her knees more than her back and really hoping now that no one was watching her or they would at the very least assume that she had been struck by some strange fit. All too soon, she reached the end of the hedge. She was half-aware of voices coming from the garden beyond the hedge and waited for a moment, trying to judge if it was someone crying out at the extraordinary agitation of a strange bonnet, but it did not seem to be. She pressed her skirts back as far as she could against her legs with one hand, crushed in one wing of her bonnet with the other, and peeped around the corner.

Her caution had been worth it. Mr. Durris was standing, quite still, about twenty yards away, one hand out almost as if to balance himself on the hedge, the other holding his hat out at an awkward angle. What on earth was he doing? Then something in his stance struck a chord in her: he was listening.

But to what?

There was nothing in the pasture to his left, except some sheep, looking shorn and dismal on the yellowing grass. Apart from Mr. Durris the path was empty as far as she could see along it. She herself had made hardly any sound, she was sure. So it must be the voices in the garden. She pulled back a little from the corner, allowed her skirts to settle out again, and focussed her hearing on the voices.

And even as she did so, the voices grew louder, as if just at that point a mild disagreement had become a full-blown quarrel. Listening was easy.

'I don't know what you think you are talking about,' came Lord Tresco's cultivated tones. 'Has the country air gone to your head, do you think?'

'There is nothing in the least wrong with my head!' came the other voice – a man's, similarly educated but sharper, less of a drawl, more incisive. Mr. Dinmore, definitely. 'If you wish for proof, I can tell you at once: I have found the cottage.'

This apparently innocent statement was met with silence. Hippolyta wondered if Lord Tresco were simply scratching his head. What cottage? Whose?

It was almost as if Lord Tresco had heard her, and she jumped when he echoed,

'What cottage are you talking about, Dinmore? Whose cottage?'

'I don't know whose cottage,' Dinmore snapped, and Hippolyta had a sudden vision of the sharp, determined teeth of a clever terrier – the kind that would rather disobey you and take the punishment later than actually do what they were told straightaway. 'But I can tell you where it is and I can make a good guess at your association with it.'

'Well, that's more than I can do, with the information you

have given me so far,' said Lord Tresco. He, by contrast, had a stubbornness about him that put Hippolyta in mind of a donkey she had once known: it would not obey an order even when it was precisely the thing it wanted to do. She had the feeling that Dinmore was on the right track, whatever track that was, and that Lord Tresco would eventually be stamping his feet and swearing his own ignorance even when every proof was set before him, in pure pig-headed stupidity. Except that pigs, as she had reason to know, were really quite clever, and at present Lord Tresco was not giving the same impression. Mr. Dinmore, growing impatient, let out a hissing breath through his teeth.

'Perhaps it was such a trifling thing for you that you do not remember. You gave me, after all, a room in your house when my knees gave way, and left a watercolour of the cottage in it. Did you not think I would recognise it?'

'I cannot even remember which picture you mean. My late mother collected rather dull watercolours from all over the country, wherever she travelled. No doubt it was one of hers, a daub a friend had given her, perhaps.'

'It was a very accurate daub, when it came to it,' said Mr. Dinmore. 'It was a remarkably similar daub to one my wife keeps in her own bedchamber. Not in prime position, I have to tell you, in case you thought it greatly valued: it is down to the side of the night table. I should think perhaps there is a stain on the wall there and she needed something to cover it.'

The needling voice did not suit him: he sounded desperate to believe what he was saying himself. But what was he trying to tell Lord Tresco? Hippolyta's heart quickened as she thought that perhaps she had been right after all, and that she was about to hear the truth of the relationship between Lord Tresco and Mrs. Dinmore. But what did a cottage have to do with it? Mrs. Dinmore when she had stayed in Ballater before had taken Braehead house, just as she and her husband had this time.

'Perhaps she had no wish for you to see it,' said Lord Tresco sulkily. 'If I had any idea what you were talking about I might be able to tell you better.'

'When I saw that your picture matched her picture, and I could guess when she had obtained it – or painted it, for she has some little talent in that direction – then I knew it must be from somewhere around here. Your trysting place, when you and she were here on your own.'

'Oh, the Devil!' cried Lord Tresco. 'Why does everyone persist in telling me I have been here before?'

'You cannot deny it: the two of you were here together. What do you intend to do about it?'

'What do I intend to do? What should I do? I still have no idea what you are talking about!'

'You and my wife! Staying here in Ballater four years ago – in that very house, no doubt! Playing at marriage, when she is married to me!'

'Don't be ridiculous, man. If we were staying in that house, what need would we have for the ruined cottage?'

'Ha!' There was a thump, as though perhaps Mr. Dinmore had overturned one of the lawn chairs in a leap towards Tresco. 'I said nothing about a *ruined* cottage!'

'You said the picture was in the bedchamber you slept in – while I had you nursed to recovery, I might remind you! That's a picture of a ruined cottage, isn't it?'

A ruined cottage? Hippolyta's mind snapped to attention. Had Lord Tresco known of the ruined cottage where Georgina seemed to have been killed? Had Mr. Dinmore, too, been there? But Mr. Dinmore was not giving her time to think.

'You said you didn't remember it!'

'It's coming back to me. A cottage in some woods, perhaps? Is that the one?' Lord Tresco's drawl was beginning to irritate even Hippolyta.

'You know very well that it was a ruined cottage in some woods. It's above Burn o' Vat.'

'Oh, well, with my leg, you know –'

'Now, perhaps, but not four years ago. You would have been perfectly capable then! And my wife has always been a hearty walker. Good Heavens, when I think of the two of you up there – when she was supposed to be here to recuperate her health! And instead the pair of you are queuing for the use of some local trysting place like – like –' Words seemed to fail him, and Hippolyta could hear gasping breath.

'It's not a local trysting place,' said Lord Tresco triumphantly. 'Nobody else was using it!'

Oh, well done! thought Hippolyta. That's the end of that pretence, then. The gasping breath turned abruptly into a roar, and there was a resounding crash from the garden. In a second, Hippolyta pressed herself into the hedge as Mr. Durris hurtled past, making for the garden gate they had both passed. She brushed off twigs and leaves, and followed him.

By the time she reached the garden gate, Mr. Durris was already approaching the two men – Hippolyta was astonished at his speed. And her next thought was that Lord Tresco and Mr. Dinmore looked completely ridiculous. Both had evidently raised their walking sticks to use as a weapon, perhaps without even thinking about it, and forgetting that they needed the sticks for more than just swagger: Lord Tresco was clutching at the garden table, while Mr. Dinmore had assumed a desperate, wide-kneed stance in which he crouched, wobbling, his stick waving uselessly in the air. They looked like two small boys ready to fight though neither had quite learned to walk.

Mr. Durris moved quickly between them, hands raised on both sides. Reluctantly, Lord Tresco lowered his stick, and used the table to balance as he retrieved one of the fallen chairs. He slumped into it without noticing that Hippolyta was nearby, and she had no intention of bringing herself to their attention. Mr. Dinmore was slower to retreat, and waggled his stick a moment more until Durris took a step towards him. Then, still glaring at Lord Tresco, he dropped his arm and edged both feet back towards the firm support of the stick, wincing as he did so. Foolish man, Hippolyta thought, taking on a confrontation like this when his knee wasn't working – even if Lord Tresco's legs were hardly in their best state, either.

Durris bent and righted the other garden chair, and gestured to Mr. Dinmore to sit. Then he took out his notebook and arranged himself midway between the two men, his back still to Hippolyta. None of them yet seemed aware that she was there: she was partly hidden by a white rose on a trellis that seemed to disguise her pale gown, and she did her best to remain motionless.

'Right,' said Durris, 'what was the reason for your unseemly behaviour, gentlemen?'

'None of your business,' snapped Mr. Dinmore, his attention still on Tresco.

'Private grounds,' agreed Lord Tresco. He did not look at Durris either.

'I'm conducting an enquiry into the murder of a young girl,' said Durris, 'and I have reason to believe that one or other of you, or perhaps both, has some information as to the case.'

'What makes you think that?' asked Dinmore. 'I barely knew the girl. Though no doubt Tresco there was intimately acquainted with her.'

'You're maligning her character,' said Lord Tresco, sitting up a little straighter, 'and you've no right to if you barely knew her. Mind, I had only just met her myself.' Any gallantry a listener might have attributed to him was blown away by this quick effort to distance himself from Georgina. Hippolyta's nose wrinkled.

Durris ignored both of them.

'Tell me about this ruined cottage,' he said.

'That's his obsession,' said Tresco. 'Some ruined cottage.'

'How do you know about it, man?' Mr. Dinmore demanded. 'Have you been eavesdropping on a private conversation?'

'Word about the village has it that you have been making enquiries about antiquities in the area – notably a ruined cottage,' said Durris blandly.

'Nothing but baseless, idle gossip. I should have expected as much from such a place,' said Dinmore in disgust. 'The sooner I gather up my wife,' he went on, with some considerable emphasis on the last two words, 'and go home to London, the better. You go on about the fresh air here: most of it is between the ears of the inhabitants.'

'You were looking for the cottage,' Durris went on, 'because you believed, for whatever reason, that Lord Tresco and Mrs. Dinmore had, on a previous visit, used it for trysts of a romantic nature.'

'Why do people keep insisting I have been here before?' demanded Lord Tresco plaintively.

'Romantic barely covers it,' said Dinmore at the same moment, then reddened unpleasantly. 'I mean, you know, trysting places. Sites of debauchery and indecency of all sorts. I imagine.' He fiddled with the head of his walking stick, and stared at the table.

'And where was this site of debauchery?' asked Durris.

Dinmore thumbed the carved wood, biting his lip.

'Up above Burn o' Vat.'

'Interesting. It's not a widely-known site, even locally.'

'Well, it's a ruin, I suppose,' said Dinmore absently.

'When did you find it?' Durris asked, his voice gentle.

'Monday morning.' The words were reluctant, but they squeezed out of Dinmore's tight lips.

'You didn't mention it to Lord Tresco till now, though, is that right?'

Dinmore's gaze flickered to Lord Tresco, and back to the table.

'No.'

'Given how angry you seem to be, I find that surprising.'

'I wanted to make sure,' said Dinmore. Hippolyta had to strain to hear him. 'So I went back this morning, the first time I could climb up there since I –' he gestured irritably at his knee.

'But why could you not make sure at the time?'

'I told you: it's a trysting place. There was a young couple already there.'

'You saw them?'

'They were fooling around. He was carrying her, pulling her up out of the ruin – the roof has tipped over, and she – they must have been hiding underneath.'

'And then what happened?'

'Well, I left. I'm no gawker, no peeping Tom! The girl was only wearing her shift!'

Durris' back stiffened.

'Tell me, Mr. Dinmore: did you see her move, at all? Or was the man carrying her, taking her full weight?'

'I don't know: I didn't wait about the place.' He thought back, though, despite himself. 'No, I don't think she made any effort at all. He was doing all the work. Larking about, the pair of them.'

'Right. And tell me this too, Mr. Dinmore: did you recognise either of them?'

'I didn't look at the girl's face. I mean, I didn't look at the girl at all.'

'And the man?'

'I admit, he was not a local. Perhaps the locals do not use it. After all, he and my wife are not local.' He jerked his head towards Lord Tresco, who was sitting up now, confused but interested.

'Then who was he?'

'I can't remember his name. But he was one of those Hendry boys – you know, the family that came on the picnic?'

Chapter Twenty-Five

Mr. Durris' back and neck relaxed. Hippolyta realised her mouth was open, and closed it: she had inadvertently clutched at the rose bush, and was astonished to see that she had managed to miss the thorns. She shook slightly as she let go.

'Did he see you?'

'I was behind some brambles, I think they were, by chance. I don't believe they saw me at all: they certainly didn't act as if they thought themselves observed.'

'Do you know which brother it was? Would you recognise the man again if you saw him?' Durris was asking. Mr. Dinmore shrugged.

'It could have been either brother. My eyesight is not so good, you know. No better than my knees. Look after your leg, Tresco: when you get to my age you'll be sorry if you don't look after it now.' His expression was pure exhausted misery. Hippolyta wondered briefly what kind of portrait Mrs. Price would make of him.

Lord Tresco still looked baffled at the conversation, and sat up in alarm when Durris turned to him.

'My lord, when were you at the ruined cottage?'

'But Dinmore just said it was the Hendry boy – or one of them – that he had seen up there! How could I possibly climb all the way up there with my leg like this? You ask that Napier fellow: he'll tell you. It was not me.'

'No, my lord, not you on this occasion. But you did know about the cottage, didn't you?'

'Not until Dinmore here came yelling and cursing at me today about it,' he said sulkily – and unconvincingly.

'When you were here before, though –'

'Was not,' said Lord Tresco.

'People are saying that you were.'

'Was not!' Tresco folded his arms jerkily. 'Was not, ever! Why doesn't anyone believe me?'

Because honestly, Lord Tresco, thought Hippolyta irritably, you sound and look like one of my little nephews squabbling with his brother over something you both know very well you have done. What a silly man!

Mr. Durris seemed to be as fed up with both men as she was. He sighed sharply, packed away his notebook and pencil, and regarded them both, one after the other. Hippolyta could not see his expression, but first Lord Tresco then Mr. Dinmore turned away. Mr. Dinmore at least had the grace to look shamefaced.

'You knew that Miss Georgina Pullman was missing,' said Durris, 'and you knew that we were searching around the area where we all – both of you included – met for the picnic last Saturday. Yet you failed to tell me or, as far as I can tell, anyone else, that you saw a man known to Miss Pullman with a woman – a woman who was not responding to his actions – somewhere in the search area two days after she disappeared. Lord Tresco, a note purportedly from you was found in Miss Pullman's belongings. Mr. Dinmore has presented information to the effect that you were in Ballater before and that you knew the ruined cottage where we have reason to believe she was killed. You persist in denying this, which is at the very least suspicious. And you, Mr. Dinmore, failed to realise or report that you almost certainly saw Miss Pullman's body being removed from the cottage to be taken to the place where it was discovered.'

'What?' cried Mr. Dinmore, instantly grey. 'Her body? Dead?'

'Had it not occurred to you?' asked Durris, a touch of bitterness in his voice. He put a hand to his forehead, as though weary of the whole business. 'I must go. You will excuse me, gentlemen.' He spun on his heel, and almost immediately saw Hippolyta behind the rose bush. To his credit, he barely flinched but strode past her back to the garden gate and she, after checking to see that both Lord Tresco and Mr. Dinmore had turned back to stare at each other, hurried quietly after him.

'Mr. Durris!'

'Mrs. Napier – of course you were listening.'

'It was hard not to.'

'Once you were in the rose bush, yes, I'm sure. Perhaps you could more easily have resisted the temptation to enter the garden in the first place?'

'And listen through the hedge, like you?' she could not help asking.

He turned at the gate and opened it, ushering her through before him – probably so that he could keep an eye on her, she thought.

'I at least am the person legally required to investigate this matter. I'm not quite sure what your excuse is.'

'I just happened to be … well, I was passing, and – and I saw you were further up the path and so I backed round the corner because I thought you would suspect me of all kinds of things if you saw me catch you up. And then, well, you shot past and I wondered what on earth you were doing.'

It was fairly feeble, but it was said with conviction, she felt. She trotted for a few paces to keep up with Mr. Durris: she was tall, but he was striding along. He said nothing.

'Where are you going? Are you going up to Pannanich to talk to the Hendrys?' she asked.

'I am walking with you back to your house, Mrs. Napier. I intend to see you enter the house and the door shut securely behind you, and then I shall go elsewhere, and I should like you to undertake not to pursue me or attempt to follow in any way. Do I make myself clear?' He stopped abruptly and turned to her. 'Well?'

'What harm have I done? They didn't even notice me!'

'Mrs. Napier: Dr. Napier has explained to me that you are … that you are in a delicate condition. If anything were to happen to you because you had been placing yourself in danger trying to interfere in my work, he would not forgive me and I should find it, Mrs. Napier, I should find it extremely hard to forgive myself. Do you understand?'

He seemed to have grown taller. She considered defying him: surely he would not really lock her in her own house? But then she thought of Patrick, and of Patrick perhaps blaming Mr. Durris, and Mr. Durris blaming himself, and for once she decided to back down. She did her very best to look innocent, finding it ironic that it seemed harder when she really was innocent.

'Very well, Mr. Durris. I promise that I shall go home, and stay there at least for now, and not attempt to follow you up to Pannanich or to interfere with you speaking to the Hendrys.'

Dignified and just a little defiant, she thought: but she had promised, and she would do it. Mr. Durris seemed satisfied, and began to walk again towards the main road. She hurried to catch up.

'Mr. Durris, do you believe Mr. Dinmore? Do you think it was Richard Hendry, or Lennox? What do you think?'

'I think Mr. Dinmore is more of a fool than he thinks he is, and that Lord Tresco is not telling the truth.' He still sounded cross, and she let him go on for some yards before speaking again.

'I agree that Lord Tresco is lying. I don't know how you would make him admit it, though. He's so stubborn!'

'It will come out eventually, no doubt,' said Durris, and she thought his mood might be softening just a little.

But he did indeed march her as far as her garden gate, and stood waiting while she entered the house and closed the door behind her. She felt her cheeks burn – mostly, she told herself, with frustration. Surely she would be useful if she went with him? She had found out all kinds of interesting information in the past, and had hardly ever come to any harm. Then she drew a deep breath and considered Patrick, and his feelings in the matter, and how his patients might feel about their physician's wife tearing about the countryside chasing murderers – all the things he had so gently complained of before – and she subsided. But she did not take off her bonnet or her gloves, and paced up and down the narrow hall for a moment, considering what she should do next. She needed distraction. She had promised Durris that she would not follow him, or impede his investigation in any way. Durris was making for Pannanich, where the Hendrys were staying. Then, to avoid all censure, she should go in the opposite direction, shouldn't she? For just a moment she was tempted to go to visit Mrs. Dinmore at Braehead, just for a word. She would be able to tell them all about Lord Tresco and whether or not her husband's suspicions were well founded – but on the other hand, was she likely to talk to Hippolyta? She had no high opinion of her, that much was clear. Did she know that her husband had been tramping about the countryside looking for the cottage in which she and Lord Tresco had had their assignations? Or was she completely innocent, as well as ignorant? Hippolyta tapped her foot on the stone floor, concentrating, but she could not think quite how to prod the truth out of Mrs. Dinmore – not yet.

She sighed. What else was in that direction? That was easy: Dinnet House, and kindly, sensible Mrs. Kynoch. Nodding briefly to herself, she opened the front door just a crack and peeped out to see that Mr. Durris had really gone. Then she slipped out as if he still might catch her, and trotted back up the road to see her friend.

She had to admit to herself that the visit was not just a social one by the time she reached the top of the green, for she had already gone over in her mind any questions she might want to ask Mabelle about Georgina, or Grace about Peter Middleton. In her mind they still had not quite cleared Peter Middleton from all involvement, not now that they had found he had been working for Mr. Dinmore, and that Mr. Dinmore had found the cottage. True, he seemed to have found it while Peter Middleton was still cooling his heels in Aberdeen, and by the time he came back Mr. Dinmore's knee had given way, but there was nothing to say that Mr. Dinmore had not contacted Middleton and told him about the cottage … no, but by that time Georgina's body had been moved, by whoever Mr. Dinmore saw on Monday morning. Could Peter have told him about the cottage? But why on earth would he do that if he had hidden Georgina's body there? Hippolyta stopped for a moment, and frowned. Could Peter Middleton be mistaken for one of the Hendry brothers? Surely not, and not, particularly, by Mr. Dinmore who had spent a good deal of time in Peter Middleton's company, and might even be expecting to see him at the cottage. He would have been more likely to mistake a Hendry for Peter Middleton than the other way around. And again, it seemed certain that Peter Middleton had been in Aberdeen while Mr. Dinmore was at the cottage. So Peter Middleton had definitely not moved the body. But could he still have killed her? But if he had, why would the Hendrys want to move the body? Well, for it to be found, perhaps. But to move it secretly? It made no sense. In fact, was there anyone the Hendrys might want to protect or harm by moving the body, if they had not killed her? She could think of no one.

She moved on, conscious that one or two passersby were regarding her with amusement. She passed Mr. Strachan's emporium and carried on past his house, past the main gate to Braehead, and up to the tree-shadowed gateway of Dinnet House. The place was peaceful and quiet, and when Mrs. Kynoch answered the door herself, as she so often did, her smile was as welcoming as ever. Hippolyta could feel some of her concern and tension slipping away.

'Come on in, Mrs. Napier! There is still some tea, I believe – we are in the garden still.' She led Hippolyta through the house once again, to the now-familiar scene of the girls attending to their afternoon stitching under parasols on the yellowing lawn. How easy it was to grow used to such a thing, she thought, yet by winter it would seem completely bizarre again, a thing that would only happen somewhere exotic, like Tobago. She smiled to herself, feeling sorry for the girls who had only arrived as the weather warmed. They would feel a shock when that winter came at last, poor things. She wondered if her confinement would be a good time to knit a number of pairs of warm gloves.

'Come, sit down!' Mrs. Kynoch was saying, pulling out a chair for her. Grace found her a clean cup and saucer, and Mabelle, apologetically, waved without standing up. She had little Ruth on her lap again. Hannah had a cushion on a rug at her feet, and was sewing steadfastly.

'Hello, Hannah, hello, Ruth!' said Hippolyta. 'How are you both today?'

Hannah leapt to her feet, and made a curtsey. Ruth struggled, too, and slid off Mabelle's lap to wobble her own curtsey. Neither smiled, nor did they seem resentful. Hippolyta did smile, deliberately, but there was still no response.

'That's all right, girls, Mrs. Napier doesn't need anything,' said Mabelle awkwardly. 'Ruth, come and finish your cake, dear!' She helped the little girl back on to her own lap. Only then did Hippolyta notice that Mrs. Price was also in the garden, sketching both girls from a short distance. Hippolyta rose and went to greet her.

'I hope you are quite well, Mrs. Price,' she began.

'Oh, much better, thank you,' sighed Adelina Price, her eyes flickering between her canvas and her subjects. 'If you ask me what I was doing the other night, I'm not even sure I know. I should be sorry for it now - upsetting everyone, particularly Hannah and Ruth. Making a fool of myself. Except that now those children are here, not with the Hendrys. That I cannot regret.'

'Do you think,' said Hippolyta, watching Hannah's studious stitching, 'that they will ever be like normal little girls? Smiling and laughing?'

'I don't believe they even speak,' said Mrs. Price. 'They seem to have no feelings. But they are very young still: perhaps, if they are loved and know that they are loved ...' Her voice grew thick and she stopped herself, and Hippolyta laid a hand on her arm briefly. Mrs. Price did not seem like the kind of woman one would embrace. Hippolyta watched her outlining the two little girls, catching, even in pencil, that wall through which it seemed they could neither speak nor feel. She wondered, suddenly, what would happen if Mrs. Price were loved and knew she was loved. She had a feeling it had not happened for a long time.

It was so peaceful in the garden that it was almost possible to forget that this was where she had seen Georgina flirting with Lord Tresco, where Grace had been so upset with Peter Middleton, where, indeed, she had heard Lennox Hendry make his disparaging remarks about his old neighbour Miss Pullman. Had it really been a Hendry moving Georgina's body last Monday morning? Had they disliked her so much? Surely not so much that they needed to follow her to Scotland and murder her!

She walked slowly back to her seat at the tea table and silently accepted a cup of tea, watching the little girls. If a Hendry had been involved in Georgina Pullman's death, would that give Mr. Durris some leverage in allowing the girls to stay here? Or to leave with Mrs. Price? Surely she was too poor to keep them: they would be more comfortable here at Dinnet House, and Mabelle was devoted to them, clearly. In fact, Mabelle seemed to have flourished in the absence of Georgina. Hippolyta paused, watching her. In fact, she thought again, Mabelle does not seem to have missed Georgina at all.

But the brief image that passed through her mind of Mabelle strangling Georgina in the cottage then persuading a

Hendry to carry the body down to the Vat was ridiculous. Mabelle was not the kind of girl for whom men perform that kind of lunatic act. Was she?

'Tell me about the Hendrys, Mabelle,' she said almost without thinking about it.

'The Hendrys? I don't know anything much about them, really,' said Mabelle. 'Only things Georgina told me.'

'Like what?'

'Oh, that they were annoying. That she'd known them all her life. That both of them had made her proposals and she had turned them down. That kind of thing.'

'Both of them? Both Lennox and Richard?'

'So she said,' said Mabelle with a shrug, then jumped as little Ruth murmured something. 'What was that, sweetheart?'

Ruth hid her face behind her hand for a moment, and from behind it they could just hear the words,

'Wet feet.'

'Wet feet?' Mabelle took her little toes in one hand. 'No, sweetheart, your feet aren't wet!'

'What an extraordinary thing to say!' said Hippolyta. 'Clever girl!' She glanced down at Hannah. Hannah had stopped stitching, staring up at her sister, but the second she saw Hippolyta watching she set to again. But it was progress, Hippolyta thought. It was something.

The sunshine was making her dozy again, and she pulled her shoulders back and stretched her neck a little. Mabelle was absorbed in Ruth's cake-eating again, but Grace sat beside her. Hippolyta took a refreshing sip of tea and gathered some of her thoughts. Grace was much prettier than Mabelle, and Peter Middleton had been devoted to her before Georgina came along. Was she the kind of girl for whom men did stupid things? The trouble was that Georgina almost certainly was – look how Peter Middleton had helped her with her arrangements for absconding, when he must at least have suspected that he was not the one she was intending to abscond with. Grace may have detested Georgina, and she had some reason to, but Peter was not the person who would have disposed of Georgina to please Grace. It did not make sense. And anyway, if he did, why did a Hendry move the body? She sighed. She wished she could have gone with Mr. Durris to talk to the Hendrys. She might even know by now whether one of them had indeed moved Georgina's body, which one, and perhaps even why. To think that Mr. Durris knew and she did not was quite maddening.

There was a clack behind her and she turned to see that Mrs. Price had folded her easel, her canvas already swathed in a cloth, her pencil, Hippolyta was amused to note, tucked into her knotted hair over one ear. In a moment Mrs. Price had come to sit at the table too. She identified her own cup from earlier, and helped herself to tea without bothering to wait to be offered.

'You'll finish the portrait at home?' Hippolyta asked. Adelina Price nodded briefly.

'As usual,' she said.

'What will become of it?'

'It depends.' She took a large sip of tea. 'It would be a good painting to auction for the funds, of course, but if it turns out as I hope it will I should like to keep it, too. But then I cannot really afford such luxuries.'

'You could make a copy,' Hippolyta suggested.

'I could. I could send a copy to the Hendrys, and see if that satisfies them for an exchange. After all, a portrait is as decorative as a little girl, and it won't age, and it won't speak, and it won't try to escape.'

Hippolyta flinched at the bitterness in her voice.

'Do ...' she was not sure if she wanted to hear the answer, 'do the Hendrys mistreat their slaves?'

Mrs. Price sat back, and the look on her face chilled Hippolyta to the bone. Adelina folded her arms, and spoke considerately.

'The Hendrys are greedy, nasty people. The old man is the worst, but Lennox is not much better. They take what they can get, from their land, from their neighbours, from their slaves. When they cannot get what they want, they bully until they do. I would not let them near a dog, never mind two little girls.'

'Yet Mr. Durris might, by law, have to return the girls to the Hendrys.'

'They are in this country now: they are not slaves. Surely he will not have to return them!'

'I'm not sure,' Hippolyta admitted. 'And nor, I think, is he.

In the absence of their parents, the Hendrys may be the girls' legal guardians.'

'But that's awful!' Mabelle could restrain herself no longer. 'How can those horrible people keep Hannah and Ruth? Stopping them from talking, stopping them from smiling ...'

'Keeping them fed, keeping them clothed,' countered Mrs. Price. 'Where does it say that a legal guardian has to make a child smile?'

Ruth emitted the quietest of soft grunts, and Mabelle leaned back.

'Oh, I am sorry, my sweet – was I crushing you?'

Ruth gazed up into her face, paused, then nodded solemnly. Mabelle's eyes widened, and she looked up at Hippolyta.

'She has never done that before! Oh, you clever thing, you!' She pulled Ruth to her for a cuddle, then released her and stroked her little face. 'Well done!'

'Perhaps today is the beginning,' said Hippolyta, trying to keep the tears in her eyes and her hand from her own stomach.

'We can only pray so,' added Mrs. Price, a little smile at her lips. But her eyes were still bleak: perhaps, thought Hippolyta, she has seen this kind of thing before too many times. And indeed, how many years had Hannah and Ruth been with the Hendrys? It could not all be undone in two or three days, whatever it was.

'Have the Hendrys been to see them here?' she asked, her eyes still on the girls.

'No, not yet. No doubt they will come to stake their claim,' said Mrs. Price. 'I doubt if they miss them – well, perhaps Miss Hendry does,' she conceded. 'As one might miss a lapdog. I suppose they spend more time with her than with anybody.'

'Do they have any duties, do you suppose?' Hippolyta asked. 'I have only seen them in attendance, never doing much.'

'Hannah's hands are a little worn,' said Mabelle. 'I think she must work, but Ruth is small yet.'

'Sewing, I suppose,' said Mrs. Price. 'She seems good at it.'

'Perhaps they will simply give up and go back to Tobago,' suggested Mabelle.

'My dear,' said Mrs. Price, 'you know what it is like there. They may indeed give up and go back to Tobago - and buy two more.'

'It seemed so natural there,' Mabelle moaned. 'How could I not have seen?'

'You were brought up to it, that is all,' said Mrs. Price, almost kindly. 'And now you have seen the alternatives, you have realised your mistake, like any right-thinking girl. It is people like the Hendrys, who know they do wrong and still carry on –'

But at that point, there was a flurry at the door to the house, and Mrs. Kynoch, face red, emerged into the garden – with the Hendrys.

Chapter Twenty-Six

Mr. Hendry led the way in, smiling grittily. Lennox and Richard followed. Hippolyta, who felt as if she had frozen to her chair, was surprised to see that Mabelle had leapt up, little Ruth still securely in her arms, and was standing between the Hendrys and Hannah, her broad skirts as firm a shield as she could make it.

'Now, now,' Mrs. Kynoch fluttered nervously around them – though Hippolyta saw that in her anxious movements she, too, effectively barricaded Mrs. Price out of sight at her seat. 'I'm sure that Mr. Hendry is not here to snatch the girls away from us, Mabelle!'

'Well, as it happens,' said old Mr. Hendry, steadier on his feet than Hippolyta had ever seen him, 'we have come to collect the lasses. We're in the position of having to leave very suddenly, and I'm afraid we cannot wait around for Mr. Sheriff's Man to make his decision. And when it's bound to go our way anyway, in law ...'

'No!' cried Mabelle, clutching Ruth tight. At the same moment, Mrs. Price sprang from behind Mrs. Kynoch. buffetting her into Hippolyta who caught her before she fell.

'No, indeed!' cried Mrs. Price. 'You shall not take them without the agreement of the sheriff's man – that's Mr. Durris, to you.'

'Oh, aye, and what are you? Some do-gooder painter that daubs out wee pictures to sell for the Great Cause? The Great Emancipation? What the devil do you think you know about life in the West Indies? Sitting in your wee parlour with your paints?'

'I've lived there,' said Mrs. Price shortly. She evidently hoped to stop the discussion there, but Mr. Hendry drew breath to speak, then hesitated, squinting at her.

'No,' he said. 'No, it canna be.' He stepped back unsteadily, glancing at his sons to see if they could see what he could see, but they were simply confused. 'It canna be,' he repeated. 'You're dead.'

'I don't believe I am,' said Mrs. Price, unhelpfully.

'You were. You were Pullman's wife, and you died.'

'I was Pullman's wife. I suppose in law I still am,' she admitted, thoughtfully. 'But in nothing else.'

'So did you take my property deliberately? I mean, because it was me?' Hendry asked, his expression calm, as if their discussion were simply academic. But he had the support of the back of a chair now, and Hippolyta could see how his knuckles whitened as he clutched it. She had not relaxed, either.

'I took the girls because they were not your property,' Mrs. Price explained. 'Yet you were treating them as such. They are not slaves when they set foot in this country.'

'They're still something I bought and paid for,' said Hendry, 'and if I have to give them over, I expect compensation. Aye, and for the money I've spent training them since.'

'Mrs. Kynoch,' Hippolyta whispered, 'is there no man about the place to protect us?'

'No, none,' said Mrs. Kynoch. 'You know I keep no manservant yet.'

'Could you send someone to find Mr. Durris? Or Patrick? Or even Constable Morrisson?' She hoped they would not have to resort to the limited talents of Constable Morrisson.

'I did,' said Mrs. Kynoch. 'The minute I saw them, I sent young Kate off fast to find Mr. Durris.'

'Oh, thank heavens!' said Hippolyta. Then she remembered that Mr. Durris had last been seen heading up to Pannanich, where he had presumably missed the Hendrys. It would take a while for Kate to find him. She tried to breathe calmly. It was all very well for Mrs. Kynoch, she thought, but here in front of them, threatening to take the little girls, was the man who they believed had moved Georgina Pullman's body. And what on earth was she supposed to do about that?

'So if you'll just hand the lasses over,' old Mr. Hendry was saying, 'then we'll be off, and no one will be injured.'

'Injured!' shrieked Mabelle, and little Ruth clung more

tightly to her neck.

'Mr. Hendry, if you are off so precipitately, where is Miss Hendry?' Hippolyta asked – if nothing else, it might delay them. 'I hope she is not unwell.' Good heavens, she thought, this was scarcely a polite drawing room.

'My sister has a headache,' said Lennox Hendry sharply.

'Brought on by the anxiety of being parted from her little maids,' added old Mr. Hendry, not one to pass up the opportunity to push his argument. 'And no doubt, if it concerns you, the lasses miss her too. So hand them over.'

Hippolyta decided that it was time to act a little more decisively. She rose from her seat and pulled herself up to her full height – slightly taller than old Mr. Hendry – and offered up a swift prayer that Mr. Durris and Patrick were indeed on their way.

'No,' she said clearly. 'We shall not hand them over. Not before we have some explanations.'

'Oh, for pity's sake!' groaned Mr. Hendry. 'How many times do I have to tell you that they're my property?'

'Not about that, unsound as it is,' said Hippolyta, venting a little of her lawyer's-daughter persona once again. 'No: I should like an explanation as to what your sons were doing on Monday morning, up at a ruined cottage above Burn o' Vat.'

'Why,' said old Mr. Hendry nastily, 'what do the silly gossips say they were doing?' But Richard Hendry had turned white, lips pressed tight shut.

'No silly gossip, sir, but a reliable witness,' said Hippolyta.

'Well then, what?'

'Shifting the body of Georgina Pullman from the cottage down into the Vat.'

Behind her there was a crash. Mabelle stood firm, but Grace had fainted, knocking into the tea table. Mrs. Kynoch clutched Hippolyta's arm, then seemed to recover herself and let go. Hippolyta paid none of it any heed, and nor, after a moment, did the Hendrys. Richard's eyes were fixed on her, but Lennox managed to maintain his cocky expression.

'And who's this reliable witness, then, eh?' he demanded. 'I think it must be some dottled old quine who wouldn't know any of us from Adam, Father. Pay her no heed.'

'Aye, you're right,' old Mr. Hendry began to say, but at

that Richard Hendry pushed forward, stumbling past his father and brother.

'No!' he shouted 'I won't have it any more! The truth must be told!'

'What?' asked his father, bewildered. 'What are you on about, boy?' Lennox grabbed Richard's arm, but he shook him off easily – too easily, Hippolyta thought, as if Lennox had not really meant it. She frowned, but Richard stood his ground.

'I did it,' he announced, and she could see that he was trembling.

'What did you do, Richard?' she asked, hoping that she sounded gentle – it seemed to work for Mr. Durris.

'I killed her. I killed Georgina Pullman, may God forgive me!' He sank to his knees, head dropped forward.

'Dinna be ridiculous, lad!' old Mr. Hendry gasped, but Lennox seemed all too ready to believe his brother.

'It was you, Dick? You fool, what have you done? You were always sweet on her. Did she turn you down?'

'She did, she did!' cried Richard, flinging his head back. 'And I couldn't bear it, after all she has put me through! The Lord forgive me, I lost control: I took her by force, and when I had finished … she was not breathing any more. I cannot keep quiet any longer. I shall confess all to Mr. Durris!'

'Goodness,' said Hippolyta, not sure what to think. It was like a play in Edinburgh. But no one was paying any attention to what she was doing. Old Mr. Hendry had turned purple.

'You disgrace! You'll no turn yourself over to any sheriff's man: I'll kill you with my own hands first!'

'Father!' Richard scrambled to his feet, struggling to escape the rain of blows that began to batter around his head and shoulders. 'Father, the law must take its course! I must be hanged!'

'You'll not live to be hanged, and bring ruin on all of us!' bawled old Mr. Hendry, laying about him with the stick with more strength than Hippolyta would ever have suspected him to have. But with a twisting movement, Richard manoeuvred out from under his arm, and ran. Lennox snatched at him as he passed, but Richard dodged and made for the house. Lennox turned to his father.

'I'll get the girls: we'll have to go after him,' he snapped.

But old Mr. Hendry shook his head sharply.

'Leave the girls to me. You take that painter. If' I'd known who she was she'd have gone long ago.' The words were flung out almost faster than Hippolyta could understand them, and in a moment Mr. Hendry's stick was in the air and there was a scream from Mabelle. She fell, and Hendry snatched up both the little girls under his arms. In the same instant, Lennox grabbed Mrs. Price and bundled her before him towards the house. Hippolyta seized the teapot and hurled it after him, but it fell short. She glanced around. Mrs. Kynoch had fallen to her knees between Grace and Mabelle – there was blood on Mabelle's gown. The other girls were clinging to each other, sobbing and wailing, not a sensible face amongst them. Hippolyta gave out an exasperated sigh.

'When Mr. Durris comes, tell him what's happened!' she shouted. 'I'm going after them! Well, one of them, at least,' she added, not sure who should have her best attention, as she ran across the lawn and flung herself against the door. It was locked.

Disbelief slowed her. Then she pulled herself together and headed for the shrubbery at the side of the house. She emerged on to the front drive just as a carriage was driven past – the carriage that the Hendrys had travelled in to the picnic. They must have been ready to leave, for the roof and rear rack were piled with luggage, and Hippolyta caught the least glimpse of Miss Hendry inside. Richard Hendry must be in there too, must he not? But then she glimpsed a mounted figure, just at the gateway – it was Richard, fleeing from them all.

A mounted man and a carriage drawn by four horses – she could not hope to catch any of them. What was she thinking? And what could she possibly do if she did catch them? But she could not stop. She ran as fast as she could, down into the village – where both rider and carriage had to slow at least through the busy daytime traffic – and she had time to see them start out on the road towards Tullich and beyond. At the inn she threw herself into the yard and cried out for a horse. A groom hurried forward with his hand already on a bridle, then took in the fact that she was a woman.

'I can't ride astride in this silly gown!' Hippolyta snapped as though it were his fault. 'Sidesaddle, please!'

She waited, trying not to tap her feet on the cobbles in her impatience, making her breathing calm. At last the horse was ready.

'He's in a bit of a feerich, Mrs. Napier,' said the groom, handing her the reins. 'Just ca' canny: he'll be fine with you.' In any case she already had the horse against the lepping-on stane and was hooking her leg over the saddle's awkward pommel. Her left foot was still finding the stirrup as she set off.

On the road she glanced back towards the village, and nearly came off the horse. Patrick and Mr. Durris were standing aghast by the inn's front door.

'Hendrys!' she cried, pointing out towards Tullich. 'Absconding with the girls and Mrs. Price!'

Then, ignoring their horrified faces, she spun back in the saddle and suggested to the horse that they might like to move.

How could she catch them now? The carriage should be fast, but it had been laden with luggage, and with four adults and two children inside, not to mention the dark-skinned driver – was he a slave, too? – on the box. She urged her mount into a trot, then a gentle canter, weaving between scattering workers and visitors along the road. Up ahead she could see a dustcloud – could that be raised by the carriage, or by a hurrying rider? She took a chance and cut across a wide pasture to shorten a corner, and made it back to the road successfully. She could see the carriage clearly now, and the single rider ahead of it. But it was still far off.

As she rode she tried to think. Which way would they go? The rider could go almost anywhere, as she had just done, cutting across fields and along narrow paths. But the carriage was of course much more restricted. It was quite a grand affair, and expensive: old Mr. Hendry would not want it ruined by scratching it on close dykes or breaking the axles on rough roads. He would like, no doubt, to stick to the toll roads where possible, and that would take him straight to Aberdeen – along a very obvious route. She bit her lip. Obvious, yes, but with a harbour at the end of it, where, as Peter Middleton had contemplated, they could take ship for almost anywhere. The Hendry sons had wandered all about the place locally, so they would know the paths around Ballater, but beyond that what would they know? She had no idea. She leaned low over the horse's neck as best she could, spoke to it soothingly, and carried on her steady canter, not too fast, but not too slow, either.

In the distance the turn to Tarland came in sight, and just approaching it, carriage and rider. The rider wheeled, gesticulating. For a moment Hippolyta wondered if Richard were going to double back, knowing it would take the carriage much longer to turn around even at a junction, and give himself up to Durris as he had promised. Then as if a spring had been touched, he darted up the Tarland road. The carriage driver laboured over the horses' reins, and the carriage turned to follow.

No doubt she would make up some ground again as the carriage would struggle on the narrow, steep road. She reached the junction herself and turned with caution, in case she had allowed herself to be drawn into a trap. She glanced behind, along the flat road she had travelled. Some distance behind her she could see two riders, moving at speed – it had to be Patrick and Mr. Durris. Feeling much braver, she tipped her horse towards the Tarland road, and headed up the hill.

It always seemed to her slightly further than she was expecting before she reached that flat area where, on the day of the picnic, all the carriages and carts had been left. She shivered now when she saw the Hendrys' carriage already there, jammed into the space and motionless. She checked her speed. The reason was obvious: a herd of sizeable and unhurried cows was heading in the opposite direction. But where was Richard Hendry? Where was the rider? Before the cows could reach her, too, she turned the horse neatly on to the path for the Burn o' Vat: it would take only a moment to see if he had gone that way, and it would be as quick to let the cows pass as to try to fight through them in case he had gone on ahead. She eased to a walk, and let the horse take the path through the birch trees.

At the Vat, Richard's horse was loose, cropping grass, just outside the entrance to the rocks. She dismounted, jarring her back more through trying to be careful than anything else, and looped her horse's reins around a tree, stroking its nose to reassure it. The other horse eyed them.

'Which way?' she wondered, only just out loud. 'Up or in?' She thought for a second, then decided to take the uphill path. Whatever was happening, she should be able to see better from there.

She climbed up the steep pathway, pausing for a moment to catch her breath before she emerged at the top. There was no sound in the woods except for the occasional bird, tempted out as the evening began to cool. Dinner time, she thought. Late again. No wonder Johanna had no wish to work for them. Ishbel was remarkably patient. She sighed, suddenly hungry, and pushed herself away from the grassy wall on which she had been leaning. For a moment she thought she heard a sound from the road: who had remained in the carriage? Were they going to follow her? It was not a pleasant thought, she decided, and it was enough of a stimulus to goad her on the rest of the way to the top of the path.

She looked about her carefully, then made her way to the edge of the Vat's rocky lip. One hand on a tree, she peeped over. Her heart battered when she saw Richard Hendry below her, contemplating the climb up out of the Vat itself. Where was he thinking of going?

'Richard!' she called out. He gave no sign of hearing. 'Richard Hendry!'

He turned and looked up at her, apparently surprised. Was he there on his own? She could not see, from here, into the arched recess below her.

'Go away, Mrs. Napier,' he called back, over his shoulder. 'No need for you to be here.'

'Mr. Hendry,' she called, undeterred, 'it wasn't you that moved Georgina's body on Monday morning. I know perfectly well, because I saw you that morning myself. It was your brother, wasn't it? So why was he pretending he knew nothing about it?'

'I don't know,' came the hollow reply. 'You'd better ask him.'

'Was Georgina's death an accident? Is that what it was, Richard? I can't see you losing your temper like that. And besides,' she drew breath, not quite comfortable with the next bit, 'she hadn't been interfered with, you know. She might have been left to look like that, but she really hadn't.'

Richard spun on the wet gravel, and stared up at her.

'You know an awful lot, Mrs. Napier,' he said sadly.

'I know it's an odd thing to lie about,' she admitted. 'Why on earth would you pretend to have done something like that? And then, why would your brother come back to make sure the body was going to be found? It doesn't make sense at all, does it? So someone is lying. Unless ... unless ...' Georgina had been an only child. The fact wandered into her mind. Georgina had been an only child, and the estate on Tobago was a fine one. What would happen to it now? The Hendrys were neighbours – and were greedy and ruthless ...

'Hippolyta!'

'Oh, Patrick!' She turned in delight. His face was ghastly: she prayed he would not be as angry with her as she undoubtedly deserved. 'You're here! Richard Hendry is down there and he says he murdered Georgina but I'm not so sure – at least, not for the reasons he said he did. And –'

'Hippolyta, look out!'

It happened as slowly as a dream. She felt her eyes widen at Patrick's frantic gesticulations. He was too far away from her. She caught a movement, so slight, to her side, and half-turned to see Lennox Hendry, a look of icy determination on his face, far, far too close behind her. And behind him another face – a woman, mouth open in shock, hands clutching at Lennox' arms. She felt the pressure of his hands on her waist, a shove so slow that surely she could spin out of the way? She tried, but she was as slow as everything else. Her back bent. Her feet left the safe woodland earth, trailing behind her as she flew out over the rocky hollow of the Vat. She waved her arms – flying? Or was she trying to tell Patrick something important? Then the trees and the rocky walls spun around her, and she fell, so, so slowly, as the ground spread greedily to catch her.

Chapter Twenty-Seven

She was aware of light before she opened her eyes. Bright sunlight, she thought. I must be in Tobago.

If I'm in Tobago, I can go and warn Mr. Pullman. I can explain all about Georgina's death, and tell him to look out for those Hendrys. They are not to be trusted.

But she was not sure quite why, and drifted off again into strange dreams of flying.

'Just good luck,' someone was saying, the next time her feet touched the ground.

'More than good luck,' said someone else. 'Much, much more.' She winced at the depths of feeling there in that sound. The voice was important to her, she knew. And comforting, and more. She opened her eyes.

'Hippolyta, my love!' Patrick was leaning over the bed, holding her hand. He touched her cheek. 'Good morning!'

'Morning?' She found she could only croak, and in a moment he had a cup of water to her lips. She sipped greedily, and cleared her throat. 'Did I miss dinner?'

Patrick laughed, and squeezed her hand.

'Dinner and breakfast. That's how we knew you were really unconscious,' he added. 'But how do you feel?'

Hippolyta considered, then squeaked in pain.

'My hand!' she cried. She squirmed to look. Her left hand was heavily bandaged, but the tips of the fingers protruding from the end of the wrappings were dark and swollen.

'You've broken a couple of bones in your wrist, I think,' said Patrick.

'Ow! How am I going …' A flood of memories struck her hard. Her wrist was a minor thing. She tangled the fingers of her

313

right hand in Patrick's. 'Patrick?'

He knew at once what she meant, and she felt him lay his free hand on her stomach.

'I think – I think everything is all right. I couldn't believe it.'

'But I fell – didn't I? I fell into the Vat. Lennox Hendry pushed me.'

'You did – but by the greatest of good luck something broke your fall. Well, the greatest of good luck for you, my love. You owe someone ... well, your thanks at least.' Grinning, he nodded across the room. Hippolyta wriggled to sit up in bed, and saw Mr. Durris standing by the window. He, too, had a bandaged hand. He nodded a little stiffly towards Hippolyta.

'Three broken fingers and four cracked ribs,' Patrick enumerated.

'Oh, Mr. Durris, I am sorry!'

'My own fault,' he said, not moving. 'The next time I shall have to let you fall.'

'I shall never forget that moment!' said Patrick. 'Seeing the pair of you flat on the ground in the Vat – it will haunt my dreams. Much worse for both of you. And to add insult to injury, you were both soaking and covered in that reddish grit that is everywhere there.'

Hippolyta tried to imagine it and realised how stiff she felt, all over. All of a sudden she wanted badly to cry. She bit her lip, knowing if she tried to speak she would only sob.

'You'll want to know about the Hendrys,' said Durris, to her relief. 'We caught old Mr. Hendry in his carriage, keeping his daughter and the maids captive. Well, to be fair we're still not sure about Rebecca Hendry, whether she was complicit or not, but I'm inclined to think that if she was it was her father's fault anyway. It's not, in the end, up to me, I'm glad to say.'

'And the sons?' asked Hippolyta, risking a few words. 'Why did they even go to Burn o' Vat? They could just have driven straight to Aberdeen.'

'It was Mrs. Price,' said Patrick. Hippolyta suddenly remembered her horrified face, the claws of her fingers sinking into Lennox Hendry's arm as he reached for her. 'A spur of the moment thing, I think. Old Mr. Hendry seemed to have realised who she was, and that she would be the only one around here who would have information about them.'

'Yes, he'd only just found out – in the garden at Dinnet House,' Hippolyta murmured. 'She told him. So it was about the estate? Is that what it was?'

'Yes,' said Mr. Durris. 'They tried to tell us that it was just Richard, that he had attacked Georgina Pullman out of – well, lust,' he said, awkward for once. 'But Mrs. Price said you hadn't seemed convinced.'

'But I couldn't see at first why he would lie. But the whole thing looked like a play – I remember thinking how like a play it was.' Her voice wobbled treacherously, and she swallowed. 'And of course it was. They had it all planned. Richard would take the blame, they would tell him what they thought of him, he would run and they would disown him – and buy the land when Mr. Pullman died, or when he found out he no longer had an heir. I suppose they might even have helped him on his way, in the end. Ow,' she finished, squirming against the pain in her arm, and the aches all over.

'Laudanum is wearing off,' said Patrick. 'I'll give you another dose. You should sleep some more.'

He brought her a wine glass, and she took the dose obediently. The room was already fading as they bade her good bye.

When she woke again she was cheered to see Mrs. Kynoch sitting by the bed, stitching.

'My dear friend,' said the little woman, laying her work down at once, 'how brave you were! And in your condition, too! If I had known I should never have let you run after them like that!'

Hippolyta smiled at the idea of little Mrs. Kynoch trying to hold her back, and possibly being dragged behind her in the process.

'How is everyone?' she asked. 'It must have been a shock, all that happening in your garden – and then the little girls and Mrs. Price being taken like that.'

'The little girls are back,' said Mrs. Kynoch with satisfaction, 'and so, for the moment, is Mrs. Price. I did offer to take in Miss Hendry, too, but Mr. Durris did not feel quite certain that he could assure me of her innocence, and in the end … well, in the end it was Hannah and Ruth who asked if she could be taken elsewhere.'

'Hannah spoke too?' Hippolyta's mind had drifted just a little but now it sprang back. She sat up so quickly her left hand protested. 'How long have I been in this bed?'

'Indeed, Ruth scarcely stops now!' Mrs. Kynoch smiled happily. 'But Hannah has been telling Mr. Durris some very sad facts about their lives with the Hendrys, and in particular some of the things they have overheard recently. I don't believe Mr. Hendry ever thought they would speak to anyone or he might have been more urgent about getting them back. Foolish man! Mabelle has given them more kindness in the last week than they have received in their lives before, and now they are beginning to be proper little girls. And they shall soon mix with girls of their own age, too, for I shall make sure they meet some of the village children to play with them. I have never had such young pupils before, but I shall have plenty of help!'

'Is Mabelle all right?' Hippolyta suddenly remembered the blow from Mr. Hendry's stick, the blood on her gown.

'Yes, though bruised. Rather pleased with herself for being brave, and for not fainting, like Grace.'

'And Mrs. Price?'

'Now she is a brave woman. Lennox Hendry had every intention of hurling her into the Vat – apparently Richard was sent ahead to make sure no one was in the Vat at the time – but after he pushed you in they seemed to think the matter was more complicated – and of course by then dear Dr. Napier was there, too, even if he must have been driven to distraction seeing you pushed over the edge. Oh!' She put a hand to her breast. 'I cannot imagine his distress! But of course Mr. Durris had brought other men with him when they followed you, so Lennox was quickly caught and they secured old Mr. Hendry very easily, I believe. His driver ran away – and so, I'm afraid, did Richard Hendry.'

'He escaped?'

'He did.' Mrs. Kynoch put out a hand to Hippolyta's good one. 'Mr. Durris has sent messengers all over the place to find him, and no doubt he would be after him himself if he were well enough. But of course he cannot ride at present: I understand,' she said, with a solemn expression, 'that Lennox Hendry cast some kind of heavy weight on top of him from the edge of the Vat.'

'So I hear,' said Hippolyta, equally grave. 'It must have been a substantial and awkward weight, whatever it was. Oh, poor Mr. Durris!' she added, unable to be completely silly about it. 'He probably saved my life, and what is he suffering for his pains!'

'Indeed,' said Mrs. Kynoch, 'and we are all very grateful to him. And to you, but now, my dear Mrs. Napier, you must take more care. No more running around, or riding fast, or placing yourself in danger. You have a greater adventure to face than all of that.'

'You sound like Patrick,' Hippolyta complained.

On Monday, her appetite somewhat restored and consequently Patrick rather less worried, Hippolyta was allowed to dress – with a good deal of help from Johanna – and sit quietly in the garden. The mild clucking of the hens was very soothing, she had to admit, and the cats arranged themselves about her in turns like little guardian angels in white fur – she shook herself at that thought, and decided that motherhood would make her much too fanciful. With her sketch book and pencils, and trees and hens and cats to observe, and tea to drink, she was surprisingly content, and was even a little cross when she heard the garden gate open. But it was Mr. Durris, who had apparently been resident in their guest room since his accident at the Vat.

'We have him,' he said, without any other greeting.

'Richard Hendry? Where?'

'Peterhead, trying to bribe a fisherman to take him down the coast. His plan was to pass Aberdeen where he thought we would be looking for him, and come in somewhere further south where he could change to a larger vessel. But Peterhead fishermen are not so easily to be distracted from their fishing,' he said with some satisfaction. 'His father arranged all, apparently – told him he was to be scapegoat but in return his father and Lennox would do their best to aid his escape, and they would follow, apparently regarding him as a disgrace to the family. I gather Lennox killed Georgina, though: and Lennox moved the body. But Richard wrote the note that lured her up to the cottage, believing Lord Tresco would follow her and meet her there.'

'What about Johnnie Boy Jo?' Hippolyta asked, a catch in her throat.

'Both of them. It took them both, I believe, to – um – arrange his body where we found it. They thought, of course, that he had seen something as he wandered the woods. Johanna was probably right, though: if he had told anyone, he was not the one who would have been believed.'

'So we have them all,' said Hippolyta, determined not to pursue that particular memory. 'Mr. Durris, will you sit and take some tea?'

'I'll take tea,' he said, 'but I'd rather not sit, if you don't mind, Mrs. Napier.'

'Oh, of course.' She bit her lip, cross at herself. 'I'll have Johanna fetch another cup and saucer.'

'Allow me,' said Mr. Durris, but at that moment the kitchen door opened and to her surprise, Johanna ushered Lord Tresco into their workaday garden. He must have come through the kitchen. Hippolyta tried to keep her face straight.

'I hope I am not intruding,' said his Lordship, easing himself into a chair when he had greeted them. 'But I hoped to enquire after at least one fellow invalid, and now I find I can share moans and groans with both of you!'

'You're very kind, my lord,' said Hippolyta. She was distracted for a moment by Johanna, and the arrangements for more tea. Lord Tresco had really come to hear at first hand the story that was circulating in the village, and as it now did not directly concern him even Mr. Durris was happy to give him an authoritative, if edited, version. The time passed pleasantly enough, even if Hippolyta was no more impressed by Lord Tresco's intellect than she had been till now. At last he rose, less awkwardly than before, and bowed.

'I am to return to London shortly,' he said. 'I have benefitted greatly from the famous fresh air of Deeside, and from Dr. Napier's care for my leg, and must resume some of my duties soon. You'll understand, Mr. Durris, that the society here has become – a little less agreeable to me over recent days, and it will no doubt be pleasanter for all if I depart. But I shall take with me very happy memories of Ballater, Mrs. Napier, despite the very sad events that have happened here.' He stopped, apparently lost in his confusion of feelings, and at last gave a little shrug. 'Perhaps I shall have the pleasure of meeting you both again in London in the future. Please do not hesitate to call if you are in town!' He bowed, and turned to leave the way he had come, then seemed to remember that that would take him back through the kitchen. He glanced around, saw the garden gate, and with obvious relief set off and let himself out into the lane at the back of the house. Durris and Hippolyta watched him go.

'Well,' said Hippolyta, 'no doubt the Dinmores will be returning to London too, so he won't escape them that easily. Yes, Johanna, you may clear.' She watched the maid for a moment, trying to remember something. 'Oh, Johanna, I'm sorry I missed your brother's funeral,' she said when it struck her. 'I hope it went well.'

'There was lots there, all kind of folks,' said Johanna, gulping. 'I never thought … I never thought they would.'

'Oh, my dear! I am pleased.' She closed her eyes for a moment, picturing the scene, tears rising to her eyes. 'And we need to have a little talk about whether or not you'll stay with us, then, soon? When you are ready.'

'No, ma'am, I'll stay. For now,' she added, in case Hippolyta should feel inclined to take her for granted. Hippolyta smiled.

'I'm glad.'

Johanna finished loading cups and saucers on to a tray.

'Was that fellow really Lord Tresco?' she asked, balancing the tray on her thin hip.

'You –' No, Hippolyta said to herself, she would leave the lesson for another day. 'Yes, it was.'

'Oh, aye. I dinna think that's the name he was using the last time he was here,' she added, flicking a cloth at the table top.

'The last time he was here?' Hippolyta repeated. She could sense Mr. Durris' close attention.

'Aye, when he was staying up at – what's it cried? Braehead? I told you I worked for some visitors before. He was staying there with yon Mrs. Dinmore. Kept himself to himself, ken, but I always heard him called Mr. Dinmore, no Lord Tresco.'

Clearly deciding that he had airs above his station, she marched off to the kitchen door, meeting Patrick on his way out into the garden.

'I met Lord Tresco outside,' he announced. 'He said he'd called in.'

'Or Mr. Dinmore, apparently,' said Hippolyta.

'Mr. Dinmore?' Patrick looked as puzzled as one would expect.

'That's what he called himself – the last time he was here,' said Hippolyta. 'According to Johanna.'

'To Johanna? Has this matter any more surprises to give us?'

'Peter Middleton and Grace are to be married, if that counts,' said Durris unexpectedly. 'But apart from that, I think all is done.'

'Then you have no excuse, madam,' said Patrick, sitting down beside his wife. 'No more excitement for you until this baby arrives safely. This time, I shall make you promise.'

'Then I promise,' said Hippolyta. 'I promise to do my best to avoid all excitement.'

'Oh, Hippolyta,' said Patrick with a sigh. 'I suppose that's the best I can hope for.'

Unusual words – some more unusual than others

Bosie	cuddle, embrace
Bothy	accommodation for farmhands
Burn	stream
Ca' canny	go carefully
Chap	knock (at a door)
Chappit	chopped
Claik	gossip, chat
Clarted	filthy
Dottled	confused
Een	eyes
Feerich	panic
Fit, fa	what, where (general replacement in North East of wh- with f-)
Gey	very
Glour	muck
Kirk	church
Kist	chest (general replacement in Scots of soft ch- with hard k-)
Lepping-on stane	
	mounting block
Loon	man
Orra loon	odd job man on farm
Quine	woman
Thrawn	stubborn

About the Author:

Lexie Conyngham is a historian living in the shadow of the Highlands. Her historical crime novels are born of a life amidst Scotland's old cities, ancient universities and hidden-away aristocratic estates, but she has written since the day she found out that people were allowed to do such a thing. Beyond teaching and research, her days are spent with wool, wild allotments and a wee bit of whisky.

You can follow her meandering thoughts on Facebook or Pinterest or at www.murrayofletho.blogspot.co.uk, and if such a thing appeals you can even sign up for a quarterly newsletter by emailing contact@kellascatpress.co.uk. And if you enjoyed this book, please leave a review where you bought it!

The Hippolyta Napier books:
A Knife in Darkness
Death of a False Physician
A Murderous Game
The Thankless Child

The Murray of Letho books:
Death in a Scarlet Gown
Knowledge of Sins Past
Service of the Heir (An Edinburgh Murder)
An Abandoned Woman
Fellowship with Demons
The Tender Herb (A Murder in Mughal India)
Death of an Officer's Lady
Out of a Dark Reflection
Slow Death by Quicksilver
Thicker than Water

The Orkneyinga Murders books:
Tomb for an Eagle
A Wolf at the Gate (coming shortly)

<u>Standalones</u>
Windhorse Burning
The War, The Bones and Dr. Cowie
Thrawn Thoughts & Blithe Bits (short stories)
Jail Fever

Printed in Great Britain
by Amazon